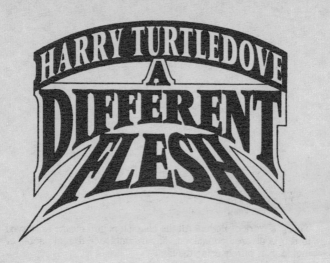

HARRY TURTLEDOVE

A DIFFERENT FLESH

D0958632

BAEN

A Different Flesh

This is a work of fiction. All the characters and events portrayed in this book are fictional, and any resemblance to real people or incidents is purely coincidental.

Copyright © 1988 by Harry Turtledove
Introduction copyright © 1988 by Nightfall, Inc.

A Baen Book

Baen Publishing Enterprises
P.O. Box 1403
Riverdale, NY 10471

ISBN: 0-671-87622-8

Cover art by Kevin Murphy

First Baen printing, September 1994

Distributed by Simon & Schuster
1230 Avenue of the Americas
New York, NY 10020

Printed in the United States of America

LESS THAN HUMAN . . .

Wingfield stepped into the clearing. The sim heard him. It rose, clutching the bloody rock in a large, knobby-knuckled hand. It was about as tall as the Englishman, and naked but for its own abundant hair. Its long, chinless jaw opened to let out a hoot of dismay.

Wingfield gestured with the pistol. Sims had no foreheads to speak of above their bone-ridged brows, but they had learned the colonists' weapons slew at a distance greater than they could cast their rocks. Usually, these days, they retreated instead of proving the lesson over again.

This one, though, stood its ground, baring broad, yellow teeth in a threatening grimace. Then the bushes quivered on the far side of the clearing, and a second sim came out to stand behind its fellow. This one carried a large, sharp-edged rock ready to hurl. It shook its other fist at Wingfield, and shouted angrily.

It was the Englishman's turn to grind his teeth. If both sims rushed him, he would never have the chance to reload either a pistol or his crossbow. And if they did kill him, they would not content themselves with the game he carried. They would eat him, too.

Raising the pistol in a final warning, he drew back into the woods. The sims' mocking cries followed him. He hated the filthy animals . . . if they were animals. Churchmen and scholars were still arguing furiously over whether sims were mere brute beasts or human beings.

At the moment, Wingfield was ready to hate them no matter what they were.

Baen Books by Harry Turtledove

The Case of the Toxic Spell Dump
Werenight
Prince of the North
Agent of Byzantium
A Different Flesh

Isaac Asimov

The Sorry Record

WHEN TWO ORGANISMS overlap too closely in a single environmental niche, they compete. It may not be purposeful—the organisms may not have the kind of brains that will make anything at all purposeful—but they will compete just the same. They will try to use the same habitats; live on the same food; and it is very likely that one will prove a bit more efficient than the other. The stronger will beat off, damage, or kill the weaker; the better hunter or forager will leave the poorer to starve.

It is one of the mechanisms of evolution, usually expressed by the cliche "survival of the fittest" (except that you define the "fittest" as the one who survives, so that you have a nice circular argument).

To get a bit closer to home . . . We don't know exactly what killed off the *australopithecines* after their having lived in eastern and southern Africa for two million years, but it may well be that genus *Homo*, wittingly or unwittingly, helped.

And *Homo erectus* may have been done in, at least to

some extent, by *Homo sapiens*, while the Neanderthal variety of the latter was in turn done in by the modern variety.

We can't put ourselves into the minds of *Homo erectus* or *Australopithecus africanus*, let alone into what might pass as the mind of *Tyrannosaurus rex*, but we know very well what our own minds are like. We have minds that make it possible for us to know what we are doing when we callously mistreat others who are very much like ourselves, and do you know what we do? We *rationalize* our cruelty, and justify ourselves, and even make ourselves sound moral and noble.

Here is the first example I know of. Immediately after the Flood (according to the Bible) Noah planted a vineyard, made wine, drank it, and was drunken. And his youngest son, Ham, the father of Canaan, didn't show the old man the proper respect. (The Bible doesn't go into detail.) Noah therefore said, "Cursed be Canaan; a servant of servants shall he be unto his brethren." (Genesis 9:25.)

In the time of King David and King Solomon, the Israelites controlled all of Canaan and enslaved the Canaanites and put them to forced labor—it was not because the Israelites were a master race and did as master races always do. Not at all. They did it (they said) because of a Biblical curse on Canaan. (One that was undoubtedly inserted into the Bible after the fact.)

Very well, then, that was ancient times, and people were primitive and knew no better.

However, in modern times, it was suggested that Ham, the youngest son of Noah, was a black and the ancestor of all the blacks that have existed since. This, of course, is entirely wrong, for the Canaanites, if we go by linguistic divisions, were as Semitic as the Israelites, the Arameans, the Babylonians, and the Arabs. They were *not* blacks.

However, it suited the slavemasters of Europe and America to pretend that Ham was black because that made black slavery a divine institution and placed the blacks under that same curse the Israelites had made use of three thousand years before. When preachers from the slave states said that the Bible enjoined black slavery, Noah's curse was what they referred to.

In fact, you don't have to refer to a particular Biblical verse to make yourself sound moral and noble. After all, when you enslave a black, you free him from his slavery to his vile superstitions, his false religions, his primitive way of life, and you introduce him to the benefits of Christianity and save his soul. Since his soul is worth infinitely more than everything else he possesses or can possess, you are doing the slave an enormous favor by enslaving him and you're earning for yourself kudos in heaven and flights of angels will sing you to your rest for being a noble slave-owner. (If you think that slaveowners didn't use this argument to justify themselves, you are very naive.)

In fact, to slaveowners, slaves were always responsible for their own slavery. To Aristotle, that great Greek thinker, those people who weren't Greeks were slaves by nature. These "barbarians" (so-called because they didn't talk "people-talk" the way the Greeks did, but made uncouth incomprehensible sounds like "bar-bar"), being natural slaves, were naturally enslaved. You do them a favor, obviously, by letting them be what they naturally are.

The very word "slave" comes, I believe, from "Slav" since to the Romans and the Germans, Slavs were slaves by nature.

It's not even just slavery. The German Nazis killed hosts of Jews, Poles, Russians, Gypsies, and others. Did they do it because they were blood-thirsty, ravening beasts? Not to hear *them* tell it. They were purifying the race and getting rid of disgusting sub-men for the benefit of true humanity. I'm sure they thoroughly expected the gratitude of all decent people for their noble deeds.

And we Americans? Well, there is a story that the Turkish sultan, Abdul Hamid II, a bloody and villainous tyrant, visited the United States once and was tackled over the matter of the Armenian massacres. In response, he looked about him calmly and said, "Where are your Indians?"

Yes, indeed, we wiped them out. It was their land but we didn't enslave them; we killed them. We killed them in defiance of treaties, we killed them when they tried to assert their legal rights under those treaties, and we killed them when they submitted and did not defend themselves. And we had no qualms about it. They were "savages" and we were doing God's work by ridding the Earth of them.

There is a (possibly apocryphal) story that after Custer's Last Stand (the Massacre at Little Big Horn—it's only a massacre when white men get killed) a Comanche chief was introduced to General Sheridan (a Northern hero of the Civil War). The Comanche said, "Me Toch-a-way. Me good Indian." To this General Sheridan is reported to have replied, "The only good Indians I ever saw were dead."—A very nice genocidal remark.

The history of human cruelty is revolting enough, but the history of human justification thereof is infinitely more revolting.

Would it be any different in an alternate world, where *Homo erectus* still existed alongside of us? Would we treat our evolutionary cousins any better than we've ever treated our own kind? Harry Turtledove takes a hard look at this question in *A Different Flesh*, and comes up with some answers we'd probably just as soon not hear.

Preface

"WHERE DO YOU get your ideas?"

I've never known a science fiction writer who hasn't been asked that question a good many times. I'm no exception. And, as is true of most of my colleagues, the answers I give often leave questioners unsatisfied. I've had ideas doing the dishes, taking a shower, driving the freeway. I don't know why they show up at times like those. They just seem to.

Sometimes ideas come because two things that by rights ought to be wildly separate somehow merge in a writer's mind. I had just finished watching the 1984 Winter Olympics when I happened to look at a Voyager picture of Saturn's moon Mimas, the one with the enormous crater that has a huge central peak. I wondered what ski-jumping down that enormous mountain, under that tiny gravity, would be like. A story followed shortly.

And sometimes ideas come because you look for them. Like most science-fiction writers, I read a lot. In late 1984, I was going through Stephen Jay Gould's excellent monthly column in *Natural History*. That month, he was showing how all surviving races of human beings are really very much alike, and idly wondering how we would treat our primitive ancestor *Australopithecus* if he were alive today.

What I think of as my story-detector light went on. How *would* we treat our poor, not-quite-so-bright relations if we met them today? I soon dismissed the very primitive *Australopithecus*. As far as anyone knows, he lived only in Africa. But *Homo erectus*, modern man's immediate ancestor, was widespread in the Old World. What if, I thought, bands of *Homo erectus* had crossed the Siberian land bridges to America, and what if no modern humans made the same trip later? That what-if was the origin of the book you hold in your hands.

The world where sims (the European settlers' name for *Homo erectus*) rather than Indians inhabit the New World is different from ours in several ways. For one thing, the grand fauna of the Pleistocene—mammoths, saber-tooth tigers, ground sloths, glyptodons, what have you—might well have survived to the present day. Sims would be less efficient hunters than Indians, and would not have helped hurry the great beasts into extinction.

Human history starts looking different too. North America would have been easier for Europeans to settle than it was in our history, where the Indians were strong enough to slow if not to stop the expansion. Central and South America, on the other hand, would have been more difficult: Spanish colonial society was based on the ruins of the American Indian empires. And Spain, without the loot it plundered from the Indians, probably would not have dominated sixteenth-century Europe to the extent it did in our history.

Also, the presence of sims—intelligent beings, but different from and less than us—could not have failed to have a powerful effect on European thought. Where did they come from? What was their relationship to humans? Having these questions posed so forcefully might well have led thinkers toward the idea of evolution long before Darwin. Sims might also make us look rather more carefully at the differences between various groups of ourselves.

To return to Gould's question: how would we treat sims? I fear that the short answer is, *not very well*. They are enough like us to be very useful, different enough from us to be exploited with minimal guilt, and too weak to resist effectively for themselves. The urge to treat them better would have to come from the ranks of humanity, and to compete against the many reasons—some of them arguably valid—for continuing exploitation.

"The proper study of mankind is man." True enough. Sims can, I hope, help us look at ourselves by reflecting our view at an angle different from any we can get in this world. Come to think of it, that's one of the things science fiction in general can do. That's why it's fun.

1610

Vilest Beast

Simia quam similis, turpissima bestia, nobis!
[The ape, vilest beast, how like us!]
—Ennius, quoted in Cicero,
De Natura Deorum

Europeans found the New World a very different land from the one they had left. No people came down to the seashore to greet their ships. Before the arrival of European settlers, there were no people in North or South America. The most nearly human creatures present in the Americas were sims.

In the Old World, sims have been extinct for hundreds of thousands of years. Fossils of creatures very much like present-day sims have been found in East Africa, on the island of Java, and in caves not far from Pekin, China. Sims must have crossed a land bridge from Asia to North America during an early glacial period of the Ice Age, when the sea level was much lower than it is now.

At the time when humans discovered the New World, small hunting and gathering bands of sims lived throughout North and South America. Their lives were more primitive than those of any human beings, for they knew how to make only the most basic stone and wood tools, and were not even able to make fire for themselves (although they could use and maintain it if they found it). Paradoxically, this very primitiveness makes them interesting to anthropologists, who see in them an illustration of how humanity's ancient ancestors must have lived.

Despite their lack of weapons more formidable than chipped stones and sticks with fire-hardened points, sims often proved dangerous to colonists in the early days of European settlement of the New World. As they learned to cope with attacks from bands of sims, the settlers also had to learn new farming techniques needed for soils and climates different from those of their native lands. Hunger was their constant companion in the early years of the colonies.

Another reason for this was the necessity of bringing all seed grain across the Atlantic until surpluses could be built up. The Americas offered no native equivalent of wheat, rye, or barley for settlers to use. Sims, of course, knew nothing of agriculture.

Nevertheless, the Spaniards and Portuguese succeeded in establishing colonies in Central and South America during the sixteenth century. The first English settlement in what is now the Federated Commonwealths was at Jamestown, Virginia, in 1607. . . .

From *The Story of the Federated Commonwealths*, by Ernest Simpson. Reproduced by permission.

AFTER THIRTY MILD English summers, July in Virginia smote Edward Wingfield like a blast from hell. Sweat poured off him as he tramped through the forest a few miles from Jamestown in search of game. It clung, greasily, in the humid heat.

He held his crossbow cocked and ready. He also carried a loaded pistol in each boot, but the crossbow was silent and accurate at longer range, and it wasted no precious powder. The guns were only for emergencies.

Wingfield studied the dappled shadows. A little past

noon, he guessed. Before long he would have to turn round and head home for the colony. He had had a fairly good day: two rabbits, several small birds, and a fat gray squirrel hung from his belt.

He looked forward to fall and the harvest. If all went well this year, the colony would finally have enough wheat for bread and porridge and ale. How he wished—how all the Europeans wished—that this godforsaken new world offered wheat or barley or even oats of its own. But it did not, so all seed grain had to cross the Atlantic. Jamestown had lived mostly on game and roots for three years now. Lean and leathery, Wingfield had forgotten what a hot, fresh loaf tasted like. He remembered only that it was wonderful.

Something stirred in the undergrowth ahead. He froze. The motion came again. He spied a fine plump rabbit, its beady black eyes alert, its ears cocked for danger.

Moving slowly and steadily, hardly breathing, he raised the crossbow to his shoulder, aimed down the bolt. Once the rabbit looked toward him. He stopped moving again until it turned its head away.

He pressed the trigger. The bolt darted and slammed into a treetrunk a finger's breadth above the rabbit's ear. The beast bounded away.

"Hellfire!" Wingfield dashed after it, yanking out one of his pistols.

He almost tripped over the outflung branch of a grapevine. The vine's main stock was as big around as his calf. Virginia grapes, and the rough wine the colonists made from them, were among the few things that helped keep Jamestown bearable.

The panic-stricken rabbit, instead of diving into the bushes for cover and losing itself there, burst past a screen of brush into a clearing. "Your last mistake, beast!" Wingfield cried in triumph. He crashed through the brush himself, swinging up the gun as he did so.

By then the rabbit was almost to the other side of the clearing. He saw it thrashing in the grass there. Wingfield paused, puzzled: had a ferret torn out its throat as it scampered along, oblivious to everything but its pursuer? Then his grip tightened on the trigger, for a sim emerged from a thicket and ran toward the rabbit.

It had not seen him. It bent down by the writhing beast, smashed in the rabbit's head with a rock. Undoubtedly it had used another to bring the animal down; sims were deadly accurate throwing sharpened stones.

Wingfield stepped into the clearing. The colony was too hungry to let any food go.

The sim heard him. It rose, clutching the bloody rock in a large, knobby-knuckled hand. It was about as tall as the Englishman, and naked but for its own abundant hair. Its long, chinless jaw opened to let out a hoot of dismay.

Wingfield gestured with the pistol. Sims had no foreheads to speak of above their bone-ridged brows, but they had learned the colonists' weapons slew at a distance greater than they could cast their rocks. Usually, these days, they retreated instead of proving the lesson over again.

This one, though, stood its ground, baring broad, yellow teeth in a threatening grimace. Wingfield gestured again, more sharply, and hoped he seemed more confident than he felt. If his first shot missed, or even wounded but failed to kill, he would have to grab for his other gun while the sim charged—and pistol-range was not *that* much more than a stone's throw.

Then the bushes quivered on the far side of the clearing, and a second sim came out to stand behind its fellow. This one carried a large, sharp-edged rock ready to hurl. It shook its other fist at Wingfield, and shouted angrily.

It was the Englishman's turn to grind his teeth. If both sims rushed him, he would never have the chance to reload either a pistol or his crossbow. The odds of stopping them with just two shots were not worth betting his life on, not for a rabbit. And if they did kill him, they would not content themselves with the game he carried. They would eat him too.

Raising the pistol in a final warning, he drew back into the woods. The sims' mocking cries followed him. He hated the filthy animals . . . if they were animals. Close to a century had passed since the Spaniards brought the first pair back to Cadiz from their coastal fortress of Veracruz. Churchmen and scholars were still arguing furiously over whether sims were mere brute beasts or human beings.

At the moment, Wingfield was ready to hate them no matter what they were.

He found the tree where he had shot at the rabbit the sims were now doubtless gulping down raw. He managed to cut himself while he was digging out the crossbow bolt with his knife. That did nothing to improve his temper. Had he shot straight in the first place, he would not have put himself in the humiliating position of backing down from sims.

Thinking such dark thoughts, Wingfield turned back toward Jamestown. He scratched at his nose as he walked along, and felt skin peel under his nails. One more annoyance—he was too fair not to burn in this climate, but found wearing a hat equally intolerable.

On his way home, he knocked over a couple of quail and one of the native beasts that looked like giant, white-faced rats but tasted much better. That improved his mood, a little. He was still grumbling when Allan Cooper hailed him from the edge of the cleared ground.

Thinking of the guard's misery made him ashamed of his own bad temper. Cooper wore a gleaming back-and-breast with thick padding beneath; a heavy, plumed morion sat on his head. In that armor, he had to be steaming like a lobster boiled in its own shell. Yet he managed a cheery wave for Wingfield. "Good bag you have there," he called.

"It should be better, by one hare," Wingfield replied, pique flaring again. He explained how he had lost the beast to the sims.

"Aye, well, no help for such things sometimes, not two on one," Cooper sighed, and Wingfield felt relief at having his judgment sustained by a professional soldier. The guard went on, "The thieving devils are robbing traps again, too. Henry Dale came in empty-handed this afternoon, swearing foul enough to damn himself on the spot."

"If swearing damns a man, Henry was smelling brimstone long years ere this," Wingfield observed.

Cooper laughed. "You speak naught but the truth there, though I don't blame him for his fury this time. Sims are worse than foxes ever were—foxes have no hands." He hefted his matchlock musket. "Without guns, we'd never keep them from our own animals. And how often have they raided the henhouse?"

"Too many times." Wingfield turned to a less gloomy subject. "How is Cecil?"

"Doing splendidly," Cooper said, his voice full of pride. "The lad will be three months tomorrow." Cecil Cooper was Jamestown's oldest child; the first ship carrying women had reached Virginia only a year before. Wingfield had a daughter, Joanna, only a few weeks younger than the guard's son.

He left Cooper and walked down the muddy path through the fields. Several rows of thatch-roofed cabins stood by the log stockade that mounted cannon. On the other side of the fortress were longer rows, of graves. More than half of the original three shiploads of colonists had died from starvation or disease. A couple of the newest burials were pathetically small: even back in England, so many infants did not live to grow up—and life was far harsher here.

But the marker that grieved Wingfield most was one of the oldest, the one showing where Captain John Smith lay. Always eager to explore, he had set about learning the countryside from the day the English landed—until the sims killed him, three months later. Without him, the settlement seemed to have a lesser sense of drive, of purpose.

Still, it went on, as people and their works do. Several colonists swung the gates of the fortress open, so others could drive in the pigs, goats, and oxen for the night to protect them from the sims and other predators. The pigs and goats, which ate anything they came across, throve in this new land. The oxen had the same gaunt look as most of the colonists.

Wingfield's cabin was in the outer row, closest to the forest. Smoke rose from the chimney as he approached. The door stood open, to let in what air would come.

Hearing her husband's step, Anne Wingfield came out to greet him. He hugged her close, so glad she had chosen to spend her life with him. She had had her pick of suitors, as was true of all the women in Virginia; men outnumbered them four to one.

She exclaimed in pleasure at how much game he had brought home. Back in London, she would have been nothing special to look at: a rather husky, dark-haired girl in her early twenties, with strong features—if anything, handsome rather than pretty. On this side of the Atlantic, though, she was by definition a beauty.

"And how is Joanna?" Wingfield asked as his wife skinned and disjointed his two rabbits and tossed the meat into the stewpot. The rabbits shared it with a small piece of stale venison from a couple of days before and a mess of wild onions, beechnuts, mushrooms, and roots. The smell was heavenly.

"Asleep now, " Anne said, nodding toward the cradle, "but very well. She smiled at me again this morning."

"Maybe next time she will do it in the night, so I may see it too."

"I hope she will."

While they waited for the rabbits to cook, they dealt with the rest of Wingfield's catch, cutting the meat into thin strips and setting them on racks over the fire to dry and smoke. After what seemed an eternity, Anne ladled the stew into wooden bowls. Wingfield licked his clean. Though matters were not so grim as they had been the first couple of dreadful winters, he was always hungry.

"I would have had another cony, but for the sims," he said, and told Anne of the confrontation.

Her hand jumped to her mouth. "Those horrid beasts!

They should all be hunted down and slain, ere they harm any more of our good Englishmen. What would I have done here, alone save only for Joanna, had they hurt you?''

"No need to fret over might-have-beens; I'm here and hale," he reassured her, and got up and embraced her for good measure. "As for the sims, if they be men, slaying them out of hand so would burden us with a great weight of sin when we are called to the Almighty.''

"They are no creatures of His," Anne returned, "but rather of the Devil, the best he could do toward making true humankind.''

"I've heard that argument before. To me it smacks of the Manichean heresy. Only God has the power to create, not Satan."

"Then why did He shape such vile parodies of ourselves, His finest creatures? The sims know nothing of farming or weaving or any useful art. They cannot even set fires to cook the beasts they run down like dogs.''

"But they know fire, though I grant they cannot make it. Yet whenever lightning sets a blaze, some sim will play Prometheus and seize a burning brand. They keep the flames alive as long as they may, till they lose them from rain or sheer fecklessness.''

Anne set hands on hips, gave Wingfield a dangerous look. "When last we hashed this over, as I recollect, 'twas you who reckoned the sims animals and I the contrary. Why this reversal?''

"Why yours, save your concern for me?" he came back. "I thank you for't, but the topic's fit to take from either side. I tell you frankly, I cannot riddle it out in certain, but am changeable as a weathervane, ever thinking now one thing, now the other.''

"And I, and everyone," Anne sighed. "But if they put you in danger, my heart cannot believe them true men, no matter what my head might say.''

He reached out to set his fingers gently on her arm. The tender gesture was spoiled when a mosquito spiraled down to land on the back of his hand. The swamps round

Jamestown bred them in throngs worse than any he had known in England. He swatted at the bug, but it flew off before the deathblow landed.

Outside, someone struck up a tune on the mandolin, and someone else joined in with a drum. Voices soared in song. The settlers had only the amusements they could make for themselves. Wingfield looked out, saw a torchlit circle dance forming. He bobbed his head toward his wife. "Would it please you to join them?"

"Another time," she said. "Joanna will be waking soon, and hungry. We could step outside and watch, though." Wingfield agreed at once. Any excuse to get out of the hot, smelly cabin was a good one.

Suitors were buzzing as avidly as the mosquitoes round the few young women who had not yet chosen husbands. Some of those maids owned distinctly fragile reputations. With no others to choose from this side of the sea, they were courted nonetheless.

"Oh, my dear, what would you have me do?" cried a roguish youngster named Caleb Lucas to a girl who, smiling, had turned her back on him. "Go off to the woods and marry a sim?" Laughter rose, hearty from the men who heard him, half-horrified squeals from the women.

"Allan Cooper says the Spaniards do that, or anyway cohabit," Wingfield told Anne. Spain held a string of outposts down to Magellan's Strait and then up the western coast of South America, to serve her galleons plying the rich trade with the Indies.

"Have they not read Deuteronomy?" Anne exclaimed, her lip curling in disgust. Then curiosity got the better of her and she whispered, "Can there be issue from such unions?"

"In truth, I don't know. As Allan says, who's to tell the difference betwixt the get of a Spanish sire and that of a sim?" Anne blinked, then burst into giggles at the bawdy slander against England's longtime foe.

Before long, both she and her husband were yawning. The unremitting labor of building the colony left scant energy for leisure or anything else. Still, Wingfield hesitated before he blew out the last lamp in the cabin. He glanced toward Anne, and saw an answering flush rise from her throat to her cheeks. She was recovered now from the ordeal of childbirth. Perhaps tonight they might start a son. . . .

He was about to take Anne in his arms when Joanna let out a yowl. He stopped short. His wife started to laugh. She bared a breast. "Let me feed her quickly, and put her back to sleep. Then, why, we shall see what we shall see."

"Indeed we shall." Wingfield lay down on the lumpy straw-stuffed bed to wait. He knew at once he had made a mistake, but fell asleep before he could do anything about it.

Anne stuck out her tongue at him when the sun woke him the next morning. She skipped back when he reached for her. "This even," she promised. "We have too much to do of the day to waste it lying abed."

He grimaced. "You have a hateful way of being right." He scrambled into trousers and boots, set a plumed hat on his head to shield him from the sun. The plume was a bright pheasant's feather from England, now sadly battered. Soon he would have to replace it with a duller turkey tail-feather.

He was finishing a bowl of last night's stew, strong but still eatable, when someone knocked on the cabin door. "There, you see?" Anne said.

"Hush."

He opened the door. Henry Dale came in. He was a short, fussy man whose ruddy complexion and tightly held jaw gave clues to his temper. After dipping his head to Anne, he said, "Edward, what say we set a few snares, today—mayhap, if fortune favors us, in spots where no knavish sims will come on them to go a-poaching."

"Good enough. Allan Cooper told me how you were robbed yesterday."

Anne's presence plainly was the only thing keeping Dale from exploding with fury. He limited himself to a single strangled, "Aye." After a few moments, he went on, "Shall we be about it, then?"

Wingfield checked his pistols, tucked a bundle of cross-bow bolts into his beltpouch, nodded. After a too-brief embrace with his wife, he followed Dale out into the bright morning.

Colonists were already weeding, hoeing, watering in the fields. Caleb Lucas shooed a goat away from the fresh, green stalks of wheat, speeding it on with a kick that brought an indignant bleat from the beast. "And the very same to you," Lucas called after it. "Damned impudent beast, you can find victuals anywhere, so why thieve your betters' meals?"

"Belike the foolish creature thinks itself a sim," Dale grunted, watching the goat scurry for the edge of the woods, where it began browsing on shoots. "It lacks the accursed losels' effrontery, though, for it will not turn on its natural masters. The sims, now, those whoreson, beetle-headed, flap-ear'd stinkards—"

Without pausing but to draw breath, he continued in that vein until he and Wingfield were surrounded by forest. As had Anne's remarks the night before, his diatribe roused Wingfield's contentious nature.

"Were they such base animals as you claim," he said, "the sims would long since have exterminated one another, and not been here for us to find on our landing."

Dale gave him a look filled with dislike. "For all we know, they well-nigh did. 'Twas not on us they began their habits anthropophagous."

"If they were eating each other, Henry, and you style them 'anthropophagous,' does that not make men of them?" Wingfield asked mildly. His companion spluttered and turned even redder than usual.

A robin twittered among the leaves. So the colonists named the bird, at any rate, but it was not the redbreast of England. It was big and fat and stupid, its underparts the color of brick, not fire. It was, however, easy to kill, and quite tasty.

There were other sounds in the woods, too. Somewhere, far off, Wingfield heard the deep-throated barking cries of the sims. So did Henry Dale. He spat, deliberately, between his feet. "What men speak so?" he demanded. "Even captured and tamed—as much as one may tame the beasts—they do but point and gape and make dumb show, as a horse will, seeking to be led to manger."

"Those calls have meaning to them," Wingfield said.

"Oh, aye, belike. A wolf in a trap will howl so piteously it frightens its fellows away. Has he then a language?"

Having no good answer to that, Wingfield prudently kept silent.

As the two men walked, they looked for signs to betray the presence of small game. Dale, who was an able woodsman when amiable, spotted the fresh droppings that told of a woodchuck run. "A good place for a snare," he said.

But even as he was preparing to cut a noose, his comrade found a track in the soft ground to the side of the run: the mark of a large, bare foot. "Leave be, Henry," he advised. "The sims have been here before us."

"What's that you say?" Dale came over to look at the footprint. One of the settlers might have made it, but they habitually went shod. With a disgusted grunt, Dale stowed away the twine. "Rot the bleeding blackguards! I'd wish their louse-ridden souls to hell, did I think God granted them any."

"The Spaniards baptize them, 'tis said."

"Good on them!" Dale said, which startled Wingfield until he continued, "A papist baptism, by Jesus, is the most certain highroad to hell of any I know."

They walked on. Wingfield munched on late-ripening wild strawberries, larger and sweeter than any that grew in England. He spotted a woodchuck ambling from tussock to tussock. This time he aimed with special care, and his shot knocked the beast over. Dale grunted again, now in approval. He had bagged nothing more than a couple of songbirds.

They did find places to set several new snares: simple

drag nooses, hanging snares made from slip nooses fastened to the ends of saplings, and fixed snares set near bushes. The latter were especially good for catching rabbits.

They also visited the snares already set. A horrible stench announced that one of those had taken a black-and-white New World polecat. Skinned and butchered to remove the scent glands, the beast made good eating. Wingfield and Dale tossed a copper penny to see who would have to carry it home. Wingfield lost.

Two traps had been sprung but held no game. There were fresh sim footprints around both. Dale's remakes were colorful and inventive.

The Englishmen headed back toward Jamestown not long after the sun began to wester. They took a route different from the one they had used on the way out: several traps remained to be checked.

A small, brown-and-white-striped ground squirrel scurried away from Wingfield's boot. It darted into a clump of cockleburs. A moment later, both hunters leaped back in surprise as the little animal was flung head-high, kicking in a noose, when a bent sapling suddenly sprang erect.

"Marry!" Dale said. "I don't recall setting a snare there."

"Perhaps it was someone else. At all odds, good luck we happened along now." Wingfield walked over to retrieve the ground squirrel which now hung limp. He frowned as he undid the noose from around its neck. "Who uses sinew for his traps?"

"No one I know," Dale said. "Twine is far easier to work with."

"Hmm." Wingfield was examining the way the sinew was bound to the top of the sapling. It had not been tied at all, only wrapped around and around several twigs until firmly in place. "Have a look at this, will you, Henry?"

Dale looked, grunted, turned away. Wingfield's voice pursued him: "What animals make traps, Henry?"

"Aye, well, this is the first we've seen, in all the time we've been this side of the Atlantic. I take that to mean the

sims but ape us, as a jackdaw will human speech, without
having the divine spark of wit to devise any such thing for
themselves. Damn and blast, man, if a dog learns to walk
upon his hinder feet, is he then deserving of a seat in
Parliament?''

"More than some who have them now," Wingfield
observed.

Both men laughed. Dale reached for the ground squirrel,
tossed it into the bag with the rest of the game he carried.
His crooked teeth flashed in a rare grin. "It does my heart
good to rob the vermin this once, instead of the other way
round."

His good humor vanished when he and Wingfield returned to the settlement. They found not only Allan
Cooper and the other three guards armed and armored, but
also a double handful more men. That morning a sim had
burst out of the woods, smashed in a goat's skull with a
rock, flung the animal under an arm, and escaped before
the startled Englishmen could do anything.

"I shot, but I missed," Cooper raid morosely.

"It's a poor trade for a ground squirrel, Henry," Wingfield remarked.

His hunting partner's scowl was midnight black. "The
mangy pests grow too bold! Just the other night they
slaughtered a hound outside the stockade, hacked it to pieces
with their stones, and were eating the flesh raw when at last
the sentry came round with his torch and spied them. He
missed, too," Dale finished, with a sidelong look at
Cooper.

"And would you care to draw a conclusion from that?"
the guard asked. His hand caressed the hilt of his rapier.

Henry Dale hesitated. As a gentleman, he was trained to
the sword. But liverish temper or no, he was not a fool;
Cooper had learned in a harsher school than his, and
survived. At last Dale said, "I draw the same conclusion as
would any man of sense: that our best course is to rid
ourselves of these pestiferous sims forthwith, as wolves and

other vicious creatures have long been hunted out of England."

"I hold to war, Henry, on being attacked, but not to murder," Cooper said. "Mind, we must seem as outlandish to them as they to us."

"Killing a sim is no more murder than butchering a pig," Dale retorted. The endless debate started up again.

Having no desire to join in another round, Wingfield took his share of the game back to his cabin. Anne was changing Joanna's soiled linen. She looked up with a wan smile. "There's no end to't."

The baby kicked her legs and smiled toothlessly at her father. He felt his own tight expression soften.

He plucked the songbirds, skinned the polecat, set the hide aside to be tanned. He gutted the birds and tossed their little naked bodies into the stewpot whole. He threw the offal outside for the pigs or dogs to find. The black-and-white polecat required more skillful butchery, for it had to be cut into pieces after the scent glands were removed.

"Thank you, dear." Anne rocked Joanna in her arms. "She's getting hungry—aren't you, sweet one? What say I feed you now, so you let us eat in peace afterwards. Can you tend to the stew, Edward?"

"Of course." He stirred the bubbling contents of the pot with a wooden spoon. Now and again he tossed in a dash of dried, powdered herbs or a pinch of grayish sea-salt.

Joanna nursed lustily, then fell asleep. The stew began to smell savory. Anne was about to ladle it into bowls when the baby wet herself and started crying again. Her mother gave Wingfield a look of mingled amusement and despair.

"Go on with what you were about," he told her. "I'll tend to Joanna." Anne sighed gratefully. Wingfield tossed the soggy linen into the pile with the rest for tomorrow's washing. He found a dry cloth, wrapped the baby's loins, and set her in her cradle. Anne rocked it while they ate.

Joanna tolerated not being held, but showed no interest in going back to sleep. She squawked indignantly when

Anne made the mistake of trying to turn her onto her belly, and remained irritated enough to stay awake even after her mother picked her up.

Her fussy cries rang loud in the small cabin. After a while, Wingfield thrust a torch into the fire. "Let's walk her about outside," he suggested. "That often seems to calm her."

Anne agreed at once. She rocked the baby in her arms while her husband held the torch high so they would not stumble in the darkness. With his free hand, he batted at the insects the torch drew.

The James River splashed against the low, swampy peninsula on which Jamestown sat, and murmured as it flowed by unimpeded to the south. Above it, on this clear, moonless night, the Milky Way glowed like pale mist among the stars of the Scorpion and the Archer. Elsewhere, but for silver points, the sky was black.

Even blacker against it loomed the forest to the north. Suddenly Wingfield felt how tiny was the circle of light his torch cast: as tiny as the mark the English had made on this vast new land. The comparison disturbed him.

From the edge of the forest came the cries of sims, calling back and forth. Wingfield wondered how much meaning lay behind them. Those bestial ululations could hardly be true speech—Henry Dale was right there—but they were much more varied, more complex, than a wolfpack's howls.

Anne shivered, though the night was warm. "Let us go back. I take fright, hearing them so close."

"I mislike it also," Wingfield said, turning round. "We are not yet here in numbers enough to keep them from drawing nigh as they wish. Be glad, though, you were still in dear England those first two years, when they thought us and ours some new sort of prey for their hunting." He touched the knife on his belt. "We've taught them better than that, at any rate."

"I've heard the tales," Anne said quietly.

Wingfield nodded. As was the way of things, though, not all the tales got told. He had been one of the men who brought John Smith's body back for burial. He knew how little of it rested under its stone, awaiting the resurrection.

To his mind, the sims' man-eating habits gave strong cause to doubt they had souls. If one man devoured another's flesh, to whose body would that flesh return come the day of judgment? As far as he knew, no learned divine had yet solved that riddle.

Such profitless musings occupied him on the way back to the cabin. Once inside, Anne set Joanna back in the cradle. The baby sighed but stayed asleep; she probably would not rouse till the small hours of the morning.

The embers in the fireplace cast a dying red glow over the single room. Wingfield stripped off his clothes; in the sultry Virginia summer, nightwear was a positive nuisance.

Anne lay down beside him. He stroked her smooth shoulder. She turned toward him. Her eyes were enormous in the dim light. "Here it is, evening," he said, at the same time as she was whispering, "This even, is it not?" They laughed until he silenced her with a kiss.

Afterwards, he felt his heart slow as he drifted toward slumber. He was hotter than he had been before, and did not mind at all; the warmth of the body was very different from that of the weather. He did not know why that was so, but it was. Anne was already breathing deeply and smoothly. He gave up thought and joined her.

He was never sure what exactly woke him, some hours later; he usually slept like a log till morning. Even Joanna's cries would not stir him, though Anne came out of bed at once for them. And this noise was far softer than any the baby made.

Maybe what roused him was the breeze from the open cabin door. His eyes opened. His hand went for his knife even before he consciously saw the two figures silhouetted in the doorway. *Thieves*, was his first thought. The colonists had so few goods from England that theft was always a problem, the threat of the whipping-post notwithstanding.

Then the breeze brought him the smell of the invaders.

The Englishmen bathed seldom; they were often rank. But this was a thicker, almost cloying stench, as if skin and water had never made acquaintance. And the shape of those heads outlined against the night—

Ice ran through Wingfield. "Sims!" he cried, bounding to his feet.

Anne screamed. The sims shouted. One sprang at Wingfield. He saw its arm go back, as if to stab, and knew it must have one of its sharpened stones to hand. That could let out a life as easily as his own dagger.

He knocked the stroke aside with his left forearm, and felt his hand go numb; the sims were devilish strong. He thrust with his right and felt his blade bite flesh. The sim yammered. But the wound was not mortal. The sim grappled with him. They rolled over and over on the dirt floor, each grabbing for the other's weapon and using every fighting trick he knew. The sim might have had less skill than Wingfield, but was physically powerful enough to make up for it.

A tiny corner of Wingfield's awareness noticed the other sim scuttling toward the hearth. He heard Anne shriek, "Mother Mary, the baby!" Bold as a tigress, she leapt at the sim, her hands clawed, but it stretched her senseless with a backhand blow.

At almost the same moment, the sim Wingfield was battling tore its right arm free from the weakened grasp of his left. He could not ward off the blow it aimed, but partially deflected it so that the flat front of the stone, rather than the edge, met his forehead. The world flared for a moment, then grayed over.

He could not have been unconscious long. He was already aware of himself, and of the pounding anguish in his head, when someone forced a brandy bottle into his mouth. He choked and sputtered, spraying out most of the fiery liquid.

He tried to sit; hands supported his back and shoulders. He could not understand why the torch Caleb Lucas held was so blurred until he raised his arm to his eyes and wiped away blood.

Lucas offered the brandy again. This time Wingfield got it down. Healing warmth spread from his middle. Then he remembered what had happened with one sim while he fought the other, and he went cold again. "Anne!" he cried.

He looked about wildly, and moaned when he saw a blanket-covered form on the floor not far from him. "No, fear not, Edward, she is but stunned," said Allan Cooper's wife Claire, a strong, steady woman a few years older than Anne. "We cast the bedding over her to hide her nakedness, no more."

"Oh, God be thanked!" Wingfield gasped.

"But—" Cooper began, then looked helplessly at his wife, not sure how to go on. He seemed to make up his mind. He and Lucas bent by Wingfield. Together, they manhandled Wingfield to his feet, guided his stumbling steps over to Joanna's cradle.

He moaned again. It was empty.

Anne sat on a hard wooden chair, her face buried in her hands. She had not stopped sobbing since she returned to her senses. She rocked back and forth in unending grief. "God, God, God have mercy on my dear Joanna," she wailed.

"I will get her back," Wingield said, "or take such a vengeance that no sim shall dare venture within miles of an Englishman ever again."

"I want no vengeance," Anne cried. "I want my darling babe again."

The colonists' first efforts at pursuit had already failed. They had set dogs on the sims' trail less than an hour after the attack. With the blood Wingfield had drawn, the trail had been fresh and clear. Only for a while, though: the ground north of Jamestown was so full of ponds and streams that the dogs lost the scent. Further tracking had had to wait for daylight—and with every passing minute, the sims took themselves farther away.

"Why?" Anne asked. The question was not directed at anyone. "Why should even such heartless brutes snatch up a defenseless babe? What are they doing to her?"

Wingfield's imagination conjured up a horde of possibilities, each worse than the one before. He knew he could never mention even the least of them to his wife.

But her first agonized question puzzled him as well. He had never heard of the sims acting as they had that night. They killed, but they did not capture—he felt heartsick anew as he worked out the implications of that.

Caleb Lucas said, "I fear me they but sought specially tender flesh." He spoke softly, so Anne would not hear.

Wingfield shook his head. The motion hurt. "Why take so great a risk for such small game?" He gritted his teeth at speaking of Joanna so, but went on, "They would have gained more meat by waiting until one of us stepped outside his cabin to ease himself, striking him down, and making away with him. If they had been cunning, they might have escaped notice till dawn."

"Wherefore, then?" Lucas asked. Wingfield could only spread his hands.

"What do you purpose doing now?" Allan Cooper added.

"As I told Anne," Wingfield said, rising. His head still throbbed dreadfully and he was wobbly on his feet, but purpose gave his voice iron. "I will search out the places where the sims encamp in their wanderings, and look for traces of Joanna. If God grant I find her living, I'll undertake a rescue. If it be otherwise—"

Henry Dale stuck his head in the cabin door. His lips stretched back in a savage grin. "—Then kill them all," he finished for Wingfield. " 'Twere best you do it anyhow, at first encounter."

"No," Wingfield said, "nor anyone else on my behalf, I pray you. Until I have certain knowledge my daughter is dead, I needs must act as if she yet lives, and do nothing to jeopardize her fate. A wholesale slaughter of sims might well inflame them all."

"What cares one pack of beasts what befalls another?" Dale asked scornfully.

Allan Cooper had a comment more to the point. "Should you fare forth alone, Edward, I greatly doubt you'd work a wholesale slaughter in any case—more likely the sims would slay you."

That set off fresh paroxysms of weeping from Anne. Wingfield looked daggers at the guard. "I can but do my best. My hunting has taught me somewhat of woodscraft, and bullet and bolt strike harder and farther than stones." He spoke mostly for his wife's benefit; he knew too well Cooper was probably right. Still, he went on, "You'd try no less were it your Cecil."

"Oh, aye, so I would," Cooper said. "You misunderstand me, though. My thought was to come with you."

"And I," Henry Dale said. Caleb Lucas echoed him a moment later.

Tears stung Wingfield's eyes. Anne leapt from her chair and kissed each of his friends in turn. At any other time that would have shocked and angered him; now he thought it no less than their due.

Yet fear for his daughter forced expedience from him. He said, "Henry, I know your skill amongst the trees. But what of you, Allan? Stealth is paramount here, and clanking about armored a poor preparation for't."

"Fear not on my score," Cooper said. "Or ever I took the royal shilling, I had some nodding acquaintance with the Crown's estates and the game on them." He grinned slyly. Wingfield asked no more questions; if Cooper had made his living poaching, he would never say so straight out.

"What will the council say, though, Allan?" Dale demanded. "They will not take kindly to a guardsman haring off at wild adventure."

"Then damnation take them," Cooper replied. "Am I not a free Englishman, able to do as I will rather than hark to seven carping fools? Every subject's duty is the king's; but every subject's soul is his own."

"Well spoken! Imitate the action of the tiger!" cried Caleb Lucas, giving back one quote from Shakespeare for another.

The other three men were carefully studying him. Wingfield said, "You will correct me if I am wrong, Caleb, but is't not so your only forays into the forest have been as a lumberer?"

The young man gave a reluctant nod. He opened his mouth to speak, but Dale forestalled him: "Then you must stay behind. Edward has reason in judging this a task for none but the woodswise."

Wingfield set a hand on Lucas's shoulder. "No sense in anger or disappointment, Caleb. I know the offer came in all sincerity."

"And I," Anne echoed softly. Lucas jerked his head in acknowledgment and left.

"Let's be at it, then," Cooper said. "To our weapons, then meet here and away." Wingfield knew the guard had no hope of finding Joanna alive when he heard Cooper warn Henry Dale, "Fetch plenty of powder and bullets." Dale's brusque nod said the same.

Before noon, the three men reached the spot where the dogs had lost the sims' scent. As Wingfield had known it would, the trail led through the marshes that made up so much of the peninsula on which Jamestown lay. By unspoken consent, he and his companions paused to rest and to scrape at the mud clinging to their boots.

His crossbow at the ready, Wingfield looked back the way he had come, then to either side. For some time now, he had had a prickly feeling of being watched, though he told himself a sim would have to be mad to go so near the English settlement after the outrage of the night before.

But Cooper and Dale also seemed uneasy. The guard rubbed his chin, saying, "I like this not. I'm all a-jitter, as I've not felt since the poxy Spaniards snuck a patrol round our flank in Holland."

"We'd best push on," Henry Dale said. "We'll cast about

upstream and down, in hopes of picking up tracks again. Were things otherwise, I'd urge us separate, one going one way and two the other, to speed the search. Now"—he bared his teeth in frustration—" 'twere better we stayed in a body."

The bushes quivered, about fifteen paces away. Three weapons swung up as one. But instead of a sim bursting from the undergrowth, out came Caleb Lucas. "You young idiot! We might have shot you!" Cooper snarled. His finger was tight on the trigger of his pistol; as a veteran soldier, he always favored firearms.

Lucas was even filthier than the men he faced. His grin flashed in his mud-spattered face. "Send me back no if you dare, my good sirs. These past two hours I've dogged your steps, betimes close enough to spit, and never did you tumble to it. Have I not, then, sufficient of the woodsman's art to accompany you farther?"

Wingfield removed the bolt from his bow, released the string. "I own myself beaten, Caleb, for how should we say you nay? The damsels back in town, though, will take your leaving hard."

"They'll have plenty to company them whilst I'm gone, and shall be there on my return," Lucas said cheerfully. "And in sooth, Edward, are we not off to rescue a fair young damsel of our own?"

"Not wondrous fair, perhaps, since the little lass favors me, but I take your meaning." Wingfield considered. "We'll do as Henry proposed before your eruption, and divide to examine the streambank. Caleb, you'll come with me this way; Henry and Allan shall take the other. Half a mile either way, then back here to meet. A pistol-shot to signal a find; otherwise we go on as best we can. Agreed?"

Everyone nodded. A sergeant to the core, Cooper muttered, "As well I don't have Caleb with me—I want a man I know'll do as he's told." Unabashed, Lucas came to such a rigid parody of attention that the others could not help laughing.

He and Wingfield hurried along the edge of the creek,

their heads down. Herons and white-plumed egrets flapped away; frogs and turtles splashed into the turbid water. "There!" Lucas said. His finger stabbed forth. The print of a bare foot was pressed deeply into the mud.

"Good on you!" Wingfield clapped him on the back, drew out one pistol, and fired it into the air. He reloaded in the few minutes before Dale and Cooper came trotting up.

Dale, who was red as a tile, grunted when he spied the footprint. "The brutes did not slip far enough aside, eh, my hearties? Well, after them!"

The trail ran northwest, almost paralleling the James River but moving slowly away. It became harder to follow as the ground grew drier. And the effort of sticking to it meant the four trackers had to go more slowly than the sims they pursued.

By evening, the Englishmen were beyond the territory they knew well. Explorers had penetrated much farther into the interior of America, of course, but not all of them had come back—and with the colony's survival hanging by so slender a thread, exploration for its own sake won scant encouragement.

At last the thickening twilight made Wingfield stop. "We'll soon lose the trace," he said, smacking fist into palm, "yet I misdoubt the sims push on still. What to do, what to do?"

Again Caleb Lucas came to the rescue. "Look there, between the two pines. Is't not a pillar of smoke, mayhap marking one of the sims' nests?"

"Marry, it is!" Wingfield turned to Allan Cooper, the most experienced of them at such estimations. "How far away do you make it?"

The guard's eyes narrowed as he thought. "The sims favor large blazes, as being less likely to go out. Hmm, perhaps two, two-and-a-half miles—too far to reach before full dark."

"All the better," Dale said. "I'd liefer come on the accursed creatures with them unawares." No one cared to disagree.

Cooper took the lead as they grew closer. "Reminds me of a scouting party I commanded outside Haarlem," he remarked, and reminisced in quiet tones until they drew within a few hundred yards of the fire.

He stopped then, and waved the others to a halt behind him. "Let me go on alone a bit," he whispered. "If they're smart as Spaniards (which says not much), they're apt to have a sentry out, and I'll need to scout a way past it."

He slipped away before Henry Dale could voice the protest he was plainly forming. Whether a poacher or not, Cooper had told the truth: he could move silently in the woods. It was too dark to see his face when he reappeared, but his whisper was smug: "The bugger's there, just so. Here, hands and knees now, after me, and he'll never be the wiser."

"That were so in any case," Dale retorted, but he lowered himself with the others.

Again Wingfield caught the thick, warm stench from the sim. It never sensed him or his comrades, who crawled past downwind—another proof Cooper knew his business. The Englishmen peered through a last thin screen of bushes at the band of sims.

Perhaps twenty-five were there. Several slept close to the fire. From time to time, a grizzled male threw a fresh branch onto it; the sim would let it get low, but never close to going out.

Along with the odors of smoke and sim, the air still held the faint flavor of roasted, or rather burnt, meat. Bones from small game lay about. Every so often a sim would pick one up and gnaw on it.

The sims ate anything. A female turned over stones and popped the grubs and crawling things it found into its mouth or handed them to the toddling youngster beside it. The firekeeper grabbed moths out of the air with practiced skill, crunching them between its teeth.

Another, younger, male was using a hammer made from a piece of antler to chip flakes from a rock it held between its knees.

Wingfield studied the sims with growing disappointment. None bore a knife wound, and he saw no sign of Joanna. The three or four infants in the band all bore a finer coat of the dark brown hair that covered their elders. One was nursing at its mother's breast and fell asleep in its arms. The female sim set it down on a pile of leaves. It woke up and started to yowl. The mother picked it up and rocked it till it was quiet again.

Allan Cooper let out the ghost of a chuckle. "Looks familiar, that."

"Aye," Wingfield whispered back. "We may as well be off. We've not found here what we sought."

To his surprise, Henry Dale said, "Wait." He had been watching a pair of sims grooming each other, hands scurrying through hair after ticks, fleas, and lice. The scratchings and pickings had gradually turned to caresses and nuzzlings. Then the sims coupled by the fire like dogs, the male behind the female. The rest of the band paid no attention.

"Shameless animals," Dale muttered, but he watched avidly until they were through.

He was, Wingfield recalled, unwed, and with his temper had enjoyed no luck among the single women at the settlement. Unslaked lust could drive a man to madness; Wingfield remembered the sinful longing with which his own eyes had followed a pretty cabin boy aboard the *Godspeed*.

But even if sure the prohibitions in Deuteronomy did not apply, he would have let sim females alone forever, no matter what vile rumor said Spaniards did. One could close one's eyes to the ugliness, hold one's nose against the stench, but how, in an embrace, could one keep from noticing the *hair . . .*?

The sound of the edge of a hand striking a wrist and a harsh whispered curse snapped Wingfield from his lascivious reverie. "Be damned to you right back, Henry!" Caleb Lucas said hotly. "Edward said no killings whilst his daughter remains stolen, and if you come to his aid you can do his bidding."

Dale picked up his pistol, which by good luck had fallen on soft grass and neither made a betraying noise nor discharged. "The filthy creatures all deserve to die," he growled, barely bothering to hold his voice low.

His face was pitiless as a wolf's. Wingfield abruptly realized Dale had never expected to find Joanna alive, but was along only for revenge. If by some stroke of fortune they should come across the baby, his comrade might prove more dangerous to her than the sims.

All he said, though, was, "My thanks, Caleb. Away now, quiet as we can. Come morning we'll hash out what to do next."

Cooper led them away from the sims by the same route they had taken in; again they passed by the lone watcher close enough to catch its reek. They camped without fire, which would have brought sims at a run. After gnawing leathery smoked meat, they divided the night into four watches and seized what uncomfortable, bug-ridden sleep they could.

When morning came, they took council. "It makes no sense," Henry Dale complained. "Where was the sim you fought, Edward? None of the beasts round their blaze showed the knifemark you said you set in him."

"I thought the same, and again find myself without answer," Wingfield said; if Dale was willing to let last night's quarrel lie, he did not intend to bring it up himself.

"Hold—I have a thought," Caleb Lucas said. Somehow he managed to seem fresh on scanty rest. "When we spied the sims' fire, we hared straight for it, and gave no more heed to the track we'd followed. Could we pick it up once more—"

"The very thing!" Allan Cooper exclaimed. " 'Sblood, we're stupider than the sims, for we acted on what we thought they'd done when the truth was laid out before us, had we only the wit to look on it."

"Shorn of the windy philosophizing, the point is well taken," Dale said.

Before Cooper had time to get angry, Wingfield said hastily, "Could you find the spot where we saw the smoke, Allan?"

"Maybe his royal highness there would sooner lead us," the guard snapped. Dale opened his mouth to reply, but Wingfield glared at him so fiercely that he shut it again. At length Cooper said, "Yes, I expect I can."

He proved good as his word, though the trip was necessarily slow and cautious to avoid foraging sims. When the Englishmen returned to the place by the two pines, they cast about for the trace they had pursued the day before.

Cooper found it first, and could not help sending a look of satisfaction at Henry Dale's back before he summoned his companions. They eagerly followed the track, which, to their growing confusion, ran in the same direction they had previously chosen.

"Cooper, we've already seen the brutes did not come this way," Dale said with an ominously false show of patience.

"No, all we've seen is that they did not reach the band. Tracks have no flair for lying." Cooper held his course; Dale, fuming, had no choice but to follow. A few minutes later, the guard stiffened. "Look here, all of you. Of a sudden, they spun on their heels and headed northeast."

"Why, I wonder?" Wingfield said. He glanced toward the column of smoke from the sims' fire, pointed. "They could easily see that from here."

"What does it matter?" That was Henry Dale. "Let's hunt down the beasts and have done with this pointless chatter."

"Pointless it is not," Wingfield said, "if it will help us in the hunting. Were you coming to a camp of your friends, Henry, why would you then avoid it?"

"Who knows why a sim does as it does, or cares? If it amuses you to enter the mind of an animal, go on, but ask me not to partake of your fatuity."

"Hold, Henry," Cooper said. "Edward's query is deserving of an answer. In war, now, I'd steer clear of a camp, did it contain the enemy."

"Are sim bands nations writ in small?" Dale scoffed.

"I tell you honestly, I do not know for a fact," Cooper replied. "Nor, Henry, do you." Dale scowled. Cooper stared him down.

The country rose as they traveled away from the James. The sims they were following stuck to wooded and brushy areas, even when that meant deviating from their chosen course. After seeing the fourth or fifth such zigzag, Cooper grunted, "Nation or no, that pair didn't relish being spotted. Soldiers travel so, behind the foe's lines."

"Even if you have reason," Caleb Lucas said a while later, ruefully rubbing at the thorn scratches on his arms, "why did the wretched creatures have to traverse every patch of brambles they could find?"

"Not for the sake of hearing your whining, surely." Had Cooper given Henry Dale that rebuke, he would have growled it. With the irrepressible young Lucas, he could not keep a twinkle from his eyes.

All the Englishmen were scratched and bleeding. Wingfield stopped to extract a briar that had pierced his breeches. The bushes around him were especially thick and thorny, their leaves a glistening, venomous dark green. Only against that background would the white bit of cloth have caught his notice.

He reached out and plucked it from its bramble without realizing for a moment what it meant. Then he let out a whoop that horrified his comrades. They stared at him as at a madman while he held up the tiny piece of linen.

"From Joanna's shift!" he said when he had calmed enough to speak clearly again. "It must be—the sims know nothing of fabric, nor even pelts to cover their loins."

"Save their own pelts, that is," Lucas grinned. Then the excitement took him too. "Proof we're on the right track."

"And proof—or at least hope—my little girl yet lives," Wingfield said, as much to himself as to the rest. "Had the sims sought no more than meat, they'd not have left the shift round her so long, would they?" He looked to the others for reassurance.

"It were unlikely, Edward," Cooper said gently. Caleb Lucas nodded. Henry Dale said nothing. Wiping his florid face with his sleeve, he pushed ahead.

Late that afternoon, near the edge of a creek, the Englishmen came upon the scaly tail of a muskrat—all that was left of the beast save for a blood-soaked patch of grass Allan Cooper found close by. "Here the sims stopped to feed," the guard judged. Further casting about revealed a sharpened stone that confirmed his guess.

"This making of tools on the spot has its advantages," Caleb Lucas said. "One need never be without."

"Oh, aye, indeed, if one has but three different tools to make," Henry Dale said sourly.

Wingfield did his best to ignore the continual bickering. He went over the ground inch by inch, searching for signs of Joanna. He finally found a spattering of loose, yellow-brown muck on some chickweed not far from the edge of the stream. His heart leaped.

The others came rushing over at his exclamation. Dale and Lucas stared uncomprehending at the dropping, but Allan Cooper recognized it at once. "The very same as my little Cecil makes, Edward," he said, slapping Wingfield on the back. "This far, your baby was alive."

"Aye," Wingfield got out, giddy with relief. His greatest fear had been that the sims would simply dash her against a treetrunk and throw her tiny broken body into the woods for scavengers to eat.

"They have her yet, I must grant it," Dale said. "Do they take her back to their fellows for tortures viler than those they might perform in haste?"

"Shut up, damn you!" Wingfield shouted, and would have gone for Dale had Cooper and Caleb Lucas not quickly stepped between them.

"Have you not called them beasts all this while, Henry?" Lucas said. "Beasts kill, aye, but they do not torture. That is reserved for men."

"Leave be, all of you," Cooper ordered in a parade-ground voice. "Yes, you too, Caleb. Such squabbling avails us nothing, the more so when a life's at stake."

The guard's plainspoken good sense was obvious to everyone, though Wingfield could not help adding, "See you remember we know it is a rescue now, Henry. I charge you, do nothing to put Joanna at risk."

Dale nodded gruffly.

The Englishmen hurried on; hope put fresh heart in them and sped their weary feet. Soon they were going down into marshier country again as they approached the York River, which paralleled the James to the north. They all kept peering ahead for a telltale smudge of smoke against the sky.

Darkness fell before they found it. They had to stop, for fear of losing the sims' trail. Wingfield drew first watch. He sat in the warm darkness, wishing he had some way to let Anne know what he had found. His wife would still be suffering the agony of fear and uncertainty he had felt until that afternoon, and would keep on suffering it until he brought their daughter home.

He refused to think of failing. He had before, when he thought Joanna dead. But having come so close, he felt irrationally sure things would somehow work out. He fought that feeling too. It could make him careless, and bring all his revived dreams to nothing.

When he surrendered sentry duty to Lucas, he thought he would be too keyed up to sleep. As it had back in his own bed, though, exhaustion took its toll; the damp ground might have been a goosedown mattress ten feet thick.

Henry Dale spotted the sims' fire first. The Englishmen were much closer to it than they had been to the one a couple of days before, for it was smaller and not as smoky. The hour was just past noon.

"We wait here," Allan Cooper decreed, "so we may approach by night and lessen the danger of being discovered."

They soon found that danger was real. A sim on its way back to the fire walked within a double handful of paces of their hiding place. By luck, it was carrying a fawn it had killed, and did not notice them.

"Ah, venison," Caleb Lucas sighed softly, gnawing on smoked meat tough enough to patch the soles of his boots.

The wait seemed endless to Wingfield; the sun crawled across the sky. To be so close and yet unable to do anything to help his daughter ate at him. But getting himself killed with an ill-considered rush would do her no good either.

The Englishmen made low-voiced plans. All had to be tentative. So much depended on where Joanna was around the fire, what the sims were doing to her (Wingfield would not let himself consider Henry Dale's notion), how many sims there were, how much surprise the rescuers could achieve.

At last the birds of day began to fall silent. The sky went gold and crimson in the west, deep blue and then purple overhead. When stars came out not far from where the sun had set, Allan Cooper nudged his fellows. "Now we move—cannily, mind."

The guard led them as they crept toward the fire. He was humming a Spanish tune under his breath. Wingfield did not think he knew he was doing it. But he had learned his soldiering against Spanish troops, and a return to it brought back old habits.

This band of sims dwelt in more open country than had the other. The Englishmen could not get very close. Half their plans, the ones involving unexpectedly bursting from the woods and snatching up Joanna, evaporated on the instant. They whispered curses and watched from the nearest shrubbery.

At first glance the scene in front of them did not seem much different from the one they had watched a couple of nights before. There were more sims here, perhaps as many as forty. Three or four males were roasting roots and bits of meat on sticks over the fire, and passing the chunks of food to sims who stood round waiting.

Another male was cutting up an animal that, with its skin removed, Wingfield could not identify. He stiffened. That was no stone tool the sim used; it was a good steel knife. Henry Dale noticed that at about the same time he did. "Damned thieving creatures," he muttered.

A female set the young one it was holding down on the ground, then rose and ambled away from the fire, probably to relieve itself. The infant followed it with its eyes and shrieked in distress. The adult came back and played with it, dandling it in its arms, rolling it about, and making faces at it. After the child was quiet, the female left it again. This time, it stayed quiet until its mother returned.

This band did not have one firekeeper as the other had. From time to time, a female or young male would come up to the blaze and toss on a branch or a shrub. The system seemed haphazard to Wingfield, but the fire never looked likely to go out.

A group of sims had gathered on the far side of the fire around something their bodies kept Wingfield from making out. Whatever it was, it mightily interested them. Some stood, others hunkered down on their haunches for a closer look. They pointed and jabbered; once one shook another, as if to get a point across. Wingfield could not help chuckling to himself—they reminded him of so many Englishmen at a public house.

Then the chuckle died in his throat, for he saw that one of the males there had a great glob of mud plastered to the hair from its rib cage. The sim moved slowly and painfully. Wingfield touched Cooper's arm. "On my oath, that is the one I fought. I knew I marked him with my knife."

"Then we tracked truly, as I thought. Good. Now we—"

Wingfield's hand clamped down tight on the guard's wrist, silencing him. From the center of that tightly packed bunch of sims had come a familiar thin, wailing cry. "Joanna!"

"How do you know 'tis not one of their cubs yowling?" Henry Dale demanded. "All brats sound alike."

"Only to a single man," Wingfield retorted, too full of

exaltation and fear to care how he spoke. Against all hope, his daughter lived, but how was he to free her from her captors? And what—the question ate at him, as it had from the onset—what had prompted the sims to steal her in the first place? .

A couple of sims stepped away to take food, opening a gap in the crowd. "There, do you see?" Wingfield said triumphantly. No matter how dirty she was (quite, at the moment), smooth, pink Joanna could never be mistaken for a baby sim.

As if to make that pikestaff-plain, one of the sim infants lay beside her on a bed of grass and leaves. Terror stabbed Wingfield as an adult ran its hand down his daughter's chest and belly, but then it did the same to the hairy baby next to her. It stared at its palm, as if not believing what it had felt.

The sim Wingfield had wounded held up one of Joanna's hands, then that of the infant of its own kind. Then it held up their feet in the same way. The other sims grunted. Some looked at their own hands and feet, then toward Joanna's. Except for size and hairiness, there was not much difference between their members and hers.

But then the sim patted Joanna's smooth, rounded head, and that was nothing like what the tiny sim next to her had. Already its brow beetled bonily, and above it the skull quickly retreated. Noticing that, one of the adults rubbed her own receding brow. She scratched, for all the world as if lost in thought.

"What are they playing at?" Henry Dale whispered harshly. Wingfield, at a loss, could only shrug.

Caleb Lucas said, "If a tribe of devils set up housekeeping outside London and we wished to learn of what they were capable, were it not wise for us to seize on a small one, knowing full well a grown devil would drag us straight to perdition?"

"Why are you dragging in devils?" Dale did not have the type of mind that quickly grasped analogies.

Allan Cooper did. "Youngster, meseems you've thrown

your dart dead center," he said. "To the sodding sims, we must be devils or worse." He stopped, then went on, sounding surprised at where that line of thought was taking him, "Which would make them men of a sort, not so? I'd not've believed it."

Wingfield paid more attention to Joanna than to the argument. She was still crying, but did not seem in dreadful distress. It was her hungry cry, not the sharper, shriller one she used when gas pained her or something external upset her.

The female sim that had scratched its head might have been the mother of the infant with whom Joanna was being compared. It took Joanna away from the wounded sim and lifted her to a breast. The baby nursed as eagerly as if it had been Anne. Wingfield told himself that was something his wife never needed to know.

He invented and discarded scheme after scheme for rescuing his daughter. The trouble was that the sims would not leave her alone. Even while she was feeding, they kept coming up to stare at her and touch her. She ate on, blissfully oblivious to everything but the nipple.

"By God, I *shall* get her back," Wingfield said.

He spoke loud enough to distract Allan Cooper. "What? How?" the guard said.

And then Wingfield knew what he had to do. "Do you three cover me with your weapons," he said, "and should the sims harm Joanna or should I fall, do as you deem best. Otherwise, I conjure you not to shoot." Before his comrades' protests could more than begin, he got up from his concealment and walked into the light of the sims' fire.

The first sim to see him let out a hoot of alarm that made the rest of the band whip their heads around. He walked slowly toward the fire, his hands empty and open; he had left his crossbow behind when he rose.

Had the sims chosen to, they could have slain him at any instant. He knew that. His feet hardly seemed to touch the ground; they were light with the liquid springiness fear gives. But the strange unreality of the moment gripped the sims no less than him. Never before had an Englishman come to them alone and unarmed (or so they must have thought, for the pistols in his boots did not show—in truth, he had forgotten them himself).

But then, the sims had never stolen a baby before.

Females snatched up youngsters and bundled them away in their arms as Wingfield passed. Lucas had it right, he thought wryly; it was as if Satan had appeared, all reeking of brimstone, among the Jamestown cabins.

He stopped a few feet in front of the male he had fought. That one had stooped to grasp a sharp stone; many of them lay in the dirt round the fire. But the sim made no move to attack. It waited, to see what Wingfield would do.

The Englishman was not sure if the sim knew him. He pointed to the plastered-over cut he had given; to the bruise and scab on his own forehead; to Joanna, who was still nursing at the female sim's breast. He repeated the gestures, once, twice.

The sim's broad nostrils flared. Its mouth came open, revealing large, strong teeth. It pointed from Wingfield to Joanna, gave a questioning grunt.

"Aye, that's my daughter," Wingfield said excitedly. The words could not have meant anything to the sim, but the animated tone did. It grunted again.

Wingfield dug in his pouch, found a strip of smoked meat, and tossed it to the sim. The sim sniffed warily, then took a bite. Its massive jaw let it tear and chew at the leathery stuff where the Englishman had to nibble and gnaw, and made its smile afterward a fearsome thing.

When Joanna finally relinquished the nipple, the sim holding her swung her up to its shoulder and began pounding her on the back. The treatment was rougher than Wingfield would have liked, but was soon rewarded with a hearty belch. The female sim began to rock Joanna, much as Anne would have.

Wingfield pointed to his daughter, to himself, and then back in the direction of Jamestown. As best he could, he pantomimed taking Joanna home. When he was done, he folded his arms and waited expectantly, trying to convey the attitude that nothing but going along with his wishes was even conceivable.

Had he hesitated, faltered for an instant, he would have lost everything. As it was, that aura of perfect confidence gave him his way. None of the sims moved to stop the female when it came forward and set Joanna in his arms.

He bowed to it as he might have to a great lady of the court, to the sim he had fought as to an earl. Holding Joanna tightly to him, he backed slowly toward the brush where his companions waited. He expected the tableau to break up at any moment, but it held. The sims watched him go, the firelight reflecting red from their eyes.

He was close to the place from which he had come when Caleb Lucas said from the bushes, "Splendidly done, oh, splendidly, Edward!" His voice was a thread of whisper; none of the sims could have heard it.

"Aye, you have the girl, and good for you." Henry Dale did not try to hold his voice down. Indeed, he rose from concealment. "Now to teach the vermin who stole her the price of their folly." He aimed a pistol at the sims behind Wingfield.

"No, you fool!" Lucas shouted. He lunged for Dale at the same moment the sims cried out in fear, fury, and betrayal. Too late—the pistol roared, belching flame and smoke. The lead ball struck home with a noise like a great slap. The sim it hit shrieked, briefly.

With a lithe twist, Dale slipped away from Caleb Lucas. His hand darted into his boot-top for his other pistol. The second shot was less deliberately aimed, but not a miss. This time the screams of pain went on and on.

By then Wingfield was among the bushes. Behind him, the sims were boiling like ants whose nest has been stirred with a stick. Some scrambled for cover; others, bolder, came rushing after the Englishman. A stone crashed against greenery mere inches from his head.

"No help for it now," Henry Dale said cheerfully, bringing up his crossbow. The bolt smote a charging sim square in the chest. The sim staggered, hands clutching at the short shaft of death. It pitched forward on its face.

More rocks flew. Wingfield turned to one side, to try to shield Joanna with his body.

Allan Cooper got to his feet. "God damn you to hell for what you make me do," he snarled at Dale. He fired one pistol, then a second, then his crossbow.

A sharpened stone tore Wingfield's breeches, cut his thigh. Had it hit squarely, it would have crippled him. The sims were howling like lost souls, lost angry souls. Dale was right—no help for it now, Wingfield saw. His pistol bucked when he fired one-handed. He did not know whether he hit or missed. In a way, he hoped he had missed. That did not stop him from drawing his other gun.

"You purposed this all along, Henry," he shouted above the din.

"Aye, and own it proudly." Dale dropped another sim with a second crossbow bolt. He turned to kick Caleb Lucas in the ribs. "Fight 'em, curse you! They'll have the meat from your bones now as happily as from mine."

"No need for this, no need," Lucas gasped, swearing and sobbing by turns. But whether or not that was true, he realized, as Wingfield had, that there was no unbaking a bread. His pistols barked, one after the other.

But the sims on their home ground were not the skulking creatures they were near Jamestown. Though half a dozen lay dead or wounded, the rest, male and female together, kept up the barrage of stones. Their missiles were not so deadly as the Englishmen's, but they loosed them far more often.

One landed with a meaty thud. Allan Cooper, his face a mask of gore, crumpled slowly to the ground.

Dale shot his crossbow again, wounded another sim. He turned to Wingfield, who was struggling to fit another bolt into his weapon's groove. "Go on!" he shouted. "You have what you came for. I'll hold the sims. As you say, I am to blame here."

"But—"

Dale whipped out his rapier. Its point flickered in front of Wingfield's face. "Go! Aye, and you, Caleb. I promise, I shall give the brutes enough fight and chase to distract 'em from you."

He sprang into the clearing, rushing the startled sims. One swung a stout branch at him. Graceful as a dancer, he ducked, then thrust out to impale his attacker. The sim gave a bubbling shriek; blood gushed from its mouth.

"Go!" Dale yelled again.

Without Joanna, Wingfield would have stood by the other Englishman no matter what he said. When she squalled at the rough treatment she was getting, though, he scrambled away into the woods. Lucas followed a few seconds later.

For as long as they could, they looked back at Henry Dale. After that first one, no sim dared come within reach of his sword. He stayed in the clearing for what seemed an impossibly long time, stones flying all around him.

At last he turned. "Catch me if you can!" he shouted, brandishing his rapier. Wingfield saw how he limped as he ran; not every stone had missed. Dale crashed through the undergrowth, going in a different direction from his comrades and making no effort to move quietly. His defiant cries rang through the night. So did the sims' bellows of rage as they pursued him.

"You make for home," Caleb Lucas urged Wingfield. "I will give Henry such help as I may."

"They will surely slay you," Wingfield said, but he knew he would not hold Lucas back. Had their positions been reversed, he would not have wanted the youngster to try to stop him.

Just then, the sims' shouts rose in a goblin chorus of triumph. Screams punctuated it, not all from an English throat. As Dale had promised, he did not die easily. Caleb Lucas sobbed.

"Come," Wingfield said softly, his own voice breaking. "Now we have but to save ourselves, any way we may."

Wingfield lay on the straw pallet in his cabin, having scant energy for anything more. After the desperate dash back to Jamestown, he was gaunt rather than lean. Insect bites blotched his face and arms; leeches had clung to his legs when he and Lucas plunged into the swamps to elude the sims.

The worshipful looks Anne sent his way went far to ease the memory of his privations. She had hardly let Joanna out of her arms since her husband had come stumbling home the night before. The baby was nursing again. She had done little else, once reunited with her mother.

The sound of weeping came through the doorway. That too had gone on since the night before, when Claire Cooper learned she was a widow.

Anne sighed. "So high a price—two good men lost, to rescue a single babe."

Wingfield nodded. Lucas and he had agreed there was no point to speaking ill of the dead. Let Henry Dale be remembered as a hero; with his folly forgotten, the tale of his undoubted bravery at the end of his time would inspire those who still lived.

Wingfield did say, "Aye, we lost a pair, but the sims paid far dearer than we." That far, at least, Dale had been right, he thought, though better none had died on either side. He went on, "Their bands range widely, but they are small; this one took a hurt from which 'twill be years recovering."

"Good!" Anne said, a fierce light in her eyes. "The sooner those foul animals are driven far from the haunts of men, the sooner we sleep at our ease of nights."

"As you've said, my dear, in the past I've taken both sides of that question, but now I will name the sims men." Wingfield spoke reluctantly but firmly.

"How can you think that, after what your own daughter suffered at their hands?" Anne ran her hand protectively over Joanna's scanty yellow hair.

"Anne, were they beasts they would have slain her. Instead, they kept her hale as best they might. Caleb feels they sought to learn of us from her, as the Spaniards have fetched sims back to Europe for learned men to study. Having thought much on what I saw, I can draw no other conclusion than that he is right."

His wife remained unconvinced. "Man or beast, what boots it in the end? We should rout out savages no less than wild beasts—or with all the greater vigor, as presenting more danger to us and ours."

"But if they be men, it were wrong to slay them out of hand, as one would so many wild dogs: our souls should suffer for't."

"What then?"

"I cannot say," Wingfield admitted. He had not thought it through; he was still exhausted from his adventures, and in any case he did not seek a quarrel with his wife. When he continued, he was musing aloud: "They are less than we; that no one may deny. Perhaps God has set them here as our natural servants. If that be so, 'twere a wicked waste to flout His will by expunging them from the earth."

To his relief, Anne let it go with a noncommittal "Hmm." She had a strong will of her own, and was not usually shy about expressing it, but with Joanna safely home she did not really care what her husband believed.

For his part, Wingfield was also willing to let the conversation flag. He kept returning to the image Caleb Lucas had summoned up, of demons settling on good English soil. Even if they purposed benevolence, how likely were their purposes to coincide with his countrymen's?

No more so, he answered himself, than that what Englishmen and sims intended would correspond. If they were human, the sims would struggle against their fate with every fiber of their being.

Not, he thought, that it would do them much good.

He closed his eyes and tried to sleep.

1661

And So to Bed

Sims made people look at themselves and their place in nature differently from the way they had before. They showed the link between humans and animals far more clearly than any creatures with which Europeans had been familiar before.

Had there been no sims—had the Americas been populated by native humans, say, or only by animals—the development of the transformational theory of life might have been long delayed. This would have slowed the growth of several sciences, biology being, of course, the most obvious of them. Speculating on might-have-beens, however, is not the proper domain of history. The transformational theory of life was first put forward in 1661. After that, humans' view of their place in the world would never be the same. . . .

From *The Story of the Federated Commonwealths*

May 4, 1661. A fine bright morning. Small beer and radishes for to break my fast, then into London for this day.

The shambles on Newgate Street stinking unto heaven, as is usual, but close to it my destination, the sim marketplace. Our servant Jane with too much for one body to do, and whilst I may not afford the hire of another man or maid, two sims shall go far to ease her burden.

Success also sure to gladden Elizabeth's heart, my wife being ever one to follow the dame Fashion, and sims all the go of late, though monstrous ugly. Them formerly not much seen here, but since the success of our Virginia and Plymouth colonies are much more often fetched to these shores from the wildernesses the said colonies front upon. They are also commenced to be bred on English soil, but no hope there for me, as I do require workers full-grown, not cubs or babes in arms or whatsoever the proper term may be.

The sim-seller a vicious lout, near unhandsome as his wares. No, the truth for the diary: such were a slander on any man, as I saw on his conveying me to the creatures.

Have seen these sims before, surely, but briefly, and in their masters' livery, the which by concealing their nakedness conceals as well much of their brutishness. The males are most of them well made, though lean as rakes from the ocean passage and, I warrant, poor victualing after. But all are so hairy as more to resemble rugs than men, and the same true for the females, their fur hiding such dubious charms as they may possess nigh as well as a smock of linen: nought here, God knows, for Elizabeth's jealousy to light on.

This so were the said females lovely of feature as so many Aphrodites. They are not, nor do the males recall to mind Adonis. In both sexes the brow projects with a shelf of bone, and above it, where men do enjoy a forehead proud in its erectitude, is but an apish slope. The nose broad and low, the mouth wide, the teeth nigh as big as a horse's (though shaped, it is not to be denied, like a man's), the jaw long, deep and devoid of chin. They stink.

The sim-seller full of compliments on my coming hard on the arrival of the *Gloucester* from Plymouth, him having thereby replenished his stock in trade. Then the price should also be not so dear, says I, and by God it did do my heart good to see the ferret-faced rogue discomfited.

Rogue as he was, though, he dickered with the best, for I paid full a guinea more for the pair of sims than I had looked to, spending in all £11.6s.4d. The coin once passed over (and bitten, for to ensure its verity), the sim-seller signed to those of his chattels I had bought that they were to go with me.

His gestures marvelous quick and clever, and those the sims answered with too. Again, I have seen somewhat of the like before. Whilst coming to understand in time the speech of men, sims are without language of their own, having but a great variety of howls, grunts, and moans. Yet this gesture-speech, the which I am told is come from the signs of the deaf, they do readily learn, and often their masters answer back so, to ensure commands being properly grasped.

Am wild to learn it my own self, and shall. Meseems it is in its way a style of tachygraphy or short-hand such as I use to set down these pages. Having devised varying tachygraphic hands for friends and acquaintances, 'twill be amusing taking to a *hand* that is exactly what its name declares.

As I was leaving with my new charges, the sim-seller did bid me lead them by the gibbets on Shooter's Hill, there to see the bodies and members of felons and of sims as have run off from their masters. It wondered me they should have the wit to take the meaning of such display, but he assured me they should. And so, reckoning it good advice if true and no harm if a lie, I chivvied them thither.

A filthy sight I found it, with the miscreants' flesh all shrunk to the bones. But *hoo!* quoth my sims, and looked close upon the corpses of their own kind, which by their hairiness and flat-skulled heads do seem even more bestial dead than when animated with life.

Home then, and Elizabeth as delighted in my success as am I. An excellent dinner of a calf's head boiled with dumplings, and an abundance of buttered ale with sugar and cinnamon, of which in celebration we invited Jane to partake, and she grew right giddy. Bread and leeks for the sims, and water, it being reported they grow undocile on stronger drink.

After much debate, though good-natured, it was decided to style the male Tom and the female Peg. Showed them to their pallets down cellar, and they took to them readily enough, as finer than what they were accustomed to.

So to bed, right pleased with myself despite the expense.

May 7. An advantage of having sims present appears that I had not thought on. Both Tom and Peg quite excellent ratters, finer than any puss-cat. No need, either, to fling the rats on the dungheap, for they devour them with as much gusto as I should a neat's tongue. They having subsisted on such small deer in the forests of America, I shall not try to break them of the habit, though training them not to bring in their prey when we are at table with guests. The Reverend Mr. Milles quite shocked, but recovering nicely on being plied with wine.

May 8. Peg and Tom the both of them enthralled with fire. When the work of them is done of the day, or at evening ere they take their rest, they may be found before the hearth observing the sport of the flames. Now and again one will to the other say *hoo!*—this noise, I find, they utter on seeing that which does interest them, whatsoever it may be.

Now as I thought on it, I minded me reading or hearing, I recall not which, that in their wild unpeopled haunts the sims know the use of fire as they find it set from lightning or other such mischance, but not the art of its making. No wonder then they are Vulcanolaters, reckoning flame more precious than do we gold.

Considering such reflections, I resolved this morning on an experiment, to see what they might do. Rising early for to void my bladder in the pot, I put out the hearthfire, which in any case was gone low through want of fuel. Retired then to put on my dressing gown and, once clad, returned to await developments.

First up from the cellar was Tom, and his cry on seeing the flames extinguished heartrending as Romeo's over the body of fair Juliet when I did see that play acted this December past. In a trice comes Peg, whose moaning with Tom did rouse my wife, and she much upset at being so rudely wakened.

When calm in some small measure was restored, I bade by signs, in the learning of which I proceed apace, for the sims to sit quietly before the hearth, and with flint and steel restored that which I had earlier destroyed. They both made such outcry as if they had heard sounded the Last Trump.

Then doused I that second fire too, again to much distress from Peg and Tom. Elizabeth by this time out of the house in some dudgeon, no doubt to spend money we lack on stuffs of which we have no want.

Set up in the hearth thereupon several small fires of sticks, each with much tinder so as to make it an easy matter to kindle. A brisk striking of flint and steel dropping sparks onto one such produced a merry little blaze, to the accompaniment of much *hoo*ing out of the sims.

And so to the nub of it. Shewing Tom the steel and flint, I clashed them once more the one upon the other so he might see the sparks engendered thereby. Then pointed to one of the aforementioned piles of sticks I had made up, bidding him watch close, as indeed he did. Having made sure of't, I did set that second pile alight.

Again put the fires out, the wailing accompanying the act less than heretofore, for which I was not sorry. Pointed now to a third assemblage of wood and tinder, but instead of myself lighting it, I did convey flint and steel to Tom, and with signs essayed to bid him play Prometheus.

His hands much scarred and callused, and under their hair knobby-knuckled as an Irishman's. He held at first the implements as if not taking in their purpose, yet the sims making tools of stone, as is widely reported, he could not wholly fail to grasp their utility.

And indeed ere long he did try parroting me. When his

first clumsy attempt yielded no result, I thought he would abandon such efforts as beyond his capacity and reserved for men of my sort. But persist he did, and at length was rewarded with scintillae like unto those I had made. His grin so wide and gleeful I thought it would stretch clear round his head.

Then without need of my further demonstration he set the instruments of fire production over the materials for the blaze. Him in such excitement as the sparks fell upon the waiting tinder that beneath his breeches rose his member, indeed to such degree as would have made me proud to be its possessor. And Peg was, I think, in such mood as to couple with him on the spot, had I not been present and had not his faculties been directed elsewhere than toward the lectual.

For at his success he cut such capers as had not been out of place upon the stage, were they but a trifle more rhythmical and less unconstrained. Yet of the making of fire, even if by such expedient as the friction of two sticks (which once I was forced by circumstance to attempt, and would try the patience of Job), as of every other salutary art, his race is as utterly ignorant as of the moons of Jupiter but lately found by some Italian with an optic glass.

No brute beast of the field could learn to begin a fire on the technique being shown it, which did Tom nigh readily as a man. But despite most diligent instruction, no sim yet has mastered such subtler arts as reading and writing, nor ever will, meseems. Falling in capacity thus between men and animal, the sims do raise a host of conundrums vexing and perplexing. I should pay a pound, or at the least ten shillings, merely to know how such strange fusions came to be.

So to the Admiralty full of such musings, which did occupy my mind, I fear, to the detriment of my proper duties.

May 10. Supper this evening at the Turk's Head, with the other members of the Rota Club. The fare not of the finest, being boiled venison and some few pigeons, all meanly done up. The lamb's wool seemed naught but poor ale, the sugar, nutmeg, and meat of roasted apples hardly to be tasted. Miles the landlord down with a quartan fever, but ill-served by his staff if such is the result of his absence.

The subject of the Club's discussions for the evening much in accord with my own recent curiosity, to wit, the sims. Cyriack Skinner did maintain them creatures of the Devil, whereupon was he roundly rated by Dr. Croon as having in this contention returned to the pernicious heresy of the Manichees, the learned doctor reserving the power of creation to the Lord alone. Much flinging back and forth of Biblical texts, the which all struck me more as being an exercise of ingenuity of the debaters than bearing on the problem, for in plain fact the Scriptures nowhere mention sims.

When at length the talk did turn to matters more ascertainable, I spoke somewhat of my recent investigation, and right well received my remarks were, or so I thought. Others with experience of sims with like tales, finding them quick enough on things practic but sadly lacking in any higher faculties. Much jollity at my account of the visible manifestation of Tom's excitement, and whispers that this lady or that (the names, to my vexation, I failed to catch) owned her sims for naught but their prowess in matters of the mattress.

Just then came the maid by with coffee for the Club—not of the best, but better, I grant, than the earlier wretched lamb's wool. She a pretty yellow-haired lass called, I believe, Kate, a wench of perhaps sixteen years, a good-bodied woman not over thick or thin in any place, with a lovely bosom she did display most charmingly as she bent to fill the gentlemen's cups.

Having ever an eye for beauty, such that I reckon little else beside it, I own I did turn my head for to follow this Kate as she went about her duties. Noticing which, Sir William Henry called out, much to the merriment of the Club and to my chagrin, "See how Samuel peeps!" Him no mean droll, and loosed a pretty pun, if at my expense. Good enough, but then at the far end of the table someone (I saw not who, worse luck) thought to cap it by braying like the donkey he must be, "Not half the peeping, I warrant, as at his sims of nights!"

Such mockery clings to a man like pitch, regardless of the truth in't, which in this case is none. Oh, the thing could be done, but the sims so homely 'twould yield no titillation, of that I am practically certain.

May 12. The household being more infected this past week with nits than ever before, resolved to bathe Peg and Tom, which also I hoped would curb somewhat their stench. And so it proved, albeit not without more alarums than I had looked for. The sims most loath to enter the tub, which must to them have seemed some instrument of torment. The resulting shrieks and outcry so deafening a neighbor did call out to be assured all was well.

Having done so, I saw no help for it but to go into the tub my own self, notwithstanding my having bathed but two weeks before. I felt, I think, more hesitation stripping down before Peg than I should in front of Jane, whom I would simply dismiss from consideration save in how she performed her duties. But I did wonder what Peg made of my body, reckoning it against the hairy forms of her own kind. Hath she the wit to deem mankind superior, or is our smoothness to her as gross and repellent as the peltries of the sims to us? I cannot as yet make shift to enquire.

As may be, my example showing them they should not be harmed, they bathed themselves. A trouble arose I had not foreseen, for the sims being nearly as thickly haired over all their bodies as I upon my head, the rinsing of the soap from their hides less easy than for us, and requiring much water. Lucky I am the well is within fifty paces of my home. And so from admiral of the bath to the Admiralty, hoping henceforward to scratch myself less.

May 13. A pleasant afternoon this day, carried in a coach to see the lions and other beasts in the menagerie. I grant the lions pride of place through custom immemorial, but in truth am more taken with the abnormal creatures fetched back from the New World than those our people have known since the time of Arthur. Nor am I alone in this conceit, for the cages of lion, bear, and camel had but few spectators, whilst round those of the American beasts I did find myself compelled to use hands and elbows to make shift to pass through the crowds.

This last not altogether unpleasant, as I chanced to brush against a handsome lass, but when I did enquire if she would take tea with me she said me nay, which did irk me no little, for as I say she was fair to see.

More time for the animals, then, and wondrous strange ever they strike me. The spear-fanged cat is surely the most horridest murderer this shuddering world hath seen, yet there is for him prey worthy of his mettle, what with beavers near big as our bears, wild oxen whose horns are to those of our familiar kine as the spear-fanged cat's teeth to the lion's, and the great hairy elephants which do roam the forests.

Why such prodigies of nature manifest themselves on those distant shores does perplex me most exceedingly, as they are unlike any beasts even in the bestiaries, which as all men know are more flights of fancy than sober fact. Amongst them the sims appear no more than one piece of some great jigsaw, yet no pattern therein is to me apparent; would it were.

Also another new creature in the menagerie, which I had not seen before. At first I thought it a caged sim, but on inspection it did prove an ape, brought back by the Portuguese from Afric lands and styled there, the keeper made so good as to inform me, shimpanse. It flourishes not in England's clime, he did continue, being subject to sickness in the lungs from the cool and damp, but is so interesting as to be displayed whilst living, howsoever long that may prove.

The shimpanse is a baser brute than even the sim. It goes on all fours, and its hinder feet more like unto monkeys' than men's, having thereon great toes that grip like thumbs. Also, where a sim's teeth, as I have observed from Tom and Peg, are uncommon large, in shape they are like unto a man's, but the shimpanse hath tushes of some savagery, though of course paling alongside those of the spear-fanged cat.

Seeing the keeper a garrulous fellow, I enquired of him further anent this shimpanse. He owned he had himself thought it a sort of sim on its arrival, but sees now more distinguishing points than likenesses: gait and dentition, such as I have herein remarked upon, but also in its habits. From his experience, he has seen it to be ignorant of fire, repeatedly allowing to die a blaze though fuel close at hand. Nor has it the knack of shaping stones to its ends, though it will, he told me, cast them betimes against those who annoy it, once striking one such with force enough to render him some time senseless. Hearing the villain had essayed tormenting the creature with a stick, my sympathies lay all for the shimpanse, wherein its keeper concurred.

And so homewards, thinking on the shimpanse as I rode. Whereas in the lands wherewith men are most familiar, it were easy distinguishing men from beasts, the strange places to which our vessels have but lately fetched themselves reveal a stairway ascending the chasm, and climbers on the stairs, some higher, some lower. A pretty image, but why it should be so there and not here does I confess escape me.

May 16. A savage row with Jane today, her having forgotten a change of clothes for my bed. Her defense that I had not so instructed her, the lying minx, for I did plainly make my wishes known the evening previous, the which I recollect most distinctly. Yet she did deny it again and again, finally raising my temper to such a pitch that I cursed her right roundly, slapping her face and pulling her nose smartly.

Whereupon did the ungrateful trull lay down her service

on the spot. She decamped in a fury of her own, crying that I treated the sims, those very sims which I had bought for to ease her labors, with more kindlier consideration than I had for her own self.

So now we are without a serving-maid, and her a dab hand in the kitchen, her swan pie especially being toothsome. Dined tonight at the Bell, and expect to tomorrow at the Swan on the Hoop, in Fish Street. For Elizabeth no artist over the hearth, nor am I myself. And as for the sims, I should sooner open my veins than indulge of their cuisine, the good Lord only knowing what manner of creatures they in their ignorance should add to a pot.

Now as my blood has somewhat cooled, I must admit a germ of truth in Jane's scolds. I do not beat Tom and Peg as a man would servitors of more ordinary stripe. They, being but new come from the wilds, are not inured to't as are our servants, and might well turn on me, their master. And being in part of brute kind, their strength does exceed mine, Tom's most assuredly and that of Peg perhaps. And so, say I, better safe. No satisfaction to me the sims on Shooter's Hill gallows, were I not there to see't.

May 20. Today to my lord Sandwich's for supper. This doubly pleasant, in enjoying his fine companionship and saving the cost of a meal, the house being still without maid. The food and drink in excellent style, as to suit my lord. The broiled lobsters very sweet, and the lamprey pie (which for its rarity I but seldom eat of) the best ever I had. Many other fine victuals as well (the tanzy in especial), and the wine all sugared.

Afterwards backgammon, at which I won £5 ere my luck turned. Ended 15s. in my lord's debt, which he did graciously excuse me afterwards, a generosity not looked for but which I did not refuse. Then to crambo, wherein by tagging *and rich* to *Sandwich* I was adjudged winner, the more so for playing on his earlier munificence.

Thereafter nigh a surfeit of good talk, as is custom at my lord's. He mentioning sims, I did relate my own dealings

with Peg and Tom, to which he listened with much interest.
He thinks on buying some for his own household, and
unaware I had done so.

Perhaps it was the wine let loose my tongue, for I
broached somewhat my disjoint musings on the sims and
their place in nature, on the strangeness of the American
fauna and much else besides. Lord Sandwich did acquaintance me with a New World beast found in their southerly
holdings by the Spaniards, of strange outlandish sort: big
as an ox, or nearly, and all covered over with armor of bone
like a man wearing chain. I should pay out a shilling or
even more for to see't, were one conveyed to London.

Then coffee, and it not watered as so often at an inn, but
full and strong. As I and Elizabeth making our departures,
Lord Sandwich did bid me join him tomorrow night to
hear speak a savant of the Royal Society. It bore, said he, on
my prior ramblings, and would say no more, but looked
uncommon sly. Even did it not, I should have leaped at the
chance.

This written at one of the clock, for so the watchman just
now cried out. Too wound up for bed, what with coffee and
the morrow's prospect. Elizabeth aslumber, but the sims
also awake, and at frolic, meseems, from the noises up the
stairway.

If they be of human kind, is their fornication *sans* clergy
sinful? Another vexing question. By their existence, they do
engender naught but disquietude. Nay, strike that. They
may in sooth more sims engender, a pun good enough to
sleep on, and so to bed.

May 21. All this evening worrying at my thoughts as a dog
at a bone. My lord Sandwich knows not what commotion
internal he did by his invitation, all kindly meant, set off in
me. The speaker this night a spare man, dry as dust, of the
very sort I learned so well to loathe when at Cambridge.

Dry as dust! Happy words, which did spring all unbid-
den from my pen. For of dust the fellow did discourse, if
thereby is meant, as commonly, things long dead. He had

some men bear in bones but lately found by Swanscombe at a gravel-digging. And such bones they were, and teeth (or rather tusks), as to make it all I could do to hold me in my seat. For surely they once graced no less a beast than the hairy elephant whose prototype I saw in the menagerie so short a while ago. The double-curving tusks admit of no error, for those of all elephants with which we are anciently familiar form but a single segment of arc.

When, his discourse concluded, he gave leave for questions, I made bold to ask to what he imputed the hairy elephant's being so long vanished from our shores yet thriving in the western lands. To this he confessed himself baffled, as am I, and admiring of his honesty as well.

Before the hairy elephant was known to live, such monstrous bones surely had been reckoned as from beasts perishing in the Flood whereof Scripture speaks. Yet how may that be so, them surviving across a sea wider than any Noah sailed?

Meseems the answer lieth within my grasp, but am balked from setting finger to't. The thwarting fair to drive me mad, worse even, I think, than with a lass who will snatch out a hairpin for to defend her charms against my importuning.

May 22. Grand oaks from tiny acorns grow! This morning came a great commotion from the kitchen. I rushing in found Tom at struggle with a cur dog which had entered, the door being open on account of fine weather, to steal half a flitch of salt bacon. It dodging most nimbly round the sim, snatched up the gammon and fled out again, him pursuing but in vain.

Myself passing vexed, having intended to sup thereon. But Tom all downcast on returning, so had not the heart further to punish him. Told him instead, him understanding I fear but little, it were well men not sims dwelt in England, else would wolves prowl the London streets still.

Stood stock still some time thereafter, hearing the greater import behind my jesting speech. Is not the answer to the riddle of the hairy elephant and other exotic beasts existing in the New World but being hereabouts long vanished their having there but sims to hunt them? The sims in their wild haunts wield club and sharpened stone, no more. They are ignorant even of the bow, which from time out of mind has equipt the hunter's armory.

Just as not two centuries past we Englishmen slew on this island the last wolf, so may we not imagine our most remotest grandsires serving likewise the hairy elephant, the spear-fanged cat? They being more cunning than sims and better accoutered, this should not have surpassed their powers. Such beasts would survive in America, then, not through virtue inherent of their own, but by reason of lesser danger to them in the sims than would from mankind come.

Put this budding thought at luncheon today to my lord Sandwich. He back at me with Marvell to his coy mistress (the most annoyingest sort!), viz., had we but world enough and time, who could reckon the changes as might come to pass? And going on, laughing, to say next will be found dead sims at Swanscombe.

Though meant but as a pleasantry, quoth I, why not? Against true men they could not long have stood, but needs must have given way as round Plymouth and Virginia. Even without battle they must soon have failed, as being less able than mankind to provide for their wants.

There we let it lie, but as I think more on't, the notion admits of broader application. Is't not the same for trout as for men, or for lilacs? Those best suited living reproduce their kind, whilst the trout with twisted tail or bloom without sweet scent die all unmourned, leaving no descendants. And each succeeding generation, being of the previous survivors constituted, will by such reasoning show some little difference from the one as went before.

Seeing no flaw in this logic, resolve tomorrow to do this from its tachygraphic state, bereft, of course, of maunderings and privacies, for prospectus to the Royal Society, and mightily wondering whatever they shall make of it.

May 23. Closeted all this day at the Admiralty. Yet did it depend on my diligence alone, I fear me the Fleet should drown. Still, a deal of business finished, as happens when one stays by it. Three quills worn quite out, and my hands all over ink. Also my fine camlet cloak with the gold buttons, which shall mightily vex my wife, poor wretch, unless it may be cleaned. I pray God to make it so, for I do mislike strife at home.

The burning work at last complete, homeward in the twilight. It being washing-day, dined on cold meat. I do confess, felt no small strange stir in my breast on seeing Tom taking down the washing before the house. A vision it was, almost, of his kind roaming England long ago, till perishing from want of substance on vying therefor with men. And now they are through the agency of men returned here again, after some great interval of years. Would I knew how many.

The writing of my notions engrossing the whole of the day, had no occasion to air them to Lord Brouncker of the Society, as was my hope. Yet expound I must, or burst. Elizabeth, then, at dinner made audience for me, whether she would or no. My spate at last exhausted, asked for her thoughts on't.

She said only that Holy Writ sufficed on the matter for her, whereat I could but make a sour face. To bed in some anger, and in fear lest the Royal Society prove as close-minded, which God prevent. Did He not purpose man to reason on the world around him, He should have left him witless as the sim.

May 24. To Gresham College this morning, to call on Lord Brouncker. He examined with great care the papers I had done up, his face revealing naught. Felt myself at recitation once more before a professor, a condition whose lack these last years I have not missed. Feared also he might not be able to take in the writing, it being done in such haste some short-hand characters may have replaced the common ones.

Then to my delight he declared he reckoned it deserving

of a hearing at the Society's weekly meeting next. Having said so much, he made to dismiss me, himself being much occupied with devising a means whereby to calculate the relation of a circle's circumference to its diameter. I wish him joy of't. I do resolve one day soon, however, to learn the multiplication table, which meseems should be of value at the Admiralty. Repaired there from the college, to do the work I had set by yesterday.

May 26. Watch these days Tom and Peg with new eyes. I note for instance them using between themselves our deaf-man's signs, as well as to me and my wife. As well they might, them conveying far more subtler meanings than the bestial howlings and gruntings that are theirs in nature. Thus, though they may not devise any such, they own the wit to see its utility.

I wonder would the shimpanse likewise?

A girl came today asking after the vacant maidservant's post, a pretty bit with red hair, white teeth, and fine strong haunches. Thought myself she would serve, but Elizabeth did send her away. Were her looks liker to Peg's, she had I think been hired on the spot. But a quarrel on it not worth the candle, the more so as I have seen fairer.

May 28. This writ near cockcrow, in hot haste, lest any detail of the evening escape my recollection. Myself being a late addition, spoke last, having settled the title "A Proposed Explication of the Survival of Certain Beasts in America and Their Disappearance Hereabouts" on the essay.

The prior speakers addressed one the organs internal of bees and the other the appearance of Saturn in the optic glass, both topics which interest me but little. Then called to the podium by Lord Brouncker, all aquiver as a virgin bride. Much wished myself in the company of some old soakers over roast pigeons and dumplings and sack. But a brave front amends for much, and so plunged in straightaway.

Used the remains of the hairy elephant presented here a sennight past as example of a beast vanished from these shores yet across the sea much in evidence. Then on to the deficiencies of sims as hunters, when set beside even the most savagest of men.

Thus far well received, and even when noting the struggle to live and leave progeny that does go on among each and between the several kinds. But the storm broke, as I feared it should and more, on my drawing out the implications therefrom: that of each generation only so many may flourish and breed; and that each succeeding generation, being descended of these survivors alone, differs from that which went before.

My worst and fearfullest nightmare then came true, for up rose shouts of blasphemy. Gave them back what I had told Elizabeth on the use of reason, adding in some heat I had expected such squallings of my wife who is a woman and ignorant, but better from men styling themselves natural philosophers. Did they aim to prove me wrong, let them so by the reason they do profess to cherish. This drew further catcalling but also approbation, which at length prevailed.

Got up then a pompous little manikin, who asked how I dared set myself against God's word insofar as how beasts came to be. On my denying this, he did commence reciting at me from Genesis. When he paused for to draw breath, I asked most mildly of him on which day the Lord did create the sims. Thereupon he stood discomfited, his foolish mouth hanging open, at which I was quite heartened.

Would the next inquisitor had been so easily downed! A Puritan he was, by his somber cloak and somberer bearing. His questions took the same tack as the previous, but not so stupidly. After first enquiring if I believed in God, whereat I truthfully told him aye, he asked did I think Scripture to be the word of God. Again said aye, by now getting and dreading the drift of his argument. And as I feared, he bade me next point him out some place where Scripture was mistaken, ere supplanting it with fancies of mine own.

I knew not how to make answer, and should have in the next moment fled. But up spake to my great surprise Lord Brouncker, reciting from Second Chronicles, the second verse of the fourth chapter, wherein is said of Solomon and his Temple, *Also he made the molten sea of ten cubits from brim to brim, round in compass, and the height thereof was five cubits, and a line of thirty cubits did compass it round about.*

This much perplexed the Puritan and me as well, though I essayed not to show it. Lord Brouncker then proceeded to his explication, to wit that the true compass of a ten-cubit round vessel was not thirty cubits, but above one and thirty, I misremember the exact figure he gave. Those of the Royal Society learned in mathematics did agree he had reason, and urged the Puritan make the experiment for his self with cup, cord, and rule, which were enough for to demonstrate the truth.

I asked if he was answered. Like a gentleman he owned he was, and bowed, and sat, his face full of troubles. Felt with him no small sympathy, for once one error in Scripture be admitted, where shall it end?

The next query was of different sort, a man in periwigg enquiring if I did reckon humankind to have arisen by the means I described. Had to reply I did. Our forefathers might be excused for thinking otherwise, them being so widely separate from all other creatures they knew.

But we moderns in our travels round the globe have found the shimpanse, which standeth nigh the flame of reasoned thought; and more important still the sim, in whom the flame does burn, but more feebly than in ourselves. These bridging the gap twixt man and beast meseems do show mankind to be in sooth a part of nature, whose engenderment in some past distant age is to be explained through natural law.

Someone rose to doubt the variation in each sort of living thing being sufficient eventually to permit the rise of new kinds. Pointed out to him the mastiff, the terrier, and the bloodhound, all of the dog kind, but become distinct through man's choice of mates in each generation. Surely the same might occur in nature, said I. The fellow admitted it was conceivable, and sat.

Then up stood a certain Wilberforce, with whom I have some small acquaintance. He likes me not, nor I him. We know it on both sides, though for civility's sake feigning otherwise. Now he spoke with smirking air, as one sure of the mortal thrust. He did grant my willingness to have a sim as great-grandfather, said he, but was I so willing to claim one as great-grandmother? A deal of laughter rose, which was his purpose, and to make me out a fool.

Had I carried steel, I should have drawn on him. As was, rage sharpened my wit to serve for the smallsword I left at home. Told him it were no shame to have one's great-grandfather a sim, as that sim did use to best advantage the intellect he had. Better that, quoth I, than dissipating the mind on such digressive and misleading quibbles as he raised. If I be in error, then I am; let him shew it by logic and example, not as it were playing to the gallery.

Came clapping from all sides, to my delight and the round dejection of Wilberforce. On seeking further questions, found none. Took my own seat whilst the Fellows of the Society did congratulate me and cry up my essay louder, I thought, than either of the other two. Lord Brouncker acclaimed it as a unifying principle for the whole of the study of life, which made me as proud a man as any in the world, for all the world seemed to smile upon me.

And so to bed.

1691

Around the Salt Lick

Europeans soon settled the Atlantic seaboard of North America. Settlement was slower in the Spanish and Portuguese colonies further south, as the harsh tropical climate of much of Central and South America posed a serious challenge to immigrants. In the seventeenth and eighteenth centuries, only New Granada and Argentina, the most northerly and southerly of the Hispanic settlements, truly flourished.

The British North American colonies, however, soon outdistanced even the most successful settlements farther south. Because the land was more like that to which the settlers had been accustomed, European farming techniques needed less adaptation than was the case in Central and South America. Moreover, the establishment of a divine-right monarchy on the French model in England made political and religious dissenters eager to leave the island—and the Crown happy to see them go. Thus a constant stream of settlers was assured.

As the seventeenth century drew toward a close, explorers were beginning to penetrate the mountain passes and push west into the North American heartland. Bands of wild sims made sure some would not find their way home, and others fell victim to spearfangs and other wild beasts. But neither sims nor beasts could halt or even slow the steady westward push of people into North America.

Still, as has always been true, the first humans to go west of the mountains faced no small danger, and had to show extraordinary resourcefulness in unfamiliar and dangerous circumstances. . . .

From *The Story of the Federated Commonwealths*

THOMAS KENTON PAUSED to look westward at land no man had seen before. The gap in the mountains revealed an endless sea of deep green rolling woods ahead. Virginia had been such a wilderness once, before the English landed eighty-odd years ago.

"But no more, eh, Charles?" he said to the sim at his side. "Virginia fills with farmers, and the time has come to find what this western country is like."

Find, Charles signed. Like most of the New World's native subhumans, he understood speech well enough, but had trouble reproducing it. Signals based on those used by the deaf and dumb came easier for him.

The sim was close to Kenton's own rangy six feet one. His eyes, in fact, were on a level with the scout's, but where Kenton's forehead rose, his sloped smoothly back from beetling brow ridges. His nose was low, broad, and flat; his mouth wide; his teeth large, heavy, and yellow; his jaw long and chinless. As an Englishman, he would have been hideous. Kenton did not think of him so; by the standards of his own kind, he was on the handsome side.

On, Charles signed, adding the finger-twist that turned it into a question. At the scout's nod, he strode ahead, his deerskin buskins silent on the mossy ground. His only other clothing was a leather belt that held water bottle, hatchet, knife, and pouches for this and that. His thick brown hair served him as well as did Kenton's leather tunic and trousers.

A turkey called from a stand of elms off to one side. Kenton felt his stomach rumble hungrily, and an instant later heard Charles's. They grinned at each other. *Hunt*, the scout signed, not wanting to make any noise to alert the bird.

The sim nodded and trotted toward the far side of the trees. Kenton gauged distances. If all went well, the shot would be only about fifty yards—a half-charge of powder should serve. He poured it into the little charge-cup that hung from the bottom of his powderhorn, then down his musket barrel it went.

Working with practiced speed, he set a greased linen patch on the gun's muzzle, laid the round ball on it, and rammed it home till it just touched the powder. Then he squeezed down on the first of the musket's two triggers, setting the second so it would go off at the lightest touch. The whole procedure took about fifteen seconds.

And it was all needless. Kenton waited, expecting the frightened turkey to burst from cover at any moment. What emerged, however, was Charles, carrying the bird by the feet in one hand and his bloody hatchet in the other. He was laughing.

"Good hunting," Kenton said. He carefully reset the first trigger, making sure he heard it click back into place. He did not begrudge the sim the kill; he welcomed anything that saved powder and bullets.

Stupid bird, Charles signed. *I get close, throw*. He pantomimed casting the hatchet. It had a weighted knob at the end of the handle to give it proper balance for the task. Even wild sims were dangerous, flinging the sharp-chipped stones they made.

The sun was going down over the vast forest ahead. "We may as well camp," Kenton decided when they came to a small, cool, quick-flowing stream. He and Charles washed their heads and soaked their feet in it. They drank till they sloshed, preferring the stream's water to the warm, stale stuff in their canteens.

Then they scoured the neighborhood for dry twigs and brush for the evening's fire. Kenton was careful to make sure trees and bushes screened the site from the west. When he took out flint and steel to set off the tinder at the end of the fire, Charles touched his arm. *Me, please*, the sim signed.

Kenton passed him the metal and stone. Charles briskly clashed them together, blew on the sparks that fell to the tinder. Soon he had a small smokeless blaze going.

When he started to pass the flint and steel back to Kenton, the scout said, "You may as well keep them; you use them more than I do, anyway."

The flickering firelight revealed the awe on Charles's face. That awe was there even though he was of the third generation of sims to grow up as part of Virginia. In the wild, sims used fire if they came across it, and kept it alive as best they could, but they could not start one. To Charles, Kenton's simple tools conveyed a power that must have felt godlike.

The scout burned his hands and his mouth on hot roasted turkey, but did not care. Blowing on his fingers, he chuckled, "Better than going hungry, eh, Charles?"

The sim grunted around a mouthful. He did not bother with any more formal reply; he took his eating seriously.

They tossed the offal into the stream. Charles had taken the first watch the night before, so tonight it belonged to Kenton. The sim stripped off his shoes and belt, curled up by the fire—with his hair, he needed no blanket—and fell asleep with the ease and speed Kenton always envied. Charles and his breed never brought the day's troubles into the evening with them. Were they too simple or too wise? The scout often wondered.

He let the fire die to red embers that hardly interfered with his night sight. The moon, rounding toward full, spilled pale light over the forest ahead, smoothing its contours till it resembled nothing so much as a calm, peaceful sea.

The ear pierced the illusion that lulled the eye. Somewhere close by, a field mouse squeaked, briefly, as an owl or ferret found it. Farther away, Kenton heard a wolf howl to salute the moon, then another and another, until the whole pack was at cry.

The eerie chorus made the hair prickle upright at the nape of the scout's neck. Charles stirred and muttered in his sleep. No one, human or sim, was immune to the fear of wolves.

The pack also disturbed the rest of a hairy elephant, whose trumpet call of protest instantly silenced the wolves. They might pull down a calf that strayed too far from its mother, but no beasts hunted full-grown elephants. Not more than once, anyway, Kenton thought.

The normal small night noises took a while to come back after the hairy elephant's cry. The scout strained his ears listening for one set in particular: the grunts and shouts that would have warned of wild sims. No camp was in earshot, at any rate. Hunting males ranged widely, though, and these sims would from long acquaintance not be in awe of men, and thus doubly dangerous.

A coughing roar only a couple of hundred yards away cut short his reverie on the sims. The scout sprang to his feet, his finger darting to the trigger of his musket. That cry also roused Charles. The sim stood at Kenton's side, hatchet ready in his hand.

The roar came again, this time fiercely triumphant. *Spearfang*, Charles signed, *with kill*.

"Yes," Kenton said. Now that the beast had found a victim, it would not be interested in hunting for others—such as, for instance, himself and the sim. In dead of night, he welcomed that lack of interest.

All the same, excitement prickled in him. The big cats were not common along the Atlantic seaboard, and relentless hunting had reduced their numbers even in the hinterlands of the Virginia colony. Not many men, these days, came to the governor at Portsmouth to collect the £5 bounty on a pair of fangs.

Kenton imagined the consternation that would ensue if he marched into the Hall of Burgesses with a score of six-inch-long ivory daggers. Most of the clerks he knew would sooner pass a kidney stone than pay out fifty pounds of what was not even their own money.

The scout snorted contemptuously. "I'd sooner reason with a sim," he said. Charles grunted and made the question-mark gesture. "Never mind," Kenton said. "You may as well go back to sleep."

Charles did, with the same ease he had shown before. Nothing troubled him for long. On the other hand, he lacked the sense for long-term planning.

Kenton watched the stars spin slowly through the sky. When he reckoned it was midnight, he woke Charles, stripped off his breeches and tunic, and rolled himself in his blanket. Despite exhaustion, his whirling thoughts kept him some time awake. This once, he thought, he would not have minded swapping wits with his sim.

Sunrise woke the scout. Seeing him stir, Charles nodded his way. *All good*, the sim signed. *Spearfang stay away*.

"Aye, that's good enough for me," Kenton said. Charles nodded and built up the fire while Kenton, sighing, stretched and dressed. Jokes involving wordplay were wasted on sims, though Charles had laughed like a loon when the scout went sprawling over a root a couple of days earlier. The turkey was still almost as good as it had been the night before. Munching on bulbs of wild onion between bites went a long way toward hiding the slight gamy taste the meat had acquired.

The way west was downhill now; the explorer and his sim had passed the watershed not long before they made camp. The little stream by which they had built their fire ran westward, not comfortably toward the Atlantic like every other waterway with which Kenton was familiar.

The scout strode along easily, working out the kinks a

night's sleep on the ground had put in his muscles. His mouth twisted. A few years ago, he would have felt no aches, no matter what he did. But his light-brown hair was beginning to be frosted with gray, and to recede at the temples.

Kenton was proud the governor had chosen him for this first western journey, rather than some man still in his twenties. "Oh, aye, a youngster might travel faster and see a bit more," Lord Emerson said, "but you're more likely to return and tell us of it."

He laughed out loud. He wondered what Lord Emerson would have said after learning of his spearfang-hunting plans. Something pungent and memorable, no doubt.

Charles stopped with a perplexed grunt, very much the sort of sound a true man might have made. *Ahead strange sound*, he signed.

Kenton listened, but heard nothing. He shrugged. His eyes were as sharp as the sim's, but Charles had very good ears. They were surely not a match for a hound's, nor was the sim's sense of smell, but Charles could communicate what he sensed in a way no animal could match.

"Far or close?" the scout asked.

Not close.

"We'll go on, then," Kenton decided. After a few hundred cautious yards, he heard the rumble too—or perhaps *felt* would have been the better word for it. He thought of distant thunder that went on and on, but the day was clear. He wondered if he was hearing a waterfall far away. "Kenton's Falls," he said, trying out the sound. He liked it.

Charles turned to look at him, then made as if to stumble over a root. The sim got up with a sly grin on his face. Kenton laughed too. Charles had made a pun after all, even if unintentionally.

The game path they were following twisted southward, bringing the edge of a large clearing into view. Kenton stared in open-mouthed wonder at the teeming, milling buffalo the break in the trees revealed. There were more of them than Virginia herds had cattle.

The beasts were of two sorts. The short-horned kind, with its hump and shaggy mane, was also fairly common east of the mountains; it closely resembled the familiar wisent of Europe. The other variety was larger and grander, with horns sweeping out from its head in a formidable defensive arc. Only stragglers of that sort reached Virginia. They were notoriously dangerous to hunt, being quicker and stronger than their more common cousins.

The rumble the sim and scout had heard was coming from the clearing; it was the pounding of innumerable buffalo hooves on the turf. Charles pointed to the herd, signing, *Good hunting. Good eating.*

"Good hunting indeed," Kenton said. Its meat smoked over a fire, a single buffalo could feed Charles and him for weeks. But the scout saw no need for that much work. With the big beasts so plentiful, it would be easy to kill one whenever they needed fresh meat.

Good hunting in another way also, the scout realized. A herd this size would surely draw wolves and spearfangs to prey on stragglers. Kenton smiled in anticipation. He would prey on them.

"Let's get some meat," Kenton said matter-of-factly. Charles nodded and slipped off the trail into the trees. The scout followed. He could just as well have led; the sim and he were equally skilled in woodscraft. But he would not go wrong letting Charles pick a spot from which to shoot.

Once away from the trail, the scout felt as though the forest had swallowed him. The crowns of the trees overhead hid the sun; light came through them wan, green, and shifting. Shrubs and bushes grew thick enough to reduce vision to a few yards, but not enough to impede progress much. The air was cool, moist, and still, with the smell of earth and growing things.

Steering by the patterns of moss and other subtle signs, Charles and Kenton reached the clearing they had spied in the distance. It was even larger than the scout had thought, and full of buffalo. More entered by way of a game track to the north that was wider than most Virginia roads; others took the trail south and west out.

Charles picked a vantage point where the forest projected a little into the clearing, giving Kenton a broad view and a chance to pick his target at leisure. "Good job," the scout murmured. Charles wriggled with pleasure at the praise like a patted hound.

But Kenton knew there was more to the sim's glee than any dog would have felt. Charles's reasoning was slower and far less accurate than a man's, but it was enough for him to understand how and why he had pleased the scout. People who treated their sims like cattle or other beasts of burden often had them run away.

Kenton shook his head slightly as he aimed at a plump young buffalo not thirty yards away. If Charles wanted to flee on this journey, he had his chance every night.

The flintlock bucked against the scout's shoulder, though the long barrel of soft iron reduced the recoil. Buffalo heads sprang up at the report; the animals' startled snorts filled the clearing. Then the buffalo were running, and Kenton felt the ground shudder under his feet. If the sound of the beasts' hooves had been distant thunder before, now the scout heard the roar as if in the center of a cloudburst. Charles was shouting, but Kenton only saw his open mouth—his cry was lost in the din of the stampede.

The cow the scout had shot tried to join the panic rush, despite the blood that gushed from its shoulder just below the hump and soaked its shaggy brown hair. After half a dozen lurching strides, blood also poured from its mouth and nose. It swayed and fell.

Several other buffalo, most of them calves, were down, trampled, when Kenton and Charles went out into the clearing, which was now almost empty. The scout took the precaution of reloading—this time with a double charge—before he emerged from the woods, in case one of the buffalo still on their feet should decide to charge.

Crows and foxes began feasting while Charles was still cutting two large chunks of meat from the tender, fat-rich hump. Soon other hunters and scavengers would come: spearfangs, perhaps, or wolves or sims. Kenton preferred meeting any of them on ground of his own choosing, not here in the open. He drew back into the woods as soon as Charles had finished his butchery. They got well away from the open space before they camped, and Kenton made sure they did so in a small hollow to screen the light of his fire from unwelcome eyes.

After he had eaten, he wiped his greasy hands on the grass, then dug into his pack for his journal, pen, and inkpot. He wrote a brief account of the past couple of days of travel and added to the sketch map he was keeping.

As always, Charles watched with interest. *Talking marks?* he signed.

"Aye, so they are."

How do marks talk? the sim asked, punctuating the question with a pleading whimper. Kenton could only spread his hands regretfully. Several times he had tried to teach Charles the ABCs, but the sim could not grasp that a sign on paper represented a sound. No sim had ever learned to read or write.

Then the scout had an idea—maybe his map would be easier than letters for Charles to understand. "Recall the creek we walked along this morning, how it bent north and then southwest?"

The sim nodded. Kenton pointed to his representation. "Here is a line that moves the same way the creek did."

Charles looked reproachfully at the scout. *Line not move. Line there.*

"No; I mean the line shows the direction of the creek. D'you see? First it goes up, then down and over, like the stream did."

So? In their deep, shadowed sockets beneath his brow ridges, Charles's eyes were full of pained incomprehension. *Line not like stream. How can line be like stream?*

"The line is a picture of the stream," the scout said.

Line not picture. Charles's signs were quick and firm. *Picture like thing to eyes. Line not like stream.*

Kenton shrugged and gave up. That had been his last, best try at getting the idea across. Sims recognized paintings, even pen-and-ink drawings. Abstract symbols, though, remained beyond their capacity. The scout sighed, got out his blanket, and slept.

Instead of returning to the clearing, Kenton decided to parallel the game track down which the buffalo had fled. Mockingbirds yammered in the treetops high overhead, while red squirrels and gray frisked along the branches, pausing now and then to peer suspiciously down at the man and the sim.

"An Englishman I met at Portsmouth told me there are no gray squirrels in England, only red ones," Kenton remarked.

No grays? Who ate them?

Kenton smiled, then sobered. There was more to the question than Charles, in his innocent ignorance, had meant. People on both sides of the Atlantic were still hotly debating the notion someone had put forward a generation before: that the struggle of predator against prey determined which forms of life would prosper and which would fail.

The scout liked the idea. To his mind, it explained why such beasts as spearfangs and hairy elephants lived in America but not in Europe, though their ancient bones had been found there. Humans, even savages, were better hunters than sims. Already, after less than a century, spearfangs were scarce in Virginia. No doubt they had been exterminated east of the ocean so long ago that even the memory of them was gone.

The thought of life changing through time horrified folk who took their Scripture literally. Kenton could not fathom their cries of protest. America had shown so many wonders the Bible did not speak of—sims not the least—that using Scripture to account for them struck him as foolish. Like most colonists, he preferred to judge truth for himself, not receive it from a preacher.

A little past noon, the scout began hearing the low rumble of many buffalo hooves again. He found a herd gathered at a salt lick, pushing and shoving each other to get at the salt like so many townswomen elbowing their way to a peddler's cart. He took out his journal and noted the lick. When settlers eventually came, they could use the salt to preserve their meat.

He had not intended to hunt that day, not when he and Charles were still carrying some of the buffalo hump. But a tawny blur exploded from the far side of the clearing and darted toward a yearling cow at the edge of the herd. The spearfang's roar sent the buffalo scattering in terror and made ice walk up Kenton's back.

The spearfang's powerful forelimbs wrapped round the buffalo's neck. Despite the beast's panic-stricken thrashing and bucking, the spearfang wrestled it to the ground. Excitement made the big cat's short, stumpy tail quiver absurdly.

The struggle went on for several minutes, the buffalo trying desperately to break free and the spearfang to hold it in place with front legs and claws. At last the spearfang found the grip it wanted. Its jaws gaped hugely. It sent its fangs slashing across the buffalo's throat. Blood fountained. The buffalo gave a final convulsive shiver and was still. The spearfang began to feed, tearing great hunks of dripping meat from the buffalo's flank.

Kenton swung up his musket, glad he had a double charge in the gun. Luckily, the spearfang was exposing its left side to him. He released the set trigger, took a deep breath and held it to steady his aim, touched the second trigger.

His flint and gunpowder were French, and of the best quality; only a farmer would use Virginia-made powder. Along with the twin triggers, they ensured that the musket would not misfire or hang fire.

The spearfang screamed. It whirled and snapped at its flank. But the wound was not mortal, for the spearfang bounded into the woods the way it had come.

"Oh, a pox," Kenton said; the shot had struck too far forward to pierce the heart. He paused to reload before pursuing the big cat. He was not mad enough to follow a wounded spearfang armed only with a brace of pistols.

As he had been trained, Charles trotted ahead to find the trail. Kenton soon waved him back to a position of safety; the spearfang had left a blood-spattered spoor any fool could follow.

That overconfidence almost cost the scout his life. Once in the forest, the spearfang doubled back on its trail. Kenton did not suspect it was there till it burst from the undergrowth a bare ten yards to his left.

Those yawning jaws seemed a yard wide, big enough to gulp him down at a single bite. He had not time to turn and shoot; afterwards, he thought himself lucky to have got off a shot across his body, his musket cradled in the crook of his elbow.

With a lighter gun, he probably would have broken his arm. But one of the reasons he carried a five-foot, eleven-pound rifle was to let him take such snap shots at need. Because of its weight, it had less kick.

The spearfang pitched sideways as the ball, which weighed almost a third of an ounce, slammed into its face just below a glaring eye. An instant later, Charles's hatchet clove the beast's skull. Kenton thought his bullet had already killed it, but was honest enough to admit he was never quite sure. His narrow escape made his hands shake so much he spilled powder as he reloaded, something he had not done since he was a boy.

Charles had to set a foot on the spearfang's carcass to tug his hatchet free. He used it and his knife to worry the fangs from the cat's upper jaw, handed Kenton the bloody trophies.

"Thanks." The scout wiped his sweat-beaded forehead with the back of his hand. "That, by God, is £5 I earned."

The sim shrugged. With his simple wants, money meant little to him. Ever practical, he signed, *Good meat back there*.

Here in this unexplored territory, £5 was of no more immediate use to Kenton than to Charles. The scout nodded, made his wits return to the business at hand. "So there is. Let's get at it." He and the sim walked back toward the buffalo the spearfang had killed.

Kenton made a semi-permanent camp near the salt lick, building a lean-to of branches and leaves for protection against the warm summer rain. He went back to the lick for both deer and buffalo, and added three more sets of spear-fang teeth in less hair-raising fashion than he had collected the first.

The hunting was so easy it required only a small part of his time. He ranged widely over the countryside, adding to his map and journal. The more he traveled, the richer he judged the land. Not only was it full of game, but the rich soil and abundant water were made for farming.

Sometimes Charles accompanied him on his journeys, sometimes he went alone. The sim traveled too, though not as widely as Kenton. Often he would bring back to camp small game he had slain himself: rabbits, turkey, a beaver, a porcupine that proved amazingly tasty once it was skinned. They made a welcome change of diet.

Saw strange thing, Charles signed after one of his solitary jaunts. *Many buffalo bones.* He opened and closed his hands several times, indicating some number larger than he could count.

He led Kenton to the spot the next morning. The scout whistled in surprise as he looked down into a dry wash at the tangle of whitened bones there. "Must be a hundred head, easy," he said.

Charles repeated the sign for an indefinitely large number. Together they scrambled down the steep side of the ravine, going slowly and often grabbing at bushes for support. Kenton tried to imagine what could have made a herd plunge down such a slope. Even at full stampede, the buffalo should have turned aside.

Then the scout was among the bones. Scavengers had

pulled apart many skeletons. Bushes were pushing through rib cages, climbing over skulls. The herd had met disaster at least a year ago, Kenton judged.

Many great legbones were neatly split lengthwise, almost all the skulls smashed open. When Kenton found a fist-sized lump of stone with an edge chipped sharp, it only confirmed what he had already guessed. He tossed the hand-axe up and down.

Charles recognized it at once. *Sims. Wild sims.*

"Aye. No animal could've gone for the beasts' brains and marrow so." Likely, Kenton thought, the subhumans had driven the buffalo into the gully. He glanced round, as if expecting to see a sim crouching behind every shrub. He had never doubted sims lived west of the mountains, but this was the first sure sign of it, and a sobering reminder.

Big killing, Charles signed, his eyes traveling the scattered bones. Kenton wondered what was going through his mind, wondered if he was proud of the slaughter his distant cousins had worked. Some Englishmen trained their sims to hate and fear the wild ones. The scout had never seen the need for that. Finding out he was wrong might prove costly.

He did his best to keep his voice casual. "Let me know before you join them, eh?"

Charles's face was troubled. *Joke?* he signed at last.

Kenton dimly realized how hard it had to be for sims to keep track of men's vagaries they could not share. "Joke," he said firmly. Charles nodded.

They spent a while longer investigating the ravine. Kenton turned up a few more stone tools, but nothing to show that the sims had come back to this immediate area since the year before. That was some relief, if not much.

When Charles wanted to go off for some purpose of his own, Kenton said only, "I'll see you back at the camp this evening." The last thing he wanted was the sim thinking he mistrusted him. He wished he had kept his mouth shut instead of letting his stupid wisecrack out.

Thinking such dark thoughts, the scout decided to return to the salt lick. The chunk of venison he had cached in a tree probably would not be fit to eat by nightfall, not in this heat. And game was so easy to come by west of the mountains that he did not have to put up with meat even a little off.

He wormed his way to his familiar cover. Excitement coursed through him as he looked into the clearing round the lick. A spearfang had just slain a plump doe and was dragging the carcass back into the bushes to feed. Almost without conscious volition, his rifle sprang to his shoulder and spoke.

The spearfang yowled with anguish as it staggered away from its kill. Kenton reloaded, hurried after it. He held his gun at the ready, although he did not think he would need it for such desperate work as before. The big cat's uncertain gait reflected a wound that would soon be fatal.

So it proved. Less than a furlong from the fallen deer, the scout found the spearfang dead, its mouth gaping in a last defiant snarl. Insects were already lighting on the carcass. They buzzed away as Kenton stooped beside it.

He set down his rifle, used his knife and a stone to pry out the beast's fangs. They were a fine pair, not much shorter than the gap between his thumb and little finger when he splayed them wide. He bound the two long canines with a rawhide thong, slipped them into his pouch with the rest.

He caught a slight motion out of the corner of his eye. Still on his knees, he turned. "See, I'll be rich yet, Char—"

The words caught in his throat. The sim behind him was naked, and shorter and stockier than his companion. It hefted a stone in its right hand.

The tableau held for several seconds. The sim stared at Kenton as if unsure it believed its eyes. The scout cursed himself for putting his musket to one side. The sim could hurl its rock before he grabbed the gun. And even at a bare twenty feet, he might miss with a pistol.

All the same, his right hand was easing toward his belt when three more sims, all adult males, slid silently out of the woods. He ground his teeth—no chance now to get rid of the lot of them.

Perhaps he could frighten them off. He drew a pistol. That alone would have sent wild Virginia sims running; they had seen too often what guns could do. But these sims knew nothing of firearms. One drew back its arm to cast its stone.

Kenton fired the pistol into the air. At the report and the burst of white smoke, the sims shouted in fright. The scout thought they would flee, but the one that had its rock ready let fly with it, and that rallied the others. They rushed at Kenton.

He dodged the missile, snatched out his other gun, and fired at point-blank range. As happens too mournfully often in the heat of action outside romances, he missed. He brought the pistol down club-fashion on a sim's head. The subhuman staggered but still surged forward to grapple with him; sims had thicker skulls than humans.

Afterward, the scout was just as glad not to remember much of his fight with the sims. What he could recall hurt. He never quite lost consciousness, but after a while he could not fight back much, either. The sims were not sophisticated enough for deliberate cruelty, but when four of them were beating him into submission the result came close enough to satisfy any but the most exacting critic.

When he came back to himself, one sim was carrying him by the feet and another with its hands dug into his armpits. He wondered why the sims had not killed him on the spot. Twisting his head, he saw that the four he had battled were only part of a larger band. There must have been ten males altogether, most of them bearing big joints of meat from the deer the spearfang had killed and from the spearfang itself.

With so much other food, he thought, they could afford to indulge their curiosity about him. Humans were as fascinating to sims as the reverse; indeed, sims had kidnapped Kenton's great-grandmother when she was a baby, and had done nothing worse than compare her with one of their own infants before her father rescued her.

Men would have made the scout walk once they saw he could. The sims kept carrying him. Before long, he decided he would rather have walked; it was quite the most uncomfortable journey he had ever taken.

The hunting party was traveling northwest. They topped a ridge and started down the other side. Kenton saw smoke in the distance. The rise must have kept him from spying it before; his exploratory jaunts had gone farther south.

He still had some hope. Along with a hind leg of the doe, one of his captors was carrying his musket. The sim had no idea it held a weapon, or at least not a firearm. It was toting the gun upside down, and now and then would swing it like a club. That might have prompted it to pick up the piece, that or its never having seen anything like the musket before.

Another sim, worse luck, had appropriated the scout's belt. The subhumans might have been ignorant of gunpowder, but they had seen Kenton use a pistol as a bludgeon. To them, his powderhorn and the hilt of his knife (which was all they had seen, as it was still in its sheath) might have made similar weapons.

The very notion of a belt was new to them. One set down the haunch it was carrying and wrapped a vine around its middle. Then it stopped, looking foolish; the chipped stone it had borne with the meat had neither handle nor sheath to attach to the makeshift waistband.

The sim that had kept its comrades from panicking when Kenton fired in the air let out a loud hoot. It pulled free another, shorter length of vine. Pushing out its lips with concentration, it wrapped one end of the vine several times around the stone tool and the other around the leafy belt.

The scout would not have cared to have a large rock knocking against his thigh at every step he took, but from their grins, calls, and embraces, all the sims seemed to be greeting the contrivance with the same rapture Englishmen would have given to a flying machine.

Twilight was near when the band of sims made its triumphal entry into the camp. Females and young came pelting forward to greet the returning hunters. They shrieked with delight when they saw the bounty of meat the males were bringing to them, then suddenly fell silent on noticing Kenton.

The sims that had carried him so long dumped him unceremoniously on the ground not far from the fire. They wrapped vines around and around his arms and legs. He was not sure they made any knots, but the tough plants were so twisted over and under each other that it hardly mattered.

Then the whole troop was all over him, touching, pinching, prodding; their heavy smell filled his nostrils. His clothing fascinated them. They kept running their fingers over the sueded leather. At first they seemed to think it part of him, but then they discovered his tunic could be unbuttoned, his trousers lowered.

The sims pointed and hooted at the relatively hairless skin they had exposed. Kenton felt a horrid stab of fear as they poked at his privates, but the examination, though rough, was not malicious. And with his bladder full to bursting, it was a relief to void himself without having to foul his trousers.

The sims also kept patting his forehead, the chief bodily difference between them and him. From their incredulous grins, they found it funny. They had obviously never seen a human before. He suspected the hunting band's curiosity was all that had saved his life back in the clearing.

"I'm not your enemy," he said, and gave the grunted greeting-call wild sims of the same troop used with one another back in Virginia. They understood it; he saw puzzlement on their heavy features that he, so plainly alien, should mimic the snort they used among themselves.

For a moment, he thought they might loose his bonds. But he was too strange for that, even if he knew their calls. And then the sim that had been carrying his belt began opening the pouches and powderhorn that hung from it,

which proved interesting enough to distract a good part of
the troop from his person.

The fine black grains of gunpowder made the sims
sneeze; some tasted the stuff, and made faces at the result.
The scout hoped they would toss the powderhorn onto the
fire. The blast might scare them away long enough for him
to get free. Of course, after a pound of gunpowder went off
close by, he might not be in any condition to try. Given his
present predicament, though, he was willing to take the
risk.

The sims poured the powder out onto the ground,
scotching that chance.

His tin water jar enthralled them a good deal more. Like
his belt, it was an idea they had not thought of. One rushed
over to a tiny creek a few hundred yards away, filled the jar,
and brought it back.

The sim that had bound the stone to the vine belt
suddenly snatched up the powderhorn. It hurried to the
streamlet and filled the powderhorn with water. Adapting a
tool from one use to another showed quicker wit than most
sims could boast.

They came to his shot-pouch next. The bullets cascaded
out. As soon as the sims discovered they were not some
queer kind of fruit, their youngsters pounced on the musket
balls, which made toys unlike the sticks, leaves, and stones
they had known before.

The older sims went on exploring the scout's gear. He
ground his teeth as they opened the leather bag that held
the canines of the spearfangs he had killed. The sims
recognized the fangs at once. Surprised hoots arose. The
sims stared wide-eyed at Kenton, unable to imagine how he
had slain so many of the big cats.

Last of all, the sims pulled his knife from its sheath. The
only sharp edges they knew were the ones they laboriously
chipped and flaked onto stone. They did not recognize the
gleaming steel blade as something familiar until one of
them closed her hand round it. She shrieked at the unex-

pected pain, gaped to see blood streaming down her fingers.

One of the males seized the knife then, by the hilt—more through luck than design. The sim brandished the weapon wildly, then suddenly stopped, realizing what it was for. Again Kenton fought panic; men likely would have tested the blade on his flesh.

But sims had minds more strictly utilitarian. The male squatted in front of one of the joints of meat the hunting party had brought back. It screeched in pleasure at the ease with which the knife slid through the flesh. Another sim stuck the carved-off gobbet on a stick and held it over the fire.

The first smell of roasting meat made most of the sims forget about Kenton. They armed themselves with sticks and dashed over to the butcher, who, grinning, was cutting chunk after chunk from the doe's hindquarters. The males jostled round the fire; such a feast did not often come their way. Females and youngsters beseechingly held out their hands. With so much food, the males were generous in sharing.

The wind had shifted till it came out of the west, filling the sky with clouds and blowing smoke from the fire straight into Kenton's face. It made him cough and his eyes water. Mixed with it, though, was enough of the aroma of cookery to drive him nearly wild. He could hear his stomach growling above the racket the sims were making.

He loudly smacked his lips, a signal sims gave one another when they were hungry. The sims who heard him sent him the same curious look they had when he imitated their greeting-call. But they did not feed him. Taking a captive was so unusual for them that they had no idea how to treat one. Any being outside their troop was not one of them, and so was entitled to nothing.

Things might have been worse, Kenton decided. Instead of begging for food, he could have *been* food. That the sims showed no signs of moving in that direction was mildly heartening, enough at any rate to help him resist his hunger pangs.

He wondered what Charles was doing. By now the sim should long since have returned to their camp, and it was late enough for him to be wondering what had happened to Kenton.

He might, the scout decided, be clever enough to visit the salt lick; Kenton went there most often. The scout could not guess what Charles would do after that. He was used to the company of humans—maybe he would try to go back to Virginia. Kenton wondered if the men at Portsmouth would believe his explanations, or kill him for doing away with his master. He hoped they would believe him; Charles deserved a better fate than disbelief would get him.

The sim might have a better chance here west of the mountains. He was an able hunter; he would have no trouble feeding himself. Eventually he should be able to find a home among the wild sims here, suspicious though they were of all strangers.

Charles would be able to show them so much that he could prove himself too valuable to exclude. Apart from the knife and hatchet he carried, he had learned a great deal in Virginia that wild sims were ignorant of. Even something as simple as the art of tying knots was unknown here. These sims, if they were like the ones along the Atlantic, would not know how to set snares. Charles might even be able to show them how to tan leather, which would give them footwear and many new tools.

All that would make the wild sims harder to push aside when English settlers began coming over the mountains. Kenton found he did not much care. He and Charles had been a team for years now; he could not find it in his heart to wish the sim anything but good, no matter what resulted afterwards.

The wind was blowing harder now, bringing with it cool, moist air. It must have felt wonderful to the sims, who because of their thick hair suffered worse than humans from the usual run of summer weather. That dislike of heat, though, did not keep them from feeding the fire with branches and dry shrubs whenever it began to get low.

The amount the sims could eat was astonishing. Because they spent so much time hungry, they were extravagantly able to make up for it when the chance came. They also let nothing go to waste, eating eyes, tongues, and lungs from the carcasses, smashing big bones and sucking smaller ones to get every scrap of marrow.

At last, a sort of happy torpor came to the encampment. Females nursed their infants. Youngsters gradually lost interest in throwing Kenton's musket balls at each other and bedded down in nests of dry grass and leaves. Most of the adults followed them before long, singly or in pairs.

A few males stayed awake. One kept the fire going. Three more went to the edge of the clearing as sentries. One of those carried a club, another a couple of chipped stones. The third, a large, hulking sim, bore Kenton's rifle. It carried the gun by the muzzle end of the barrel and swung it menacingly every minute or so, as if daring anything dangerous to come close.

The clever sim sat cross-legged by the fire not far from the scout. It stared down at the dagger it held in its lap. From time to time it would run a hand along its chinless jaw, the very image of studious concentration.

Kenton felt a touch of sympathy; the sim could study the knife till doomsday without learning how it was made. At that moment the sim looked his way. It shook its head, exactly as a frustrated man might: it was full of questions, and had no way to ask them.

Some of the wild Virginia sims had learned sign-speech from runaways and used it among themselves, but it had not come over the mountains. The wild troops had so little contact with one another that ideas spread very slowly among them.

The sim picked up a stone chopper, took it in its left hand and the knife in its right. The crudeness of its own product next to the other must have infuriated it, for it suddenly scrambled to its feet and hurled the stone far into the night.

All three of the males standing watch whirled at the sound of the rejected tool landing in the bushes. The clever sim let out an apologetic hoot. The others relaxed.

The clever sim came over to glare at Kenton. The scout thought what a man would be feeling, confronted with skills and knowledge so far ahead of anything he possessed—and confronted with a being like and yet unlike himself. Sims were less imaginative than humans, but surely some of that combination of anger, fear, and awe was on the subhuman's face.

Anger quickly came to predominate. Kenton uselessly tightened his muscles against the knife thrust he expected.

He hardly noticed the first raindrop that landed on his cheek, or the second. Even when a drop hit him in the eye, it distracted him only briefly from his fearful focus on the blade in the sim's hairy hand.

The sim shook its head in annoyance as the rain began. To it, too, the early sprinkles were but an irritation. As the rain kept up, though, it forgot Kenton, forgot the knife it held. Its cry of alarm brought the rest of the troop bounding from their rest.

For a moment, Kenton wondered if the clever sim had gone mad. But soon he understood its concern, for the rain grew harder. The fire began to hiss as water poured down on it—and no wild sim could start a fire once it went out.

Because that was so, the sims had had to learn to keep their flames alive even in the face of rain. Some of the males held hides above the fire to shield it from the storm. Females dug ditches and built little dams of mud so the water on the ground would not get the fuel wet.

Their efforts worked for a time. The sims with the hide shield coughed and choked on the smoke it trapped, but they did not leave their post. The fire continued to crackle.

Kenton all but ignored it. His mouth was wide open, to catch as much of the rain as he could. The sims had given him no more water than food, and his throat felt raspy as a file. It took a while to get enough for a swallow, but every one was bliss.

The downpour grew heavier, the wind stronger. Soon it was blowing sheets of water horizontally. The sims' hides were less and less use. They wailed in dismay as the fire went out. Kenton could hardly hear them over the drumming of the rain. He was glad they had not dumped him face down; he might have drowned.

The storm lasted through the night, and began to ease only when light returned. Drenched, Kenton was relieved the rain was warm; had the cloudburst come, say, in fall, he would have been all too vulnerable to chest fever. He imagined it carried off many of the sims.

They huddled together, sodden and miserable, around their dead fire, their arms up to keep some of the rain from their faces. Now and then one would let out a mournful, keening cry that several others would echo. It reminded the scout eerily of a wake.

When the rain was finally over, the clever sim raked through the ashes, searching for hot coals that might be coaxed back to life. But the storm had been too strong; everything was soaked. As the sims saw they were indeed without the heat to cook their food and, in days to come, to keep them warm, they broke out in a fresh round of lamentation.

Kenton wondered if they would seek to have him restart the blaze. If that meant getting free of them, he would do so in an instant. He would have offered, if they understood his speech or if he could have used his arms to gesture. But they did not even look his way; it did not occur to them that *anyone* could start a fire. His strangeness, and the curious tools he bore, were not enough to overcome that automatic assumption.

Slowly, morosely, the sims began to pick up the usual business of the camp. A grizzled male chipped away at a chunk of flint to shape a new hand-axe. Females dug roots with sticks and went into the nearby forest after early-ripening berries. Youngsters turned over rocks and popped whatever crawling things they found into their mouths.

A hunting party set out, armed with an assortment of wooden clubs and sharp stones. The sim with Kenton's musket apparently decided the long gun would be too clumsy to swing in tight quarters, for it exchanged the rifle for a stout bludgeon. The scout shook his head, relieved that the sim did not grasp what the musket could do.

The clever sim did not go with the band of hunting males. Its arms were filthy to the elbows from grubbing in the ruins of the fire. It kept staring at Kenton, as if he were a puzzle to be pieced together. When a couple of toddlers came over and prodded him; it bared its formidable teeth and shouted so fiercely that they tumbled backward in fright.

It came over and squatted by him; it made squelching sounds as it sat in the mud. "I am not your enemy," Kenton said, as he had the night before.

It grunted. He thought it sought to converse with him, but his words meant nothing to it. Sims came to understand human speech, but their own calls in the wild, even eked out by gestures, did not make up a language. The clever sim felt the lack, yet was powerless to remedy it. Had his arms been free Kenton might have, but he needed dumb show to ask to be released, and could not use it until he had been. Contemplating that paradox led only to discomfiture.

If the sim and he could not converse, though, only one thing was likely to happen to him. No sims he knew kept captives, and the treatment he was getting here showed this troop to be no different. His flesh might not be so toothsome raw as roasted, but he did not think that would save him.

The way the clever sim was licking its lips now as it looked at him told him it had come to the same conclusion. The only reason he could find for its not killing him immediately was to keep his meat fresh for the hunting party when they came back. That did little to improve his spirits. He was getting thirsty again, too, and very hungry.

The day dragged on. The clever sim no longer bothered to keep the troop's youngsters away from Kenton. The small indignities they inflicted in their curiosity added to his misery. Still, human children would have done worse.

He heard a rustling in the woods, from the direction in which the hunters had gone. The old male who had been making tools gave the grunted greeting-noise. Kenton turned his head as the clever sim moved toward him, his knife in its hand. He expected the returning hunters would be the last thing he ever saw.

Then the old sim and several females cried out in alarm. The clever sim sucked in its breath in a harsh gasp. Coming into the clearing was not one of the hunters—it was Charles instead.

Charles's eyes went wide when he saw Kenton lying tied in the mud by the drowned fire. He was too far away for the scout to read his expression clearly. Kenton wondered what was going through his mind, observing his master bound and helpless in the hands of his wild cousins. Was he tempted to throw in his lot with them? How could he help it, with the scout's vulnerability so displayed? Superior wit was not all that let humans rule sims; their aura of might played no little role.

If Kenton's weakness gave Charles qualms, the sim from Virginia was as disturbing to the wild sims. The scout's clothes and possessions were strange to them, but so was he himself. Charles was of their own kind, yet he too wore a belt and buskins, and bore tools of the same alien sort as Kenton's.

The clever sim glanced from the knife he was holding to the one swinging at Charles's belt, and to the bright steel head of the hatchet Charles carried. The clever sim's face was the picture of bewilderment. Kenton could hardly blame it. It had seen its world turned upside down twice now in two days.

Raising the hatchet in a plain warning gesture, Charles advanced into the clearing. Females and young scurried away from him. He was more frightening than Kenton, and not just because he was free. The familiar turned bizarre is always harder to face than something wildly different.

Charles strode toward Kenton, the hatchet still held high. The scout spoke through lips dry from thirst and fear: "Good to see you again." He had all he could do to hold his voice steady. Nothing, he knew, might more quickly ingratiate Charles with the wild sims than slaughtering him.

Charles surveyed the encampment. The clever sim was the only male there of vigorous years. When it saw that Charles understood Kenton, it scowled fiercely and tightened its grip on the scout's knife.

Kenton had no choice but to wait to see what Charles would do. But Charles also seemed unsure, staring from the scout to the clever sim and back again. At last his left hand moved in a sign Kenton understood: *Trouble*.

"Trouble indeed," Kenton said, though he could not tell whether Charles meant the sign for him or it was simply the sim's equivalent of talking to himself. Daring to hope hurt, as an arm that has fallen asleep will tingle when the blood rushes in again.

Then Charles signed, *I help*, and squatted over him to cut his bonds. The clever sim shouted angrily and brandished the scout's knife. Charles shouted back, but drew away from Kenton. Had it just been the clever sim and he, the hatchet would have given him all the advantage he needed. But though none of the other sims was his match individually, together they could overwhelm him.

"Give them something to think about," Kenton exclaimed suddenly. "The storm put out their fire—start it again."

The way Charles's face lit was almost enough to kindle a blaze by itself. He deliberately turned his back on the clever sim, doing it with as much aplomb as any nobleman scoring off some rival. In spite of everything, Kenton could not help smiling; here was something unexpected that Charles had learned in Virginia.

Charles knelt and took out his tinderbox. The scout

heard him strike flint and steel together several times, saw him bend further to blow to life the sparks that had fallen on his tinder. Then, with a satisfied snort, Charles stepped away.

Because he had no dry fuel close by, he had made a pile of all the powdered bark and lint in the tinderbox. The little fire crackled briskly.

The wild sims stood transfixed, as if turned to stone. Then one of the old males hooted softly, the most nearly awed sound Kenton had ever heard from a sim's throat. The old male scrabbled through the remains of the dead fire for wood dry enough to burn. Having found a couple of sticks, it approached the blaze Charles had set, glancing at him as though for permission. When he did not object, it set the sticks on the fire. After a while, they caught.

Half a dozen wild sims dashed off after more fuel. The rest crowded toward the blaze, drawn to the flames like moths.

Not even the clever sim was immune to the fascination. This time it did not object when Charles stooped and began cutting Kenton's bonds.

The scout grimaced at the sting of returning circulation he had imagined a few minutes before. He clenched and unclenched his fingers and toes, trying to work feeling back into them. All the same, it was some minutes before he could stand. When he finally did, he had to clutch undignifiedly at his trousers; their sueded leather had stretched from the soaking it had taken.

He did not think he could get his knife back from the clever sim, but did go over to where the other male had discarded his musket. With his powder spilled and bullets scattered, he had only the one shot till he got back to his pack, but that was better than nothing. And the wild sim had been right, in its way—at need, the rifle would make a good club.

Kenton also gathered up the spearfang canines, although to his annoyance one had disappeared in the mud. He had come by them through hard, dangerous hunting, and they represented wealth too great and too easily portable for him to abandon.

Though the scout hurried, Charles waited with barely concealed impatience. *We go?* he signed, adding the emphatic gesture to the questioning one.

"Indeed we do!" Kenton wanted to be as far from the encampment as he could when the hunting party returned.

The clever sim watched them withdraw. Its massive jaw muscles worked. The scout could all but taste its frustration. It had met beings and found tools and skills beyond any it could have imagined, and here, after only a brief moment, they were vanishing from its life again.

That proved more than it could bear. With a harsh cry, it rushed Kenton and Charles. The scout flung his musket to his shoulder, but hesitated with his finger still on the first trigger. The males in the hunting party had heard gunfire before; the sound of a shot would surely bring them on the run.

Charles had no such worries. His arm went back, then forward. The hatchet spun through the air. It buried itself deep in the clever sim's chest.

The clever sim shrieked. It wrenched the hatchet out, heedless of the blood that gushed from the wound. The clever sim flung the hatchet back at Charles, but its throw was wild. It staggered on rubbery legs, sat heavily. Kenton could hear how its breath bubbled in its throat.

The rest of the wild sims came out of their trance round the fire. They shouted and hooted. Hands groped for stones to throw. Saving his single bullet against desperate need, Kenton ran. Charles fled with him, stopping only to seize the hatchet from where it lay on the ground. Red streaked the gray steel blade.

Kenton never found out whether the clever sim lived or died. He was everlastingly grateful it was the only robust male at the encampment. He and Charles outdistanced the gray-hairs and youngsters that tried to pursue them. They might not have had such good fortune if tested against the members of the hunting band, the more so as the scout's abused limbs could not carry him at full speed.

Kenton knew the troop's hunters would be expert trackers. They would have to be, living as they did from what they could run down. And so, no matter how urgently he wanted to put distance between himself and the camp, he and Charles did not neglect muddling their trail, doubling back on their tracks and splashing down streams so they would not leave footprints.

A large bullfrog sat on a half-submerged log, staring stupidly, as Kenton and Charles drew near. Too late, it decided to leap away. The scout grabbed it and broke its neck.

A bit farther on, they came upon clumps of freshwater mussels growing on some rocks. Charles used his knife and Kenton borrowed his hatchet to sever the byssi by which the shellfish moored themselves.

By then it was nearly dark. Neither of them knew the countryside well enough to head back toward the camp by night. They would have to shift camp anyway, Kenton realized; it was too close to the salt lick. The wild sims would surely scour that whole area in search of them. The scout hoped he could recover his pistols from the spot where he had killed the spearfang.

All that, though, could wait. Finding a hiding place for the night came first. A hollow with a rock pile down one side proved suitable, after Kenton stoned to death a fat rattling-snake that had been nesting among the rocks.

Fire? Charles signed.

The scout considered the lay of the land. "Yes," he said, "a small one." If the wild sims came close enough to spot a tiny blaze by night, they would be on top of him anyway. And while he did not mind eating raw mussels, even hungry as he was he wanted to roast the frog and snake.

His stomach still growled when he was done with his share, but he felt better for it. He licked his fingers clean of grease and looked across the fire at Charles, who was still worrying tiny fragments of meat from a frogleg with his tongue.

In the dim, flickering red light, the sim's eyes were sunk in pits of shadow, unreadable. "Charles," Kenton began, and then stopped, unsure how—or if—to go on.

Charles tossed the bones, by now quite naked, to one side. He gave a low-voiced, questioning hoot.

"I thank you," the scout said.

Charles grunted, a noncommittal sound.

Kenton almost let it rest there. His curiosity, though, was too great. People had been trying to understand sims—and to see how close sims could come to understanding them— for close to two centuries. And so the scout asked, "Why did you decide to rescue me?"

The skin moved on Charles's brow-ridges; a man would have been wrinkling his forehead in concentration. *You, I come here together*, he signed. *We go back together*.

The scout wondered if that indeed was the whole answer. Because they were less imaginative than men, sims rigidly followed plans. Kenton had often talked about the return trip; perhaps Charles had simply been unable to conceive of anything else happening, and had acted as he did more for the picture of the future the scout had outlined than for Kenton's sake.

Kenton's lips twisted wryly; there was a thought to put him in his place. He persisted, "It would have been easier and less risky for you to join the wild sims."

He knew he was treading on dangerous ground. Back in Virginia, many sims fled to the wild troops that still lurked in the backwoods. There was always the risk of putting ideas in Charles's head that had not been there before.

The sim surprised him with an immediate gesture of rejection. *Not leave you*, Charles signed. *You, me, together, good. Years and years—not want end.*

"I thank you," Kenton said again. Had he followed the course of some colonists—who treated their sims as much like beasts as possible—he was sure he would have been shared among the wild sims in raw gobbets, with Charles likely joining the feast.

But the sim, to his surprise, was not done signing: *Not want to live with wild sims. Want to live with people. Wild sims boring*—an enormous yawn rendered that—*not know houses, not know music, not know knives, not know bread.* Charles sniffed with the same disdain a Portsmouth grandee would have shown on learning his daughter's prospective bridegroom wore no shoes and shared a cabin with his mule.

Kenton burst out laughing. Charles snorted indignantly. The scout apologized, both in words and with the customary sim gesture: he smacked his lips loudly and spread his hands, meaning he had intended no harm. Charles accepted, once more with a lord's grace.

Inside, though, Kenton kept chuckling, though he was careful not to show it. He did not want to hurt Charles's feelings. But how on earth, he wondered, was he going to explain to Lord Emerson that he had been saved because his sim was a snob?

1782

The Iron Elephant

The Americas proved to possess a number of animals unlike any with which Europeans had been familiar: the ground sloth, the spearfang, and the several varieties of armadillo, of which the largest was bigger than a man. Others, such as the hairy elephant, had counterparts in distant areas of the Old World but still seemed exotic to early generations of settlers.

Just before the American colonies broke away from English tyranny and banded together to form the Federated Commonwealths of America, however, efforts began to exploit the hairy elephant's great strength in a new way. The first rail systems, with waggons pulled by horses, appeared in England at about this time to haul coal from mines to rivers and canals. Hairy elephants began their railroad work in this same capacity, but soon were pulling other freight, and passengers as well.

In the decades following the creation of the republic, railroads spread across the country. Because the

97

Federated Commonwealths is so much larger than any European nation, such a web of steel was a vital link in knitting the country together. By 1780, tracks had reached across the New Nile. The mighty river remained unbridged, but ferry barges joined the settled east with the new lands that were just beginning to be farmed.

But the hairy elephant's trumpet was not destined to remain the characteristic sound of the railroads. Coal mining also resulted in the development of the steam engine. At first used only in place, to pump water from the mines, the steam engine soon proved capable of broader application. Soon the hairy elephants that had been for more than a generation the mainstay of the American railway system began to feel the effects of mechanical competition.

From *The Story of the Federated Commonwealths*

THE TRAIN RATTLED east across the prairie toward Springfield. Prem Chand kept his rifle across his knees, in case of sims. From his perch atop Caesar, the lead hairy elephant, he could see a long way over the grassland.

"We should make town in another hour," Paul Tilak called from Hannibal, the trail beast. "An easy trip, this one."

Prem Chand turned around. "So it is, for which I am not sorry." He and Tilak were both small, light-brown men with delicate features. Their grandfathers had come to America when the English decided to see if elephant handlers from India could tame the great auburn-haired beasts of the New World.

The two dozen waggons stretched out behind the pair of elephants showed that the answer was yes, though the Federated Commonwealths had been free of England for a generation. With people even then beginning to settle west of the New Nile, no country across the sea could hope to enforce its will on its one-time colonies.

"Sim!" Tilak shouted suddenly. "There, to the north!"

Prem Chand's head whipped round. He followed his friend's pointing finger. Sure enough, the subhuman was loping along parallel to the train, about three hundred yards away. Prem Chand muttered something unpleasant under his breath. Sims might have no foreheads to speak of, but they had learned how far a gun could shoot with hope of accuracy.

"Shall we give him a volley?" Tilak asked.

"Yes, let us," Prem Chand said. Three hundred yards was not quite impossibly long range, not with more than a dozen rifles speaking together. And the sim's arrogant confidence in its own safety irked the elephant driver.

He waved a red flag back and forth to make sure the brakemen posted on top of every other car saw it. Tilak peered back over his shoulder. "They're ready."

Prem Chand swung the flag down, snatched up his rifle. It bellowed along with the others, and bucked against his shoulder. The acrid smell of gunpowder filled his nose.

The hairy elephant beneath him started at the volley. It threw up its trunk and let out a trumpeting roar almost as loud as the gunshots. Prem Chand shouted, "*Choro*, Caesar, *choro*: stop, stop!" Elephant commands were the only Urdu he still knew. His father had preferred them to English, and passed them on to him.

He prodded Caesar behind the ear with his foot, spoke soothingly to him. Being on the whole a good-natured beast, the elephant soon calmed. Tilak's Hannibal was more excitable; the other driver had to whack him with a brass *ankus* to make him behave. Hannibal's ears twitched resentfully.

Prem Chand peered through the smoke to see whether all that gunfire had actually hit the sim. It hadn't. The subhuman let out a raucous hoot, shook its fist at the train, and bounded away.

Prem Chand sighed. "I do not like those pests, not at all. One day I would like to unharness Caesar and go hunting sims from elephant-back."

"Men only began settling hereabouts a few years ago," Tilak said resignedly. "Sims will be less common before long."

"Yes, but they are so clever it's almost impossible to root them out altogether. Even on the eastern coast, where the land has been settled for a hundred-fifty years, wild bands still linger. Not so many as here west of the New Nile, true, but they exist."

"Mere vermin fail to worry me," Paul Tilak said. He put a hand to his forehead to shade his eyes. "We should be able to see Springfield soon."

"Oh, not yet," Prem Chand said. But he also looked ahead, and saw the thin line of black smoke against the sky. Alarm flashed through him. "Fire!" he shouted. "The town must be burning!"

He dug his heels into Caesar's shoulders, yelled, *"Mall-mall:* go on!" He heard Tilak using the elephant goad to urge Hannibal on. The two beasts had to pull hard to gain speed against the dead weight of the train. Prem Chand hoped the brakemen were alert. If he had to slow suddenly, they would need to halt the waggons before they could barrel into the elephants ahead of them.

The line of smoke grew taller, but no wider. Prem Chand scratched his head. Funny kind of fire, he thought.

"What's burning?" a farmer called as the train rolled by—farms sprouted like mushrooms along the tracks close to town, though they were still scarce farther away. Prem Chand shrugged. Even then, in the back of his mind, he might have known the truth, but it was not the sort of truth he felt like facing before he had to.

Then he could see Springfield in the distance. Its wooden buildings looked quite intact. The smoke had stopped rising. The prairie breezes played with the plume, dispersing it.

Houses, stables, a church, warehouses passed in swift succession. Prem Chand guided Caesar into the last turn before the station. *"Choro!"* he called again. Caesar slowed. The brakemen worked their levers. Sparks flew as the waggons' iron wheels squealed on the track. The train pulled to a halt.

"Seventeen minutes ahead of schedule," Paul Tilak said with satisfaction, checking his pocket watch. "No one will be able to complain we are late on this run, Prem."

"No indeed," Prem Chand said. "But where *is* everybody?" Their being early was no reason for the eastbound side of the station to be empty—they had been in sight quite a while. Where were the men and tame sims to unload the train's freight? Where were the people coming to meet arriving passengers? Where were the ostlers, with fodder and water and giant currycombs for the elephants? Come to think of it, where had the small boys who always gawked at the train disappeared to?

Prem Chand tapped Caesar's left shoulder, as far down as he could reach. The hairy elephant obligingly raised its left leg. Prem Chand shinnied down to the broad, leathery foot, then dropped to the ground.

A passenger stuck his head out the window of a forward waggon. "See here, sir," he called to the elephant driver, "what is the meaning of this? I am an important man, and expect to be properly greeted. I have business to transact here before I go on to Cairo." He glared at Prem Chand as if he thought everything was his fault.

"I am very sorry, sir," Prem Chand said politely, which was not at all what he was thinking. "I will try to find out."

At that moment, a door in the station house opened. Finally, Prem Chand thought, someone's come to take a look at us. It was George Stephenson, the stationmaster, a plump little man who always wore a stovepipe hat that went badly with his build.

"What is the meaning of this?" Prem Chand shouted at him, stealing the pompous passenger's phrase. "Where are the men to take care of the elephants?" To a driver, everything else was secondary to that.

Stephenson should have felt the same way. Instead, he blinked; the idea did not seem to have occurred to him. "I'll have Willie and Jake get round to it," he said grudgingly.

"Get round to it?" Prem Chand clapped a hand to his forehead in extravagant disbelief. "How else will they make enough money for their whiskey? What is wrong with this town today? Has everyone here gone out of his mind?"

"Not hardly," Stephenson said. He was looking at Caesar and Hannibal in a way Prem Chand had never seen before. Was that pity in his eyes? "We've just seen the future, is all. Maybe you better take a peep too, Prem, so as you and Paul there can start huntin' out a new line of work."

Then Prem Chand did know what had happened, knew it with a certainty that gripped his guts. Even so, he had to make Stephenson spell it out. "You mean—?"

"Ayah, that's right, Prem. One o' them newfangled steam railroad engines has done come to Springfield. How do you propose outdoin' a machine?"

The pennant tied to the front of the steam engine called it "The Iron Elephant." To Prem Chand, the name was an obscene parody. The upjutting smokestack reminded him of Caesar's trunk, yes, but that trunk frozen in rigor mortis. Painting the boiler red-brown to imitate a hairy elephant's pelt did not disguise its being made of iron. And the massive gears and wheels on either side of that boiler seemed to Prem Chand affixed as an afterthought, not parts of the device in the way Caesar's great legs were part of the elephant.

Besides, the thing stank. Used to the clean, earthy smell of elephant, Prem Chand's nostrils twitched at the odors of coal smoke and damp, cooling iron.

Had he been able to get closer, he thought, he probably would have been able to find other things to dislike about the Iron Elephant. As it was, he had to despise the contraption at a distance. Almost everybody in Springfield had jammed into the westbound side of the station to stare at the steam engine.

Stephenson turned to Prem Chand, saying, "I know you'll want to meet Mr. Trevithick, the engine handler, and compare notes. He's been waiting here for you. Come on, I'll take you to him.'' He plunged into the crowd, using his weight to shove people aside.

Meeting this Trevithick person was the last thing Prem Chand wanted. He also had a schedule to keep. He grabbed Stephenson by the shoulder. "Of course he's been waiting—he only has that damned engine. Me, I have an entire train to see to. You have my elephants fed, this instant. You have them watered. You unload what comes off here, and get your eastbound freight on board. Get your passengers moving. If I am one minute late coming into Cairo on the New Nile, I will complain to the company, yes I will, and with any luck we will bypass Springfield afterwards.''

He knew he was bluffing. Likely Stephenson did too, but he could not afford to ignore the threat. Without a rail stop, Springfield would wither and die. With poor grace, he started pulling station hands out of the crush and shouting for passengers to get over to the eastbound track. The press of people thinned, a little.

"Satisfied?" the stationmaster asked ironically.

"Better, at any rate," Prem Chand said.

"One fine day soon you won't be able to throw your weight around just on account of you drive elephants, Prem. When steam comes in, we won't need stables, we won't need the big hay yards. This operation'll run on half the people and a quarter the cost.'' Stephenson rubbed his hands at the prospect.

"And what do you do, pray tell me, when one of these engines breaks down? Whom will you hire? How much will you have to pay him? More than your ostlers or a leech, I would wager. And how long will the repairs take? Caesar and Hannibal are reliable. What sort of schedule will you be able to keep up?''

"The Iron Elephant's reliable too," Stephenson insisted, though Prem Chand's objections made him sound as if he were also trying to convince himself. But his voice steadied as he went on. "It's steamed all the way out from Boston in Plymouth Commonwealth without coming to grief. I reckon that says somethin'."

In spite of himself, Prem Chand was impressed: that was more than 1,300 miles. Still, he said scornfully, "Yes, hauling nothing but itself and its coal-waggon." No passenger coaches or freight waggons stood behind the Iron Elephant. "How will it do, pulling a real load?"

"I don't know anything about that. Like I told you before, fellow you want to talk to is the engine handler. Come on, Prem—you may as well. You know they'll be a good while yet over on the other side."

"Oh, very well." Prem Chand followed Stephenson as the stationmaster forced his way through the crowd, which had thinned more while they argued.

"Mr. Trevithick!" Stephenson called, and then again, louder, "Mr. Trevithick!" A pale, almost consumptive-looking young man standing by the traveling steam engine lifted his head inquiringly. "Mr. Trevithick, this here is Mr. Prem Chand, the elephant driver you wanted to see."

"Ah!" The engine handler broke off the conversation he was having, came hurrying over to pump Prem Chand's hand. "They spoke very well of you in Cairo, sir, when I was arranging permits to travel this line—said your Caesar and Hannibal were first-rate beasts. I see they were right; you're here a good deal ahead of schedule." Like any railroad man, Trevithick always had a watch handy.

"Thank you so very much, sir." Prem Chand saw he was going to have to work to dislike this man; Trevithick was perfectly sincere. Looking into his intense blue eyes, Prem Chand suspected he was one of those people who always said just what they thought because it never occurred to them to do anything else.

"Call me Richard—couldn't stand going as Dick Trevithick, you know. And you're Prem? Shouldn't be any stuffiness between folks in the same line of work."

Again Prem Chand realized that he meant it. As gently as he could, he said, "Richard, it is a line of work that you and that—thing"—he could not make himself call it the Iron Elephant—"are trying to get me out of."

"Am I? How?" Trevithick's surprise was genuine, which in turn surprised Prem Chand. "Who better to work the railroads under steam than someone long familiar with them as an elephant driver? Everything about them will be the same, except for what pulls the waggons."

"And, Richard, with all respect, everything about iron and wood is the same, except when I need to start a fire. I've spent a lifetime learning to care for elephants; what good will that do me in dealing with your boiler there?"

"A child could manage the throttle. And we have a whole new kind of boiler in the Iron Elephant, with tubes passing through it to heat the water more effectively. And the cylinders are almost horizontal; they work much better than the old vertical design did." Trevithick glowed with enthusiasm, and plainly wanted Prem Chand to catch fire too. "Why, on level ground, with the extra power the new system gives, we can do close to thirty miles an hour— practically flying along the ground!"

Had Stephenson named the figure, Prem Chand would have called him a liar on the spot. He did not think Trevithick a man given to exaggeration, though. Thirty miles an hour! He tried to imagine what the wind would be like, whipping in his face: as if he were on a madly galloping racehorse, but for some long time, not just the few minutes the beast would take to tire.

"How about that, Prem?" Stephenson put in, nudging him in the ribs. "Only way you'd get Caesar and Hannibal moving that fast'd be to drop 'em off a roof."

Prem Chand grunted. He thought of the stationmaster's boasts about how much he could cut back his operation. The elephant driver smiled sardonically at Trevithick's naivete. Everything would be the same, would it?

"Thirty miles an hour is a marvelous speed, Richard; it is most marvelous indeed. But that is unloaded, I take it. What can your steam engine"—he *would not* call it the Iron Elephant, not even for politeness' sake—"do pulling a load of, say, fifty tons?"

"Tell him, Mr. Trevithick." This time the engine

handler was the recipient of Stephenson's conspiratorial elbow.

He did not seem to notice. The gleam in his eyes turned inward as he calculated. At last he said, "That is a great deal of weight. Does your team really pull so much?" For the first time, his voice held a trace of doubt.

"They can, yes," Prem Chand said proudly.

"Truth to tell, I have to wonder if the machinery could stand it. But I think we should be able to do something on the order of three miles an hour, not counting stops for water or for any breakdowns that might happen."

"Three miles an hour? Is that all?" George Stephenson sounded more betrayed than disappointed.

"If that." Trevithick looked amused. "Now you see why I tend to put more stress on the engine's top speed."

Prem Chand, though, was still impressed, and worried. His beloved elephants were faster, but they were only flesh and blood. They had to rest, where the steam engine could go on and on and on. And yet, he thought, *if I can show everyone how the elephants outdo this stinking contraption—*

"Richard, load your train up, and I will load mine, and I will race you from here to Carthage."

"A race, eh?" Trevithick's bright eyes glowed. "How far is this Carthage place from here?"

"Fifty-three miles, a tiny bit south of west. The railroad ends soon after it."

"Hmm." Prem Chand watched the engine handler go into that near-trance of concentration again. When he emerged from it, he gave the elephant driver a respectful look. "That will be a very close thing, Prem. You know how embarrassing—and I mean financially as well as in the sense of a blow to my pride—it would be for me to lose?"

Prem Chand returned a bland shrug. "You've come all this way from Plymouth, Richard, to show off your iron-mongery. How embarrassing would it be for word to get out that you refused a challenge from your competition?"

Trevithick laughed out loud. "You misunderstand me. I

have no intention of refusing. When shall we start?"

"Tomorrow morning?"

"What?" George Stephenson let out a howl. "You're eastbound for Cairo tomorrow morning, Prem! What about your precious schedule?"

"Well, what about it? If this steam engine comes in and replaces Caesar and Hannibal, then I will have to do as you suggested before and find other work, so it will not matter if the company fires me. But if elephants are better than machinery, the company should know that too. They will thank me more for finding that out than they will be angry with me for being late. And besides, George, why should you worry? Don't you own the town hotel?"

Stephenson suddenly looked crafty. "Well, yes, now that you mention it, I do."

"Here is a man who thinks of everything," Trevithick said admiringly. "I wonder if I ought to race against you after all—no, my friend, only a joke. But tomorrow morning will be too soon. We will have to load up waggons so both our trains carry equal weight. . . . George, you live here, unlike either Prem or myself. Can you hire some sims from the locals to help the ones at the station here with that work?"

"Reckon so." Stephenson gave Trevithick a sidelong glance. "So long as I ain't payin' for it, that is."

Prem Chand gulped; he was never going to be rich on an elephant driver's salary. But Trevithick said, "I'll cover it, never fear. What I don't make up on bets will come back in the long run through the ballyhoo this race will cause."

"Whatever you say. All I know is, you can't put no ballyhoo in the bank. Them folks are partial to gold."

"Who isn't?" Trevithick chuckled.

Prem Chand went back to the other side of the station to stop the unloading of his train—the less that came off, the less that would have to be put back tomorrow. The straw boss who oversaw Stephenson's gang of sims looked at him as if he were crazy. "First you was screaming nobody was doing anything, now you're screaming on account of they are. Can't you make up your fool mind?"

"Truly I am sorry, Mr. Dubois." Prem Chand had always thought the straw boss more capable than Stephenson, and treated him accordingly.

Dubois only grunted in disgust, then turned and shouted to the dozen sims that were unloading sacks of grain from the waggons. He gave hand signals to back his oral instructions. Sims could follow human speech, but had trouble imitating it. They much preferred to use gestures, and many overseers gave orders both ways, taking no chances on being misunderstood.

That care paid off now. One of the sims gaped in disbelief at the overseer. Its long, chinless jaw fell open to reveal yellow teeth bigger and stouter than any man's. It ran a hand over what would have been a human's forehead, but was in the sim only a smooth slope behind bony brow-ridges.

Back, it signed, adding the little gesture that turned the word to a question. Prem Chand usually had some trouble following hand-talk, but the sim made the sign so em-phatic—the way a man might shout an objection—that he understood it with ease.

Back, Dubois signed firmly. *Put bags back.*

The sim scratched its hairy cheek, let out a wordless hoot of protest. It signed, *Bad. Very bad. Work all gone.* From its point of view, Prem Chand supposed it had a point. But under Dubois's uncompromising eye, it and its comrades began putting the produce back aboard the train.

"What are they doing, Prem?" Paul Tilak demanded. "That should go in the warehouses here—look at the bill of lading. And why were they so slow getting here in the first place? Where was everyone, and why is everyone so excited?"

Very much the same set of questions, Prem Chand thought wryly, that he had thrown at George Stephenson. They had the same answer, too: "Steam engine."

"Damnation!" Tilak shouted, so loudly that Hannibal let out an alarmed snort and swung its shaggy head to see what was wrong with its driver. "It is all right, really it is," Tilak reassured him. The elephant snorted again, doubtfully, but subsided.

"These accursed engines will be the ruination of us," Tilak said.

"I hope not."

"Of course they will." Tilak was gloomier by nature than Prem Chand. He noticed Dubois's gang of sims again. "What *are* they doing, Prem?"

Prem Chand told him. Tilak's jaw dropped. He frowned. "I do not know if we can beat this Trevithick, Prem, if his machine performs as he says it will."

"He does not know if he can beat us, either, which makes for a fair trial. Cheer up, Paul. Even if we lose, how are we worse off? What will happen? The company will buy engines, just as it would without any race at all. But if we win, perhaps they will not."

Tilak looked unconvinced. Before the argument could go further, the passenger who had bothered Prem Chand from the coach window now grabbed him by the arm. "See here, sir! Do I understand you to mean that this train will not proceed to Cairo, but rather is returning to Carthage?"

"I am afraid that is correct, sir." As gently as he could, Prem Chand shook free of the man's grasp. "I am so very sorry for any inconvenience this may—"

"Inconvenience?" the man exclaimed. His face was almost as red as his waistcoat. "Do you know, sir, that I stand to lose out on a very profitable investment opportunity if I am delayed here?"

That was too much for Prem Chand. The deference that was part of his railroading persona went by the board. He stuck his face an inch from the passenger's nose and bellowed, "God damn you to hell, do you know that I stand to lose out on a job I have loved for twenty-five years and that my father and grandfather held before me? I piss on your investment opportunity, and for a copper sester I'd black your eye, too!"

Tilak quickly stepped between them before they could

start a fight. The passenger stamped away, still yelling threats.

Prem Chand looked toward his beloved elephants. The ostlers had set out big wooden tubs of water for them. "Derr!" he shouted to Caesar: "Splash!" He thrust out his arm, pointing to the obnoxious fellow with whom he'd been quarreling.

Caesar snorted up a big trunkful of water and let it go in a sudden shower—that drenched Prem Chand. Tilak and Dubois got wet too, and hopped back swearing. The fellow the elephant driver had intended to soak got off unscathed.

"It has been that kind of day," Prem Chand sighed. "Fetch me a towel, please, someone."

Instead of starting the next morning, as Prem Chand had proposed, the race did not begin until three days later. Part of the delay was from loading waggons so that the elephants and the steam engine would pull about the same amount of weight. The rest came from dickering over conditions.

Since the flesh-and-blood elephants were ready at once, while the Iron Elephant had to build up steam, Trevithick wanted Prem Chand not to start until the engine could move. This the elephant driver indignantly refused, on the grounds that the start-up delay was an inherent part of the mechanical device's function. Public opinion in Springfield backed him, and Trevithick gave way.

But Prem Chand had to yield in turn on the load the Iron Elephant would have to haul. He wanted the weight of the waggons added on to that of the engine and coal-waggon. Trevithick, though, neatly turned the tables on him, pointing out that the Iron Elephant naturally got lighter as it traveled and consumed its fuel. The coal, he said, should count as part of its initial burden. He won his point.

Most of Springfield was there to see the race begin. The Iron Elephant was on the regular westbound track; Caesar and Hannibal took the track usually reserved for eastbound trains. Trevithick doffed his dapper cap to Prem Chand. The elephant driver returned a curt nod. Trevithick was not a bad sort. If anything, that made matters worse.

The mayor of Springfield cried, "Are all you gentlemen ready?" He held a pistol in the air. It would have taken more pull than a steam engine or a couple of hairy elephants put out to keep His Honor away.

Hearing no objections, he fired the starting gun. Caesar's ears flapped at the report. *"Mall-mall!"* Prem Chand shouted. Behind him, he heard Paul Tilak give Hannibal the same command, and emphasize it with a whack of the elephant goad.

The hairy elephants surged forward as far as their harness would allow. Then, grunting with effort, they lowered their heads, dug in their big round feet, and pulled for all they were worth. Fifty tons of dead weight was a lot even for such powerful beasts to overcome.

From the other track, Prem Chand heard the clatter of coal being shoveled into the Iron Elephant's firebox. He did not look over. He knew his train would get rolling first, and intended to wring every inch out of his advantage. *"Mall-mall!"* he shouted again.

The spectators started to slide out of his field of vision. "We're moving!" he and Tilak shouted in the same breath. *"Mall-mall!"* In his urgency, Prem Chand used the *ankus* on Caesar. The elephant shook his head reproachfully.

Each step Caesar and Hannibal took came more easily than the one before. Horses paralleled the track, as riders came along to watch the race. Prem Chand looked back over his shoulder. The Iron Elephant still had not moved.

"We may do this yet!" he called to Paul Tilak. He hoped so. He had bet as many big silver denaires as he could afford—and perhaps a few more—on the great animal straining beneath him.

"We shall see," was all Tilak said. As far as Prem Chand knew, he had not made any bets for the elephants. He had not made any against them, either. Had he done so, Prem Chand would have kicked him off Hannibal even if it meant putting an unschooled oxherd aboard the beast. He had already fired one brakeman—he wanted no one with him who had a stake in losing.

Buildings hid the Iron Elephant as Caesar and Hannibal pulled their train round a curve. They had made a good quarter of a mile and were approaching the outskirts of town when Tilak said, "The machine is coming after us."

Prem Chand looked back again. Sure enough, a plume of steam and smoke was rising above the train station. The elephant driver grunted, sounding very much like Caesar. "Whatever Trevithick does, we are still faster, so long as we are moving. What worries me is that he will go all night."

"Do you want us to try that?" Tilak asked.

"No," Prem Chand said regretfully; he had thought long and hard about it. "If we do, Caesar and Hannibal will be worth nothing tomorrow. Even as is, I am not sure they will be able to match today's pace. And I am so afraid they will have to. If Trevithick's engine works as he hopes, we will have to catch him from behind."

Soon they were out among farms once more. Cows and sheep stared incuriously as the hairy elephants tramped past. Rifle-toting farmers guarded their stock. Even so close to Springfield, sims were a constant nuisance. They might not have the brains of humans, but they were too clever to trap.

Prem Chand decided he was going to get a stiff neck if he kept turning around to look back, but he could not help it. He had to see the Iron Elephant in action. Here it came, with its train behind it. He put a spyglass to his eye for a better view.

He thought it even uglier moving than stationary. Shafts connected to its pistons drove small gears at either side of the back of the engine. Those, in turn, meshed with larger gears in front of them, and the larger gears joined with the ones on the outside of the engine's four wheels. Smoke belched from the stack as the contraption crawled along. Even from close to half a mile away, Prem Chand could hear it chug and wheeze and rattle. It reminded him more of a flatulent iron cockroach than an elephant.

When he said that out loud, Tilak chuckled, remarking, "The farm animals would agree with you, it seems."

Prem Chand had been too busy studying the Iron Elephant to pay attention to them. A quick glance showed his fellow driver to be right. The livestock had reacted to their own train as they would have toward a couple of mules hauling a waggon past, which is to say they did not react at all.

The noisy, smoky, stinking steam engine was something else again. Animals' ears went up in surprise, then back in alarm. Terrified flocks pounded across the fields, farmers trying without much luck to halt them and now and then pausing to shake their fists at the Iron Elephant.

"I never thought of that," Prem Chand exclaimed. "How can these machines ever accomplish anything, if sheep and cattle and horses will not go near them?"

"Trevithick has come this far," Paul Tilak pointed out, which made Prem Chand give him a dirty look.

The sun climbed the sky. One by one, the townsfolk who had ridden out to watch the race began turning back for Springfield. It was not the sort of event to be easily watched. Neither contestant moved very fast, and they were drawing steadily farther apart. The only drama lay in who would finish first, but the answer to that was still more than a day away.

This time Tilak was the one who looked back. What he saw raised even his unsanguine spirits. "They have broken down!" he shouted.

Prem Chand slapped the spyglass to his eye. Sure enough, the Iron Elephant was barely limping along. Less smoke poured from the stack, and what there was had changed color.

The brakemen raised a cheer. "Come on, Caesar!" "Go, Hannibal, go!" "Run that hunk of tin back to the blacksmith's shop where it belongs!"

But Prem Chand kept watching. As he had been certain, Richard Trevithick was not a man to yield tamely to misfortune. The engine handler worked furiously on his machine. Once he leaped away; Prem Chand saw one of his henchmen rush up to help him bandage his hand. Together they plunged back to their repairs. After a while, the Iron Elephant picked up speed again.

All the same, Caesar and Hannibal gained on the steam engine with every step they took. They were pulling magnificently now, their heads down, their double-curved tusks—bigger by far than those of the Indian elephants Prem Chand's grandfather had fondly remembered—almost dragging the ground.

A small stream ran not far from the tracks. "They should water themselves," Tilak said.

Prem Chand hated to stop for any reason, but knew his friend was right. He raised a signal flag to warn the brakemen to stop, called, "*Choro!*" to Caesar. Tilak echoed him. The brakes squealed as they halted. The two elephant drivers unharnessed their beasts and rode them over to the creek. "I'd like to see Trevithick do *this* when his boiler runs dry," Prem Chand said. Tilak nodded.

Caesar and Hannibal lowered their trunks into the water. They squirted it down their throats, a good gallon and a half at a squirt. Tilak had been right—they were thirsty. They drank close to thirty gallons each before they slowed down.

Their exertion had also made them hot. "*Derr-tol!*" Prem Chand called: "Squirt water on your back." Caesar did. Prem Chand scrambled forward onto the hairy elephant's head to keep from getting soaked.

As the elephant drivers led their charges back to the train, Caesar and Hannibal used their trunks to uproot a couple of bushes and stuff them into their mouths. They had eaten well before the race started and would be fed again come evening, but they were not the sort of animals to miss any chance for a snack.

"*Mall-mall!*" Prem Chand shouted, and the train headed west once more.

Behind them, the smoke that marked the Iron Elephant sank lower and lower in the east. Finally Prem Chand had to use the spyglass to see it. It never quite disappeared, though, any more than an aching tooth that has stopped hurting for the moment ceases to give little reminders of its presence.

The farms that ran west along the railway from Spring-field began to peter out. Not many ran east from Carthage; the tracks had reached it only a few years before. Between the two towns was a broad stretch where the four bands of iron ran through still-virgin prairie.

A herd of big-horned buffalo grazed north of the tracks. It was not one of the huge aggregations of spring or fall, when migrating throngs made the ground shake and could delay a train for hours or days as they crossed the rail line. Prem Chand knew some of his brakemen were swearing because the buffalo were out of rifle range. He did not care himself; he did not eat beef.

A pronghorn pranced daintily by, a good deal closer than the buffalo. A gun barked. Caesar jerked beneath Prem Chand; he heard Paul Tilak cursing and pounding Hanni-bal back under control.

When Prem Chand could spare a moment, he saw the pronghorn lying in the grass, kicking. He raised an eye-brow, impressed at the shooting. The little antelope was at least as far away as the sim a whole volley had missed on the way to Springfield.

Several men swung down from the waggons to pick up the pronghorn. All but one—presumably the fellow who had killed it—had rifles at the ready. The waist-high plains grass could hide almost anything: sims, wolves, a spear-fanged cat.

The brakemen had to run hard to catch up to the train with their booty. None of them called to Prem Chand to slow down. They knew what the odds were for that.

The elephant driver had his cap pulled low to shield his eyes from the westering sun when the train went by another creek. "What do you say we stop here?" Tilak called. "Hannibal is tired."

Prem Chand did not want to stop for anything, but he could feel that Caesar was not pulling as powerfully as he had earlier in the day. The hairy elephants were so large and strong that it was hard to think they could wear out, but they did. Elephant drivers forgot it at their peril, and their beasts'.

"We will stop," Prem Chand sighed.

They made a big fire to keep off purely animal predators, and set guards in case any sim hunting-band nearby was without flint and steel. Trappers and hunters who traded with the subhumans for pelts always got more for fire-making tools than anything else: before humans came to the New World, sims kept fires going if they found them but did not know how to kindle flames themselves. Now, most of them could.

It was not the sort of thing to take for granted, though.

Roasting pronghorn made Prem Chand's nostrils twitch and his belly rumble. Before he thought about food for himself, he saw to Caesar. The hairy elephant drank nearly as much as it had earlier in the day. Prem Chand lugged out bales of hay and set them in front of Caesar. As he watched, a couple of hundredweight vanished down the beast's throat. He gave Caesar a cabbage for a treat. A single crunch and it was gone.

Not far away, Paul Tilak was similarly tending Hanni-bal. He glanced over to Prem Chand. "We are lightening our train somewhat, also," he said.

"Well, so we are," Prem Chand admitted, "but not as much as Trevithick." He wondered how far behind the Iron Elephant was; as the eastern sky darkened, the smoke plume became indistinguishable against it.

The pronghorn proved gamy and tough, but it was more appetizing than the salt pork Prem Chand had brought from Springfield. He washed it down with beer. The crew emptied more than one barrel. In that way too, Prem Chand thought wryly, the train was getting lighter.

He spread his bedroll under him. The night was too fine and fair to need more in the way of covers than a mosquito net. He fell asleep in seconds, as he usually did after a day aboard Caesar. The next thing he expected to see was dawn streaking the eastern sky with pink and gold.

When he woke and found darkness all around him, his first fuzzy thought was of marauding beasts or sims. His hand slid automatically toward the rifle beside him as he sat up.

He was not the only one awake; the whole camp was stirring. In the red light of the fire's embers men looked this way and that, wondering like Prem Chand where the trouble lay. The elephant driver scratched his head. He saw nothing amiss, heard no cries or gunshots to show someone beset.

All the same, his ears had wakened him. The chugging rumble from out of the east grew louder as he listened. It sounded different against night's stillness from the way it had in Springfield, but he did not take long to figure out what it was.

"That damned steam engine," someone muttered, putting his thoughts into words.

Soon he could see it as well as hear it. The smoke shooting up from its stack was laced with glowing sparks. "By day in a pillar of cloud, and by night in a pillar of fire," a brakeman quoted.

Caesar and Hannibal trumpeted as the Iron Elephant drew level with them, but it made more noise than both of them together. Through the hiss and clatter, Prem Chand heard Trevithick call, "See you in Carthage, sleepyheads!" His crew whooped as they passed their competitors.

They got back curses aplenty. "We will see who sees whom!" Prem Chand shouted. By then the Iron Elephant had gone a good deal farther down the track; Prem Chand heard that Trevithick replied, but could not make out his words.

Paul Tilak asked the most important question in the world just then: "What time is it?"

Prem Chand squinted to read his watch by fading firelight. "Half past two."

"Two and a half hours to sunrise," Tilak mused. "They will have a lead of seven miles or so if we wait."

Everyone looked at Prem Chand. He could see people

making the same mental calculations he was. "We stay," he said at last. "We can catch them before noon, a few miles outside Carthage. And if we race them now we risk running the elephants into the ground. They worked hard yesterday, and they need as much rest as they can get."

The brakemen accepted his decision without argument, as he would have taken their word over anything concerning the waggons. Tilak, though, took him aside and said quietly, "I hope we *can* catch them. Hannibal was flagging badly there at the end yesterday."

"Caesar too." Prem Chand hated to make the admission, as if saying it out loud somehow made it more real. He was, however, far from giving up hope. "The steam engine has its problems too—I thought it would. If it were running as well as Trevithick claimed it could, it would have been here hours ago."

"And if it had, we could have waved goodbye to the race."

"That is true. But it passed us now, not then. We, at least, know how far we can hope to go on any given day. What will that smelly piece of ironwork do to schedules?"

"It has certainly played the very devil with mine." Tilak yawned. "I am going back to bed."

"There, for once, my friend, I cannot argue with you," Prem Chand said. His only consolation was reflecting that Trevithick probably needed sleep even more than he did.

After eating enormously at sunrise, Caesar and Hannibal seemed eager to pull. The train rattled forward at a pace better than Prem Chand had expected. The Iron Elephant's plume of smoke, which had shrunk behind them the day before, now grew larger and blacker and stood taller in the sky as they gained. Only a couple of hours passed until the steam engine's train became visible, a long, black centipede stretched out along its track.

"Go ahead and run, Richard," Prem Chand called, though Trevithick, of course, could not hear. "You cannot run fast enough."

The engine handler must have seen his rival's train and disliked the rate at which it was gaining. He must have tied down a safety valve, for more smoke poured from the Iron Elephant's stack. All the same, the flesh-and-blood beasts continued to gain.

Closer and closer they came. Now they were only a mile behind, now half a mile. And there, heartbreakingly, they stuck. Caesar's and Hannibal's morning burst of energy faded. However much Prem Chand and Paul Tilak urged them on, they could come no closer. And as the elephant drivers watched and cursed, the Iron Elephant began to pull away once more.

Prem Chand felt like weeping from frustration. Through his spyglass, the men aboard the Iron Elephant seemed close enough to reach out and touch. Yet as he watched helplessly, they drew ever farther from him. He refused to lower the spyglass, cherishing the illusion it gave of a neck-and-neck race. And so he was watching still when the Iron Elephant slid into a pit.

Prem Chand stared, not believing what he saw. He knew how hastily this stretch of the railbed had been laid; it had only gravel underneath it, not a good solid foundation of stone and rammed earth. All the same, he had crossed the same stretch of track only a few days before, and there had been no storms since to undermine it.

But something had. Paul Tilak saw what it was. "Sims!" he shouted. Suddenly and most uncharacteristically, he burst out laughing. "Their trap caught a harder-skinned elephant than they bargained for!"

Once Prem Chand's attention was diverted from the train ahead, he too saw the subhumans rushing to the attack. Some carried wooden spears, their points fire-hardened. Others bore clubs, still others held stones chipped sharp that they could throw a long way. He spied the glint of a few axeheads and steel knives, perhaps stolen, perhaps gotten in trade.

Tilak was right: the sims would not gorge on hairy elephant, as they hoped. But they were not fussy about what they ate—brakeman would do well enough. And with everyone thrown in a heap by the Iron Elephant's sudden and unexpected stop, only a couple of men were able to shoot at the charging hunters. After that it was a melee, and the sims were stronger, fiercer, sometimes even better armed than their foes.

Prem Chand threw up the red flag to warn his crew, then yelled "*Choro!*" as loud as he could. The train stopped. "Get Hannibal out of his harness!" he told Paul Tilak. Prem Chand was already unbuckling the thick leather straps that linked Caesar to Hannibal. He stood up on his elephant's back, called to the train crew, "Grab your rifles and climb onto the two beasts. It is a rescue now!"

The brakemen scrambled down from their waggons and rushed forward. Hairy elephants were better haulers than carriers; Caesar and Hannibal could bear only five men apiece. As he had at the Springfield station, Prem Chand made Caesar lift a foreleg to serve as a step. "You, you, you, and you," he said, pointing at the first four men to reach him. They swarmed onto the elephant.

Just behind them, Tilak was making a similar chant. Hannibal trumpeted at taking on unfamiliar passengers, but subsided when Tilak thwacked its broad head with the elephant goad.

"Follow us as closely as you can," Prem Chand told the disappointed latecomers from the back of the train. Then he dug in his toe behind Caesar's ear. "*Mall-mall!*" he shouted: forward!

Even with the burden it was carrying, the hairy elephant shot ahead, as if relieved to be free of the burden of the train. Its gait shifted from its usual walk to a pounding rack, with hind- and foreleg on the same side of its body advancing together.

Most of the brakemen had ridden elephants before, but not under circumstances like these. They clutched at Caesar's harness to keep from being pitched off. In spite of everything, one did fall. He rolled away, clutching his ankle. The hairy elephant's left hind foot missed his head by inches.

They were a bit more than half a mile from the Iron Elephant, three or four minutes at the elephants' best pace, which they were certainly making. When they had covered about half the distance, Prem Chand told one brakeman, "You shoot."

"No chance to hit at this range," the fellow protested.

"Yes, but we will remind the sims we are coming, and you will be able to reload by the time we get there."

"Never tried reloading on top of an elephant before," the brakeman said darkly, but he raised the rifle to his shoulder and fired. Caesar trumpeted in surprise. So did Hannibal, a moment later.

Some of the subhumans had already started to break and run—two carried a man's corpse between them, while another fled with a body slung over its shoulder. But others were still fighting, and one stubbornly kept trying to shove a spear into the metal side of the trapped steam engine. Prem Chand had to stop himself from giggling: Paul Tilak had certainly been right about that.

Against men, even men carrying firearms, the sims might have kept up the battle, at least for a little while. But the hairy elephants were the most fearsome beasts on the plains. The sight of two bearing down like an angry avalanche was too much for the subhumans. They took to their heels, hooting in dismay.

The last to run off was the one that had tried to slay the Iron Elephant. Baring its teeth in a furious grimace, it hurled a sharp stone at Caesar before seeking to get away. The rock fell far short, but by then the sim was within easy rifle range. Prem Chand's bullet sent it sprawling forward on its face.

He felt more like a general than like an elephant driver. With gestures and shouted commands, he sent Hannibal and the men he thought of as his foot soldiers after the retreating sims. He walked Caesar up to the head of the rival train.

The brakeman to the contrary, reloading on elephant-back was possible—but then, Prem Chand had more practice at it than the other man did. He fired at a sim. To his disgust, he missed. Many sims were down now, either dead or under cover in hollows the tall grass concealed.

The railroad men moved up cautiously. A couple went ahead to reclaim a body the sims had dropped in their flight. Prem Chand was dismayed to see no sign of the corpse the pair of sims had been carrying; the subhumans who survived this raid, curse them, would not go altogether hungry.

The elephant driver wondered if the body was Trevithick's. He had yet to spot the steam-engine man, and he was close to the upended Iron Elephant. After digging their pit under the rails, the sims had covered it with branches and then covered them over with dirt and gravel so they looked like the rest of the roadbed. Prem Chand shivered. He might well have led Caesar straight into the trap.

He got down from the hairy elephant, walked over to the hole in the ground. The rails had buckled as they tried and failed to support the Iron Elephant. It was tilted at a steep angle, almost nose down in the pit. A real elephant, which did not carry its weight on the rails, would have taken a worse fall.

A dead sim lay half in, half out of the pit. Prem Chand looked down into it. "Hello, Prem, very good to see you indeed," Richard Trevithick said. He held a pistol club-fashion in his bandaged left hand; his right arm hung limply. "I'm afraid you'll have to help me out of here. I think I broke it. Oh, and congratulations—you seem to have won the race."

"I had not even thought of that," Prem Chand said, blinking. He turned to his crew. "Get me a length of rope. Tie one end to Caesar's harness and toss the other down to me." He slid into the pit.

In India, he thought, hazily remembering his grandfather's stories, there would have been sharpened stakes sticking up from the bottom. Luckily, the sims had not thought of that.

He got to his feet, brushed off himself and Trevithick. "You shot the sim up there?"

The engine handler nodded. "Yes, and then spent the rest of the fight hiding under the Iron Elephant, while another of the creatures tried to kill it." He laughed ruefully. "Not very glorious, I'm afraid. But then, neither was falling out of the cab when the engine went down. If I hadn't been leaning back for another shovelful of coal, I never would have got this." He tried to move his arm, winced, and thought better of it.

"But you would have been out in the open, then, and the second sim might have speared you instead of your machine," Prem Chand pointed out.

"Something to that, I suppose."

A rope snaked into the hole. Prem Chand tied it around Trevithick's body under his arms. "Is it hooked up to Caesar?" he called.

"Sure is," a brakeman answered.

"Good. *Mall-mall!*"

The rope went taut. Prem Chand helped Trevithick scramble up the sloping side of the pit while the elephant pulled him out. The engine handler yelped once, then set his teeth and bore the jouncing in grim silence. Prem Chand yelled "*Choro!*" as soon as Trevithick was out, then crawled slowly after him.

"You didn't need to get us clean the first time," Trevithick remarked.

"You are quite right. My apologies. I will dirty you again, if you like," Prem Chand said, deadpan.

Trevithick's expression was half grin, half grimace. Then he looked around, and dismay replaced them both. Down in the pit, he had not been able to see the fight that had raged up and down the length of his train. Most of the bodies spilled on the ground, most of the blood splashed on waggons and grass, belonged to sims—but not all.

"Oh, the poor lads," the engine handler exclaimed.

Some of the survivors of his crew had joined Prem Chand's men in pursuit of the sims, which made his losses appear at first even worse than they were. But Trevithick, pointing with his left hand, counted four bodies, and one of his brakemen added, "Pat Bailey and One-eye Jim is dead, but we can't find 'em nowheres."

"Filthy creatures," Trevithick muttered.

Prem Chand knew he was not talking about the missing men. Trying to give what consolation he could, he said, "This sort of thing will not happen hereabouts much longer. Soon this part of the country will be too thickly settled for wild sim bands big enough to attack a train to flourish."

"Yes, of course. That's been happening for more than 150 years, since settlers came to Virginia and Plymouth. It does little good for me at the moment, however—and even less for One-eye Jim and Patrick Bailey."

Prem Chand had no good answer to that. He led Trevithick over to Paul Tilak, who knew enough first aid to splint a broken arm. Ignoring an injured man's howls, Tilak was washing a bleeding bite with whiskey. "Don't be a fool," he told the fellow. "Do you want it to fester?"

"Couldn't hurt more'n what you just done," the man said sullenly.

"That only shows how little you know," Tilak snorted. He moved on to a brakeman with a torn shirt and blood running down his chest. "You are very lucky. That spear could as easily have gone in as slid along your ribs." He soaked his rag at the mouth of the whiskey bottle. The brakeman flinched.

"There's one attention I won't regret being spared," Trevithick said, waiting for Tilak to get round to him.

"I do not doubt that." Prem Chand's eyes slipped back to the Iron Elephant. "Richard, may I ask what you will do next?"

The engine handler followed his rival's glance. "I expect we'll be able to salvage it, Prem, with the help of your elephants. The damage shouldn't be anything past repair." His face lit with enthusiasm. "And back in Boston, my brother is working on another engine, twice as powerful as the Iron Elephant. If I'd had that one here, you never could have stayed close to me!"

"In which case, you and your crew probably would all be dead now," Prem Chand said tartly.

But in spite of his sharp comeback, he felt a hollowness inside, for he saw that the future belonged to Trevithick. As surely as humans displaced sims, steam engines were going to replace hairy elephants: it was much easier to make an engine bigger and stronger and faster than it was an elephant. A way of life was ending.

He let out a long sigh.

Trevithick understood him perfectly. "I told you once, Prem, it won't be so bad. There will always be railroads, no matter what pulls the trains."

"It will not be the same."

"What is, ever?"

"He has you there, Prem," Tilak put in.

"Maybe so, maybe so," Prem Chand said. "Our grandfathers, who sailed halfway round the world to come here, would have agreed with you, I am certain. But do you know what hurts worst of all?"

Trevithick and Tilak shook their heads.

"When that second engine comes into Springfield, I am going to have to admit George Stephenson is right!"

1804

Though the Heavens Fall

Large-scale agricultural production was very important in several southeastern commonwealths. Indigo, hemp, and cotton—especially the latter, with its vast export market—were grown on plantations that, because they naturally did not have modern farm machinery, required a great many laborers to raise and gather in the crops.

Most of these field laborers were sims. The number of sims in North America had increased greatly since Europeans began settling in the New World, simply because agriculture is so much more efficient a way of producing food than the nomadic hunting life the native subhumans had formerly practiced. There was enough to feed both the swelling human population and the sims—which, now sometimes for many generations, had been tamed to serve humans.

Large labor forces of sims were not the only characteristic of eighteenth- and early nineteenth-century southeastern plantation agriculture. Because sims proved unsatisfactory household staff (and also, on

occasion, to supplement their number in the fields),
black human slaves were imported from Africa.

Shamefully, slavery is a human institution at least as
old as civilization itself. It was accepted in ancient
Mesopotamian society; by the Hebrews; by the
Greeks; and even by the Romans, whose republic is
the prototype for the Federated Commonwealths.
Philosophers developed elaborate justifications for the
institution, most based on the assumption that one
group of people—generally speaking, the group that
owned the slaves in question—was superior to another
and that the latter, therefore, deserved their
enslavement.

Such speculation may perhaps have been excusa-
ble in the days when humans knew only of other
humans. Differences in skin color, features, or type of
hair must have seemed large and important in those
days. But when contrasted to sims, it quickly becomes
obvious that even the most dissimilar groups of humans are very much alike. Accordingly, in the Federated Commonwealths the institution of slavery was
faced with a challenge to its very *raison d'être* unlike
any it had known in the Old World. . . .

From *The Story of the Federated Commonwealths*

JEREMIAH SWEPT THE feather duster over the polished top
of his master's chest of drawers. Moving slowly in the
building heat of a May morning in Virginia, he raised the
duster to the mirror that hung above the chest.

He paused to look at himself; he did not get to see his
reflection every day. He raised a hand to brush away some
dust stuck in his wooly hair. His eyeballs and, when he
smiled, his white, even teeth gleamed against the polished
ebony of his skin.

"You, Jeremiah!" Mrs. Gillen called from the next room.
"What are you doing in there?"

"Dusting, ma'am," he answered, flailing about with the

feather duster so she would see him busy if she came in to check. Unlike the sims that worked in the fields, house-slaves rarely felt the whip, but he did not intend to tempt fate.

All Mrs. Gillen said, though, was, "Go downstairs and fetch me up a glass of lemonade. Squeeze some fresh; I think the pitcher's empty."

"Yes, ma'am." Jeremiah sighed as he went to the kitchen. On a larger estate, other blacks would have shared the household duties. Here he was cook, cleaner, butler, and coachman by turns, and busy all the time because there was so much to do.

He made a fresh pitcher of lemonade to his own taste, drank a glass, then added more sugar. The Gillens liked it sweeter than he did.

"Took you long enough," Jane Gillen snapped when he got upstairs. He took no notice of it; that was simply her way. She was in her early thirties, a few years older than Jeremiah, her mousy prettiness beginning to yield to time.

"Oh, that does a body good," she said, emptying the glass and giving it back to him. "Why don't you take the rest of the pitcher out to my husband? He and Mr. Stowe are in the south field, and they'll be suffering from the sun. Go on; they'll thank you for it."

"Yes, ma'am," he said again, this time with something like enthusiasm. He returned to the kitchen, put the pitcher and two glasses on a tray, and went out to look for his master and the overseer.

A big male sim was chopping logs into firewood behind the house. It stopped for a moment to nod to Jeremiah as he went by.

He nodded back. "Hello, Joe," he said, a faint edge of contempt riding his words. He might be a slave, but by God he was a man!

Joe did not notice Jeremiah's condescension. Muscles bulged under the thick coat of hair on the sim's arms as it swung the axe up for another stroke. The axe descended.

Chips flew. One flew right over Joe's head, landed in the dust behind the sim.

Jeremiah chuckled as he walked on. Had he been wielding the axe, the chip would have caught him right in the forehead and probably made him bleed. But sims had no foreheads. Above Joe's deep-set eyes was only a beetling ridge of bone that retreated smoothly toward the back of his head.

More sims worked in the fields, some sowing hemp seeds broadcast on the land devoted to the farm's main cash crop, others weeding among the growing green stalks of wheat. They would have done a better job with lighter hoes, but the native American subhumans lacked the sense to take proper care of tools of good quality.

Mostly the sims worked in silence. Now and then one would let its long, chinless jaw fall open to emit a grunt of effort, and once Jeremiah heard a screech as a sim hit its own foot instead of a weed. But unlike humans, the sims did not talk among themselves. Few ever mastered English, and their own grunts and hoots were too restricted to make up a real language.

Instead, they used hand signs like the ones the deaf and dumb employed; those came easier to them than speech. Jeremiah had heard Mr. Gillen say even the wild sims that still lurked in the forests and mountains two centuries after colonists came to Virginia used hand signs taught them by runaways in preference to their native calls.

Charles Gillen and Harry Stowe were standing together, watching the sims work. Gillen turned and saw Jeremiah. "Well, well, what have we here?" he said, smiling. He was a large man, about the same age as his wife, with perpetually ruddy features and a strong body beginning to go to fat.

"Lemonade, sir, for you and Mr. Stowe." Jeremiah poured for each man, handed them their glasses.

Gillen drained his without taking it from his lips; his face turned even redder than usual. "Ahh!" he said, wiping his mouth. "Now that was a kindly thought, and surely it's no part of your regular duties to go traipsing all over the farm looking for me." He rummaged through the pockets of his blue cotton breeches. "Here's a ten-sester for your trouble."

"I thank you very much, sir." Jeremiah's trousers did not have pockets. He stowed the small silver coin in a leather pouch he wore on a thong round his neck under his shirt. The hope for just such a reward was one of the things that had made him eager to go to his master. Besides, it beat working.

He did not mention that the lemonade had been Mrs. Gillen's idea. Even if her husband found out, though, he would not take the ten-sester back; he was a fair-minded man.

Harry Stowe kept his glass in his left hand as he drank. His right hand held his whip, as it always did when he was in the field. The whip was a yard-long strip of untanned cowhide, an inch thick at the grip and tapering to a point.

Stowe was a small, compact man with fine features and cold blue eyes that never stopped moving. He snarled an oath and stepped forward. The whip cracked. A sim shouted in alarm, clutched at its right arm.

"Oh, nonsense, Tom," Stowe snapped. "I didn't hurt you, and well you know it. But damn you, have more care with what you do. That was wheat you were rooting out there, not a weed."

The sim understood English well enough, even if it could not speak. Its hands moved. *Sorry,* it signed. Its broad, flat features were unreadable. When it went back to weeding, though, it soon uprooted another stalk of wheat.

Stowe's hand tightened on the butt of the whip until his knuckles whitened. But he did not lash out. His shoulders sagged. "In a man, that would be insolence," he said to Charles Gillen. "But sims cannot, will not attend as a man would. I could wear out my arm, my cowskin, and my temper, sir, and not improve them much."

"Your being here at all keeps them working, Harry. We shouldn't expect them to be fine farmers," Gillen replied.

"When men first came to Virginia, they found the sims here unable to make fire, with no tools but chipped stones."

"You are an educated man, to know such things," the overseer said. "For myself, all I know is that they do not work as I would wish, and so waste your substance. I wish you could afford to have niggers in the fields. I would make fine farmers of *them*, I wager." He looked speculatively toward Jeremiah.

The house-slave wished he could become invisible; suddenly he was not glad at all he had come out to the fields. He stretched out his hands to his master. "Mr. Gillen, you wouldn't treat me like no sim, would you, sir?" The wobble of fear in his voice was real.

"No, no, Jeremiah, don't fret yourself," Gillen reassured him, sending a look-at-the-trouble-you-caused glance Stowe's way. "I find it hard to imagine a circumstance that would force me to use you so."

"Thank you, sir, thank you." Jeremiah knew he was laying it on thick, but he took no chances. Not only was labor in the fields exhausting, but he could imagine nothing more degrading. Even as a slave, he had a measure of self-respect. One day he hoped to be able to buy his liberation. The ten-sester his master had given him put his private hoard at over eighty denaires. Maybe he would buy land, end up owning a few sims himself. It was something to dream about, anyway. But if Gillen worked him as he would a sim, would he not think of him in the same way, instead of as a person? He might never get free then!

Why, his master had already turned his back on him and was talking politics with Stowe as if he were not there. "So whom will you vote for in the censoral elections this fall, Harry?"

"I favor Adams and Westerbrook: two men from the same party will work together, instead of us having to suffer through another five years of divided government like this last term."

"I don't know," Gillen said judiciously. "When the Conscript Fathers wrote the Articles of Independence after we broke from England in '38, they gave us two censors to keep the power of the executive from growing too strong, as it had in the person of the king. To me that says they intended the two men to be of opposing view, to check each other's excesses.''

"To check excesses, aye. But I'm partial to a government that governs, not one that spends all its time arguing with itself.''

Gillen chuckled. "Something to that, I suppose. Still, don't you think—"

Jeremiah stopped listening. What did politics matter to him? As a slave, he could no more vote than a sim could. His head hung as he made his slow way back to the house.

Mrs. Gillen saw him dawdling, and scolded him. She kept an eye on him the rest of the day, which meant he had to work at the pace she set, not his own. That, he thought resentfully, was more trouble than a ten-sester was worth. To make things worse, he burnt the ham the Gillens, Stowe, and he were going to have for supper. That earned him another scolding from his mistress and a contemptuous stare from the overseer.

At sunset, Stowe blew a long, unmusical blast on a bugle, the signal for the sims to come in from the fields for their evening meal. Their food was unexciting but filling: mostly barley bread and salt pork, eked out once or twice a week, as tonight, with vegetables from the garden plot and with molasses. The sims also ate whatever small live things they could catch. Some owners discouraged that as a disgusting habit (Jeremiah certainly thought it was; stepping on a well-gnawed rat tail could be counted on to make his stomach turn over). Most, like Charles Gillen, did not mind, for it made their property cheaper to feed.

"Never catch me eating rats, not if I'm starving," Jeremiah said as he blew out the candle in his small stuffy room. He listened to make sure the Gillens were asleep. (Stowe had his own cottage, close by the log huts where the sims lived.)

When he was sure all was quiet, the slave lifted a loose

floorboard and drew out a small flask of whiskey. Any sim caught with spirits was lashed till the blood ran through the matted hair on its back. Jeremiah ran the same risk, and willingly. Sometimes he needed that soothing fire in his belly to sleep.

Tonight, though, he drank the flask dry, and tossed and turned for hours all the same.

Spring gave way to summer. The big sim Joe stepped on a thorn, and died three weeks later of lockjaw. The loss cast a pall of gloom over Charles Gillen, for Joe was worth a hundred denaires.

Gillen's spirits lifted only when his son and daughter returned to the farm from the boarding schools they attended in Portsmouth, the commonwealth capital. Jeremiah was also glad to see them. Caleb was fourteen and Sally eleven; the slave sometimes felt he was almost as much a father to them as Charles Gillen himself.

But Caleb, at least, came home changed this year. Before, he had always talked of what he would do when the Gillen farm was his. Jeremiah had spoken of buying his own freedom once, a couple of years before; Caleb had looked so hurt at the idea of his leaving that he never brought it up again, for fear of turning the boy against it for good. He thought Caleb had long since forgotten.

One day, though, Caleb came up to him when the two of them were alone in the house. He spoke with the painful seriousness adolescence brings: "I owe you an apology, Jeremiah."

"How's that, young master?" the slave asked in surprise. "You haven't done nothing to me." And even if you had, he added silently, you would not be required to apologize for it.

"Oh, but I have," Caleb said, "though I've taken too long to see it. Do you remember when you told me once you would like to be free and go away?"

"Yes, young sir, I do remember that," Jeremiah said cautiously. Any time the issue of liberation came up, a slave walked the most perilous ground there was.

"I was too little to understand then," the boy said. "Now I think I may, because I want to go away too."

"You do? Why could that be?" Jeremiah was not pretending. This declaration of Caleb's was almost as startling as his recalling their conversation at all. To someone that young, two years was like an age.

"Because I want to read the law and set up my own shingle one day. The law is the most important thing in the whole world, Jeremiah." His voice burned with conviction; at fourteen, one is passionately certain about everything.

"I don't know about that, young master. Nobody can eat law."

Caleb looked at him in exasperation. "Nobody could eat food either, or even grow it, if his neighbor could take it whenever he had a mind to. What keeps him from it, even if he has guns and men and sims enough to do it by force? Only the law."

"Something to that," Jeremiah admitted. He agreed only partly from policy; Caleb's idea had not occurred to him. He thought of the law only as something to keep from descending on him. That it might be a positive good was a new notion—one easier to arrive at for a free man, he thought without much bitterness.

Enthusiasm carried Caleb along. "Of course there's something to it! People who make the law and apply the law rule the country. I don't mean just the censors or the Senate or the Popular Assembly—though one day I'll serve, I think—but judges and lawyers too."

"That may be so, young master, but what will become of the farm when you've gone to Portsmouth to do your lawyering, or up to Philadelphia for the Assembly?" Jeremiah knew vaguely where Portsmouth was (somewhere southeast, a journey of a week or two); he knew Philadelphia was some long ways north, but had no idea how far. Half as far as the moon, maybe.

"One day Sally will get married," Caleb shrugged. "It will stay in the family. And lawyers get rich, don't forget. Who knows? Maybe one day I'll buy the Pickens place next door to retire on."

Jeremiah's opinion was that old man Pickens would have to be dragged kicking and screaming into his grave before he turned loose of his farm. He knew, however, when to keep his mouth shut. He also noticed that any talk about his freedom had vanished from the conversation.

Nevertheless, Caleb had not forgotten. One day he took Jeremiah aside and asked him, "Would you like me to teach you to read and cipher?"

The slave thought about it. He answered cautiously, "Your father, I don't know if he'd like that." Most masters discouraged literacy among their blacks (sims did not count; no sim had ever learned to read). In some commonwealths—though not Virginia—teaching a black his letters was against the law.

"I've already talked with him about it," Caleb said. "I asked him if he didn't think it would be useful to have you able to keep accounts and such. He hates that kind of business himself."

The lad already had a good deal of politician in him, Jeremiah thought. Caleb went on, "Once you learn, maybe you can hire yourself out to other farmers, and keep some of what you earn. That would help you buy yourself free sooner, and knowing how to read and figure can only help you afterwards."

"You're right about that, young sir. I'd be pleased to start, so long as your father won't give me no grief on account of it."

The hope of money first impelled Jeremiah to the lessons, but he quickly grew fascinated with them for their own sake. He found setting down his name in shaky letters awe-inspiring: there it was, recorded for all time. It gave him a feeling of immortality, almost as if he had had a child. And struggling through first Caleb's little reader and then, haltingly, the Bible was more of the same. He wished he could spend all his time over the books.

He could not, of course. Chores around the house kept him busy all through the day. Most of his reading time was snatched from sleep. He yawned and did not complain.

His stock of money slowly grew, five sesters here, ten there. Once he made a whole denaire for himself, when Mr. Pickens's cook fell sick just before a family gathering and Charles Gillen loaned Jeremiah to the neighbor for the day. From anyone else, he would have expected two or even three denaires; from Pickens he counted himself lucky to get one.

He did not save every sester he earned: a man needs more than the distant hope of freedom to stay happy. One night he made his way to a dilapidated cabin that housed a widow inclined to be complaisant toward silver, no matter who brought it.

Jeremiah was heading home, feeling pleased with the entire world (except for the mosquitoes), when the moonlight showed a figure coming down the path toward him. It was Harry Stowe. Jeremiah's pleasure evaporated. He was afraid of the overseer, and tried to stay out of his way. Too late to step aside into the bushes—Stowe had seen him.

"Evening, sir," Jeremiah said amiably as the overseer approached.

Stowe set hands on hips, looked Jeremiah up and down. "Evening, sir," he echoed, voice mockingly high. There was whiskey on his breath. "I'm tired of your uppity airs— always sucking up to young Caleb. What do you need to read for? You're a stinking slave, and don't you ever forget it."

"I could never do that, sir, no indeed. But all the same, a man wants to make himself better if he can."

He never saw the punch that knocked him down. Drunk or sober, Stowe was fast and dangerous. Jeremiah lay in the dirt. He did not try to fight back. Caleb's law descended swiftly and savagely on any slave who dared strike a white man. But fear of punishment was not what held him back now. He knew Stowe would have no trouble taking him, even in a fair fight.

"Man? I don't see any man there," the overseer said. "All I see's a nigger." He laughed harshly, swung back his foot. Instead of delivering the kick, though, he turned away and went on toward the widow's.

Jeremiah rubbed the bruise on the side of his jaw, felt around with his tongue to see if Stowe had loosened any of his teeth. No, he decided, but only by luck. He stayed down until the overseer disappeared round a bend in the path. Then he slowly rose, brushing the dust from his trousers.

"Not a man, huh?" he muttered to himself. "Not a man? Well, let that trash talk however he wants, but whose sloppy seconds is he getting tonight?" Feeling a little better, he headed back to the Gillen house.

Summer wore on. The wheat grew tall. The stalks bent, heavy with the weight of grain. Caleb and Sally returned to Portsmouth for school. The sims went into the fields to start cutting the hemp so it could dry on the ground.

The sickness struck them then, abruptly and savagely. Stowe came rushing in from their huts at sunrise one morning to cry to Charles Gillen, "Half the stupid creatures are down and choking and moaning!"

Gillen spilled coffee as he sprang to his feet with an oath. Fear on his face, he followed the overseer out. Jeremiah silently stepped out of the way. He understood his master's alarm. Disease among the sims, especially now when the harvest was just under way, would be a disaster from which the farm might never recover.

Jane Gillen waited anxiously for her husband to return. When he did, his mouth was set in a tight, grim line. "Diphtheria," he said. "We may lose a good many." He strode over to the cupboard, uncorked a bottle of rum, took a long pull. He was not normally an intemperate man, but what he had seen left him shaken.

As Jeremiah washed and dried the breakfast dishes, he felt a certain amount of relief, at least as far as his own risk was concerned. Sims were enough like humans for illnesses to pass freely from them to the people around them. But he had had diphtheria as a boy, and did not have to worry about catching it again.

A sadly shrunken work force trooped out to cut the

hemp. Charles Gillen set Jeremiah to boiling great kettles of soup, that being the easiest nourishment for the sick sims to get past the membranes clogging their throats. Then Gillen hurried back out to the sim quarters, to do what little doctoring he could.

The first deaths came that evening. One was Rafe, the powerful woodcutter who had replaced Joe. Not all his strength sufficed against the illness that choked the life from him. The tired sims returning from the fields had to labor further to dig graves.

"I always feel so futile, laying a sim to rest," Gillen told Jane as they ate a late supper that Jeremiah had made. "With a man, there's always the hope of heaven to give consolation. But no churchman I've ever heard of can say for certain whether sims have souls."

Jeremiah doubted it. He thought of sims as nothing more than animals that happened to walk on two legs and have hands. That made them more useful than, say, horses, but not much smarter. He rejected any resemblance between their status and his own; he at least knew he was a slave and planned to do something about it one day. His hoard had reached nearly ninety denaires.

The next day, even fewer of the sims could work. Charles Gillen rode over to the Pickens farm to see if he could borrow some, but the diphtheria was there ahead of him. Mr. Pickens was down with it too, and not doing well.

Gillen bit his lip at the small amount of hemp cut so far. Jeremiah had had just enough practice ciphering over the farm accounts to understand why: the cash Gillen raised from selling the hemp was what let him buy the goods his acres could not produce.

After supper that evening, Gillen took Jeremiah aside. "Don't bother with breakfast tomorrow, or with more soup for the sims," he said. "Jane will take care of all that for a while."

"Mrs. Gillen, sir?" Jeremiah stared at his master. He groped for the only explanation he could think of. "You don't care for what I've been making? You tell me what you want, and I'll see you get it."

A gentleman to the core, Gillen replied quickly, "No, no, Jeremiah, it's nothing like that, I assure you. You've done very well." Then he stopped cold, his cheeks reddening, plainly embarrassed to continue.

"You've gone and sold me." Jeremiah blurted out the first—and worst—fear that came to his mind. Every slave dreaded the announcement that would turn his life upside down. And Charles Gillen was on the whole an easygoing master; any number of tales Jeremiah had heard convinced him of that.

"I have not sold you, Jeremiah. Your place is here." Again Gillen's reply was swift and firm; again he had trouble going on.

"Well, what is it, then?" Jeremiah demanded. His master's hesitations set them in oddly reversed roles, the slave probing and seeking, Gillen trying to evade the way Jeremiah did when caught at something he knew was wrong. Having the moral high ground was a new and heady feeling.

He did not enjoy it long. Brought up short, Gillen had no choice but to answer, "I'm sending you out to the fields tomorrow, Jeremiah, to help cut hemp."

With sick misery, the slave realized he would rather have been sold. "But that's sim work, Mr. Gillen," he protested.

"I know it is, and I feel badly for it. But so many of the sims are down with the sickness, and you are strong and healthy. The hemp must be cut. It does not care what hand swings the sickle. And I will not think less of you for working in the fields—rather the contrary, because you will have helped me at a time of great need. When the day comes that you approach me to ask to buy your freedom, be sure I shall not forget."

Had he promised Jeremiah manumission as soon as the hemp-cutting was done, he would have gained a willing worker. As it was, though, the slave again protested, "Don't send me out to do sim work, sir."

"And why not?" Gillen's voice had acquired a dangerous edge.

"Because—" Jeremiah knew he was faltering and cursed himself for it, but could not do anything about it. Charles Gillen was a decent man, as decent as a slave owner could be, but he was also a white man. He knew himself the equal of his fellow farmers and townsmen; his son dreamed of being censor of the Federated Commonwealths one day. He was immeasurably far above both blacks and sims.

Jeremiah also felt the gulf between himself and his master, of course. Even gaining his freedom would not erase all of it—certainly not in Gillen's eyes. But Jeremiah also saw another gulf, one with him at the top looking down on the sims below.

From Charles Gillen's lofty perch, that one was invisible. But it was immensely important to Jeremiah. Even a slave could feel superior to the subhuman natives of America, could pride himself on things he could do that they would never be capable of. Learning his letters was something of that sort, a reminder that, even if his body was owned, his spirit could still roam free.

And now Gillen, without understanding at all what he was doing, was shoving him down with the sims, as if there were no difference between him and them. Harry Stowe would see no difference either, indeed would relish getting his hands on Jeremiah. He had made that quite clear.

That was bad enough, but the white men already looked down on Jeremiah. He had some status, though, among the blacks of the neighborhood. It would disappear the instant he went out to the fields. Even the stupid sims would laugh their gape-mouthed, empty-headed laughs at him, and think him no better than themselves. He would never be able to trust his authority over them again.

All that passed through his mind in a matter of seconds, along with the realization that none of it would make sense to Gillen, certainly not when measured against the denaires the farmer was losing every day. "It just wouldn't be right, sir," was the weak best Jeremiah could do.

He knew it was not good enough even before he saw Gillen's face cloud with anger. "How would it not be right? It pains me to have to remind you, Jeremiah, but you are my slave, my personal chattel. How I employ you, especially in this emergency, is my affair and mine alone. Now I tell you that you shall report to the field gang tomorrow at sunrise or your back will be striped and then you will report anyway. Do you follow me?"

"Yes, sir," Jeremiah said. He did not dare look at Gillen, for fear his expression would earn him the whipping on the spot.

"Well, good." Having got his way, Gillen was prepared to be magnanimous. He patted Jeremiah on the shoulder. "It will be only for a few days, a couple of weeks at most. Then everything will be back the way it was."

"Yes, sir," Jeremiah said again, but he knew better. Nothing would ever be the same, not between him and other blacks, not between him and the sims, and not between him and Gillen either. One reason Gillen was a bearable master was that he treated Jeremiah like a person. Now the thin veil of politeness was ripped aside. At need, Gillen could use Jeremiah like any other beast of burden, and at need he would. It was as simple as that.

When Jeremiah lifted the loose board in his room, he found his little flask of spirits was empty. "I might have known," he muttered under his breath. "It's been that kind of day." He blew out his candle.

He was already awake when Stowe blasted away on the horn to summon the sims—and him—to labor. He had been awake most of the night; he was too full of mortification and swallowed rage to sleep. His stomach had tied itself into a tight, painful knot.

His eyes felt as though someone had thrown sand in them. He rubbed at them as he pulled on breeches, shoes, and shirt and went out to the waiting overseer.

Stowe was doling out hardtack and bacon to the sims still

well enough to work. "Well, well," he said, smiling broadly as Jeremiah came up. "What a pleasure to see our new field hand, and just in time for breakfast, too. Get in line and wait your turn."

The overseer watched for any sign of resistance, but Jeremiah silently took his place. The hardtack was a jawbreaker, and the bacon, heavily salted so it would keep almost forever, brought tears to his eyes. If his belly had churned before, it snarled now. He gulped down two dippers of water. They did not help.

The sims' big yellow teeth effortlessly disposed of the hardtack biscuits. The salt in the bacon did not faze them either. Jeremiah's presence seemed to bother them a good deal more. They kept staring at him, then quickly looking away whenever his eyes met theirs. The low-voiced calls and hoots they gave each other held a questioning note.

Those calls, though, could convey only emotion, not real meaning. For that, the sims had to use the hand signs men had given them. Their fingers flashed, most often in the gesture equivalent to a question mark. Finally, one worked up the nerve to approach Jeremiah and sign, *Why you here?*

"To work," he said shortly. He spoke instead of signing, to emphasize to the sim that, despite his present humiliation, he was still a man.

Harry Stowe, who missed very little, noted the exchange. Grinning, he sabotaged Jeremiah's effort to keep his place by signing, *He work with you, he work like you, he one of you till job done. No different.* "Isn't that right?" he added aloud, for Jeremiah's benefit.

The slave felt his face grow hot. He bit his lip, but did not reply.

Stowe's message disturbed even the sims. One directed hesitant signs at the overseer: *"He man, not sim. Why work like sim?"*

"He's a slave. He does what he's told, just like you'd better. If the master tells him to work like a sim, he works like a sim, and that's all there is to it. Enough dawdling, now—let's get on with it."

The overseer distributed scythes and sickles to his charges, carefully counting them so the sims could not hold any back to use against their owners—or against each other, in fights over food or females. Jeremiah wished he had a pair of gloves; his hands were too soft for the work he was about to do.

He knew better than to ask for any.

As he started down a row of hemp plants, he saw the sims to either side quickly move past him. It was not just that they were stronger, though few men could match the subhumans for strength. They were also more skilled, which was really galling. Bend, slash, stoop, spread, rise, step, bend . . . they had a rhythm the black man lacked.

"Hurry it up, Jeremiah," Stowe said. "They're getting way ahead there."

"They know what they're doing," the slave grunted, stung by the taunt. "Turn one loose in my kitchen and see what kind of mess you'd get." To his surprise, Stowe laughed.

Jeremiah soon grew sore, stiff, and winded. He did not think he could have gone on without the half-grown sim that carried a bucket of water from one worker to the next. At first it would not stop for him, passing him by for members of its own kind. A growl from Stowe, though, fixed that in a hurry.

Reluctantly, Jeremiah came to see that the overseer did not use his charges with undue harshness. To have done so would have wrung less work from them, and work was what Stowe was after. He treated the sims—and Jeremiah— like so many other beasts of burden, with impersonal efficiency. The slave even wished for the malice Stowe had shown on the path that summer night. That, at least, would have been an acknowledgment of his humanity.

Before long, he found out what it meant to have such wishes granted. "Spread the hemp out better once you cut it," Stowe snapped. Jeremiah jumped; he had not heard the overseer come up behind him. "Spread it out," Stowe repeated. "It won't dry as well if you don't."

"I'm doing as well as the sims are," Jeremiah said, nodding toward the long, sharp, dark-green leaves lying to his right and left.

Stowe snorted. "I could wear out my whip arm and they'd still be slipshod. I expect better from you, and by Christ I'll get it." His arm went back, then forward, fast as a striking snake. The whip cracked less than a foot from Jeremiah's ear. He flinched. He could not help it. "The next one you'll feel," the overseer promised. He paused to let the message sink in, then moved on to keep the sims busy.

Jeremiah had a shirt of dark green silk. He mostly wore it for show, when his master was entertaining guests. He had never noticed it was the exact color of hemp leaves. Now he did, and told himself he would never put it on again.

The day seemed endless. Jeremiah did not dare look at his hands. He did know that, when he shifted them on the handle of the sickle, he saw red-brown stains on the gray, smooth wood.

Craack! "God damn you, Jeremiah, I told you what I wanted!" Stowe shouted. The slave screamed at the hot touch of whip on his back. "Oh, stop your whining," the overseer said. "I've not even marked you, past a bruise. You keep provoking me, though, and I'll give you stripes you'll wear the rest of your life."

Several sims watched the byplay, taking advantage of Stowe's preoccupation to rest from their labor. *Work more, work better*, one signed at Jeremiah. Its wide, stupid grin was infuriatingly smug.

"Go to the devil," Jeremiah muttered. For once, he hoped sims had souls, so they could spend eternity roasting in hellfire.

He thought the day would never end, but at last the sun set. "Enough!" Stowe shouted. This time Jeremiah had no trouble understanding the sims' whoops. He felt like adding some himself.

Stowe collected the tools, counting them as carefully as

he had in the morning to make sure none was missing. His chilly gaze swung toward Jeremiah. "I'll see you tomorrow come sunrise. Now that you know what to do, I won't have to go easy on you anymore." The whip twitched in his hand, ever so slightly.

"No, sir, Mr. Stowe, you surely won't," Jeremiah said. The overseer nodded, for once satisfied.

Jeremiah had been afraid he would have to sleep in the sim barracks, but Stowe did not object when he went back to his room in the big house. Probably hadn't thought of it, the slave decided. He stopped at the kitchen for leftovers from the meal Jane Gillen had cooked. They were better than what the sims ate, but not much. His lip curled; he had forgotten more about cooking than Mrs. Gillen knew.

His hands felt as if they were on fire. He could not ignore them any more. There was a crock of lard in the kitchen. He rubbed it into both palms. The fat soothed the raw, broken skin.

Jeremiah went to his room. His back twinged again when he took off his shirt. Stowe knew exactly what he was doing with a lash, though; he had not drawn blood. But Jeremiah remembered the overseer's warning. His aching muscles contracted involuntarily, as if anticipating a blow that was sure to come.

Looking back, Jeremiah thought that unwilled, mortifying twinge was what made him do what he did next. "I don't care how white he is, he ain't gonna get the chance to whip me again," he said out loud. He put his shirt back on, took out the pouch with his hard-saved sesters and denaires, opened the door, stepped into the hallway, shut the door behind him.

He could have gone back with no one the wiser, but from that moment on he was irrevocably a runaway in his own mind. Being one, he stopped in the kitchen again, to steal a carving knife. He had held that blade in his hand a hundred times with the Gillens or their children close by, and never thought of lifting it against them. "No more," he whispered. "No more."

And yet, as he left the dark and quiet house, he had trouble fighting the paralyzing tide of fear that rose inside him. He had his place here, his known duties and expectations. His master had let him earn the money he was carrying just so he could buy his freedom one day.

He turned back. His hand was on the doorknob when the pain that light touch brought returned him to his purpose. How was it really his place, he wondered, if Gillen could take it from him whenever he chose?

The question had no answer. He walked down the wooden steps and into the night.

Eleven days later, he came down the West Norfolk Road into Portsmouth. He was ragged and dirty and thin and tired; only on the last day had he dared actually travel the highway. Before that, fearing dogs and hunters on his track, he had gone by winding, back-country paths and through the woods.

Those held terrors of their own. Spearfangs had been hunted almost to extinction in Virginia years ago. Almost, however, was the operative word; Jeremiah had spent an uncomfortable night in a tree because of a thunderous coughing roar that erupted from the undergrowth a few hundred yards to his left.

He also had an encounter with a wild sim. It was hard to say which of the two got a worse fright from it. In the old days, Jeremiah had heard, sims would hunt down and eat any humans they could catch. But now, brought low by gunpowder and by man's greater native wit, the wild sims were only skulking pests in the land they had once roamed freely. And when this one saw the knife Jeremiah jerked out, it hooted and fled before it had a chance to hear his teeth chattering.

After those adventures and a couple of more like them, he wished he had taken his chances on hounds and trackers. With them, at least, he knew what to expect.

Portsmouth was the biggest town he had ever seen, ever imagined. By the bay, masts of merchantmen and naval vessels made a bare-branched forest against the sky. The gilded dome of the commonwealth capitol dominated the skyline. Jeremiah did not know that was what it was. He only knew it was grand and beautiful.

People of every sort swarmed through the streets, paying no attention to one more newly arrived, none-too-clean black man. Even the four sims bearing a rich trader's sedan chair looked down their broad, flat noses at him. And no wonder, he thought. Charles Gillen was a long way from poor, but he did not own a suit of clothes half so fine as the matched outfits of silk and satin the sims were wearing.

Jeremiah blessed the half-thought-out notion that had brought him to the city. Among these thousands, how could anyone hope to find one person in particular? His confidence took a jolt, though, when he passed a cabin whose sign declared: "JASON BROS: RUNAWAY SIMS AND NIGGERS CATCHED." The picture below showed a sim treed by hounds with improbably sharp teeth and red mouths. Jeremiah shuddered and hurried on.

Before long, his grumbling stomach forced him to face another problem. On the road, he had raided fruit trees and stolen a couple of chickens, eking them out with fruits and berries. He did not think he could get away with that kind of provisioning for long in Portsmouth. Food was harder to get at and thieves more likely to be hunted down. He could eat for a while on the money he had with him, but he would have to find work if he did not want to deplete it. The twenty sesters he paid for a bad breakfast only reinforced the truth of that.

Here he would not have turned down the kind of hard manual labor that had made him run away in the first place. He would have been doing it for himself, of his own free will, and he reasoned that employers who wanted only strong backs would ask few questions.

But no such hauling or digging or carrying jobs were to be had: sims did them all, for no more wages than their keep. "You must be just off the farm, to think you can get that kind of job and get paid for it," a straw boss said.

Jeremiah's heart leaped into his mouth, but the man went on, "If you have a skilled trade, now, like carpenter or mason, I can use you. How about it?"

Jeremiah had used saw and chisel and plane often enough on the Gillen estate, but he said, "Sorry, sir, no," and left in a hurry. The straw boss's chance reference to his real status, even if nothing was behind it, made him too nervous to stay.

He wandered aimlessly through Portsmouth for a while, marveling at the number of buildings that would have dwarfed the Gillen house, till then the grandest he had known. One imposing marble structure near the capitol had an inscription over the columned entranceway. It was in large, clear letters, but even when he spelled it out twice it made no sense: FIAT IUSTITIA ET RUANT COELI. He shrugged and gave it up.

Not far away, down a winding side street, stood a dilapidated clapboard building with a sign nailed to the front door. The sign was hard to read because it needed painting, but the words, at least, made sense: ALFRED P. DOUGLAS, ATTORNEY AT LAW.

Jeremiah was about to pass on by when he remembered Caleb Gillen's talk about lawyers and how important they were. Maybe an important man would have work for him. And if the important man got too nosy, well, important men tended to be fat, and he could probably outrun this one. He walked up and knocked on the door.

"It's open," someone with a deep voice called from inside. He sounded important. Jeremiah turned the knob and walked in.

The man rummaging through the pile of books by his desk was fat, but that ended his resemblance to anything Jeremiah had imagined. He was about thirty, with a straggling mustache and a thick shock of greasy black hair. His breeches had a hole in the knee; one shoe had a hole in the sole. His shirt was no cleaner than Jeremiah's.

Whatever he was digging for, he must have decided he wasn't going to find it. He made a disgusted face, looked up at Jeremiah. "And what can I do for you today, sir?"

Jeremiah almost fled, as he had from the straw boss. No white man had ever called him sir, even in mockery. This did not sound like mockery. He took a chance, stayed. "I'm looking for work from you, sir."

"I'm sorry; I don't need a clerk right now." Douglas muttered something to himself that Jeremiah did not catch.

"I didn't mean that kind of work, sir." Jeremiah tried to keep his mouth from falling open. The fellow thought he wanted to study law under him! "I meant cleaning, cooking, straightening up." He looked around. "You'll excuse me for speaking so bold, sir, but this place could do with some straightening up."

Douglas grunted. "You're right, sir; as I said just now"—that must have been the mutter—"what I need is someone to make sense of this mess. You'll not be able to do that, I promise, if you have no letters."

"I can read, sir, some, and write a bit," Jeremiah said, and then had the wit to add as an afterthought, "Mr. Douglas."

Douglas grunted again. "You slave or free?"

Ice ran down Jeremiah's back. "Free," he answered, and got ready to bolt if Douglas asked for papers to prove it.

All the lawyer said, though, was, "Good. I'd sooner line your pockets than your master's. What do I call you?"

"Jeremiah." Realizing a second too late that if he was free he should also have a surname, he gave the first one that popped into his head. "Jeremiah, uh, Gillen."

Douglas showed no sign of noticing the slip. He plopped his bulk into an overstuffed armchair. The springs groaned in protest. "All right, Mr. Gillen, I'll try you, damn me if I don't. Put that stack there into some kind of order and I'll take you on."

The stack was the one the lawyer had been pawing through. Jeremiah knelt beside it. He almost gave up at once, for the books' titles were full of long, incomprehensible words: legal terms, he supposed. But before panic set in, he remembered the ABC Caleb Gillen had drilled into him, and the way Caleb's father kept the books in his library. If he arranged these alphabetically by author, he could not go far wrong.

"Here you are, sir," he said a few minutes later. He held out a handful of coins. "And here are the, uh, ninety-one sesters mixed in with the books."

Douglas stared, then burst into laughter. "Keep them, my friend, keep them. I'd say you've earned them, the more so as I'd long since forgotten they were there. It was honest of you to offer them back—but then who wouldn't be honest with a prospective employer watching?" That last so perfectly summed Jeremiah's thoughts when he found the money that he eyed Douglas with fresh respect.

The lawyer took more care inspecting the books than he had over the coins. He had to correct a mistake Jeremiah had made, and the black's heart sank for fear he would be turned down. But all Douglas said was, "Be more careful next time. Three denaires a week suit you?"

"Yes, sir!" The wage was a long way from kingly, but Jeremiah did not feel sure enough of himself to bargain. If he bought fresh food and did his own cooking, he thought he could scrape by.

Then Douglas went on, "You cook, you say?" At Jeremiah's nod, he broke into a grin that turned his heavy features boyish for a moment. "Then board with me, why don't you? I've rattled round my house since the swamp fever took my Margaret two years ago." The memory made him somber again. "Help me keep the place neat, and I'll buy supplies for both of us. You deal with them then: if I'm not the worst cook in the commonwealth, he's not been born yet. Do we have a contract?"

"A deal, you mean? Yes, sir!" Jeremiah clasped Douglas's outstretched hand. The lawyer's grip was soft but strong. Jeremiah felt like turning handsprings. With room and board taken care of, three denaires wasn't bad money at all.

Jeremiah spent the rest of the day getting things off the floor so he could sweep it clean of crumpled papers, dust, apple cores, nutshells, and other garbage. Douglas's indifference to filth left his fastidious soul cringing.

He found another denaire and a half in loose change. The lawyer let him keep that too, though he warned, "Bear in mind my generosity doesn't extend to gold, if there is any down there." The thought of coming across a goldpiece made Jeremiah work harder than ever; only later did he think to wonder whether that was what Douglas had had in mind.

He had gotten down to bare wood in a few places when Douglas had a visitor, a tall, lean, middle-aged man who wore a stovepipe hat to make himself seem even taller. "Ah, Mr. Hayes," Douglas said, setting aside the document he had been studying. "What can I do for you, this fine afternoon?"

Hayes glanced at Jeremiah. "Buy yourself a nigger? Doesn't seem like you, Alfred."

"He's free; I hired him," Douglas said, his color rising. "Mr. Hayes, Jeremiah Gillen. Jeremiah, this is Zachary Hayes." Hayes nodded with the minimum courtesy possible and did not offer to shake hands. Jeremiah went back to work. He was not used to respect from whites, and so did not miss it.

"I came on a gamble," Hayes said, turning away from Jeremiah with obvious relief. "I daresay you own the most law books in the city, and keep them in the worst order. Have you a copy of William Watson's *Ten Quodlibetical Questions Concerning Religion and State* and, if so, can you lay your hands on it?"

"The title rings a bell—having heard it, how could one forget it?" Douglas said. "As for where it might be, though, I confess I have no idea. Jeremiah, paw through things and see what you come up with, will you?"

Hayes made a sour face and folded his arms to wait, plainly not expecting Jeremiah to find the book. That scorn spurred him more even than Douglas's earlier mention of gold. He dove under tables, climbed on a shaky chair to reach top bookcase shelves. On one of those, its calfskin spine to the wall, he found Watson's tome. He wordlessly handed it to Hayes.

"My thanks," Hayes said—not to him, but to Douglas. "I'll have it back to you within a fortnight." He spun on his heel and strode out.

Douglas and Jeremiah looked at each other. They started to laugh at the same time. "Don't mind him," the lawyer said, clapping Jeremiah on the back. "He thinks niggers are stupid as sims. Come on; let's go home."

The house almost made Jeremiah regret his new employment. Douglas had spoken of needing help to keep the place neat; only someone with his studied disdain for order would have imagined there was any neatness to maintain. The house bore a chilling resemblance to his office, except that dirty clothes and dirtier pots were added to the mix.

The only thing that seemed to stand aloof from the clutter was a fine oil painting of a slim, pale, dark-eyed woman. Douglas saw Jeremiah's eyes go to it. "Yes, that's my Margaret," he said sadly; as Jeremiah would learn, he never spoke of her without putting the possessive in front of her name.

The kitchen was worse than the rest of the house: stale bread, moldy flour, greens limp at best, and salt pork like the stuff Charles Gillen's sims ate. Jeremiah shook his head; he had looked for nothing better. He pumped some water, set a chunk of pork in it to soak out some of the salt. Meanwhile, he got a fire going in the hearth. The stew he ended up producing would have earned harsh words from his former owner, but Douglas demanded seconds and showered praise on him.

"Let me start with good food, sir, and I'll really give you something worth eating," Jeremiah said.

"I don't know whether I should, or in six months I'll be too wide to go through my own front door," Douglas said, ruefully surveying his rotund form.

Jeremiah had to sweep off what he was coming to think of as the usual layer of junk to get at his cot. It was saggy and lumpy, nowhere near as comfortable as the one he'd had on the Gillen estate. He didn't care. It was his because he wanted it to be, not because it had to be.

He slept wonderfully.

As the months went by, he tried more than once to find a name for his relationship with Alfred Douglas. It was something more than servant, something less than friend. Part of the trouble was that Douglas treated him unlike anyone ever had before. For a long while, because he had never encountered it before, he had trouble recognizing the difference. The lawyer used him as a man, not as a slave.

That did not mean he did not tell Jeremiah what to do. He did, which further obscured the change to the black man. But he did not speak as to a half-witted, surly child, and he did not stand over Jeremiah to make sure he got things done. He assumed Jeremiah would, and went about his own business.

Not used to such liberty, at first Jeremiah took advantage of it to do as little as he could. "Work or get out," Douglas had told him bluntly. "Do you think I hired you to sit on your arse and sleep?"

But he never complained when he caught Jeremiah reading, which he did more and more often. In the beginning that had been purely practical on Jeremiah's part, so as to keep fresh what Caleb Gillen had taught him. Then the printed page proved to have a seductive power of its own.

Which is not to say reading came easily. It painfully taught Jeremiah how small his vocabulary was. Sometimes he could figure out what a new word meant from its context. Most of the time, he would have to ask Douglas.

" 'Eleemosynary?' " The lawyer raised his eyebrows. "It's a fancy word for 'charitable.' " He saw that meant nothing to Jeremiah either, simplified again: " 'Giving to those who lack.' What are you looking at, anyhow?"

Jeremiah held up a law book, wondering if he was in trouble. Douglas only said, "Oh," and returned to the brief he was drafting. When he was done, he sanded the ink dry, set the paper aside, and pulled a slim volume from the shelf (by this time, things were easy to find).

He offered the book to Jeremiah. "Here, try this. You have to walk before you can run."

"*The Articles of Independence of the Federated Commonwealths and the Terms of Their Federation*," Jeremiah read aloud.

"All else springs from those," Douglas said. "Without them, we'd have only chaos, or a tyrant as they do these days in England. But go through them and understand them point by point, and you've made a fair beginning toward becoming a lawyer."

Jeremiah stared at him. "There's no nigger lawyers in Portsmouth." He spoke with assurance; he had gotten to know the black part of town well. It boasted scores of preachers, a few doctors, even a printer, but no lawyers.

"I know there aren't," Douglas said. "Perhaps there should be." When Jeremiah asked him what he meant, he changed the subject, as if afraid he had said too much.

The book Douglas gave Jeremiah perplexed and astonished him at the same time. "This is how the government is put together?" he asked the lawyer after he had struggled through the first third.

"So it is." Douglas looked at him keenly, as if his next question was to be some kind of test. "What do you think of it?"

"I think it's purely crazy, begging your pardon," Jeremiah blurted. Douglas said nothing, waiting for him to go on. He fumbled ahead, trying to clarify his feelings: "The censors each with a veto on the other one, the Popular Assembly chose by all the free people and the senators by— I forgot how the senators happen."

"Censors and commonwealth governors become senators for life after their terms end," Douglas supplied.

Jeremiah smacked his forehead with the heel of his hand. "That's right. And the censors enforce the laws and lead the armies, but only if the Senate decides to spend the money the armies need. And it's the Popular Assembly that makes the laws (if the Senate agrees) and decides if it's peace or war in the first place. If you ask me, Mr. Douglas, I don't think any one of 'em knows for certain he can fart without checking the *Terms of Federation* first."

"That's also why we have courts," Douglas smiled. "Why do you suppose the Conscript Fathers arranged things this way? Remember, after we won our freedom from England, we could have done anything we wanted."

Having had scant occasion to think about politics before, Jeremiah took a long time to answer. When he did, all he could remember was the discussion Charles Gillen and Harry Stowe had had the spring before. "For the sake of argufying?" he guessed.

To his surprise, Douglas said, "You know, you're not far wrong. They tried to strike a balance, so everyone would have some power and no one group could get enough to take anybody else's freedom away. The Conscript Fathers modeled our government on the mixed constitution the Roman Republic had. You know who the Romans were, don't you, Jeremiah?"

"They crucified Jesus, a long time ago," Jeremiah said, exhausting his knowledge of the subject.

"So they did, but they were also fine lawyers and good, practical men of affairs—not showy like the Greeks, but effective, and able to rule a large state for a long time. If we do half so well, we'll have something to be proud of."

The discussion broke off there, because Zachary Hayes came in to borrow a book. Now that Jeremiah had Douglas's library in order, Hayes stopped by every couple of weeks. He never showed any sign of recognizing why he had more luck these days, and spoke directly to Jeremiah only when he could not help it.

This time, he managed to avoid even looking at the black man. Instead, he said to Douglas, "If you don't mind, you'll see me more often, Alfred. I've a new young man studying under me, and long since gave away my most basic texts."

"No trouble at all, Zachary," Douglas assured him. Once Hayes was gone, Douglas rolled his eyes. "That buzzard never gave away anything, except maybe the clap. I guarantee you he sold his old books—probably for more than he paid for them too; no denying he's able."

Jeremiah did not answer. He was deep in the *Terms of*

Federation again. Once the Conscript Fathers had outlined the Federated Commonwealths's self-regulating government, they went on to set further limits on what it could do.

Reading those limits, Jeremiah began to have a sense of what Douglas had meant by practical ruling. Each restriction was prefaced by a brief explanation of why it was needed: "Establishing dogmas having proven in history to engender civic strife, followers of all faiths shall be forever free to follow their own beliefs without let or hindrance." "So that free men shall not live in fear of the state and its agents and form conspiracies against them, no indiscriminate searches of persons or property shall be permitted." "To keep the state from the risk of tyranny worse than external subjugation, no foreign mercenaries shall be hired, but liberty shall depend on the vigilance of the free men of the nation."

On and on the book went, checking the government for the benefit of the free man. Jeremiah finished it with a strange mixture of admiration and anger. So much talk of freedom, and not a word against slavery! It was as though the Conscript Fathers had not noticed it existed.

Conscious of his own daring, Jeremiah remarked on that to Douglas. The lawyer nodded. "Slavery has been with us since Greek and Roman times, and you can search the Bible from one end to the other without finding a word against it. And, of course, when Englishmen came to America, they found the sims. No one would say the sims should not serve us."

Jeremiah almost blurted, "But I'm no sim!" Then he remembered Douglas thought him free. He did say, "Sims is different than men."

"There you are right," Douglas said, sounding uncommonly serious. "The difference makes me wonder about our laws at times, it truly does." Jeremiah hoped he would go on, but when he did, it was not in the vein the black had expected: "Of course, one could argue as well that the sims' manifest inequality only points up subtler differences among various groups of men."

Disgusted, Jeremiah found an excuse to knock off early. One thing he had learned about lawyers was that they delighted in argument for its own sake, without much caring about right and wrong. He had thought Douglas different, but right now he seemed the same as the rest.

A gang of sims came by, moving slowly under the weight of the heavy timbers on their shoulders. He glowered at their hairy backs. Too many white men were like Zachary Hayes, lumping sims and blacks together because most blacks were slaves.

As it had back on Charles Gillen's estate, that rankled. He was no subhuman . . . and if Hayes doubted what blacks really were, let him get a sim instead of the fancy cook he owned! Soon enough he'd be skeletal, not just lean. Jeremiah grinned, liking the notion.

Another party of sims emerged from a side street. This group was carrying sacks of beans. Neither gang made any effort to get out of the other's way. In an instant, they were hopelessly tangled. Traffic snarled.

Because all the sims had their hands full, they could not use their signs to straighten out the mess. Their native hoots and calls were not adequate for the job. Indeed, they made matters worse. The sims glared at each other, peeling back their lips to bare their big yellow teeth and grimacing horribly.

"Call the guards!" a nervous man shouted, and several others took up the cry. Jeremiah ducked down an alleyway. He had seen enough of sims' brute strength on the farm to be sure he wanted to be far away if they started fighting.

The town did not erupt behind him, so he guessed the overseers had managed to put things to rights. A few words at the outset would have done it: "Coming through!" or "Go ahead; we'll wait." The sims did not have the words to use.

"Poor stupid bastards," Jeremiah said, and headed home.

"Mr. Douglas, you have some of the strangest books in the

world, and that is a fact," Jeremiah said.

Douglas ran his hands through his oily hair. "If you keep excavating among those boxes, God only knows what you'll come up with. What is it this time?"

"*A Proposed Explication of the Survival of Certain Beasts in America and Their Disappearance Hereabouts,* by Samuel Pepys." Jeremiah pronounced it *pep-eeze.*

"*Peeps,*" Douglas corrected, then remarked, "You know, Jeremiah, you read much better now than you did when you started working for me last summer. That's the first time you've slipped in a couple of weeks, and no one could blame you for stumbling over that tongue twister."

"Practice," Jeremiah said. He held up the book. "What is this, anyhow?"

"It just might interest you, come to think of it. It's the book that sets forth the transformational theory of life: that the kinds of living things change over time."

"That's not what the Bible says."

"I know. Churchmen hate Pepys's theories. As a lawyer, though, I find them attractive, because he presents the evidence for them. *Genesis* is so much hearsay by comparison."

"You never were no churchgoing man, sir," Jeremiah said reproachfully. He started to read all the same; working with Douglas had given him a good bit of the lawyer's attitude. And he respected his boss's brains. If Douglas thought there was something to this—what had he called it?—transformational theory, there probably was.

The book was almost 150 years old, and written in the ornate style of the seventeenth century. Jeremiah had to ask Douglas to help him with several words and complex phrases. He soon saw what the lawyer meant. Pepys firmly based his argument on facts, with no pleading to unverifiable "authorities." Despite himself, Jeremiah was impressed.

Someone squelched up the walk toward Douglas's door: no, a couple of people, by the sound. It was that transitional time between winter and spring. The rain was still cold, but Jeremiah knew only relief that he did not have to shovel snow anymore.

Douglas had heard the footsteps too. He rammed quill into inkpot and started writing furiously. "Put Pepys down and get busy for a while, Jeremiah," he said. "It's probably Jasper Carruthers and his son, here for that will I should've finished three days ago. Since it's not done, we ought at least to look busy."

Grinning, Jeremiah got up and started reshelving some of the books that got pulled down every day. He had his back to the door when it swung open, but heard Douglas's relieved chuckle.

"Good to see you, Zachary," the lawyer said. "Saves me the embarrassment of pleading guilty to nonfeasance."

Hayes let out a dry laugh. "A problem we all face from time to time, Alfred; I'm glad you escaped it here. Do you own an English version of Justinian's *Digest*? I'm afraid the Latin of my young friend here isn't up to his reading it in the original."

The volume happened to be in front of Jeremiah's face. He pulled it from the shelf before Douglas had to ask him for it, turned with a smug smile to offer it to Hayes's student.

The smile congealed on his face like fat getting cold in a pan. The youngster with Hayes was Caleb Gillen.

The tableau held for several frozen seconds, the two of them staring at each other while the lawyers, not understanding what was going on, stared at them both.

"Jeremiah!" Caleb exclaimed. "It's my father's runaway nigger!" he shouted to Hayes at the same moment Jeremiah bolted for the door.

Pepys's book proved his undoing. It went flying out from under his foot and sent him sprawling. Caleb Gillen landed on his back. Before he could shake free of the youngster, Hayes also grabbed him. The lawyer was stronger than he looked. Between them, he and Caleb held Jeremiah pinned to the floor.

Panting, his gray hair awry, Hayes said, "You told me he was a free nigger, Alfred."

"He said he was. I had no reason to doubt him," Douglas answered calmly. He had made no move to rise from his desk and help seize Jeremiah, or indeed even to put down his quill. Now he went on, "For that matter, I still have no reason to do so."

"What? I recognize him!" Caleb Gillen shouted, his voice breaking from excitement. "And what if I didn't? He ran! That proves it!"

"If I were a free nigger and someone said I was a slave, I'd run too," Douglas said. "Wouldn't you, young sir? (I'm sorry; I don't know your name.) Wouldn't you, Zachary, regardless of the truth or falsehood of the claim?"

"Now you just wait one minute here, Alfred," Hayes snapped. "Young master Caleb Gillen here told me last year of the absconding from his father's farm of their nigger, Jeremiah. My only regret is not associating the name with this wretch here so he could have been recaptured sooner." He twisted Jeremiah's arm behind his back.

"That you failed to do so demonstrates the obvious fact that the name may be borne by more than one individual," Douglas said.

"You see here, sir," Caleb Gillen said, "I've known that nigger as long as I can remember. I'm not likely to make a mistake about who he is."

"If he is free, he'll have papers to prove it." Hayes wrenched Jeremiah's arm again. The black gasped. "Can you show us papers, nigger?"

"You need not answer that, save in a court of law," Douglas said sharply, keeping Jeremiah from surrendering on the spot. He was sunk in despair, tears dripping from his face to the floor. Once sent back to the Gillen estate, he would never regain the position of trust that had let him escape, and probably would never be able to buy his freedom either.

Hayes's voice took on a new note of formality. "Do you deny, then, Alfred, that this nigger is the chattel of Charles Gillen, Caleb's father?"

"Zachary, one lad's accusation is no proof, as well you know." Douglas took the same tone; Jeremiah recognized it as lawyer-talk. A tiny spark of hope flickered. By illuminating the dark misery that filled him, it only made that misery worse.

Overriding Caleb Gillen's squawk of protest, Hayes said, "Then let him be clapped in irons until such time as determination of his status may be made. That will prevent any further disappearances."

"I have a better idea," Douglas said. He unlocked one of his desk drawers, took out a strongbox, unlocked that. "What would you say the value of a buck nigger of his age would be? Is 300 denaires a fair figure?"

Above him, Jeremiah felt Caleb and Hayes shift as they looked at each other. "Aye, fair enough," Hayes said at last.

Coins clinked with the sweet music of gold. After a bit, Douglas said, "Then here are 300 denaires for you to acknowledge by receipt, to be forfeit to Master Gillen's father if Jeremiah should flee before judgment. Do you agree to this bond? Jeremiah, will you also agree to that condition?"

"Caleb, the decision is yours," Hayes said.

"Jeremiah, will you give your word?" the boy asked. He waved aside Hayes's protest before it had well begun, saying, "I've known him to be honest enough, even if a runaway." He slightly emphasized *known*, and glanced toward Douglas, who sat impassive.

"I won't run off from here, I promise," Jeremiah said wearily.

"Get off him; let him up," Caleb said. He did so himself. Hayes followed more slowly. Jeremiah rose, rubbing at bruises and at a knee that still throbbed from hitting the floor.

"May I borrow your pen?" Hayes asked Douglas. When he got it, he wrote a few quick lines, handed the paper to the other lawyer. "Here is your receipt, sir. I hope it suits you?"

"Be so good as to line out the word 'absconder' and initial the change, if you please. It prejudges a case not yet decided."

Hayes snorted but did as he was bid. Douglas dipped his

head in acknowledgment. After taking up the money, Hayes said, "Come along, Master Gillen. If Alfred wants to play this game, we shall settle it in court, never fear. Oh, yes— don't forget the copy of the *Digest* your nigger was kind enough to find for you." With that parting shot, he and Caleb swept out of the office.

Jeremiah stared miserably at the floor. Douglas said, "I suppose it's no good asking for a miracle. You don't happen to be a free nigger named Jeremiah who just coincidentally looks exactly like that lad's father's nigger Jeremiah?"

"No, sir," Jeremiah muttered, still not looking up.

"Well, we'll have to try a different tack, then," Douglas said. He did not sound put out; if anything, he sounded eager.

More than anything else, that made Jeremiah lift his head. "You purely crazy, Mr. Douglas, sir? They'll have me in irons and hauled away fast as the judge can bang his gavel."

"Maybe, maybe not." Douglas remained ponderously unruffled.

"Shit!" Jeremiah burst out. "And why did you give your bond on me? I could've broke out of jail maybe, gone somewheres else. How can I run off now?"

Douglas chuckled. "Caleb Gillen's right: you are honest enough, even if a runaway. If that were me in your shoes, I'd've been out the door like a shot, no matter what promises I made. But I gambled you wouldn't, because I think we just might get you really free yet."

"You're crazy, Mr. Douglas," Jeremiah repeated. A few seconds later, he asked in a small voice, "Do you really think so?"

"We just might."

"I'd give anything! I'll pay you. I've got 150 denaires saved up, almost. You can have 'em. If I'm free, I can make more." Jeremiah knew he was babbling, but couldn't help it.

"You'll stay, knowing that if we lose you'll be re- enslaved?"

That was a poser. At last, Jeremiah said, "Even if I run,

someone'll always be after me to drag me back. If we win, I won't have to look over my shoulder every time I sit with my back to the door. That's worth something."

"All right, then. I'll take your money. Not only do I need it after going bond for you, but having it in my pocket will give you an incentive to stay in town." Douglas looked knowingly at Jeremiah.

The black felt his cheeks go hot. Maybe he really was honest; once Douglas had given Hayes the money, it had not occurred to him that he could still run away. Once admitted, however, the idea was in his head for good. If things looked grim enough in court, he told himself, he might yet disappear.

For the life of him, he could not see how the upcoming hearing could do anything but send him back to Charles Gillen. After all, he was an escaped slave. He did not doubt his master could prove it. So why was Douglas willing to take the case before the judges?

When Jeremiah got up the nerve to ask, Douglas did not answer right away. He heaved his bulk up out of his chair, walked over to pick up the volume of Pepys the black had tripped on when he tried to escape. He examined it carefully to make sure it had not been damaged. Then he came over and slapped Jeremiah on the shoulder. "Be a man," he said. "Be a man, and we'll do all right."

True spring sweetened the air as Jeremiah and Douglas made their way to the Portsmouth courthouse. Jeremiah pointed up at the inscription over the entrance, the one that had baffled him when he arrived in the city. "What does that mean?" he asked Douglas.

"*Fiat iustitia et ruant coeli?*" The lawyer seemed surprised for a moment at his ignorance, then laughed. "Well, no reason to blame you for knowing even less Latin than Caleb Gillen, is there? It means, 'Let there be justice, though the heavens fall.' "

Jeremiah admired the sentiment without much expecting to find it practiced. If there were justice, he would not be a slave, but he had a fatalistic certainty he soon was going to be one again. Douglas's optimism did little to lighten his gloom. Douglas was always an optimist. Why not, Jeremiah thought bitterly. *He* was free.

A sim with a broom scurried out of the way to let Jeremiah pass. His spirits lifted a little. Even as a slave, he had known there was more to him than to any of the subhumans. His shoulders straightened.

He needed that small encouragement, for he felt how hostile the atmosphere was as soon as he followed Douglas into the courtroom. Hayes had made sure the case was tried in the newspapers constantly during the month since it began. Prosperous-looking white men filled most of the seats: slave owners themselves, Jeremiah guessed from the way they glared at him. Free blacks had only a few chairs; more stood behind the last row of seats.

Hayes, Charles and Caleb Gillen, and Harry Stowe were already in their places in front of the judges' tribunal. Jeremiah tried to read the elder Gillen's face. The man who had owned him for so long sent him a civil nod. He thought about pretending he did not recognize him, decided it would do no good, and nodded back. Hayes, who missed very little, noticed. He smiled a cold smile. Jeremiah grimaced.

"Rise for the honorable judges," the bailiff intoned as the three-man panel filed in from their chambers. In their black robes and powdered wigs, the judges all seemed to Jeremiah to be cut from the same bolt of cloth.

To Douglas, who had argued cases in front of them for years, they were individuals. As the judges and the rest of the people in the courtroom sat, he whispered to Jeremiah, "Hardesty there on the left has an open mind; I'm glad to see him, especially with Scott as the other junior judge. As for Kemble in the middle, only he knows what he'll do on any given day. He has a habit of changing his mind from case to case. That's not good in a judge, but it can't be helped."

A second look was plenty to warn Jeremiah to beware of

Judge Scott. The man had a long, narrow, unsmiling face, a nose sharp and thin as a sword blade, and eyes like black ice. Even when young, he would not have changed his mind often, and he had not been young for many years.

Hardesty's features were nondescript but rather thoughtful. High Judge Kemble looked like a fox. He had a sly mouth, a sharp nose, and wide blue eyes too innocent to be altogether convincing. Jeremiah would have bet he was rich.

"What case, bailiff?" he asked in a mellifluous tenor.

The bailiff shuffled papers, though both he and the judges knew perfectly well what case it was. He read, "An action brought by Charles Gillen, a citizen of the Commonwealth of Virginia, to regain the services of his absconded black slave Jeremiah, the said Jeremiah stating himself to be a freeman and so not liable to provide said services."

Kemble nodded, Hardesty scribbled something, Scott looked bored. The High Judge glanced toward Hayes. "The plaintiff may present his opening remarks."

The lawyer rose, bowed to Kemble and to each of the junior judges in turn. "May it please the honorable judges, we propose to prove that the nigger seated at the defendant's bench is and has been the slave of our client Charles Gillen, that he did willfully run away from the estate of Charles Gillen, and that he has received no manumission or other liberation to entitle him in law to so depart."

"What evidence will you produce to demonstrate this claim, sir?" Kemble intoned.

"I have beside me here the owner of—"

"I protest the word, your excellencies," Douglas broke in. "For all that he borrows books from me, Mr. Hayes is surely too learned to assume what he wishes to prove."

"The *claimed* owner," Hayes amended before the judges could comment. "The *claimed* owner of this *claimed* slave" (Douglas winced at the sarcasm) "and his son and his overseer, all of whom can identify the individual in question. I shall also produce a bill of sale demonstrating the chattel status of that individual." He sat down, looking as smug as a scrawny man can.

Judge Kemble glanced toward Douglas. "And how does the defendant plan to refute the evidence that counsel for the plaintiff shall put forward?"

The lawyer waited for Jeremiah's hesitant nod before he spoke. The magnitude of what they were about to undertake still terrified the black, though they had hashed it out together and agreed it was the best chance to squeeze justice from the court. As Douglas had said, "If you hit something, hit it hard."

For all his brave front, Douglas must have felt a trifle daunted too. His voice was uncharacteristically nervous as he replied, "May it please the honorable judges, we do not seek to refute the plaintiff's evidence. Indeed, we stipulate it as part of the record."

All three judges had to work together to quiet the courtroom. Cries of "Sellout!" from the few black spectators rose above the buzz of the rest of the audience. The judges stared at Douglas as they wielded their gavels: Hardesty in surprise, Kemble in frank speculation, and Scott resentfully, as if the lawyer had awakened him for no good reason.

Zachary Hayes also spent a few seconds gaping at his colleague. He recovered quickly, though, exclaiming, "If our evidence be admitted, then the case is proven for us. May I ask your excellencies to order the nigger bound over for return to his rightful owner?"

"Bailiff—" Judge Scott began.

Kemble overrode him. "A moment, please. Surely, Mr. Douglas, you could have chosen an easier way to surrender. Why this one?"

"Surrender, your excellency? Who spoke of surrender?" Douglas's voice was at its blandest now, and Hayes's face suddenly clouded with suspicion. Douglas went on, "To stipulate that Jeremiah was held in involuntary servitude does our case no harm, as our contention is and shall be that such servitude is not only involuntary but contrary to law."

"On what ground, your excellencies?" Hayes waved the documents he had intended to introduce. "These are all executed according to proper form."

Douglas leaned down to whisper to Jeremiah, "Here we go—no turning back now." The lawyer took a deep breath, faced the judges, and said slowly, "On the grounds that for any man to hold another man in slavery clearly contravenes the Articles of Federation and must therefore have no standing in law anywhere in the Federated Colonies.

The court was silent for a few seconds, while judges, opponents, and audience worked through the legal language to the implications behind it. Hayes furiously shouted, "Your excellencies, I protest!" at the same time as a black man raised a whoop and a white growled, "You hush your mouth there or I'll hush it for you!"

Getting quiet back took longer this time, and the bailiff and court scribe had to eject a couple of particularly obstreperous people. Finally, with some sort of order restored, Judge Scott brought down his gavel and said, "To me, the plaintiff's protest has merit, despite the defense's attempts at obfuscation. This small, open-and-shut case is not one from which to adduce large legal principles."

"Is it not?" Judge Hardesty spoke for the first time. "The principle would appear germane to the issue at hand."

"As Judge Scott has seen, your excellency," Hayes continued his protest to Kemble, "this is but a desperate effort on the part of the defense to shift the case away from the area where they are weakest: the truth. Its merits are clear as they stand; no need to go beyond them."

"On the contrary," Douglas said. "The claim I make is of paramount importance here. If one man may in law own another, when does application of that right end? What would the feelings of the plaintiff and his comrades be, were they at this side of the court, hearing my client lay claim to their services?"

"Any nigger wants me to slave for him'd have to kill me first," Harry Stowe snarled.

Judge Kemble's gavel crashed down, loud as a pistol shot. "Sir, that will be the last such outburst from you. You look to have seen the inside of a courtroom once or twice, enough to have learned the rules of behavior here." The chief judge glowered at Stowe until the overseer dropped his eyes and mumbled agreement. Kemble nodded. "Very well, then; we'll overlook it this time. As for the motion of the defense, however, we rule it is relevant to this case and will hear arguments based thereon." He used the gavel again.

As Hayes rose, he seemed to be fighting to hold his temper. His voice came out steady as he asked for a two-day extension "to study the new situation." Kemble granted it and adjourned the court.

Back in Douglas's office, Jeremiah was jubilant. "That Stowe hurt Mr. Gillen more'n we did?" he grinned. "Without him opening his fool mouth that way, the judge wouldn't have got mad and gone along with your motion."

"Associating with me has made you cynical," Douglas said, drawing the cork from a bottle of whiskey and taking a long swig. "Ahh! Better. Actually, I think you're wrong there. Ruling against us, Kemble probably would have lost on appeal, and he's too clever to leave himself open for anything like that. He'll let us hang ourselves instead of doing the work for us."

That assessment shattered the black's cheery mood. "We ain't won yet, then?"

"A skirmish," Douglas shrugged. "You aren't back in the fields, are you? But no, we haven't won. The real fight is just starting."

When Jeremiah's case reconvened, the courtroom was even more packed than it had been before. At the bailiff's command, the people who had managed to gain seats rose to honor the judges. Those at the back—blacks again, mostly—had been standing for some time already, and would keep on until court adjourned.

Judge Kemble rapped for order. Slowly, silence descended. Kemble nodded to Zachary Hayes. "You may begin, sir."

"Thank you, your excellency," Hayes said, rising.

"Though I regret the necessity of belaboring the obvious, still it may not be amiss to remind some of the citizens of the Federated Commonwealths of the principles upon which it was built."

He sent a sour glance toward Alfred Douglas before continuing, "I shall not even attempt to cite the precedents sanctioning slavery. Suffice it to say they are both numerous and ancient, dating back on the one hand to the Old Testament, the foundation of our faith; and on the other hand to the history and institutions of the wise and noble Greeks and Romans, upon whose usages we have modeled our own."

Listening, Jeremiah felt his heart sink. Hayes sounded too knowledgeable, too self-assured. The black's nails bit into his palms. He should have run while he had the chance. All Douglas wanted to do was show off how brilliant he was. Why not? If he lost the case, it would not hurt *him* any. *He* would not be the one hauled away in chains.

Douglas might have been reading his thoughts. He leaned over and whispered, "Don't give up just yet. He's not saying anything I didn't expect him to."

"All right." But Jeremiah remained unconvinced.

Hayes was saying, "At first glance, it might seem strange that the Federated Commonwealths, whose pride is in upholding the freedom of their citizens, should also countenance slavery. Yet when properly examined, no inconsistency appears. More than two thousand years ago, Aristotle demonstrated in the *Politics* that some men are indeed slaves by nature, and that it is only proper for them to serve so that, by enjoying the fruit of their labors, the rest may be truly free.

"How may we judge those who are slaves by nature? Whenever two groups of men differ widely, so that the inferior group can do no more than use their bodies at the direction of their superiors, that group is and ought to be slaves by nature: they reason only enough to understand what they are told, not to think new thoughts for themselves.

"Finally, for us a kindly providence has distinguished this class of individuals by their dusky skins and other features different from our own, to make display of their servile status. This being the case, I trust your excellencies shall soon bring an end to the farce we have seen played out here, and that you shall return this nigger Jeremiah to the station God has intended for him." Conscious of a job well done, Hayes sat.

"Mr. Douglas, you may reply," Judge Kemble said.

"Thank you, your excellency," Douglas said, slowly getting to his feet, "although I naturally hesitate to do so when my learned opponent, as he has demonstrated, is on such intimate terms with the Almighty." Judge Scott's gavel crashed to stifle the small swell of laughter in the court; Hayes gave Douglas a distasteful look.

The younger lawyer brushed a lock of his thick, dark hair back from his forehead. He went on, "I should also like to congratulate Mr. Hayes for the scholarship and energy he has expended to justify the ownership of one man by another. I only find it a pity that he has wasted so much ingenuity over an entirely irrelevant result. 'The mountains labor, and bring forth a ridiculous mouse.' "

This time, all three judges used their gavels, though Jeremiah saw Judge Hardesty's mouth twitch. Hayes sprang out of his chair as if he had sat on a pin. "See here, your excellencies!" he cried. "If this mountebank has a case to make, let him make it, instead of mocking mine."

"The entire proceeding of the defense has skated on thin ice," Judge Scott observed.

"Your excellency, I hope to demonstrate otherwise," Douglas said hastily; not all the sweat that beaded on his face came from Portsmouth's humid heat. "If the court will indulge me, I believe I can do so by summoning two individuals to the witness-box. One is currently in the courtroom; the other, whom I should like to call first, is just outside."

The judges conferred briefly among themselves. "Bunch of damned nonsense!" Jeremiah heard Judge Scott say. He saw the jurist's powdered wig flap indignantly. But after a few minutes, Judge Kemble said, "You may proceed."

"I thank you, your excellency," Douglas said. "I should like the bailiff to fetch in a certain Rob, whom he will find, I expect, sitting against the wall opposite this courtroom."

Bearing a martyred expression—the things half-smart lawyers put him through!—the bailiff went out into the hallway. Jeremiah heard him call, "Rob?" He returned a moment later, his face now frozen. Accompanying him was a male sim, the hair on its head and back and chest grizzled with age.

"Mr. Douglas, I do not know what you are playing at, but I assure you I am no longer amused," Judge Kemble snapped. "You know perfectly well that no testimony by a sim is valid in a court of law, they being incompetent to understand or take oath."

"Yes, your excellency, I am aware of that," Douglas answered. "It was for that very reason that I summoned Rob (who belongs to a friend of mine) before you. The presence of sims on these shores, you see, has a vital impact on the question of slavery."

"Why? Are you planning to liberate them next?" Judge Scott asked.

Such sarcasm from the bench was dangerous. "No, your excellency," Douglas replied at once. "I believe it just that they serve mankind. But their just service points out the injustice of forcing men to similar servitude."

"I fail to see how," Scott grumbled.

"Then let him show us, if he can," Judge Hardesty suggested softly. His partner's face did not clear, but Scott kept to himself the protest he still plainly felt. After glancing at Judge Kemble, Hardesty said to Douglas, "You may proceed."

"Thank you, your excellency." Douglas pointed toward Rob, who sat calmly in the witness-box, looking rather bored and working its massive jaws to help pass the time. "Here we have a being gifted with intelligence—"

"Not much!" someone called from the audience, which raised a laugh and made the judges pound loudly for order.

Jeremiah spent the next several minutes looking down at the table in front of him, until he trusted his control over his features once more. Douglas, he knew, had paid the fellow three denaires for that interruption.

The lawyer's face revealed nothing of his machinations. "—gifted with intelligence," he repeated, "though of a lesser sort than our own. Its existence is not to be denied; in the wild, sims craft crude tools of stone, and attempt to imitate ours, in a fashion no brute beast could match.

"But as most of you know, they have no language of their own, and most fail to master the English tongue. Can you speak, Rob?" Douglas asked, turning to the sim.

Its previously placid face grew tense as it struggled against its own slow wits and balky muscles. "Y-y-y-yess," it got out at last, and sat back, proud and relieved. *Speak good*, it added with signs.

"So you do," Douglas acknowledged. He concentrated on the judges again. "Had I bid the sim read to us from the simplest children's primer, of course, it would have been helpless, as it would have been to write its name. No man has yet succeeded in teaching sims their letters."

"And no man yet has taught a turtle to waltz," Zachary Hayes broke in. "What of it? The issue here is niggers, not sims. Perhaps my distinguished opponent needs reminding of it."

"Yes, Mr. Douglas, we have been patient for some time now," Judge Kemble said. "We shall not be pleased if this course of yours leads nowhere."

"It leads to the very heart of the issue, your excellency," Douglas assured him. "For consider: in the slavery of ancients, what was their chiefest concern? Why, just as the learned Mr. Hayes has demonstrated—to define who might rightfully be a slave, and who was properly free. The great Aristotle developed the concept my opponent discussed so well, that of the slave by nature. Here, in the person of Rob and in his kind, we see exactly what the Greek sage intended: a being with a body strong enough for the tasks we set, yet without wit enough to set against our will.

"Aristotle admitted that in his day, the most difficult thing to determine was the quality of mind that defined the natural slave. And no wonder, for he was trying to distinguish among groups of men, and all men far more resemble each other than they differ from sims. In these modern times, we have a true standard of comparison.

"Mr. Hayes put forth the proposition that the physical appearance of niggers brands them as slaves. That is the same as saying painted plaster will satisfy the stomach because it looks so good. In this court, should we not examine essence rather than exterior? To do so, I should like to summon my client Jeremiah to the witness-box."

While Douglas was signing to Rob that it could go, Hayes sprang up, exclaiming, "I protest this—this charade!"

"On what grounds, sir?" Judge Kemble said.

"On the grounds that it is obviously a trick, rehearsed well in advance, intended to make this nigger out to be Aristotle, Charlemagne, and the Twelve Apostles all rolled into one!"

"Aye, there's a stink of collusion in the air," Judge Scott rumbled.

"How say you, Mr. Douglas?" Kemble asked.

Douglas's smile was beatific, the smile of a man whose enemy has delivered himself into his hands. "Your excellency, I say that even if I were to admit that charge—and I do not; I deny it—it would only help my own case. How could I conspire with Jeremiah unless he had the brains to plot along with me?"

Hayes opened his mouth, closed it again. His eyes were wide and staring. Judge Hardesty let out a most unjudicial snort, then tried to pretend he hadn't. Judge Scott looked grim, which meant his expression changed not at all. Stifled whoops and cheers came from the blacks at the back of the courtroom. Judge Kemble gaveled them down.

"You may proceed, sir," was all he said to Douglas. The lawyer dipped his head, waved Jeremiah forward to take the oath. As Jeremiah raised his hand, he thought Douglas might remind the judges that he, unlike a sim, was able to do so. But Douglas knew when to be subtle. The fact itself spoke louder than anything he could say about it.

Facing the courtroom was harder than Jeremiah had expected. Except for those of the few blacks, he was hard pressed to find a friendly face. The whites in the audience regarded him with looks ranging from stony disapproval to out-and-out hatred. Harry Stowe was part of the latter group.

Next to him sat the two people Jeremiah knew best here, Charles and Caleb Gillen. The habits of years died hard; it hurt Jeremiah to see the contempt on the face of the man who had owned him, and to see his master's son scowling at him as at Iscariot. He started to smile, then let his face freeze. They would re-enslave him without a qualm if the judges said they could. That made them no friends of his.

Douglas produced a small, thick book and presented it to Zachary Hayes, "Would you care to open the Bible at random, sir, so Jeremiah may read the passage you select?"

The older lawyer drew back from the book as if it had come from the devil, "You'll not make me part of your trickery, sir! Like as not, you've had him memorize Scripture for the sake of looking good here."

"Again you prove what you'd sooner oppose," Douglas said. "If Jeremiah were stupid as a sim, he wouldn't be able to memorize the Good Book. You'll make a man of him in spite of yourself."

He turned to the bench. "Would one of you care to make the selection, your excellencies? I don't want any possibility of deceit in this, for such as Mr. Hayes to tax me with."

To Jeremiah's surprise, Judge Scott took the Bible from Douglas. The lawyer's face fell when he saw that Scott did not open the book just anywhere, as he had suggested, but went hunting for a specific passage. "Here," the judge said. "Let him read *this*." He stabbed at the section he wanted with his thumb, adding for the record, "This is the seventh chapter of First Chronicles."

Jeremiah certainly had not memorized it; he had no idea

what was in the passage. But when Douglas handed him the Bible, he understood why the lawyer had gone expressionless. The chapter was one of those collections of begats that crop up every now and then, and full of names more obscure than most.

Having no choice, he gulped and plunged in, " 'And of the sons of Issachar, Tola, and Puah, Jashub, and Shimron, four. And the sons of Tola: Uzzi, and Rephaiah, and Jeriel, and Jahmai, and Ibsam, and Shemuel. . . .' " He read slowly and carefully, often pausing to sound out an unfamiliar name. He knew he sometimes stumbled, and hated himself for it, but Judge Scott had set too wicked a trap for him to escape unscathed.

He fought his way through the sons of Bilhan (Jeush, Benjamin, Ehud, Chenanah, Zethan, Tarshish, and Ahishahar), the sons of Shemida (Ahian, Shechem, Likhi, and Aniam), and the sons of Asher (Imnah, Ishvah, Ishvi, and Beriah, to say nothing of their sister, Serah). He almost broke down on Pasach, Bimhal, and Asvath (the sons of Japhlet). But his voice rose in triumph as he came at last to the sons of Ulla—Arah, and Hanniel, and Rizia.

" 'All these,' " he finished, " 'were the children of Asher, heads of the fathers' houses, choice and mighty men of valour, chiefs of princes. And the number of them reckoned by genealogy for service in war was twenty and six thousand men.' "

He closed the Bible. The courtroom was very quiet. Douglas walked up and took the book from him. Judge Scott looked down at his hands, up to the plaster of the ceiling, anywhere but at Jeremiah.

"I think you can go back to our table now, Jeremiah," Douglas murmured.

Jeremiah's feet hardly seemed to touch the ground as he returned to his place. He heard Caleb Gillen whisper to his father, "I'm so sorry, sir. It's my fault he can read at all. I went and put ideas in his head, and see the thanks we get."

There was enough truth in that to sting, a little. Yes, Caleb had taught Jeremiah to read, but he was forgetting, in the way that was so easy for someone used to thinking of people as belongings, that Jeremiah had wanted to be free long before he could pick out the word "liberty" on the printed page. Caleb had been willing enough to help last summer, when Jeremiah's goal seemed indefinitely far away. Now that it was here, Caleb was finding he did not like it so well.

"Mr. Hayes?" Judge Kemble said, and then again, more sharply, "Mr. Hayes?"

Jeremiah had thought Hayes would have to give in— despite having worked so long for Douglas, he was still naive about lawyers. Hayes slowly rose, long and angular. He made a production out of stretching.

"Begging your excellency's pardon," he said, perfectly self-possessed. "I was woolgathering there. In considering this case, you must remember that it bears on not a single individual but, by the census of '98, close to a million persons of African descent. What of their masters' property rights? Further, assuming that by some mischance they should become free, how are they to provide for themselves? And how will they take their place in a society of free men? Freedom bestowed as a gift will mean nothing to them, as they will have done nothing to earn it."

Judge Hardesty nodded thoughtfully. That frightened Jeremiah, who had come to think of the quiet judge as being on his side. "What are we going to do?" he asked harshly.

Douglas might as well not have heard him. He waited till he was sure Hayes had finished, then heaved his bulk upright. "When a man shifts his argument from principle to expediency," he remarked, "trust neither. My learned opponent is looking to sow panic where none need exist; he speaks as if we were on the point of civil war. Why do we have courts, if not to treat our abuses before we need the medicine solders give?"

"Very pretty," Hayes said. "You answer none of the points I raised, but very pretty nonetheless."

"Had you not interrupted me, I would have answered,"

Douglas replied sweetly. "I don't presume to make the law, but I can offer some suggestions. You quoted the ancients when it suited your purpose. They had their ways of dealing with freed men, and of easing them into the life of the state. Perhaps some of the first generation would remain as clients to their one-time masters, working for a wage for some length of time before severing all obligations. Given a few years and good will, the thing can be done painlessly."

Hearing Douglas propose curtailing his freedom made Jeremiah scowl. He hated the thought of going back to work for the Gillens, even as a free man. But a moment's reflection reminded him that before he had been willing enough to stay on as a slave, so long as he was treated well and had some hope of buying his liberty one day. He had run away from maltreatment, not slavery.

And, he realized, other blacks would not face the problem of ex-owners with grudges as deep-seated as the Gillens' against him. Or would they? . . .

Zachary Hayes might have picked the thought from his brain. "Painlessly, eh?" he sneered, turning Douglas's word against him. "You can make all the laws you like, sir, but how do you propose making the good white men who built the Federated Commonwealths accept their niggers as their equals?" There was the heart of things, dragged out naked and bleeding.

Before Douglas could get up to respond, Jeremiah found himself on his feet. "Your excellencies, can I say something?"

Judge Kemble glanced toward Douglas, who looked startled but shrugged. "Is it germane?" the judge asked sternly.

"Sir?"

"Does it apply? Has it a bearing on the case here?"

"Oh. Yes, sir, that it does. Indeed it does."

"Very well. Be brief."

"Thank you, sir." Jeremiah took a deep breath. "Seems to me, sir, a lot of white folks needs to look down at niggers on account of they need to feel they're better'n somebody.

But even if you did free every nigger tomorrow, made 'em just the same as whites to the law, those whites would still know they were higher in the scheme of things than sims.

"Your excellencies, one of the things helped me get by so long as a slave was knowing the sims were there below me. Truth to tell," he went on, drawing on his thoughts of a few minutes before, "I didn't leave the Gillen farm till they stopped treating me like I was a man and worked me like a sim in the fields. That's purely not right, sirs, making a man into a sim, and if slavery lets one man do that to another, why, it's not right either. That's all."

He sat as abruptly as he had risen. Douglas leaned over and patted him on the back, murmuring, "Out to steal my job? You just might do it."

"Huh," Jeremiah said, but the praise warmed him.

The arguments went on; Hayes was not one to leave a case so long as he had breath to talk. But he and Douglas were hammering away at smaller points now, thrashing round the edges of things. Douglas got in only one shot he thought telling, a reminder of the historic nature of the case.

"That's for Kemble's sake," he told Jeremiah during a recess. "Letting him think people will remember his name forever for the sake of what he does here can't hurt."

Jeremiah thought about that, and contrasted it to Caleb Gillen's picture of the law as a vast impersonal force poised over the heads of miscreants. He preferred Douglas's way of looking at things. People were easier to deal with than vast impersonal forces.

Jeremiah Gillen walked down Granby Pike toward the Benjamin and Levi Bank of Portsmouth. Money jingled in his pocket. Even if the Conscript Fathers of Virginia decided to set up a clientage system like the one Alfred Douglas had outlined the year before, by now he had enough money to buy himself out of any further service to the family that had once owned him.

Hayes was still appealing his case, of course, sending up

writ after writ based on Judge Scott's narrow interpretation of the law. But Judge Hardesty had been as narrowly for Jeremiah as Scott was against him, and Judge Kemble's ringing condemnation of human slavery would be hard to overturn. Douglas had been dead right about him, Jeremiah thought—he must have decided the eyes of history were on him.

A sim struggling along with a very fat knapsack bumped into Jeremiah. "Watch where you're going, you brainless flathead," he snapped.

The sim cringed. It managed to get one hand free of its burden for a moment to sign, *Sorry.* Then it staggered on.

Jeremiah felt briefly ashamed. After all, were it not for sims, blacks would have been at the bottom of things, the target of everyone's spleen.

He almost went after the subhuman to apologize, but the sim would never have understood. And that was exactly the point.

He kept on toward the bank.

Trapping Run

The range where bands of wild sims could continue to live their lives much as they had before Europeans came to North America continued to shrink as human settlements pushed westward. Few bands remained entirely untouched by human influence. Sign-talk, for example, spread from band to band, even in areas where no people had ever been seen, because it was a conspicuously better means of communication than the subhumans' native assortment of noises and gestures.

Some trappers and explorers were friendly with the wild sims through whose lands they passed. Others, manifestly, were not. Bands of sims, naturally, often responded in kind, being well-disposed toward humans if the first person they met had been friendly to them, and hostile even to those who would not have harmed them if their first experience with humans had been a bad one. In this as in so much else, sims revealed how closely they resembled people.

In colonial days, and in the early years of the

Federated Commonwealths, sims' differences from us counted for more than their similarities. This was an attitude not without its good points for, as we have seen, it helped emphasize the essential likeness of all races of people. It also resulted, however, in the ruthless exploitation of sims by humans and, on and beyond the frontier, sometimes in sims' being hunted as if they were no more than wild beasts.

Trappers acquired a particularly evil reputation for their treatment of sims. And yet, as events transpired, it was a trapper who began what came to be known as the sims' justice movement. . . .

From *The Story of the Federated Commonwealths*

SILENT AS DRIFTING smoke, the sim stepped into the forest clearing where Henry Quick made his camp. The sim's hairy hand grasped a steel knife; its arms were bloody to the elbows.

Something—perhaps the first hint of its strong odor cutting through the damp sweetness of the air in the clearing—told Quick of its presence. He turned. He was a dark, stocky man whose deliberate motions belied his name.

"Sit by the fire," he said, though he knew his words were wasted. It did not matter. As he spoke, his fingers moved in the hand-talk even the wild sims here beyond the Rockies used these days. Their mouths could not shape human speech, but hand-talk let them convey far more complex ideas than did their native hoots and grunts and cries.

As the sim hunkered down beside him, Quick shook his head, surprised he had spoken at all. When he was out on a trapping run he seldom talked, even to himself, and when he did he was as apt to use signs as words.

He shrugged. Nothing wrong with talking, if he felt like it. As if to prove the point to himself, he spoke out loud again: "What do you have there for me?" Once more, his fingers echoed his words; not enough people yet crossed the mountains for the sims hereabouts to have learned to understand English.

The sim grinned, displaying broad yellow teeth. *Good fur*, it signed. Its gestures were less crisp than Quick's, not as fully realized; in their transmission through who knew how many bands of sims, the signs had grown sketchy, attenuated. But Quick followed its meaning, as a city man will grasp his country cousin's rude dialect. And, of course, the marten fur the sim held out spoke for itself.

Good fur, Quick agreed after examining it. The sim had done a neat, careful job of case-skinning, cutting from the center of the hind claws up the hind legs, across the anus and belly, and down the forelegs. The soft, plushy pelt had no extra knife holes in it to lower its value. The sim had either caught the marten in a snare of its own devising or, much more likely, brought it down with a well-flung stone.

Under their beetling brow ridges, the sim's eyes grew intent. *You give how much?* it signed.

Quick considered. *You*—he repeated the sign to make it apply to the whole band, not just the sim in front of him— *have flint, steel*.

Have, the sim echoed. Along with signs, fire-making tools had spread to the wild sims. When humans had settled North America more than two centuries ago, the native subhumans had known how to use fire and keep it alive, but not how to start it if ever it went out. Their wits, though weaker than people's, were not dull enough to miss the advantage of that.

Want hatchet? Quick asked.

Show. The sim's wide, hairy face remained impassive, but its member rose to betray its eagerness. "Get their peckers up and you got a deal" was an adage everyone who traded with sims knew.

Quick rose, ambled over to his pack, took out three hatchets. *Pick*, he offered. All three were heavier, in both head and handle, than he would have cared for himself. Sims, though, were stronger than men, and did not care for tools as humans did. Clumsy ones suited them fine.

The sim hefted all three, chose one, swung it through the air, and let out a hoot of delight. It walked over to a sapling, chopped it down with a few hard swings. Then it checked the edge of the hatchet head with its thumb. It hooted again. *Still sharp, no chips,* it signed. *Good.* In spite of its metal knife, it was still used to the chipped stones sims made for themselves.

Good, Henry Quick agreed. He had paid fifty sesters for the hatchet back in Cairo; the marten fur would be worth easily twenty times as much. Some people in the cities of the Federated Commonwealths called that robbery. Quick did not see it that way. Back on the other side of the mountains, hatchets were easy to come by, marten furs much less so. The situation was reversed here. Accounts balanced.

Too, back in the cities of the Commonwealths, Quick would have had to put up with the stink of coal smoke, railroad noise, and the endless presence of people. He had little use for pointless chatter. Maybe that was one reason he got on well with sims: they lacked the brains to talk when they did not have something to say.

Some trappers, Quick knew, treated sims like wolves or foxes or any other vermin, and hunted them savagely. Sims robbed traps, no doubt of that. They were hungry all the time, and meat already caught was easy meat. Quick was sure the sim in the clearing with him had eaten the marten's carcass as soon as the pelt was off it.

In a way, Quick followed the reasoning of the trappers who went after sims. Because of their hands and wits, sims made devilish thieves. But those same hands and wits made them dangerous enemies. By the nature of things, trappers traveled alone or in small groups. The ones who came down hardest on sims often never returned.

Quick had always felt that making them into allies worked better. His initial expense was greater because of the trade goods he bought before every journey, but he thought he got more furs by enlisting the sims' aid than by harassing them. He found a trap robbed every now and again, yes, but more often were cases like this one, sims doing his hunting for him.

The subhuman flourished the hatchet again, making the air sigh. *Good,* it signed, and left the clearing with no more farewell than that. Henry Quick was not offended; he had scant use for ceremony himself.

He stretched the skin, fur side in, on a piece of wood, and set it aside to dry. He did not have many marten pelts back at his base camp, which made him doubly glad for this one.

He also thought he would have to be a lot hungrier than he was, to want to eat marten meat.

He walked the trap line to check the snares he had set within a couple of miles of the clearing. Blazes he had cut on trees at eye level guided him from one trap to the next. As far as he knew, sims had not figured out what blazes were for. He had several sets of traps within the territory this band wandered, each grouped around a clearing. He tried to make a complete circuit every couple of weeks or so, to make sure none of the beasts he caught decomposed enough to harm their pelts.

His nose guided him to the first trap. He shook his head in annoyance. The trap must have taken a victim almost as soon as he reset it the last time through. He was doubly annoyed when he found the metal jaws holding only a striped ground squirrel, whose skin would have been worthless even if fresh. Doubly disgusted, he threw the little corpse away, set the trap again, stuck on a fresh suet bait, and went on to the next one.

Something, probably a bird but maybe a sim, had stolen the bait from that trap without springing it. Quick sighed and replaced it. The bait on the trap after that was still intact. Quick sighed again; he'd have to think about moving it.

When he neared the next trap, he heard a wild, desperate thrashing. He drew his pistol and sidled forward, soft leather boots sliding soundlessly over dirt and grass, leaves and twigs. Catching a sim in the act of robbing a trap would be tricky; finding one caught in a trap might be worse, for that could turn the whole band against him.

His breath hissed out in relief as he saw that the trap held only a fox. The animal must have been fighting the spiked iron teeth for some time. It was nearly exhausted, and lay panting as Quick approached. His mouth tightened. This was the part of his job he tried not to think about; taking a dead animal from a trap was much easier than dealing with a live one there.

No help for it, he thought. On his belt by his pistol he carried a stout bludgeon for times such as this. He set the gun down, drew it out. The fox's yellow eyes stared un-blinkingly at him. Next to the torment of its trapped and broken leg, he was as nothing. He brought down the bludgeon once, twice. The fox writhed and twitched for a few minutes, then sighed, almost in relief, and lay still.

He sat not far from the body, waiting for it to cool and the fleas and other pests to leave it. Then he pried apart the jaws of the trap, rolled the fox onto its back, and began to skin it. He always took pains at that, and took extra ones today, with the memory of the marten fur still fresh—he did not want any sim's work to outdo his.

So intent was he that he had almost finished before he realized he was not alone. A sim stood a few paces away, intently watching him. It was a female, he saw with some surprise—unlike the males, they did not usually stray far from the clearing where a band was staying. He kept away from that clearing. Of all his traps, this one was probably closest to it, but it was still a good mile away.

Female sims, Henry Quick thought, were not so brutal-looking as males. Their features were not as heavy, and the bony ridges above their eyes were less pronounced. That did not mean the sim would have made an attractive woman. It lacked both forehead and chin, and short reddish hair covered more of its face than Quick's brown beard concealed of his own.

Like all sims, it wore no clothes, but like all sims, it was hairy enough not to need them. Even its breasts were covered with hair, though the pinkish-brown nipples at their tips were exposed. It had an unwashed reek like that of the one that had traded Quick the marten pelt.

Take skin? it signed. That, at any rate, was what Quick thought it meant. He had trouble being sure; it could not use its fingers well because its hands were full of roots and grubs, and its gestures were blurry in any case.

Yes, he answered.

He must have understood correctly, for its next question was, *Why club, not noise-stick?* It pointed at his pistol.

Not want hole in skin, he signed.

It rubbed its long jaw as it considered that, then grunted, exactly like a person who got an unexpected answer that was still satisfying.

As if putting a hand to its face had reminded it of the food it carried, it popped a grub into its mouth, chewed noisily, and swallowed. Like most wild sims, it was on the lean side. Quick glanced down at the fox carcass. To him, it was so much carrion. Not to sims. *Want meat?* he asked.

Me? It pointed to itself, brown eyes wide with surprise. Male sims hunted, females gathered; probably, Quick thought, this one had never taken anything bigger than a mouse or ground squirrel. But it did not need much time to decide. *Want meat,* it signed firmly, leaving off the gesture that turned the phrase into a question.

Quick handed the fox's body to the sim. It gave a low hoot as it stared at the unaccustomed burden it held. It turned to leave, then looked back at the trapper, as if it expected him to take back the bounty he had given. *Keep. Go,* he signed. It hooted again and slipped away.

Henry Quick went in a different direction, off to check his next trap. As he walked, he chuckled quietly to himself. There would likely be consternation among the sims tonight, especially if the males had had a luckless day at the chase.

The trapper paused for a moment, frowning. He did not want his gift to land the female sim in trouble. Among humans, that might happen if a woman stepped into men's territory. With sims, on reflection, he did not think it would. Being less clever than humans, sims lacked much of their capacity for jealousy. Their harsh lives also made them relentless pragmatists. Meat would be meat, no matter where it came from.

Quick found a rabbit in his last trap. It was freshly dead. He skinned it, cleaned it, and brought it back to the clearing.

His pack of trade goods was undisturbed. Had he been one of the trappers who habitually maltreated sims, he would not have dared leave it behind . . . but then, had he been one of that sort, he would not have dared travel alone in this land where men had not yet settled.

He started his fire again, spitted the rabbit on a stick, and held it over the little blaze. The savory smell the lean meat gave off made his nostrils twitch and his mouth grow suddenly wet. He smiled, wondering what roast fox smelled like.

When he woke the next morning, he rolled up his blanket and went over to wash in a creek that ran near the clearing. The water was bitterly cold; he shivered all the way back to his campfire, and stood gratefully in front of it until he was dry. No wonder sims did not bathe, he thought as he dressed. And this was still August, with the days hot and muggy. In another month, though, snow could start falling among the peaks of the Rockies, the ultimate source of his little stream. He would have to think about heading back to inhabited country soon, unless he wanted to spend a long, cold winter living with the sims.

"Not bloody likely," he said out loud. No trapper had a lot of use for his fellow humans, but Quick ached to spend a couple of days with good bouncy company in a bordello. He was bored with his hand.

His next set of traps surrounded a clearing a few miles northwest of this one. The way was blazed, and to guide him if he got lost he had a sketch map and a list of landmarks he had made when he first scouted this territory. Except for the ones he had given them, none of the places hereabouts had names. No other man, so far as he knew, had seen them.

The behavior of the local sims certainly argued for that.

They had neither fled from him on his first appearance nor attacked him on sight. Having no hostile memories to overcome made establishing himself much easier than it would have been otherwise.

As if thinking of the sims had conjured them up, Quick heard a crashing in the undergrowth off to one side of him and the hoarse, excited cries of several males. They must have been chasing something big, most likely a deer. They were tireless trackers, and more skilled even than an outdoorsman like Henry Quick. They had no guns with which to kill at a distance, but had to rely on thrown stones and spears either tipped with fire-hardened wood or made from a knife, gained in trade, lashed to the end of a sapling.

The sims' voices rose in a chorus of triumph. They would eat well tonight, and for the next couple of days. Quick's stomach rumbled. He was not so sure of a good meal himself. When he got to the clearing that formed the center for his next set of traps, he set down his pack and went out to do some hunting of his own.

He came back near sunset, seething with frustration beneath the calm shell he cultivated. The sims had had more luck than he. He was carrying a squirrel by the tail, but there wasn't much meat on a squirrel. He made a fire, coated the squirrel with wet clay, and set it among the flames to bake.

When he thought it was done, he nudged it out of the fire with a stick and began breaking the now-hard clay with the hilt of his dagger. The squirrel's fur and skin came away with the clay, leaving behind sweet, tender meat ready to eat.

Quick, unfortunately, also remained quite ready to eat after the squirrel was gone. Along with his trade goods, he still had about ten pounds of dried, smoked buffalo meat in his pack. He worried every time he decided to gnaw on a strip—he might need it later. He was only a little hungry now, he told himself severely. He turned his back on the pack, avoiding temptation.

A noise in the darkness beyond the edge of the clearing sent ice darting up his back and made him forget his belly.

He grabbed for his rifle, peering out to see what sort of beast was prowling round his camp. Light came back red from wolves' eyes, green from those of a spearfang. Even with the gun in his hand, he shivered at the thought of confronting one of the great cats at night.

Try as he would, he saw nothing. A moment later, he realized why. A male sim stepped into the flickering circle of light his campfire threw. Like the eyes of humans, sims' eyes did not reflect the light that reached them.

The male came toward him slowly, deliberately. He saw it was the one that had brought him the marten fur. It carried its knife in one hand, the hatchet he had traded it in the other. Neither weapon was raised, and the sim showed no hostility. Still, Quick stayed wary. No sim had ever visited him at night before.

He did not set aside his rifle until the sim put down what it carried. Even then he had misgivings. Sims were stronger than people; if this one chose to grapple with him, he was in trouble.

But it had only freed its hands so it could use signs. *You give food*, it signed, amplifying, *Meat. You give to female*.

Yes, Quick agreed. *I not eat fox, not want to*—He hesitated. Hand-talk had no way to express *waste*; the concept was alien to the sim mind. —*put aside*, he finished lamely.

Why not eat fox? Meat good, the sim signed, and the trapper's tight nerves finally eased a bit. Still, the male's next question took him by surprise: *Hungry now?*

Yes, he signed again, with a rueful glance in the direction he had thrown the squirrel's small bones.

Then he was surprised all over again, for the sim signed, *You come with me to our fire, eat there.*

Go there? he asked, not quite believing he had seen correctly. He had always made a point of staying away from the clearing the sims used as their own. That was partly what with people he would have called politeness, but more the simple desire not to draw unwelcome attention to himself. Well, he seemed to have drawn attention, but not of the unwelcome sort.

Come to our fire, the sim repeated. Although almost every wild band owned flint and steel now, fire and the memory of the time when they had not been able to make it still loomed large in sims' lives. *Fire* meant to this male what *home* meant to Henry Quick.

I come, he signed, stepping toward the sim.

It picked up its weapons, signed *Follow,* and plunged into the woods. Quick followed, as best he could. Again he was reminded how wild sims perforce became masters of forest craft. The sim glided along so quietly that he felt slow and clumsy by comparison; sometimes only its lingering odor let him stay close to it. He suspected it could have gone faster had it not been leading him.

Blinking on in front of his nose, a firefly made him jump. Other than that, the forest was impenetrably dark. The sim pressed on with perfect confidence.

Just when Quick was beginning to wonder if anything lay behind that confidence, he scented woodsmoke on the breeze. The sim must also have caught the smell, for it said *"Hoo!"*—a breathy, throaty noise, the first sound it had made all night—and hurried ahead. A moment later, Quick smelled charring meat along with the smoke. He hurried too, and soon saw light ahead.

The male hooted before it entered the clearing where its band was staying. Answering calls came back to it. They made Henry Quick think of shouts heard on the breeze, with the words blown away but the sense—here, welcome—remaining.

Quiet fell as the trapper stepped into the open area. With the male sims, it was a measuring sort of silence. Quick had encountered most of the dozen or so of them as they and he hunted; he had traded tools for furs with more than half of them. Meeting them as a group, though, emphasized the differences between him and them as solitary contacts could not.

The females and youngsters, on the other hand, had never seen him before, except for the one to whom he'd given the fox carcass. Their stillness was more than a little fearful. But they were curious too. A child (for the life of him, Quick could find no better word, especially since young sims, like grown females, had a more human semblance than did grown males) of perhaps seven came up to him. It touched his suede trousers and tunic, then looked up at him, the picture of puzzlement. *Strange skin*, it signed.

A couple of males growled warningly, and one hefted a stone as Quick stretched out his arm. All he did, though, was roll up the fringed sleeve of his tunic to show what lay beneath. *No hair*, he signed. That was not strictly true, but by sim standards he might as well have been bald. *Put on animal skins instead. Warm.*

The youngster felt the trapper's bare skin, jerked its hand away with a grimace. *Hair better*, it signed.

Startled, Quick burst out laughing. The sims laughed too, loud and long. The male that had been holding a stone threw it on the ground, came over to Quick, and hugged him hard enough to make his ribs creak. He wished he could have taken more credit for winning acceptance, but was glad to get it no matter how it came.

The male that had brought him tugged him toward the fire. *Eat*, it signed, and the trapper needed no further invitation.

One leg still remained from the carcass of a buck—likely, Quick thought, the one he had heard the males chasing. The rest was bones, the big ones split to get out the marrow and the skull crushed for the sake of the brains.

A grizzled male had charge of the meat. As Henry Quick came over, the sim picked up a chipped stone and began to carve off a chunk for him. He started to offer his own steel knife instead, but stopped when he saw the stone tool gliding through the leg of venison. A steel knife lasted almost forever, was easy to hone again and again, and did not chip. None of that, however, meant stone could not be sharp.

Quick's eyes widened slightly at the size of the piece the old sim gave him. *Too much*, he signed. *Not eat all.*

The sim shrugged and grunted. *Someone*, it answered. *Someone will if you don't*, Quick thought it meant. Even the single gesture had been hesitant. The trapper wondered when hand-talk had reached this band. Maybe it was so recently that the old sim had already been grown and only learned it imperfectly, as a man will have trouble speaking a foreign language he acquires after his youth.

Watching the meat bubble and brown as he held it on a stick over the fire drove such speculation from his mind. Beside him, the sim that had brought him here was roasting an even larger piece. Less patient with cooking than he, it jerked its gobbet away from the flames, tossed it from hand to hand until it was cool enough to eat, then tore off one great bite after another. The venison disappeared with astonishing haste.

Quick sat beside the sim and tried valiantly to match its pace, but its bigger teeth and bigger appetite meant he was outclassed. Since they starved so much of the time, sims made the most of good days like this one. The trapper was groaningly full by the time half his piece was gone, yet by then the male had almost finished and showed no signs of slowing down.

He was thinking of offering it what was left of his venison when another sim touched him on the knee. He turned round to see the female he had met the day before. The female held out its left hand in a begging gesture, signing *Meat?* with the right.

He cut off a piece and gave it to the sim. Two youngsters were begging from the male next to him, which gave them some scraps. A little one that could hardly toddle came up to one of the children with its hand out, and in turn received a few tiny fragments of meat. It stared at the trapper as it ate.

The male turned to Quick. *More*, it signed, getting up and walking over to pluck a handful of whortleberries off a pile of branches heavy with the large, purple-blue fruit. The trapper ate a few himself; their tart sweetness cut through the greasy film coating the inside of his mouth.

Both males and females freely took the berries; no begging was involved. Only dearly won meat required that. Though they usually shared their prey, the males who hunted had some prior claim on it. With a burst of pride that made him feel foolish a moment later, Quick realized the female sim had treated him as if he were a hunter himself, a dominant member of the band.

Despite that acceptance, he remained an object of curiosity. That, he knew, was natural enough—he was probably the first *live* creature ever to share the band's campsite. If they changed their minds about him, he might not stay that way, either. Sims sometimes ate sims from other bands and, when they could catch them, people too. A good many such grisly episodes punctuated man's westward expansion across America.

But this group found him only interesting. The grizzled elder that tended the meat ran its hands over his clothes, as fascinated by the soft suede as the youngster had been. *Make*, it signed, and then, after obvious painful groping for the sign, *How?*

Skins cut to arms, legs, chest. Not stink—rub tree bark— not any tree, right tree. As a trapper, he knew how to tan hides; what he could not do was put it in terms the sim understood. *Show one day*, he promised. If a sim saw something done, it could copy as well as a human. But sims would not improve on a process, as humans might.

Show, the old sim agreed. It pointed to Quick's fancy silver belt buckle. *Show?*

Regretfully, he shook his head. He knew nothing of metalworking, save that it was too complex for the subhumans to fathom.

His person fascinated the sims as much as his gear. They pointed at his gray eyes, then at their own, which were uniformly dark. He had to roll up his sleeve several times, and take off his boots to show that under them his feet were like theirs, if less battered and callused. His forehead, though, intrigued the sims most. They kept patting at it to compare it to their own heads, which sloped sharply back from their brow-ridges instead of rising.

He shuddered at the idea of eking out a living with so few
resources to use to challenge nature. He shuddered even
more when he thought of doing so through the winters
hereabouts. On the face of it, it seemed impossible. The
female to whom he had given the fox carcass was close by.
He signed, *How live, when snow come?*

Bad, the sim signed, repeating for emphasis. *Hard. Cold.
Hungry. Many die in cold.* A shiver illustrated the idea. Far
more fluent with her signs than the elder had been, the
female went on, *Dens like bears'—brush, branches. Still
cold. Make fire. Still cold. Cold. Cold. Cold.* The sim's eyes
widened with dread. Winter was a worse enemy than
spearfang or bear.

With their bellies full, though, the sims, never reflective
in the first place, did not care to look ahead. The youngsters
ran through the clearing, wrestled with one another, and
pestered their elders, for all the world like so many unruly
children back in Cairo or Portsmouth or Philadelphia.
Some of the adults made beds of branches and leaves, curled
up, and went to sleep, ignoring the youngsters' squawks
and shouts. A mother nursed a baby. The old sim and a
young adult male squatted by the fire, chipping stones. The
young adult absently swatted at a youngster that disturbed
them. When it came back to watch what they were doing,
the male let it stay.

Other adults had a different idea for passing the time.
Three or four couples paired off and mated. The rest of the
sims paid them no particular attention, nor did they seem
to feel the lack of privacy. When a running youngster was
about to crash into one pair, the male reached out from its
position on its knees behind the female to fend off the little
one.

Henry Quick found the rutting sims no more interesting
than did the rest of the band. He had been away from
women a long time, but not long enough to think of a sim
as a partner. He would as soon have coupled with a pack
mare.

Some trappers, he knew, did that. Some mated with sims, too. He knew what he thought of them: the same as most people thought. "You son of a sim" would start a fight anywhere in the Commonwealths.

Thus he was taken by surprise when the female sim to whom he had given the fox meat touched him on the leg again, this time much higher up than before. *Want—?* the female signed. The last gesture it used was not a standard part of hand-talk, but not easy to get wrong, either.

To remove any possible misunderstanding, the female crouched on hands and knees, looking back over its shoulder at him. Neither that nor the sight of its cleft between hairy and rather boyish buttocks did anything to rouse his ardor.

No, he signed; hand-talk was not made for tact. He softened his refusal as much as he could: *You, I not same.*

The sim, luckily, seemed more curious than angry. *Not fit?* it asked, eyeing his crotch as if to gauge what his trousers concealed. He left that unanswered. He had seen enough sims to know their masculinity was hardly so rampant as jokes and stories made it out to be, but he was no more than average that way himself.

Not want—? the female signed after a moment, and used that gesture of its own invention again.

Full, Quick temporized. He patted his stomach.

Apparently that impeded performance among sims too, because the female gave a small, regretful hoot. *Later?* it signed.

The trapper shrugged and spread his hands. *You, I not same,* he repeated. The female shrugged too, and went off to get a few more whortleberries. To Henry Quick's relief, it did not come back to him. He'd meant to imply that men and sims were so different no offspring could come from a mating. He did not know whether the sim was bright enough to follow that. He did know it was a lie.

He had never seen a crossbreed. The repugnance almost everyone felt for coupling with the subhumans had a lot to do with that: few of mixed blood were born. Fewer still lived. The human parents in the matings usually made sure of that, to save themselves from disgrace. The ones that did survive were good for driving lawyers to distraction, and for a host of tales whose truth the trapper was in no position to judge.

He yawned. Back by his own campfire, he would have been asleep hours ago. Here he had neither his own blanket nor the nests sims made for themselves. He stretched out on the ground. The big blaze the sims had going was plenty to keep him warm. He was tired enough not to worry about sleeping soft. He rolled over, threw aside a twig that was poking his cheek, and knew nothing more till the sun rose.

He woke with a crick in his neck and a bladder full to bursting. He walked into the bushes at the edge of the clearing to relieve himself. By the smell, and by the way his boots squelched once or twice on the short journey, the sims were not so fastidious.

They had already begun their endless daily round of foraging. Henry Quick was glad to see that the importunate female was gone from the campsite. Otherwise, he thought with wry amusement, it might have wanted to go into the bushes with him to see just what sort of apparatus he had.

The males, who hunted in a group rather than scattering one by one, were still by the fire. The trapper went up to the one that had guided him here. *Good food,* he signed.

He had a spare bootlace in one of the pouches that hung from his belt. He dug it out. Yes, it was long enough for him to cut a couple of lengths from the end and still do what he wanted with it. He cut off the extra pieces, tied them to the main length at one end, and made loops at the other end of each. Then he tied the makeshift belt round the sim's middle.

Carry knife, axe, he signed. *Have them to use. Have hands free.* The sim did not seem to understand. It rubbed its chinless jaw, staring at Quick, but made no move to put the tools in the loops.

The old grizzled male looked from the trapper's belt to the leather lace he had given the other sim. Its eyes lit. It let out a soft hiss of wonder; Quick remembered making that very same noise when, as a boy, he had seen his first steam railroad engine.

The grizzled sim stepped forward, took the knife from the younger male's hand, and thrust it through one loop. Then it pointed, first at the hatchet, then at the second loop. It gave an imperative barking call, pointed again. It might never have learned hand-talk well, Henry Quick thought, but its years had given it a wisdom of its own.

After it repeated its gestures a third time, the younger sim finally got the idea. It pushed the hatchet handle into the vacant loop; the head kept the hatchet from falling through. The sim looked at its empty hands, at the tools it still had with it. Suddenly it grinned an enormous grin. *Good,* it signed at Quick. *Good. Good. Good.*

Have more? another male asked. *Make?*

No more. Henry Quick apologetically spread his hands. He suggested, *Make from plants, from skins—*

The old sim could follow hand-talk, no matter how much trouble it had using the gestures. *Make,* it signed, and pointed to itself. Before long, Quick suspected, every sim in the band, or at least every hunting male, would be sporting a belt. Some would be made of vines and would break, others of green hides that would stink and get hard and wear out quickly. They would be better than no belts at all, he supposed.

He was pleased to have found something to give in exchange for the feast of the night before. Sims had so little that he was surprised they had offered to share, in spite of his earlier gift. Now they were less likely to resent him for accepting.

In daylight, the journey back to his trap line took less than half as long as it had by night. When he returned to the clearing where his latest camp was, he checked his pack. No sims had been near it, though they never would have had a better chance to steal. On the other hand, he thought, smiling, they'd had plenty just as good.

He went the round of the traps near the clearing, reset the

ones that needed it, and dealt with the couple of furs he had
taken. He should have had one more; a trap still held the
bloody hind leg of a ringtail. That was all that was left of
the black-masked beast, though. When he first saw the
tracks around the trap, he thought the sims had robbed him
after all. Then he noticed the claw marks in front of the
toes. A bear had taken the chance to seize prey that could
not flee.

He swore, but resignedly; that sort of thing had happened
to him many times before, and would again. Bears could be
as big a nuisance as sims. Some bands of sims, like the one
in whose territory he was now, could be made to see that
working with him got them more than robbing him did.
The only thing a bear understood was a bullet.

A grouse boomed, somewhere off among the spruces.
Henry Quick forgot about the bear, at least with the front
part of his mind. He sidled toward the noise. The grouse's
dull-brown feathers concealed it on its perch, but not well
enough. He got almost close enough to knock it down with
a club before he shot it.

He bled and gutted the bird, handling the gall bladder
with care so it would not break and spill its noxious
contents into the body cavity. He wished he were back at his
base camp; the grouse would be better eating after hanging
for several days. But he was on the move, and had no time
for such refinements. The dark, rich meat would be plenty
good enough tonight.

So it proved, though he roasted it a couple of minutes too
long; grouse was best rare. He would have liked to flavor it
with some bacon instead of crumbs from his salt beef, but
the rashers he'd brought were long gone; he'd eaten them as
soon as they began to go rancid.

Picking his teeth with the point of his knife, he laughed
at himself. All this fretting about fancy cooking was a sure
sign he'd been in the wilderness too long. That night he
dreamt of eating pastry full of fruit and cream until he had
to cut a new notch in his belt, in its own way as sensual a
dream as his more usual imaginings of sweet-scented girls

reaching up to him from featherbeds thick enough to smother in.

Waking hungry to a blanket in the middle of a forest clearing was hard. Even eating what was left of the grouse did not help much, though it would have been an expensive luxury if ordered in a cafe east of the mountains. Too much of what he did involved things that were expensive luxuries east of the mountains. What he craved were the luxuries he could *only* get back there.

The intensity of that craving ended up undoing him. The next clearing around which he had a set of traps was over on the west side of the one the sims used. The trail he had blazed to it swung a lot farther north than it had to, so he could give the sims' clearing a wide berth. Now that the subhumans had shown how friendly they were, he decided to take the direct route. If he did that the rest of the time he was there, he thought, he could save several days' travel and set out for the fleshpots of the east that much sooner. The sims, he told himself, would not mind.

Nor did they. He happened on a party of hunting males not long after he set out. Several saw him, and nodded his way as they might have to one of their own band. But he had not reckoned on the bear.

For all his woodscraft, the first he knew of it was when it loomed up on its hind legs like some ancient, brooding god, not fifty feet from him. In that moment he had a good shot at its chest and belly, but he held his fire. Bears, even silvered bears like this one, rarely attacked without being provoked.

But it did not do to count on a bear, either. This one peered his way. He was close enough to see its nostrils flare as it took his scent. It gave an oddly piglike grunt, dropped to all fours, and barreled toward him.

He threw his rifle to his shoulder, fired, and ran. The bear screamed. He heard its thunderous stride falter. But it still came on, roaring its pain to the world and crashing through bushes and firs like a runaway railroad engine. And in a sprint a bear, even a wounded bear, is faster than a man.

Henry Quick wished he had time to reload. Back in Plymouth Commonwealth, he had heard before he set out on this trapping run, they had most of the kinks out of a repeating rifle. He would have given five years' worth of furs to have one now. He threw away the gun he did have so he could run faster. If he lived, he'd come back for it.

He never remembered feeling the blow that shattered his right leg. All he knew at the time was that, instead of sprinting in one direction, he was suddenly spinning and rolling through the undergrowth in a very different one. That saved his life. The bear had to change directions too, and it was also hurt.

In the second or two its hobbling charge gave him, he jerked out his pistol, cocked it, and squeezed the trigger. He seemed to have forever to shoot. His hand was steady, with the eerie steadiness the shock of a bad injury can bring. The bear's mouth gaped in a horrible snarl; the pistol ball shattered a fang before burying itself in the beast's brain. The bear sighed and fell over, dead.

"God, that was close," the trapper said in a calm, conversational voice. He started to pull himself to his feet—and the instant he tried to put any weight on his leg, all the pain his nervous system had denied till then flooded over him. He fainted before he could shriek.

The sun had moved a fair distance across the sky when he came back to himself. The moment he did, he wished he could escape to unconsciousness again. He tasted blood, and realized he had bitten his lip. He had not noticed. That pain was a trickle, set against the all-consuming torrent in his leg.

Tears were streaming down his face by the time he managed to sit up; the world had threatened to gray out several times in the process. His trouser leg was wet too, not only from where he'd pissed himself while unconscious but also farther down, where the bear had struck him. Blood was soaking through the suede.

He held himself steady with one hand in a thorn bush while he walked the other down his leg to the injury. Something hard and sharp was pressing against the inside of his trousers. He groaned, this time not just from the pain. With a compound fracture—and heaven only knew how much other damage in there—he would soon be as dead as if the bear had killed him cleanly. He wished it had. This way hurt worse.

His hands shook so badly that he took a quarter of an hour to reload his pistol. A lead ball would end his misery no less than the bear's. But after the weapon was ready, he did not raise it to his head. If he had been able to charge it with powder and wadding and bullet, how could pain's grip on him be absolute?

He began to drag himself toward the bear. That took longer than loading the gun had, though the body was only a handful of paces from him: he passed out several times on the way. At last he reached the carcass. If he was going to try to live, he would need to eat. The bear was food, for as long as it stayed fresh.

The pistol ball left no visible wound, now that the bear's mouth was closed in death. Quick's first shot, with the rifle, had torn along the left side of the beast's neck and lodged in its shoulder. It might have been a mortal wound, but not quickly enough to do the trapper any good.

He tried to push the point of his broken shinbone back into his flesh, and failed repeatedly: the pain was too much to stand. He did drag himself to a sapling close by the bear's carcass and cut it down with his knife. Then, using the lace from his left boot, he tied the sapling to his leg. It was not much of a splint, but it was a little better than nothing. With it on, the broken pieces did not grind together quite so agonizingly.

He set out to make a fire, against the coming chill of night and the chill of his damaged body and for cooking a bloody gobbet he had worried off the bear's shoulder. He was still crumbling dry leaves for tinder when the hunting party of male sims came upon him.

He did not realize they were there until they were almost on top of him. Along with their crude weapons, they carried squirrels and rabbits, a snake, and a couple of birds:

not a great day's bag by any means. They looked in wonder from Henry Quick to the bear and back again. *You kill?* one asked. After a little while, he recognized it as the male that had brought him the marten fur.

Understanding its hand-talk and responding took all the concentration and strength the trapper had. *I kill bear,* he answered. *Bear hurt me—break leg bone.*

The sims grimaced. One gave an involuntary hiss of pain. Another pointed at the rude splint. *Why stick?*

Hold bone pieces still. Hurt less. Quick changed the subject; his leg did not hurt much less. He waved at the dead bear. *Cut up meat—take to your fire.* He could not hope to eat a twentieth part of it before it spoiled.

The sims could have done what they wanted with the bear no matter what he said, but his free giving of it seemed to take them aback. *Come with us, eat with us again?* signed the male he knew.

He had prayed it would ask that. The band of sims, he knew, was his only hope of living through the winter, though he had scorned the thought not long before. It was his only hope of living longer than a few days, come to that. Even if his leg healed well, he would not be able to travel for months. And with the injury he had, he had a bad feeling it would not heal well.

A male with a broken front tooth was signing at the one he knew best: *Kill,* it urged. *More meat.*

Kill, another male agreed. *No hunt, no walk. Lie by fire, eat. Cold soon. No food to give. No good to us. Kill.*

In other circumstances, Quick might have agreed with those sims. He would be a burden for the band, and one more mouth to feed when they went hungry themselves. Unless he could find a way to make himself valuable to them, he was done for. *Take me to fire, then take all tools in pack,* he offered.

One of the sims, unfortunately, was smart enough to see the flaw in that. *Kill, then take tools,* it signed.

He almost gave up then. Like a bullet, a spear going into his chest or a club breaking his head would put him out of his pain. But he had not shot himself, and he did not want to end as a feast for subhumans. He forced his battered wits to work. *Take me to fire, make more tools.* That was the best he could do. If it did not appeal to the sims, he was dinner.

The male that had brought him the marten pelt hooted. *Make noise-sticks?* it asked. He could see the eagerness on its broad features.

No, he signed, hating to have to do it. But even had he had metal to hand, he did not know how to make a gun. *Use noise-stick to kill game near fire.*

He happened to think of bows and arrows. They were rare in the Commonwealths, but some rich men back east liked to hunt with them, claiming they were more sporting than guns. Quick cared nothing for sport. He was interested in surviving. *Make thing like noise-stick, but quiet,* he signed.

Kill far like noise-stick? the male asked.

Not that far. Farther than spear.

The sims shouted at one another, not so much arguing as trying to intimidate. Finally the male that had brought Quick the marten fur signed *Take,* and pointed at him. He tried without much luck to stifle a shriek as two sims hauled him upright. Others fell to butchering the bear. Soon they were toting slabs of meat bigger than those a man could easily carry.

That strength also helped the pair over whose shoulders Quick had draped his arms. All the same, the journey to the band's clearing was a nightmare. It would have been dreadful even with careful men hauling the trapper. It was worse with sims. They were not deliberately cruel, but they were careless. Several times his broken leg hit the ground so hard he thought it would fall off. He rather wished it would. Mercifully, he passed out again before the hunting party got home.

The anguish when his bearers let him down like a sack of meal brought him back to himself. Sims were all he could see as he peered blearily upward. Their thick odor clogged his nostrils.

He felt blood flowing down his leg again. The thought of getting the sims to set the broken bone made him sweat cold, but leaving it untended was worse. *Take off stick*, he signed. *Take off boots, pants.* The sims grunted in puzzlement; the hand-talk gesture for trousers meant nothing to them, since they had never seen any except his. He pointed at his pair, and they understood. *Fix bone, put stick back on, put another stick on, hold bone in place.* He thought of something else. *Hold me down. I yell, you do anyhow.*

The sims hooted in dismay when they saw how he was hurt. *He die,* a female signed flatly.

He live, he make for us, answered the male he knew.

He live. That was another female. After a moment, he recognized it as the one that had wanted to couple with him. Well, no danger of that now, he thought, and even in his torment almost laughed.

The grizzled sim pushed forward. *Make?* it signed. *Good. Live.* That was the most sign-talk the trapper had ever seen from it.

He turned his head away. The sight of his red-smeared white tibia sticking through his flesh was making him even sicker than he felt already. *Push bone into leg,* he signed. *Make straight, like other leg.*

Till then, he had only thought he knew what pain was. Again, the sims were not cruel on purpose; again, that did not help. No one could have set the fracture without hurting him badly. That the would-be healers were inexperienced subhumans made things worse, but perhaps not by much.

Some unmeasurable time later, his agony lessened, if only by a tiny fraction. He chose to believe that was because the two pieces of bone were properly aligned. If not, he knew he could bear no more. His throat was raw from screaming; he could feel the blood slick on his hands, where his nails had bitten into his palms.

Tie sticks on, he signed. *Tie tight. Hold bones in place.* His senses failed him before the sims were done. This time they did not return to him at once.

When at last he woke again, the sun was in his eyes. It

was in the wrong part of the sky. It was, he realized, the next morning. His leg felt dreadful, which was a marvelous improvement on how it had felt the day before.

He looked around. Most of the sims were long gone from the clearing, the males to hunt, the females to forage. Youngsters ran around. A couple of aging females kept an eye on them, as did the grizzled male. It chipped at stones, stuck the ends of saplings into the fire so they would make stronger spear points.

The female that had wanted him came out of the woods. Its arms were full of berries and roots; it carried a small dead snake in its left hand. When it saw he was conscious, it set down its prizes and came over to stoop beside him. After a moment it rose again, to return with a chunk of charred bear meat. *Eat*, it signed.

His stomach twisted. He was not ready for food, but he had a raging thirst. *Water*, he signed. His trousers still lay beside him. He took his canteen off his undone belt. A little water, none too fresh, sloshed in it. He drained the canteen, held it out to the female sim. *Fill*, he signed, and then discovered he had to explain how—the idea had never occurred to the sim.

It hurried away, returning quickly; the stream was not far away. The chill, sparkling water flowing down Quick's throat was one of the most delicious things he had ever felt. He gave the female the canteen for a refill. He felt warm, though the day was still early.

He saw a thick branch, not far from the fire, and a hatchet lying on the ground close to it—the sims knew nothing of rust. The grizzled sim was watching him with interest. *Chop*, he signed to it, indicating with his hands a length of about eight inches.

It eagerly picked up the hatchet, and fell to work with a will. When it was done, it handed him the piece of wood. *Make?* it signed, more curiosity on its face than he expected to find in a subhuman.

He began hollowing out the branch with his dagger. The work took most of the day. It was interrupted when he had to move his bowels. He could do nothing but lie in his own filth. After a while, an old female, wrinkling its broad, flat nose, got a handful of leaves and carried the dropping away. He hoped the sim would clean him too, but it did not. Sighing, he went back to his carving.

When the rude cup was done, he explained with signs what it was good for. The grizzled male took some time to understand. When at last it did, it hurried off to test the marvel for itself. It came back with a wide grin on its face. Standing where he could see it, it held the cup over its head and poured water into its mouth from arm's length. It got wet, but it did not seem to care.

The female that had wanted him returned from another foraging trip. It handed him another piece of cold cooked bear meat. *Eat*, it signed again. This time he felt ready to try. The flesh tasted like beef, but was greasier. His stomach, long empty, churned uneasily.

His bowels moved again not long after that. The young female dealt with the mess in the same way the old one had before. It came back, though, with more leaves, and did a rough job of wiping him.

Thanks, he signed. It only grunted; the gesture meant nothing to it. Back in the settled parts of the Commonwealths, where sims served humans, polite phrases had come into hand-talk. They had not, however, become part of the rough, abridged version this band used. Quick shook his head, sorry he could not express the gratitude he felt.

The last thing he remembered when he fell asleep that night was seeing the grizzled sim hard at work on another cup. The one he had made was in front of it. Every so often it would pick his up and study it, as if to remind itself what it was doing.

The trapper woke before sunrise, shivering. He had thought of the pain in his leg as a fire before; now it was hot in the most literal sense. He put a hand to his forehead. Fever, he thought. It was the last coherent thought he had for a long time.

He never knew how long he lay in delirium; the hours

and days stretched and twisted like taffy. Every once in a while, something would lodge in his memory. He recalled a young sim bending over to peer down at him, its solemn face so close to his that it filled his field of vision. A mite was crawling across its cheek. The mite seemed more interesting to him than the little sim.

He remembered telling the male that had brought him the marten fur how to get coffee stains out of linen. He went into great detail, though the sim knew nothing of either coffee or linen and understood not a word of English. Using hand-talk never occurred to him. After a while, the sim went away. Quick kept on talking until his mind clouded again.

He remembered being fed two or three times, all of them by the female that had wanted him. The first time, he choked on a piece of meat and had to struggle to spit it out. After that, the sim gave him only soft, pasty food. He watched it chewing meat and fruit before passing them on to him, as if he were a just-weaned infant. He knew he should have been disgusted, but he lacked the strength. He did not spit out the food, either.

Quick heard deep, racking coughing, and marveled that his lungs and throat were not raw. Only gradually, over a couple of days, did he realize he was not the one coughing. A little after that, the noise stopped, or he stopped noticing it; he did not figure out which until much later.

He remembered the female shaking him back into foggy awareness of the world around him. It held a plant in front of his face, a plant with downy, gray-green leaves, each cut into blunt lobes and teeth. The flower heads held many small, tubular, pinkish-white flowers. They were sere and brown now, well past their peak. Dusty maiden, the plant was called—one of the thousands of little nondescript shrubs that grew in the woods.

He laughed foolishly; he was a good way past his peak too, he thought. "Not quite ready for flowers, though," he said out loud. The sense of the words brought him closer to real consciousness. He was not far from being ready for flowers, and knew it.

The female held the root against his lips. *Eat*, it signed over and over until he opened his mouth. It thrust the root in. He gagged, bit down. Dirt crunched between his teeth. So did the root. It tasted horrid. When he tried to spit it out, the female sim held a hand over his mouth and would not let him. It kept signing *Eat*. With no other choice, he did. Tears of rage and weakness filled his eyes.

The next thing he remembered was thinking it had started to rain. But when he opened his eyes, the sun was shining. Yet he was wet. Sweat covered every inch of his body. It dripped from his nose and trickled through his beard and matted hair. He put a hand to his forehead. It was cooler. His fever had broken. He drifted away again, but into something closer to natural sleep than to the oblivion in which he had wandered before.

When he woke again, the female sim was trying to feed him another plant like the last one, but even more bedraggled. This time, the sim broke off the root and forced it into his mouth, the taste was just as bad as he remembered, but, gagging, he got the thing down. After he had swallowed, the female brought him a cup of water and held his head while he drank it. He did not think the cup was the one he had made.

He had another sweating spell during his next sleep, and stayed awake some little while when he came out of it. The female sim seemed to have taken over his nursing. It greeted him with yet another dusty maiden plant. He no longer tried to fight its ministrations. Enough of his wits were back for him to realize that, however acrid and revolting the roots it was giving him tasted, they were doing him good.

He came awake again at dawn, thinking how hungry he was. He tried to raise himself up on an elbow. The effort left him gasping before he finally succeeded. But no matter how weak he was, he was at last in command of his faculties once more.

He took stock of himself, looking down the length of his body. He whistled, soft and low. "No wonder I'm hungry," he said out loud, his voice a rusty croak. The fever had melted the flesh from his bones. Every rib was plainly visible (he had no idea when the sims had taken off his tunic), and his legs were bird-scrawny.

The splints, he saw with relief, were still on his right calf. It ached fiercely, but now the pain was at a level he could bear. Yellow serum oozed from the scab where the bone had stabbed through his skin, yet his right leg felt not much warmer than the other one. Despite the splints, the leg had a kink in it that had not been there before.

He did not care. He was healing. A limp—even a cane the rest of his life—would be a small price to pay. He marveled that he was alive at all.

Because the agony in his leg had diminished, he was able to take stock of his other bodily shortcomings, which were considerable. He felt raw, running sores on his back and buttocks, not surprising when he had been lying there so long. There were more on the insides of his thighs, from imperfectly cleaned wastes. But he was not lying in a great, stinking pool of his own filth. The sims must have dragged him from spot to spot in their clearing. He had no memory of it.

Most of the subhumans were already out looking for food. One of the old females that kept an eye on the youngsters while their parents foraged walked in front of him. *Food,* he signed.

The old female fell back a pace. *"Hoo!"* it said in surprise; he must have been an inert lump so long that the sims no longer expected anything else from him. The old female brought him some berries. They were the unripe and overripe ones none of the subhumans had wanted. Again, Henry Quick did not care. Half-starved as he was, they tasted wonderful.

He tried to roll on his side, but even splinted, even beginning to mend, his leg would not let him. His bedsores (he could think of no better name for them) snarled as his weight came back down on them. He was not going anywhere, even so short a distance, for a while yet. He abandoned the slender dream he'd let grow again of getting back across the mountains before the snow fell.

The female sim that had been caring for him returned,

bearing what looked like a chunk of log. The old female gave an excited hoot, pointed to Quick. Seeing him conscious, the other sim dropped its burden and dashed over to him.

It had also been carrying another dusty maiden plant. This time he took the plant from the sim's hand and ate it before he could be told to. Whatever was in that root was better medicine than most of what the doctors back in Cairo had. When he had choked it down, he signed *Eat?*

Eat, the female sim echoed, grinning hugely. One of the hatchets from Quick's pack was lying close by. The sim struck the log it had brought in. Punk flew; the log was old. Two or three more strokes served to split it. It was full of big, fat beetle larvae. They squirmed in the dirt. Youngsters came running up to pop them into their mouths.

The female sim skewered several grubs on a twig, held them over the fire, and brought them to Quick. The trapper gulped, then sighed. If he was going to live with sims, he would have to live like a sim, and that was that. He screwed his eyes shut, but he ate. Perhaps hunger seasoned the grubs, for he did not find them as disgusting as he expected. Compared to the medicinal root, they were delicious.

The female sim fetched him a cup of water. He wondered how many times it had done that while his wits wandered. Few human nurses would have been so patient.

The water made his bladder fill up. He did not want to piss himself, not now when he was awake. He called to the female sim. When he had its attention, he signed, *Fill cup with piss from me? Not piss on ground here.*

"Hoo," the sim said softly, as the subhumans often did when meeting an idea they had not thought of. The sim held a cup between his legs. It took hold of his penis to put the tip inside the cup as matter-of-factly as if it were handling his toe. Urinating without fouling himself was another of the pleasures that accompanied healing.

He thought of something. *Not drink from this cup,* he signed. *This cup—piss only.*

"Hoo," the female said again.

For all his improvement, the trapper still slept as much
as a young child. He was asleep when the hunting party of
males returned, a little before sunset. When he woke the
next morning, most of them were gone again. The male
that had brought him the marten pelt, however, crouched
beside him, plainly waiting for him to rouse.

That waiting was as far as politeness went among sims.
They had no small talk. As soon as the male saw Quick's
eyes on it, it signed. *Make thing like noise-stick.*

Quick frowned. He had hoped the sim had forgotten the
promise he'd made as he thrashed on the ground in
anguish. He had only the vaguest idea of how to make a
bow, to say nothing of arrows. Unfortunately, the sim
remembered. He would have to learn.

If it was going to propel an arrow, a bow had to be of
springy wood. The trapper pointed to one of the spruces at
the edge of the clearing. *Fetch me little tree like that,* he
signed. He held his hands about four feet apart. The sim
went into the woods. It soon came back with a sapling such
as he had described. A knife lay close enough for him to
reach it. He began cutting branches off the trunk. The sim
watched for a while, then decided nothing was going to
happen right away. It picked up its hatchet and a stout club
and went off to hunt.

Because Quick was stuck on his back, trimming the
sapling was a slow, awkward job. He managed to twist
enough to prop himself up on his left elbow. He used his
left hand to hold the fragrant trunk and carved away with
his right, but things still did not go well. He looked round
for the grizzled sim. The old male could help, and would
probably be interested in what he was up to.

He did not see the old male. Thinking back, he had not
seen it since his wits came back. When the female that cared
for him returned from a foraging trip, he asked about it.
Dead, the female signed, a thumbs-down gesture old as the
Roman arena. The sim amplified it with a racking burst of
coughs. Quick recalled the paroxysms he had heard in his
delirium.

Once more he was frustrated because he could not make the polite expressions of sympathy speech would permit. After some thought, he signed *Bad for band.*

Bad for band, the female agreed. *Toolmaker.* All sims could use and make tools, of course, but as with people, some were better than others. The grizzled sim had lived long enough to gain a great deal of experience, too. If it had not passed on all it knew, the band would indeed suffer. Henry Quick wondered how much he could help there. What hurt the band would also hurt him.

By the end of the day, he had the trunk of the spruce bare of branches and a notch carved in either end. *Good help,* he signed to the female. It smiled back at him. He realized he had to make a conscious effort to smell it these days, probably, he thought, because by now his own odor was as strong as its.

About then the males came back. They were smeared with blood but triumphant; they carried a plump doe already cut in pieces. The females and youngsters greeted them with glad cries. The band would feast tonight.

The male that had brought Quick the marten fur ambled over and picked up the would-be bow. It scowled, eyebrows working on the heavy brow-ridges. *Not like noise-stick,* it signed ominously. Had it had a sign for *fake,* it would have used it.

Not like, the trapper admitted, adding *Do like, when done.* The sim grunted a noise redolent of skepticism. Quick's eye fell on the hind leg from which another male was carving chunks. He had intended to use another bootlace as a bowstring, but he had only two, and the sims would need more bows than that . . . assuming he could make any at all. Sinew might serve in place of leather.

Save— he signed, and then paused, grinding his teeth: he did not remember the sign for "sinew." Eventually, by pointing to the tendons in his own wrist and at the back of the sim's ankles, he put across his meaning. The male gave him a dubious look no butler would have been ashamed of, but went over to the sim acting as butcher and passed the message along. That male shrugged as if to say the trapper was daft, but eventually set beside him several glistening white lengths, each with bits of flesh still clinging to it.

He did not work on the bow for several days after that. His fever returned. It was not strong enough to drive him into delirium, but it did leave him shivering and miserable. He glumly crunched the dusty maiden roots the female sim brought him and wished he felt more like a human being, or even a healthy sim.

Because he was still aware of his surroundings, he really noticed then the care the female sim gave him. It fed him, got him water, cleansed him, hauled him from place to place to keep him from lying in his own dung. It might not have been as gentle as a human nurse, but it was more conscientious than most.

Not only was this spell of fever less severe than the last had been, it was shorter. Yet even after Quick began to feel better, he kept waking up chilled. Only when he saw the sims also clutching themselves, building thicker piles of bedding, and huddling close to the fire did he understand that the weather was changing. Autumn was drawing near, and hard on its heels would come winter.

The sims did what they could to get ready for it. They brought in stones and brush, which they began to work into a windbreak. As the days went by, it grew thicker and taller and extended all the way around the clearing, with a couple of thin spots through which the sims could push. They also stacked up great heaps of firewood; once the snow started, it would not be so easy to collect. Quick's hatchets helped them there. They could not have cut so much wood with their crude tools alone.

Some of them even realized it. The male that had brought him the marten pelt hefted its hatchet when it saw he was watching and signed, *Good*.

It was less happy, however, over the trapper's efforts to make arrows that were worth anything. Finding really straight lengths of branch was hard enough. Getting points on them proved worse. Because the sims used stone tools,

Quick had assumed they could easily chip out little stone arrowheads. But the tools they were used to making were hand-sized choppers and scrapers. They had never done the fine, tiny flakework arrowheads required. If Quick had shown them how, they could have duplicated his efforts. He had no skill in shaping stone, though, and soon discovered that knowing what he wanted was very different from knowing how to make it.

By the time the first frost appeared on the windbreak, he no longer worried about getting knocked over the head for failing to produce. If the sims decided to do that, he could not stop them, but that fatalistic certainty was only a small part of what gradually let him relax.

Far more important was that the sims accepted him. They had grown accustomed to him lying by the fire, and no longer saw him as much different from themselves, except that he could not move. His chief worry now was what would happen if a youngster tripped over his broken leg while playing. Where the young sims had once crowded up to gape at him, now they were so careless around him that he sometimes wondered if they remembered he was there.

The leg still hurt. It also itched savagely; he rubbed the flesh round the healing gash raw until he understood the itch came from far within. He healed despite the itch, little by little. Milestones were small, but he treasured them: the day he could sit up, the day he could roll onto his side to air the sores on his back and behind, the day those sores started to scab over.

Milestones or not, he remained immobile, save when a sim dragged him along. Except for his annoyingly troublesome work on the bow, he had little to do but lie by the fire and watch the members of the band. Just as they accepted him, so he came to think of them more and more as individuals, as people, rather than as subhumans, animals to evade or exploit.

Looking back, he supposed the beginning of that process came when he finally decided that thinking of "the male that had brought him the marten skin" by that clumsy handle was more trouble than it was worth. He decided to call it Martin and have done. Giving the sim a man's name helped him think of it as being more like a man.

One by one, he named all the sims. Most of his names were just tags in his own mind. The sims had so much trouble reproducing the sounds of English that they could not use his names themselves, which made him hesitate to apply them. Martin, however, soon learned what noise meant him. (With a man's name, Martin was also harder to think of as *it*.)

The female that cared for Henry Quick also rapidly figured out what names were for. He called her Sal.

Even though he continued to improve, he knew how dependent on her he still was. He whittled away at a couple of branches, slowly turning them into crutches, but he was not ready to try them yet. A fall, a slip, would put paid to weeks of slow recovery. In any case, he had nowhere to go now that the weather was changing.

Sal went right on caring for him as she had all along. She also got better and better as his assistant in the effort to unravel the secrets of the bow. She would have been better yet, he thought glumly, had her mentor been worth a damn. She copied his blunders faithfully, one by one, but stopped making them as soon as he did. He knew a lot of people back in the Commonwealths who, having settled on a particular mistake, would keep making it till the end of time.

He also knew a lot of people who would have turned up their noses—in the most literal sense—at the continuing unpleasant labor involved in disposing of his wastes and getting the filth off him afterwards. Sal never faltered. In the days when he was still on his feet, he had improvised a good many strange wipes for his hindquarters, but in that regard Sal's ingenuity outdid his. He was grateful, and sometimes amused. He would never have thought of using grouse feathers, for instance.

Sal also kept using that same wooden cup to help him

pass water. He sometimes thought the simple desire to piss while upright would be what finally drove him to his feet. He was glad he had the sense to recognize that urge as a sign of returning health, and did not try to act on it too soon.

Another sign came not long afterward, on a day where, even by the fire, the wind held a chilly promise of the snow that would come soon. As he had countless times before, Quick called Sal's name and asked for the cup. She finished working the seeds out of a couple of pinecones she had found, brought it over to him.

She took him in hand, again as she had so often before. What happened then, though, was new and strange, for he felt himself stiffening at the sim's touch.

It was hard to say which of them was more surprised. Henry Quick had been lustful enough out on the trap line, but there is nothing like a compound fracture of the leg and a long bout of fever to make a man put aside such concerns.

Had Sal ignored his rise, simply put his penis in the cup and waited, the moment would have passed. The sim seemed about to do just that, then paused, looked down, and quietly said, *"Hoo!"*

Quick started to sign for Sal to take her hand away, but the sim, still perhaps more in the spirit of experimentation than anything else, stroked him for the first time with deliberate intent. His recovering body responded to the touch before his mind could will it not to. And in any event, once he was fully, rampantly, and so unexpectedly erect, his mind had very little to say.

The sim swung astride him, lowered onto him. He gasped; entering Sal felt no different from having a woman. Even so, seeing her there above him, hairy, chinless, and heavy-browed, made him shut his eyes in a spasm of revulsion.

Yet the act went on, whether he watched or not. And indeed, closing his eyes, regardless of the reason, made matters seem much more familiar. He felt the thick hair on Sal's thighs and buttocks as she rode him, but that sensation was distant, insignificant, when set against the explosion building in his loins. Nor were the small, wordless noises the sim made unlike the ones he had heard in bedrooms back in the Commonwealths. Too often those were from women who sighed more for his coins on the dresser than for himself; the sim had no such art.

No wonder, then, that his hips bucked of themselves, or that his hands reached out to take hold of Sal's breasts. He almost jerked them away again, for the hair that covered all the breasts but the nipples reminded him he was in no bedroom now. Then climax swept over him, and for an endless instant he did not care where he was.

Sal rolled away as soon as he was through. He kept his eyes shut, trying to sort things out; he felt simultaneously as fine and as wretched as he could ever recall.

He opened his eyes. Sal was looking at him. He nodded, not yet trusting either speech or hand-talk. The sim nodded back. *Good,* Sal signed.

"All right," the trapper said, surprising himself as usual when he spoke out loud. His equanimity was coming back. How many times had he told himself that if he was going to live with the sims he would have to live like a sim? A wry grin settled on his face. Eating grubs was all very well, but he had not expected to take things quite this far.

Again? Sal asked, and no grin, no matter how wry, could survive that question. Once he could explain it away, even to himself, as something beyond his control. Repeating the act, though, would be committing himself to what he, along with almost everyone in the Commonwealths, thought of as disgusting.

And yet the coupling had not been the sordid sort of masturbation he imagined mating with a mare or ewe might be. Sal had been a partner in the act, not a mere uncomprehending receptacle for his lust. Indeed, that he was being asked whether he wanted to go again said a good deal. In the end, the question, more than anything else, was what decided him.

"All right," he repeated. The sim could not have understood his words, but got the meaning from his tone. As sims were wont to do, Sal took him literally, and at once set about restoring his manhood. He thought that would be futile so soon after the first round, but his body, long deprived, proved him wrong. The sim mounted him again. Normally he preferred riding to being ridden, but his leg made that not worth thinking about.

This time the joining was slower, less fervent. Quick left his eyes open. The sims in the clearing were paying hardly more attention to him and Sal than they would have to a pair of their own kind, and the difference, he judged, was not prurience, only curiosity about how he performed. Once they saw he functioned much like them, they went back to whatever they had been doing.

He still did not look much at Sal, concentrating instead on what he was feeling. As before, that was like in its essence to having a woman, but now he noticed the peripheral differences more. The hairiness of the sim's body distracted him once or twice. Only later did he wonder if his own relatively smooth skin was as strange to her.

He did notice the sim's strength when she—in the middle of coupling, he could not think of Sal as it—grasped him as they mated. He had never bedded a woman at least as strong as he was.

That thought diverted Quick's attention again. He wondered how the males would react to his joining the band in this last, most intimate sense. Some had partners who mated more or less steadily with them, but the dominant males of the hunting party, Martin and two or three others, also coupled with the unattached females of the band. Now the trapper was part of that hierarchy. He wondered where he fit. He could not hunt. He could not even walk. If he was to gain importance, it would have to come through his wits.

Anyway, he thought as sensation built toward release, it was too late to worry now.

But afterward he worked away on the bow and arrows with more concentration than he had shown for several days. Nor could he stifle a twinge of alarm when Martin loomed over him, hands on hips, to inspect what he was up to. But the sim, as usual, was businesslike. *Sticks fly?* Martin asked.

Henry Quick shrugged. It was always a good question. After endless effort, he had figured out how to chip reasonably small, reasonably sharp arrowheads—they were better points than he got by simply whittling away at the tip of the arrow, at any rate. Now he was having trouble making the miserable arrows go straight.

The first ones he'd tried just spun crazily, which was good for making the sims laugh but not much else. Then he vaguely remembered that proper arrows had feathers at the back to make them fly true. Getting feathers was no problem. The sims threw rocks well enough to bring down a lot of birds. But getting the feathers to stay on the arrows was a whole different question. The sims knew nothing about glue, and Quick did not know how to make it either.

So far his best solution was cutting thin grooves in the shafts and sliding the feathers into them. That was not nearly good enough. Once in a while, one of his arrows would fly straight and thwock into a tree with enough force to stick, which made the sims hoot appreciatively. More often, a feather would come out in flight, which made the arrow behave as if it were trying to dodge its target instead of hitting it.

Sal continued to help in his bow-building efforts, and to care for him as she had been doing. She never understood much English besides her name, but he passed a lot of time talking first to her, then with her, in hand-talk. They did best at the purely pragmatic level. She understood why the people back in the Commonwealths wanted the furs he had come to trap. *Furs warm*, she signed, running a hand over his relatively naked skin. *No hair, need warm.* She stroked her own red-brown hair to emphasize the contrast. Her hair had grown thicker, almost furry, as the season changed.

When Quick tried to explain that people coveted furs for their beauty as well as their warmth, he ran into a blank wall. Sims did have an aesthetic sense of sorts, but it was limited to things they made themselves. A fur was just a fur.

He did better getting across the idea of rarity. Begging for food was a simple kind of bargaining, and the sims had learned he would give them his strange and wonderful metal tools in exchange for furs. *In my band,* he signed, *many tools, few furs. Here many furs, few tools. You want tools, we want furs.*

Sal nodded. *Why few furs there?* she asked. Her hand-talk was far more fluid than it had been when he first met her band. She, and to a lesser extent the rest of the band, had also learned from Quick a number of signs they had not known before.

Many people, he answered. *Much hunting.*

Sal understood that. A band of sims that grew too large for its territory to support soon shrank again from starvation.

Some parts of life in the Commonwealths—railroads, steamboats—Quick did not even try to explain. Getting across the idea of a house, a permanent place to live, was hard enough, as was describing domesticated plants and animals. To Sal, it all seemed a vision of unparalleled abundance. *Warm place to sleep?* she signed. *Plenty to eat? No hunting?*

The trapper nodded, admitting it.

Why come here? Sal asked.

To get furs, was the only answer Quick could put across. Wanderlust meant nothing to the sim; Sal's band knew a territory perhaps twenty miles square as intimately as anyone could, but nothing of the world beyond it. Explaining that he often found the company of his fellow men oppressive was also next to impossible.

You, they fight? Sal asked.

No, he signed, but then, after thinking about it, had to add, *I stay with other men long time, maybe fight.* He knew how impatient he could get with people's foolishness. He really did not have that problem with the band of sims. They were not smart enough to make idiots of themselves on purpose; what brains they had, they had to use.

He wanted to do something for Sal, to show his gratitude in a more permanent, more substantial way than their coupling. After the first few times, he had stopped worrying about whether those matings constituted bestiality. That was more because he thought of himself as a member of the sim band than because he suddenly reckoned her human, but the effect was the same: he concentrated on their similarities rather than their differences.

The problem was that the sims lived at the barest subsistence level. Things that would have been appropriate back in the Commonwealths were incomprehensible and so valueless here. Before he fully realized that, Quick spent a good deal of time whittling a piece of pine into the shape of a spearfang. Sal looked at it when he proudly presented it to her. She was interested; she had never seen an image before. But she was not really pleased.

Inspiration struck when the trapper saw how the hunting party of males behaved when they came into the clearing on a day after the snow had begun to fall. The sims threw down the carcasses they had brought into the clearing, then, as one, rushed to put their feet as close to the fire as they could.

Quick smelled singeing hair, but did not blame the sims a bit. For him, even healthy, going out into the snow barefoot would have meant at the very least losing toes to frostbite. The sims' feet were hairy above and had thickly callused soles, so that risk was less for them. Nothing, however, could make such shoeless travel anything but icy.

The females, Sal among them, also had to brave the winter to forage and to cut firewood. Henry Quick suddenly realized that, while his boots did not have laces anymore, they were much better than nothing. Before Sal went out the next time, he showed her how to put them on her feet.

She did not like them; they must have felt strange and confining. But when she came back, her broad grin gleamed like the snow that still clung to the load of fir branches she was carrying. *Warm*, she signed unbelievingly, pointing to her feet. *Warm.* She let out a loud hoot of glee, bent down beside Quick to hug him and plant exuberant kisses on his face and shoulders. *Warm,* she signed again. *Feet warm.*

Quick felt warm himself, no easy trick that winter. He was glad he had found a gift that made her happy.

The boots also made the other sims jealous. Quick tried to fix that as fast as he could; he did not want Sal to suffer when he'd only meant to help. The only solution he came up with involved sacrificing his trousers, which he could not wear anyhow. They made several pairs of improvised footgear, not as good as real boots but far superior to bare feet, even hairy, leathery bare feet.

His makeshift cordwainery let Sal keep the boots that had been his. That relieved him a great deal, but only for a few days.

Martin had probably the best set of makeshifts. Once he was convinced they did some good, he signed, *All hunters need.*

Leather gone, Quick answered. Martin gave a dissatisfied grunt. The trapper hoped the sim would not demand the tunic off his back. He needed it. Also fearing the big male would take his boots away from Sal, the trapper suggested, *Make foot things from skins of animals you kill.*

Skins stink fast, Martin signed.

Quick remembered promising to show the grizzled sim how to make leather. Now, in a way, he could keep that promise. *Rub skins with bark from spruce,* he signed. *Then stink slow, maybe not stink.*

Martin grunted again. *Do,* he signed. Before long, Quick was doing as much skinning, scraping, and curing as he had working the trap line. He had been a lot of things before, but never a cobbler for sims.

The cold, wet weather made his leg hurt worse, but with a different kind of pain, one he suspected would be with him the rest of his life: he knew several men with healed broken bones who were the best prophets of rain for miles around. Now at last he felt himself definitely on the mend. The successive triumphs were small but satisfying: he treasured the day he sat up by himself, the day he rolled over, the day he coupled with Sal with him on top. His sticks were still awkward, and so was she. That was not a posture sims often used. Neither, come to that, was female atop male; most often they mated from behind, like beasts.

Like any other beasts, Quick realized he would have thought before his enforced sojourn here. Yet they learned far more than beasts. That applied to other things than seeing the utility of boots. Every so often, around the fire, the trapper would notice the subhumans joining as he and Sal did. He smiled every time. That was not one of the things he had intended to teach them.

Without the fire and the windbreak, the band of sims could not have survived. In the worst storms none of them went out, except to gather more wood. They huddled in their bedding close by the fire, hugging one another for extra warmth. Often they went a couple of days without food. They were used to going hungry.

Quick was not. His belly began to preoccupy him even more than his leg. Whenever the hunting party came back with game, his stomach heralded their arrival with growls a wolf would have been proud of.

Thanks in no small part to his hatchets, the fire never went out, nor did the sims have to sacrifice the windbreak or rob it so it became threadbare. Indeed, the females and youngsters cut so much more wood than they had been able to before that the band often used the piles of fragrant branches to thicken and restore their beds before using them to feed the fire. Quick had done that himself on the trapping line; fir branches made a fine mattress on which to lay a blanket.

Being now without a blanket, the trapper happily joined the sims in burrowing among the branches and using them to hold his body warmth. His nose grew so used to the thick, resinous smell of fir that he had to make a conscious effort to notice it. He found that the sap that oozed from the branches was easier to clean from his relatively smooth skin than to get out of the sims' hair.

The sims spent a fair amount of time grooming one another under any circumstances; it was as much a part of their social lives as back-fence chatter was back in the Commonwealths. Quick did not mind taking part. Getting Sal's hair smooth and neat pleased him. He made an absent mental note to carve out a comb when he had the chance. The sap he cleaned from her hair left his hands constantly sticky, and spit did not take it off.

For a while he accepted that as just another nuisance. Then his whoop made sims all over the clearing jump. If spit did not dissolve the resin, neither would water. Now feathers would stay where he put them.

He had a couple of dozen shafts finished by the time Martin came into the clearing, staggering under the weight of the fawn in his arms. Quick was no archer, and was doubly hampered by having to shoot sitting down. Nevertheless, he sent several arrows close to a treetrunk that stood farther away than anyone could throw a stone.

His wrist raw and red from being lashed by the sinew bowstring, he handed the bow to Martin. The sim had used it only a couple of times before, but already showed signs of being a better marksman than Quick. Martin grunted when the first two arrows went where he aimed them, then said *"Hoo!"* as a third followed.

He shot again, as if to reassure himself it was no fluke, then thrust the bow back at the trapper. *Make more,* he signed. Quick had won over the skeptic.

With Sal's help, Quick went from cobbler to bowyer and fletcher. He had finished a handful of crude bows and close to a hundred arrows before he paused to wonder about what he was doing. Men had always pushed forward across America as they pleased, not least because sims lacked the weapons to fight back. A bow was nowhere near as potent as a gun, but it was vastly better than anything the subhumans had had before. Not only that, it was simple enough for them to make and care for themselves, which was not true of firearms.

After some thought, he decided it did not matter. For one

thing, ideas did not move quickly from one band of sims to the next: how recently this band had acquired hand-talk showed that. For another, even with bows the sims could hardly become more than a nuisance. And finally, staying alive now counted far more than any hypothetical trouble in the future. In such matters, the trapper was an eminently practical man.

He grinned from ear to ear when the hunting party began coming back with more game than they ever had before. *Not need close*, one signed, holding a rabbit with blood on its white fur in front of Quick's face. The male kissed the trapper's cheek, then patted his own belly. *Kill from far, eat good.*

Save for a single infant, not a sim had died this winter, though it was the desperate time of year for the wild bands. Quick was amazed at the difference the extra fuel and now the extra food made.

But winter was also the desperate time of year for the other predators that roamed the woods. One morning a female started to push aside a chunk of the windbreak, then shoved back the piled branches with a shriek of fright. A wolf bayed in anger and frustration and hunger. Around the windbreak, the rest of the pack took up the chorus. The sims were besieged.

Sal shivered, next to Quick. Cold had nothing to do with it. *Wolves stay*, she signed. *Stay, stay, stay. We hungry, hungry. We go out, they eat. They eat enough, then finally go.*

The rest of the sims seemed sunk in the same fearful depression. None showed any sign of trying to drive the wolves away, nor did they reach for the bows that lay by the fire. Their wits were slower than humans' after all, Quick saw: they had trouble grasping that what served so well on the hunt would also defend them.

He was sure they would eventually have worked it through for themselves, but lacked the patience to wait. He shouted till he had Martin's attention. His voice also roused the devil's choir outside the windbreak, but he did not care about that. *Take bows, arrows,* he signed. *Shoot wolves.* He rendered that by pantomiming drawing a bow back to his ear. *Shoot wolves, those you not shoot run away.*

The big male rubbed his long, chinless jaw as he wrestled with the idea. He sprang to his feet with a wordless yell, ran for the weapons. He dashed to the windbreak, peered through. Quick heard a snarl from the far side. The wolf was not afraid of a sim, especially not with a barrier between them.

Martin aimed the bow through a gap in the branches. He let fly. The wolf's fierce growls turned to a yowl of agony that went on and on. The howls from the rest of the pack stopped abruptly.

Quick feared and hated wolves: after sims, they were the most dangerous creatures in the woods. A bear or a spearfang, of course, was more than a match for a wolf, but a pack of wolves would run even a spearfang off its prey. Had the trapper been able to stand, he would have gone to the windbreak to fire his rifle and pistol at the beasts.

The sims proved able to deal with things on their own. Martin dashed to another hole in the windbreak. He shot again. A wounded wolf ki-yied in pain. That was enough to send more males rushing up to grab the rest of the bows and arrows. In minutes, several more wolves had been hit, and the rest of the pack was in full retreat. The male sims took clubs and spears outside the windbreak to finish off the animals they had wounded.

Roast wolf tasted much better than Quick had thought it would.

A few days later, the weather turned clear and unseasonably warm. The trapper, with the aid of Sal and of the crutches he had fashioned weeks before, stood up for the first time since the sims had brought him into the clearing. The effort even a couple of steps required left him weak and gasping. His left leg was, from lack of use, almost as feeble as his right, which he still did not try to touch to the ground.

But he was upright at last. The sense of freedom that

brought was intoxicating. He leaned over and kissed Sal on the lips. He had never done that before. The motion almost made him fall. Sal steadied him. They both laughed. He kissed her again. This time they did slide to the ground, carefully, still laughing, and ended up coupling.

Afterward Sal got up to gather wood, leaving Quick by himself; she took pleasure in the act, but knew nothing of lazing in the afterglow. A smile still on his lips, Quick watched her retreating form.

There, he thought, goes a hell of a woman. Hearing the word in his own mind brought him up short. It had been a while since he took a real look at how he felt about her.

That her body pleased him had been a surprise, but was no longer. Now he noticed her hairiness, her features, hardly more than had she been black or had very blue eyes. He was used to her, as one person grows used to another.

What did surprise him was how much he liked her. He knew that had grown from her caring for him, but there was more to it now. Her happiness mattered to him: why else had he given her his boots, and worried so much over whether Martin would take them away that he devised substitutes?

And if he desired her, and at the same time wanted to gladden her in other ways—He startled himself by speaking out loud. "If that's not love, I don't know what the devil is."

The summer before, using that word in connection with a sim would have seemed as ridiculous as thinking of a female sim as a woman. He shrugged, not so disturbed as he expected to be. Living as part of the band had changed his perspective.

Sims weren't human, he thought, but they were people. He nodded slowly, pleased with the distinction. The sims had been living in these woods for who knew how many years. For the first time, Quick felt guilty over the way humans were supplanting wild sims all across the continent. Even tame sims depended on their masters' whim for security. The trapper had trouble finding that right, but at the same time did not know what else could have happened.

The more the sims hunted with bows, the deadlier they grew. The males brought in such an unending stream of game that the clearing constantly smelled of cooking meat. The whole band began to lose the gauntness that went with winter.

None of them, though, was fat; to Quick, a fat wild sim was a contradiction in terms. So he thought, at any rate, until he noticed Sal's belly beginning to protrude. Yet she showed no extra flesh on her limbs or in her face. The trapper scratched his head and kept on trying to get about with his crutches.

His right leg was never going to be the same. There was an enormous knot of bone where the leg had been broken and had not healed straight, which made it a little shorter than its mate. Quick stumped patiently back and forth, putting as much weight on it as he could. Day by day it bore more, but he knew he had made his last trapping run. He would need a stick for the rest of his life.

He was exercising—his mind, he would have sworn, somewhere far away—when the reason Sal was putting on weight dawned on him. He sat down heavily. No matter how often his body had joined with hers, he had never thought issue might spring from it. In hindsight, that was stupid. In hindsight, of course, a lot of things were stupid.

He stayed on his haunches, lost in his own thoughts. When Sal came back from a foraging trip, she gave him a reproachful look. *Not walk?* she asked.

No. Henry Quick pointed at her. *Baby in you?*

She glanced down at herself. The bulge was obvious, so obvious that Quick again kicked himself for not figuring out what it meant before. She signed, *Baby in me.*

She did not say anything about him being the father, though since that first time she had rarely coupled with any partner but him. After a moment, he realized he had never seen any sim in the band use the sign for father. They valued mating for its own sake, not for the sake of children, and had never made the connection between the two.

He wondered what to do, and wished he were callous enough for her pregnancy to make no difference to him. He had intended to head back toward the Commonwealths as soon as the snow melted. Now . . . it would not be so easy. *You want me stay here?* he signed.

Where go? Sal asked.

To men like me.

Sal frowned. One of him was strange enough; visualizing many of his kind took more imagination than she had. At last she signed, *Winter not gone.*

"Only too right it's not," Quick said aloud. Even on a mild day like this one, the breeze made his teeth chatter. At first he thought Sal had changed the subject, but after a moment he realized such subtlety was beyond her. She'd simply pointed out that, whatever he decided to do, he wasn't going to do it tomorrow, or the day after either.

He thought about what staying with the sims and never going back to the Commonwealths would be like. He cared for Sal as he had for no woman on the other side of the Rockies, and she was carrying his child. That counted for something, but he was not sure in which direction it swung the balance. Son of a sim was a bad enough thing to call a man, but father of a sim . . . ? Still, he could be like a god if he chose to stay. There was so much the sims did not know—

He laughed at himself. Like a god, was it? A god who huddled naked, cold, and stinking in fir branches, who ate whatever was alive (or had been lately) and was glad to get it, who could not even use his own speech but had to content himself with a clumsy, limited makeshift? Anyone who bought godhood on those terms deserved to think he had it.

That the trapper lived hardly better than the sims while in the field did not enter into the equation. He deliberately chose those hardships to escape from his fellow men for a time, and to earn the money to live high when he got back to civilization. Until now, he had never imagined staying west of the mountains. Without Sal, he would have had no doubts.

Without Sal, he would have been dead months before, and would not be in this quandary.

She touched his arm. Under their shelf of bone, her brown eyes were troubled. Male sims were not normally quiet and reflective. Sal had accepted that Henry Quick sometimes was, but had also come to know him well enough to tell when his thoughts troubled him. *You good?* she asked. Even after trading signs with him for so long, she could not come closer than that to probing his feelings.

He spread his palms, a gesture that meant neither yes nor no.

She rummaged about, offered him some half-frozen cattail roots she had found. *Eat*, she signed, as if food could ease mental as well as physical distress. He sighed and declined. Sal made another gesture. He acted on that one, but afterward, no matter how sated his body was, his mind would not rest.

How could it be love, he wondered, when he could not even express the idea to Sal? But what else was it? He had no answer, not even for himself. He turned to Sal. *You want me to go?* he asked.

It was her turn to hesitate. Finally she signed, *Do good for you.* He tugged at his beard, frowning; sometimes sims' statements were oracular in their obscurity. At last he decided she was telling him that the most important thing was his own happiness, a curious mirroring of his own feelings toward her. And if that wasn't love, what else was it?

But even if it was, was it worth abandoning the Commonwealths for good? He knew a fair number of men who had given up the lives they had known to stay with a woman with whom they had fallen in love. Once the first flush faded, most came to regret it.

Something else occurred to the trapper. He was the first man to enter this part of the wilderness, but he would not be the last. He did not have to wonder what the newcomers would think of him: just what he would have thought before the bear wrecked his leg. Tales of Quick the sim-lover might get him remembered forever, but not in a way he wanted. What else was he, though?

He did not even think of taking Sal back to the Commonwealths with him. He knew the ostracism that would bring, the more so as she carried his child. She did not deserve to face that. Apart from it, too, he doubted she could adapt to life east of the Rockies. She was a creature of the wilds, no less than the marten or the spearfang. If he chose to live with her, it would have to be here.

He bit down on his lip till he tasted blood, then slowly made himself relax. As Sal had reminded him, winter was a long way from over. Nothing he decided now could be final; he would be rehashing it endlessly for weeks to come. Best to put it aside as well as he could, and wait to see what those weeks would bring.

That sadly indecisive and unoriginal conclusion was enough to grant him rest at last.

Whenever the weather was clear enough and warm enough to let him, Quick kept exercising, working to put strength back in his long-inactive legs. He got to the point where he could stump about on his crutches with Sal lending him strength and balance. Then, a good many days later, he managed to hobble along with but a single stick. Most of the time, though, he spent as he had the beginning of the winter—under cover.

Martin stayed on good terms with the trapper. That was partly because of the bows and arrows Quick kept turning out. By now the sims' products—especially the arrowheads—were as good as anything he could make, but he had more leisure than they in which to make them. Moreover, Martin must have realized that without Quick the band never would have known of bows and arrows in the first place.

The sim kept drawing the trapper out, hoping to pick up more ideas the band could use. Quick racked his brains, but came up with little. No matter how free-ranging a life he lived in the wild, most of what he knew depended in some part on civilized techniques he could not match here, or on domesticated plants and animals that were equally unobtainable.

He had never thought of things as basic as wheat and

flax, sheep and cattle, as being elements of civilization until he tried to change a way of life without them.

Most of the other males let Quick alone. That was not so much hostility as uncertainty over where he fit into the band. His status could hardly have been more confusing: he had gone from being a powerful outsider to a helpless cripple. As if that were not bad enough, as a helpless cripple he had come up with a notion none of them could have matched.

Had they been men, he knew he could have expected trouble over Sal. He had already seen, though, that that sort of possessiveness was much weaker among sims. The males, then, did not object when he took his share of the meat they brought in, and let it go at that.

Among themselves, they jockeyed for position as they always had. Quick was just as glad not to be involved in that. The males' squabbles reminded him of nothing so much as small boys squaring off to fight. Even perfectly healthy, he would not have relished the prospect of getting into a face-to-face screaming match with a wild male—not without his pistol handy, at any rate.

Yet for all the shrieks and gestures, for all the fury and bared teeth, few tiffs actually ended with the combatants rolling and punching and kicking and biting on the ground. Like a lot of small-boy fights, most were games of bluff and counterbluff, good for letting off steam but not changing the status of either participant.

Through the winter, Martin stayed atop the hierarchy. Not only was he in his physical prime, but he also enjoyed the added prestige the success of Quick's devices brought him. The band had fared well in what was usually a time of privation, and the sims recognized that and gave credit for it.

Most did, at any rate. Like humans, some were unwilling to accept anything for which they were not responsible themselves. Three or four males, of middling to fairly high status in the hunting party, began hanging around together. They had been the last ones to start using the bow.

Their leader, as much as they had one, was the male with the broken tooth who had wanted to kill Quick and eat him when the hunters came on him after the bear broke his leg.

Since then, and especially since he began to recover, it had had even less to do with him than its fellows, though every so often he would catch it watching him out of the corner of its eye. Because of its almost regal aloofness and because, although not old, it was going bald, he finally named the male Caesar; it was one of the last ones to pass from *it* to *he* in his mind.

Caesar and his companions all had that same sidelong way of looking at Martin. Quick was slower to put a motive to it than he would have been with men, but at last he had no doubts: they were studying their leader, looking for weakness.

If Martin noticed, he gave no sign. When the trapper did his best to warn him, the sim's only response was to tap himself on the chest as if to say, I can deal with any of them.

The days were growing longer more quickly now; Sal's belly grew more quickly too. Snow turned to icy rain. Quick found that worse than the blizzards that had gone before. The windbreak and the nest of branches had done a fair job of shielding the band—and the trapper—from the snow, which piled up in drifts and lay on top of the nest.

The rain, by contrast, trickled through and made everyone shiveringly miserable. It also threatened to put out the fire. That was not quite the catastrophe it would have been for sims before the days of flint and steel, but it would not have been pleasant. Not only would the blaze have been hard to get going again with everything soaked, but the sims would have suffered from the cold, blustery weather while it was out.

A couple of males held hides over the fire. Others, at Quick's urging, dug channels to guide the rainwater on the ground away from the burning branches and sticks. A small chorus of "*Hoo*"'s went up as the sims saw the water being turned aside. Sal squeezed the trapper in delight.

They were coupling less often now; her interest waned as

her pregnancy advanced. Quick had wondered, with a cold-bloodedness that disturbed him, whether he would stop fancying her once he had to resort to his hand again. He found it was not so. As he had before they first joined in body, he cared for her for herself, not for her anatomy.

Nor did she grow aloof from him in any way but mating. The embrace she gave him after the storm was but one example of that. She stayed by him most of the time when she was not out foraging; brought him tidbits from her trips (by now he seldom worried about eating them, whatever they were); and helped him get about, though he was more and more mobile on his own.

She also spent a good deal of time, as was only natural, preoccupied with the child growing within her. *Baby soon,* she would sign, patting her belly or her breasts, which had also swollen some in anticipation of nursing.

Once Quick signed, *Baby look like you and like me.* He touched his forehead, ran his hand along the relatively hairless skin of his arm. Ever since he realized Sal was pregnant, he had wondered which of them the child would more closely resemble. He did not know. He had never seen any crossbreeds, and the wild stories whispered about them varied enough that he could not tell where truth lay. Some claimed crosses could pass as humans, others that they were brutes unable to speak.

The whole concept of fatherhood was alien to Sal. *Baby from me, baby like me,* she insisted, and kept repeating her gestures until Quick gave up. He did not press her for long. Sims had been giving birth to sims for as long as there had been sims; no wonder Sal could not look forward to anything different.

Martin remained the dominant male in the band. Perhaps in reaction to Quick's warning, perhaps on his own, he began to be more touchy around Caesar and what the trapper could not help thinking of as his clique. For their part, they placated him, bending their heads and holding out their hands, palms up, when he shouted at them or brandished a weapon. As with most confrontations among sims, that was plenty to settle things. Martin would turn his back and swagger away, satisfied he was still cock o' the walk.

Henry Quick shared the big male's exuberance, but only to a point. He could not help noticing that the members of the hunting party who backed Martin were nowhere near so closely knit as Caesar's followers. Caesar by himself was no match for Martin; Caesar and several comrades probably were.

Rain came more and more often. Black patches of dirt began to appear. The evergreens lost their white mantles, while buds grew on branches bare for months. Quick heard geese crying far overhead, and on clear days saw V's of black specks flying north against the blue sky.

He wondered, as he had once in a while through the winter, if anyone missed him back in the Commonwealths. Trapping was a risky business, and every year many who tried it never came back. If he did return to civilization, he would be a nine days' wonder. Was that reason enough to make the trip? He doubted it. He also doubted whether he could finish his life among the sims, even loving one. For better or worse, he and they were different.

Unable to decide what to do, he let day follow day, hoping events would solve his problem for him. He got stronger; with his stick, he was not much slower or more awkward than an old man. He could even hobble a couple of steps without it, though his left leg had to take almost all of his weight.

With that success, he began thinking hard about what travel would mean. The idea of depending on archery to feed himself was appalling. His powderhorn was still half full. He had done his best to keep rifle and pistol dry through the winter, greased them with animal fat, and used dirt and gravel to scour away the rust that did appear. He began substituting the rifle for his stick. The extra weight tired him, but he managed.

He hated to burn powder and waste bullets on test shots, but he would sooner find out whether his guns worked in a setting where his life did not depend on the answer. One morning he loaded them, pointed the pistol into the air, lowered it again. *Big noise,* he signed, warning the females and youngsters in the clearing.

Noise-stick, Sal amplified. The sims had learned the year before that Quick carried noisy weapons that could slay at a distance. Few except the hunting males, though, had heard them. Of course, the trapper thought as he squeezed the trigger, they might not hear one now.

He felt like cheering when the gun went off. The recoil was easier to take than he'd expected, easier even than he remembered; his arms had become very strong from bearing so much of his weight through his crutches.

The sims shrieked. Some clapped hands to ears. Youngsters ran to their mothers. "Big noise" was easier to say than to experience. Even Sal jumped, though she recovered quickly. *Noise-stick good?* she signed.

Good, Quick answered. He fired the rifle. It also worked; its kick almost knocked him over. The report was louder than the pistol shot had been, but the sims did not make quite such a fuss over it—this time they knew what he was warning them about.

He reloaded both guns. If he did decide to leave, they would make all the difference in the world.

The females and youngsters had a great deal to tell the males when the hunting party returned. Hands fluttered, and in their excitement the sims hooted and yelled to add emphasis to their gestures.

After the commotion died down, Martin came over to Henry Quick. He asked the same question Sal had: *Noise-sticks good?*

The trapper agreed they were.

Hunt with us? the sim asked.

Too slow, not keep up.

Martin rubbed his jaw. He could not disagree with that. At length he signed, *Give me noise-stick.*

Quick had expected something of the sort. *You not work noise-stick,* he signed. To make sure he was not lying, he had surreptitiously removed the flints from his guns while the females were carrying on. He did not resist when Martin took the pistol away from him.

The sim knew what the trigger was for, but only a click rewarded him when he pulled it. He tried the rifle, with the same result. Growling in frustration, he shoved them back at Quick and stalked away. The trapper made sure the sim was not looking before he restored the flints to their places.

The next morning, most of the hunting party set out early, as they usually did. Martin hung back. He walked up and down examining the windbreak, plainly trying to decide whether it was time to turn it into firewood.

Caesar and two members of his clique also stayed behind. As far as Quick could see, they were not doing anything in particular. He practiced his walking, limping along leaning his right side on his rifle and carrying his pistol in his left. The morning was humid, so his leg hurt more than usual.

When Martin turned away from the windbreak and spotted the other males still in the clearing, he shouted angrily at them. *Go! Hunt!* he signed, his gestures quick and peremptory. He was still wearing the makeshift belt Quick had made for him from a bootlace. He yanked free a dagger, waved it in the air.

Quick expected Caesar and his followers to go meekly on their way, as they always had before. They did not. Maybe they had planned it among themselves, maybe they simply noticed they were three to Martin's one. They held their ground and yelled back.

Instantly pandemonium filled the clearing. Several females ran to Martin and added their yells to his. Almost as many, though, backed Caesar and his two comrades. Quick stood off to one side and wished his hands were free so he could cover his ears. Sal, he thought, would have favored Martin, but she was already off in the woods.

The two groups of sims, still shrieking, drew closer to each other. Caesar, perhaps given courage by the males at his back, did not shrink as Martin approached. Instead he advanced to confront Martin, windmilling his arms and shouting as loudly as his opponent. The encounter was at a level too basic for either of them to bother with signs; their innate responses were what counted now.

All the same, the quarrel might have ended peaceably, or with no more than pushes and shoves. Most incidents among sims did. But when Martin reached out to push Caesar away, he still had the sharp steel dagger in his fist. It scored a dripping line down the other sim's chest.

Caesar shrieked again, a cry full of pain, surprise, and fury. Martin might have finished him at that moment, but instead stared for an instant, as much taken aback as his foe, at the blood running through Caesar's hair. An instant was all Martin got. Fast as a striking snake, Caesar bent down, grabbed a branch, and slammed it into the dominant male's side. Then he sprang for Martin. They fell together, biting and gouging and kicking.

Henry Quick had not thought the din could get louder. He found he was wrong. The sims gathered in a tight knot around the two battling males. They were all screaming at the top of their lungs, and beginning to struggle with one another.

One of Caesar's supporting males also had a knife. He shoved a female aside, almost pitching her into the fire, and stooped over the two main combatants. He slashed at one of them, presumably Martin. An anguished bellow arose, loud enough to be heard through the chaos all around.

Quick limped forward. That Martin had to fight for his life was one thing, that he should be beset by two at once something else again. The male was raising an arm to bring down the dagger again. The trapper shifted his weight to his left foot; that leg would have to bear most of it for a moment. He used the stock of his rifle to knock the knife out of the sim's hand, then hit him in the temple with it.

That second blow might have felled a man, but sims had heavier skulls and thicker muscles over them. The male blinked, shook his head, spat blood. He grabbed Quick by the shoulders and threw him to the ground. A burly lumberjack might have matched it, but the sim was half a foot shorter than Quick.

The trapper landed heavily; the rifle came out of his hand and bounced away. Pain flared in his ribs and in his bad leg. That's what you get for sticking your nose in, he thought blurrily. But the male was not done with him. The sim seized his rifle, lifted it high, and stamped toward him, plainly intending to beat him to death.

Quick still held on to his pistol. He cocked it with desperate haste and fired. He aimed for the sim's chest. The ball took the male in the belly instead.

The noise of the shot shocked the sims into momentary silence. Nothing else, perhaps, could have distracted them so effectively from their own quarrels. Leaning up on one elbow, Quick saw one of the two males around whom the bigger squabble had revolved also sitting up, pushing away the inert body of his foe. Martin had won the fight; blood was still flowing from a score of Caesar's wounds. Yet by the way he moved, the victor was also badly hurt.

Quick spared him hardly a glance, though. The trapper's horrified attention—and that of all the sims in the clearing—was drawn to the male he had shot. Quick had heard tales of the agony of gutshot men. Now he saw it firsthand.

The sim rolled and thrashed, hands clutched to the hole above and to one side of its navel. Blood trickled between its fingers. Soon more came from its anus. When it emptied its bladder a moment later, that discharge too was red. The sim shrieked and wailed.

Several females came running from the woods; the gunshot drew those who had not heard the sound of the fight. Sal was the last of them; her bulging belly made her move slowly. Quick was glad to see her, and even gladder she had not been in the clearing before.

He struggled to his feet. His right leg groaned but did not scream; he had not rebroken it. He picked up his rifle and hobbled over toward Martin. When Sal came up to help him as she had so many times before, he gratefully let her bear some of his weight. The other sims, their eyes still on the awful spectacle of the male he had shot, stepped out of his way. None of them signed to him. None of them seemed to want to have anything to do with him.

Pain twisted Martin's face. His hairy hide was scraped away in a dozen places to show raw, bleeding flesh. Caesar had bitten half of one ear away. Martin was holding his ribs with one hand, and had the other at the back of his left heel.

When the trapper saw that, and saw how the sim's left calf was bunched but his foot limp, he had a sinking feeling that made him forget his bruises. Against all odds, he had recovered from his own crippling injury, at least enough to get about. Martin never would, not when he was hamstrung.

Martin took his hands from his wounds, signed *Fix leg?* His eyes were full of desperate appeal. They held Quick's.

Seeing how Martin's thoughts paralleled his own only made Henry Quick feel worse. Behind the trapper, the male he had shot screamed on, unceasing and dreadful. *Not fix*, Quick had to sign.

Sal stared at him in amazement. *Fix*, she signed firmly. *Use sticks. Sticks fix your leg, sticks fix his leg.*

Not fix, the trapper repeated miserably. *His leg not hurt same way.* How could he explain that the splints only held the pieces of his shattered leg together while the bone healed, but that you could splint a cut tendon from now till doomsday and it would never mend? He could not, not with the limited hand-talk Sal knew.

And if he could, she would not have believed him. *Sticks*, she signed, and stepped away from him to get a couple.

At least she was doing something constructive. The rest of the sims in the clearing wandered about dazed, like men and women who had been through a train wreck. Quick could see why. In the space of a few minutes, the band had suffered disaster. Two prime males were dead (even if one might go on making horrid noises for hours). The dominant male was at best crippled; at worst, if his wounds went bad, he would join Caesar and his follower. The hunting party, never more than a dozen strong to begin with, would take years to recover.

Worse, Quick knew the catastrophe would not have happened in the same way had he not become part of the band. The fight between Martin and Caesar would not have turned savage had Martin not been holding the sharp steel knife, the tool he'd got from the trapper: it would have remained one of the shove-and-bluff contests typical among sims. Maybe Caesar would have backed down, maybe Martin. No one would have been much hurt either way.

The subhumans lacked a good part of the trapper's reasoning ability. They seemed to have reached the same conclusions he had, though, whatever the means they used to get there. All through the winter, they had treated Quick like one of them. Now they drew apart from him. He saw at once he was no longer one of the band.

Being rejected by mere sims should not have hurt Quick. It did. The trapper's fate had been too intimately tied with theirs for too long for him to be indifferent to their feelings about him.

That was especially true in one case. Quick's gaze went to Sal, who was still busy putting a splint on Martin's leg. *Better?* she signed when she was through.

Martin's breath hissed through clenched teeth. He shrugged, as if he did not want to say no but hurt too much to say yes. Quick knew he was not going to get better, with or without the splint.

Sal got to her feet awkwardly. She patted her swollen belly in annoyance, almost in reproach. Most of her attention, though, remained on Martin. At last she looked away. Her eyes met the trapper's. She looked at him, at the male he had shot (who was still ululating piteously), at Martin, at Caesar (whose skin was pierced in so many places it would have been worthless as a pelt). When she glanced Quick's way again, it was with no more warmth than if she had been looking at a stone. That told him the last thing he needed to know.

If the sims had decided to tear him to pieces, he could not

have stopped them. They ignored him instead. Perhaps they thought ostracism a worse punishment. In their small bands, with each member knowing all the others so intimately, that made some sense. Quick was never sure. Living like a sim, he found at last, could not make him think like a sim.

He reloaded his pistol, put his powderhorn, ammunition pouch (which also held flint and steel), a knife, and a hatchet on his belt. Leaning on his rifle, he took a couple of limping steps toward the edge of the clearing, then turned back. No matter what the band did to him, he could not stand having the wounded sim's shrieks pursuing him through the woods. He aimed carefully, shot the male in the head.

He reloaded again, limped away. The sims still did not try to stop him. He looked back at Sal a last time, and at the unborn child he would never see now, the child that would live out its life with its mother's band.

Maybe that, at least, was for the best, he told himself, and not just because of the social strictures in the Commonwealths against such babies. In the world of humans, a child half sim would always be at a disadvantage, slower and stupider than its fellows. But in the world of sims, a half-human child might prove something of a prodigy, and earn a place in the band higher than any it could look for east of the mountains.

He did not know that was so. He could only hope. The woods closed in behind him, hiding the clearing from sight.

The tavern was hot and noisy. Henry Quick knocked back a whiskey with reverent pleasure. He was wearing clothes he had left behind before he set out on his last trapping run. He had been in civilization a month, and regained some of the weight he'd dropped in his slow, painful journey east and south. All the same, his tunic and the breeches that should have been tight flopped on him as though meant for a larger man.

"Have another," James Cartwright urged. The fur dealer had been generous with Quick, giving him a room in his own house and a place at his table. Quick knew he had an ulterior motive. He did not mind. Even Martin had had an ulterior motive.

The trapper caught a barmaid's eye, held up his empty glass. The girl looked bored, but finally nodded and went off for a bottle. She was blonde, smooth-skinned, and pretty. Quick could easily imagine sharing a bed with her. Caring afterward was something else again.

"Your health," he said to the fur dealer when he had been resupplied. He drank again, sighed contentedly.

"Now, then, Henry," Cartwright said, seeing that look of relaxation on the trapper's face, "you really ought to tell me more about the clearing where your cache of furs is. They'd be worth a pretty pile of silver denaires, I dare say."

"So they would, so they would," Quick admitted, "but drunk or sober, I have nothing to say to you about them. You can test it if you like; I'll sponge up as much as you care to buy."

"Worse luck for you, I believe it." But, laughing, the fur dealer signaled for another round. After it arrived, he turned serious again. "Henry, I just can't fathom why you're being so pigheaded. It's not as if you could hope to get those pelts back for yourself. Moving the way you do, you needed a special miracle to make the trip out once. You can't be thinking of going in again for them."

"Oh, I can think about it," Quick said; the urge to get away would never leave him. But whenever he tried to walk, even now, he knew long journeys were really behind him.

"Why, then?" Cartwright persisted.

The liquor had loosened Quick's tongue enough to make him willing to justify himself out loud. "Because of the sims," he said. "That band deserves to have men leave them alone, instead of flooding in the way they would after they found my trail and took out my furs. Those sims took me in and saved me, and they've had enough grief for it already."

"They're just sims, Henry," Cartwright said. He knew

the trapper's story, as much of it as Quick had told. No one knew about Sal; no one knew about the child. No one ever would.

"They were here first, John," Quick said stubbornly. "It's not their fault they're stupider than we are. Having them work fields and such is one thing; we can make better use of good land than they ever could. But let them keep the backwoods. Some of them ought to stay free."

"Maybe you won't want to go trapping after all," Cartwright observed. "You sound like you've got yourself a new mission in life."

Quick hadn't thought of it in quite those terms. He rubbed his chin. He'd shaved his beard, but wasn't yet used to feeling smooth skin again. At last he said, "Maybe I do, at that. Sims aren't animals, after all."

A hunter sitting at the next table turned round at his words. He grinned drunkenly. "You're right there, pal. They give better sport than any damned beasts." He hooked a thumb under his necklace, drawing Quick's eye to it. The cord was strung with dried, rather hairy ears.

It took four men to pry Quick's hands from the fellow's throat.

1988

Freedom

There can be no doubt that the labor of sims contributed greatly to the growth of the Federated Commonwealths of America. As we have seen, this was true in agriculture. It was also the case in the huge factories of the nineteenth and early twentieth centuries: simple, repetitive tasks proved to be within the capacity of the native subhumans. Their treatment at the dormitories next to these factories was all too often worse than any suffered by human workers, who had both the wit and the political ability to combine to improve their conditions.

These workers' alliances were early supporters of the sims' justice movement. If factory owners could use sims instead of people, rewarding them with no more than what was frequently inadequate food and shelter, then wages for all workers were depressed. Only the fact that humans greatly outnumbered sims prevented this problem from being even worse than it was.

The steady growth of technology, however, did at least as much to change conditions for sims as did political agitation. Farming grew increasingly mechanized, and machines gradually began taking over many of the simple factory jobs sims had formerly performed. This transformation also affected humans, of course. But most succeeded in changing with the times, and in finding new positions in emerging high-technology industries. This option was not open to sims.

Even with improved technology, the sims' justice movement has continually faced a serious problem: sims, while more than beasts, manifestly are less than men and women. Defining a middle ground, and an appropriate role for sims in modern society, has never been easy; the movement itself has fragmented several times over attempts to do so. In recent years, though, the area of research has drawn attention from almost all factions of the sims' justice movement.

Because they are so like people in so many ways, sims have since their discovery been used for experiments where humans could not in good conscience be employed. Sometimes this has resulted in glorious successes: witness the sim Abel, who orbited the earth six months before the first man to do so. Sometimes, as in the case of certain nineteenth-century medical research conducted without benefit of anesthesia, words cannot convey the horror suffered by sims.

And yet, it cannot be denied that much good has accrued to humanity through the testing in sims of new surgical techniques and various methods of immunization. Whether this good outweighs the suffering that sims are intelligent enough to feel but not fully to understand must, in the end, be decided by each person for him- or herself. Society as a whole still feels that it does; research with sims, under properly controlled conditions, continues. There remains, though, a vocal minority that cannot in its conscience justify what it perceives as abuse of intelligent creatures. . . .

From *The Story of the Federated Commonwealths*

Dr. PETER HOWARD stepped to the podium with the brisk strides of a man who did not believe in wasting any time, ever. Yes, I have something to say, his walk proclaimed—I'll say it and get out and get back to work, and once you've heard it you can do what you like with it.

Television lights glared overhead; flashbulbs from newspaper photographers made even the determined Dr. Howard blink repeatedly. As soon as he reached the rostrum, he tapped on the microphone for quiet. When he did not get it right away, a frown made his long, thin face longer.

He tapped again, louder this time, and said, "I'd like to begin with a short statement, if I could. I don't want to spend more time here in Philadelphia than I have to. I want to get down to Terminus and back to work."

The reporters gradually quieted. They still were not fast enough to suit Howard, who began when the room in the Hall of the Popular Assembly was still buzzing with talk: "I have some progress to report in our efforts to find a cure for acquired immune deficiency syndrome, more commonly known as AIDS."

That got him silence, but only a moment's worth. Then the buzz became a roar. A whole new fusillade of flashbulbs went off. Howard held up his hand, as much to protect his eyes as to ask to be allowed to go on.

Finally, he could. "I do not yet *have* a cure," he said firmly. Setting off hysteria was the last thing he wanted to do. The reporters who had leaped to their feet sat down again. Good, Howard thought: having ridden an emotional roller coaster in two sentences, maybe they would settle down now and listen.

He said, "As you know, the HIV virus that causes AIDS attacks the body's immune system, specifically the white blood cells called T-lymphocytes. Without these cells to fight off infection, the body becomes vulnerable to opportunistic diseases it would otherwise repel. Eventually, one of them proves fatal to the patient.

"At the Terminus Disease Research Center, we have developed a drug we are calling an HIV inhibitor, or HIVI for short. In the laboratory, HIVI seems to help prevent the virus from gaining a foothold in the body's T-cells, and strengthens the effectiveness of the antibodies the immune system produces to fight AIDS. Let me show you what we have achieved."

He gestured in the direction from which he had come, his hands shaping words almost everyone in the chamber followed as easily as speech: *Out here. Now*. A sturdy male sim emerged to join him at the podium. "This is Matt," Howard said.

More flashbulbs popped. Matt lowered his head so that his heavy brow-ridges protected his eyes from the bursts of intolerable light. "How do you feel, Matt?" Howard asked. He signed the words as he spoke them, to make sure the sim would understand.

Feel good, Matt answered with his hands; like almost all sims, he found sign-talk much easier than true speech.

"Matt feels good now," Howard said. "Sadly, six months ago he was much less well." The doctor waved a hand. The lights dimmed; a large screen dropped into place behind him and Matt. Howard waved again. At the far end of the hall, a slide projector came on.

The hall grew truly quiet at last. Into that silence, Howard said, "This was Matt six months ago." The sim on the slide was sadly different from the one who stood before the reporters in the flesh. The Federated Commonwealths— the world—had seen too many cases of AIDS for them to mistake this one. The image of the emaciated sim, his once-thick hair falling out in clumps all over his body, was a vivid—and dreadful—illustration of why in Africa AIDS was simply called "the slims."

Howard went on, "Two days after that picture was taken, Matt began receiving HIVI. Today, his T-cells are nearly normal, as are his immune responses. He does not even know he still has AIDS."

Feel good, Matt signed again.

The reporters could not stand it anymore. "Why isn't this a cure, then?" one of them shouted.

"Because—as I was about to say," Howard added pointedly, "the AIDS virus is still in Matt's bloodstream. He can still transmit it to others—other sims in his case, I suppose, but in theory to humans as well—through sexual relations. And if he stops receiving HIVI injections, the symptoms of AIDS will return. Now"—he emphasized the word—"I will respond to questions."

The frantically waving hands reminded him of storm-lashed treetops. He chose one at random. "Yes, you in the third row, with the blue ruffled tunic."

"How many sims have died of AIDS in the course of your experiments?" the man asked.

Howard pursed his lips. He had expected questions of that sort. With the demonstrators marching outside the Hall of the Popular Assembly, he would have been an idiot not to. But he had hoped not to have to deal with them so soon. He should have listened to his colleagues down in Terminus, and planted a few people to ask the questions he wanted asked. He had always been headstrong, though. He thought he could deal with anything. Now he'd have to.

"My program, to date, has seen the expiration of twenty-eight sims," he answered steadily.

His luck was not all bad. The reporter simply followed up by asking, "Wouldn't it have been better to use shim-panses than sims in your research?"

"Other than sims and men, shimpanses are the only creatures in which the AIDS virus will grow," Howard acknowledged. "But there are several objections to their use in AIDS research. Most obvious, of course, is the fact that most of them must be caught wild in Africa and then shipped to the FCA. That makes the supply uncertain and expensive, all the more so because of the growing instabil-ity in the African states as the AIDS epidemic debilitates them. Sims, being native to America, are easily available.

"There are also other reasons for preferring them to shimpanses. Biologically, sims are much closer to humans than shimpanses are: as we all know, mixed births between sims and humans are perfectly possible."

The reporters muttered in distaste. Everyone knew that,

but it was something seldom mentioned outside of dirty jokes. Howard suspected there would be shocked gasps in living rooms all across the Federated Commonwealths: talking about sex between people and sims was not standard television fare.

"Also, of course," the doctor finished, "sims have the advantage of being able to report symptoms to us, something of which shimpanses are incapable." He pointed to another reporter. "Yes?"

"Isn't that part of the problem, Dr. Howard?" the fellow asked. "How do you feel about deliberately subjecting twenty-eight intelligent creatures to the grim, lingering death AIDS brings?"

"I had hoped some of you might perhaps be interested in the success—or at least the partial success—of HIVI, rather than in the failures that preceded it," Howard said sharply.

"I am, Dr. Howard," the reporter said, "but that's not the question I asked."

Howard scowled out at the audience, but saw everyone nodding along with the reporter. If some of these people had their way, he thought with sudden hot anger that he did his best to conceal, he'd be lucky to be able to work with shimpanses, let alone sims.

He chose his words with care; he had not come up to Philadelphia to antagonize the press. "I always regret sacrificing any, ah, creatures in the laboratory but, particularly in the case of what is, as you say, a grim disease such as AIDS, I feel justified in doing whatever I must to save people's lives."

"But sims—" the reporter persisted.

Howard cut him off. "—are not people. The law has never regarded them as such. They are different from animals, true, but they are also very different from us. The sims in my research project were purchased with an appropriation from the Senate for that express purpose. Everything I have done has been in accordance with all applicable regulations. And that is all I have to say on *that* topic." He looked toward another reporter. "Yes?"

"What makes HIVI more effective against AIDS than earlier drugs?"

Howard nodded to her and smiled his thanks. At last, a sensible question. "We're still not entirely sure, Mistress, ah—"

"Reynolds."

"Mistress Reynolds, but we believe that the chief improvement has to do with the way HIVI interacts with the T-cells' outer membranes and strengthens them, making them more resistant to penetration by the AIDS virus. HIVI was developed from—"

Round and round, round and round—Ken Dixon was getting sick of carrying his picket sign. He also did not like the way the greencoats were gathering in front of the Hall of the Popular Assembly. He could not read their faces, not with the mirrored visors on their helmets. But their body language said they were going to break up the demonstration soon.

"Killing sims is murder!" he chanted. He'd been calling that for a couple of hours now, since before Dr. Howard's news conference convened. His throat felt sore and scratchy.

A man walking on the part of the sidewalk the demonstration wasn't using caught his eye. "Not under the law, it's not," he said. He looked prosperous and well-fed, nothing like a sim who'd been given AIDS on purpose.

Likely a lawyer himself, Dixon thought scornfully; Philadelphia was lousy with them. While the chant went on around the young man, he broke it to say, "The law is wrong."

The probable lawyer fell into step beside him. "Why?" he asked. "Sims aren't people. If using them will help us rid ourselves of this terrible disease, why shouldn't we?"

Dixon frowned. At the planning meeting for this protest, he'd worried out loud that people would say just what this plump fellow was saying, that the threat of AIDS would let people justify the horror of the Terminus labs. He'd been argued down then, and now gave back the reasoning the rest of the steering committee had used against him: "Howard's AIDS research is just a fragment of what we're talking about here. If you allow it, you set a precedent for allowing all the other cruelty that sims have suffered since people first came to America: everything from working them to death on farms and in mines to hunting them and killing them for sport." He screwed up his face to show what he thought of that kind of sport.

"Sims were here," the plump man shrugged. "We used them to do the work we didn't care to do for ourselves. We still do. Why not?"

The man's question grated on Dixon all over again, but he thought before he answered; the fellow was not a fool. "In the old days we needed them, I admit. I'm not saying what we did then was right—far from it—but it was understandable. It isn't anymore, not with machines to do sim-work, and do it better, faster, and cheaper than sims ever did."

"You'd send them all to the preserves, then?"

"That would be the ideal solution," Dixon said cautiously. Most of the people marching with him would have given the plump man a *yes* at once. Three big tracts of land—together they were as large as a fair-sized commonwealth—one in the Rockies, one on the plains, and one in the northwest woods, gave wild sims and their way of life a last stronghold in the FCA.

Trouble was, even a small band of wild sims needed a large territory on which to forage. There wasn't enough land to accommodate the subhumans who now lived in civilized country, even assuming they wanted to trade their lives for ones like those of their ancestors.

"And in this not-so-ideal world?" the plump man asked, his raised eyebrow telling Dixon he knew all the objections that had popped into the demonstrator's mind.

"As much freedom as they can handle," Dixon said. He jerked his chin at the Hall of the Popular Assembly. "At least freedom from being made into lab animals just because they're too much like us."

That eyebrow, damn it, climbed higher. " 'As much freedom as they can handle,' " the plump man echoed. "I can't imagine a more dangerous gift, for either the sims or the people who give it to them." His eyes followed Dixon's stubborn chin to the portico of the Hall. Someone was handing the greencoat chief a rolled-up piece of paper. The fellow resumed, "I would say, for example, that our esteemed constabulary has just been granted all the freedom it can handle."

"Yes," Dixon said unhappily. He knew a writ when he saw one. Somebody on the committee had fouled up; the legal side was supposed to keep the greencoats off people's backs until the protest broke up by itself.

He turned to say that to the man who'd been walking with him. The fellow wasn't there anymore. Dixon spotted him walking purposefully down the street in the direction he'd been going before he fell in with the demonstration. From the plump man's perspective, that made good sense. Dixon was tempted to disappear himself.

The greencoat chief put a hailer to his mouth. The static that belched from it as he turned it on made everybody look his way who hadn't already. One of his assistants ceremoniously unrolled the writ.

"Uh-oh, trouble," Melody Porter said from in front of Dixon. They'd been in a lot of the same classes at the Philadelphia Collegium since they were both freshmen—almost four years now, he thought, bemused. They'd been in a lot of demonstrations together, too. Melody was even more strongly committed to justice for sims than he was. She came by it honestly; she was the great-great-granddaughter of Henry Quick, the trapper who'd really founded the sim justice movement.

In an altogether different vein, Dixon thought marching behind her was one of the things that made protests worthwhile.

After a few more seconds of fumbling, the boss greencoat finally got the hailer working. His aide handed him the legal paper. *Pro bono publico,* he intoned, his amplified voice filling the square with formality. Dixon wondered how many horrors had been perpetrated "for the public good."

"Pro bono publico," the greencoat repeated for the sake of the record and for the benefit of everyone this side of complete nerve-dead deafness. Then he got down to business: "A court has declared this rally a danger to public order. Those who do not disperse in the next five minutes will be liable to arrest."

The blunt demand jerked the protesters out of their chant. People shouted back at the greencoat: "We're peaceable! Why aren't you?" "Can't stand to hear the truth, eh?" And a cry that started a new chant: "Justice for sims, and for people too!" Even so, Dixon noticed that the marchers' picket signs, which had been steady, began to jerk as if pelted by hailstones. People were having second thoughts. Few were leaving, though.

The officer with the hailer knew his job. He kept the pressure on, loudly announcing each minute as it went by. The greencoats shook themselves out into a skirmish line.

"Time's up," the chief announced. The line moved forward. Dixon took off his spectacles and stuck them in the hip pocket of his breeches. Sometimes these affairs stayed polite, sometimes they didn't. The world turned blurry.

A greencoat emerged out of the blur. He was carrying a club. His voice conversational, matter-of-fact, he asked Dixon, "You going to take off, kid?"

Before he answered, he heard Melody loudly say "No" to what had to be the same question. That killed the few shreds of hesitation he had left. "No," he said, trying to sound as firm as Melody had.

The greencoat only shrugged. "I arrest you, then, for constituting a danger to public order." Formal language done, he went on, "Come along quietly?"

"Sure."

"All right, then. Put down your sign—you won't get an extra trash-strewing charge on account of it." Dixon did.

He put his spectacles back on. The greencoat waited till he was done, then gave him a light shove. "Over that way. Come on." He sounded more bored than anything else, Dixon thought, a little resentfully. Justice for sims was too important to be handled as part of someone's routine.

Even with his spectacles, Dixon did not see what went wrong. Maybe a protester whacked a greencoat with a picket sign. Maybe a greencoat thought one was going to, and swung first. Maybe a greencoat swung first for the hell of it.

However it happened, it happened fast. What had been a civil process turned ugly all at once. Demonstrators swung at greencoats, and pushed them away when they tried to arrest them. Like the genie in the legend, once violence was out of the bottle, it did not want to go back in.

The greencoat who was urging Ken Dixon along suddenly pushed him in the back, hard. He went down to his knees. His carefully replaced spectacles flew off his nose. He heard a crunch as a greencoat running toward the brewing fight smashed them with his boot.

Melody screamed as she got the same treatment he just had. "Leave her alone!" he shouted. He tried to get to his feet to go help her.

A club exploded against the side of his head. He went down. He tried to get up again, but his legs didn't want to do what he told them. He had made it to all fours when a greencoat landed on him, knocking him down again.

"You're not going anywhere!" the greencoat bawled in his ear. It was *his* greencoat; he recognized the voice. He was irrationally pleased he was able to recognize anything.

The greencoat yanked his arms out from under him. His chin hit the pavement. The greencoat jerked his arms behind his back, clapped manacles on his wrists. He had thought the roaring pain in his head left him immune to other hurts. The bite of the manacles' metal teeth convinced him otherwise in a hurry.

"*Now* come on, you stinking sim-lover!" the greencoat shouted. He hauled Dixon to his feet, frog-marching him toward a constabulary motorcoach. Two more greencoats were waiting at the steps. They grabbed him, flung him inside.

He almost fell over somebody inside the motorcoach. A moment later, somebody almost fell over him. Crawling with his hands locked behind him was almost impossible. Because he had to, he managed to lurch his way up onto one of the motorcoach's hard, comfortless seats.

"Are you all right, Ken?" He hadn't even seen Melody on the seat in front of him. Concern in her voice, she went on, "You're bleeding."

"I suppose so," he said vaguely; he felt something warm and wet trickling down his cheek and jaw. He leaned his head against the bar-reinforced glass of the window. Then he looked at Melody again. Above one ear, blood matted her short, sandy hair. "So are you."

"I know." Despite the blow she'd taken, she still had her wits about her, and she was furious. "The bastard groped me, too, when he was wrestling with me to get the manacles on. I clawed him pretty good, I think, before he finally managed to."

"Good for you." Dixon leaned against the window again; talking and thinking hurt. Someone sat down beside him. He hardly noticed. He was watching the greencoats finish off the demonstration. Protesters outnumbered constables, but the contest was never in doubt. The demonstrators hesitated before they fought, and when they did it was by ones and twos. The greencoats did not hesitate at all, and worked together. A few demonstrators managed to flee; most were seized and hauled off to the motorcoaches.

"Maybe it's for the best," Melody said. "This way our side of the message is sure to reach the television news tonight, along with Dr. Howard's rationalizations."

"Maybe," was all Dixon could manage. After a while, the greencoats slammed the motorcoach's doors shut. Its engine roared to life. It rattled through the streets of Philadelphia, toward the lockup.

The two sims separated. Matt lay back on the bed. The

female—it was the one called Jane, Dr. Howard saw when she turned her face toward the monitor camera—stayed on hands and knees beside him. After a surprisingly short time, Matt's vigor returned. He got behind her and fell to again.

"Don't they ever quit?" a technician asked, pointing at the screen. A whole bank of monitors let the investigators at the Disease Research Center watch the sims they studied without disturbing them.

"What else do they have to do?" Howard asked. "They aren't likely to sit around reading books, you know."

The technician laughed, but persisted. "This is the third time they've been at it today, and it's only"—he glanced at his pocket watch—"a little past two."

Howard shrugged. "Weren't you ever a randy eighteen-year-old? That's what Matt is, or the equivalent. Sims age a little faster than we do, so he's probably about at his peak now at fourteen. And up until not so long ago he was deathly ill, so I dare say he's making up for lost time too."

"Well, maybe," the technician said. Howard walked down the row of television screens to check on some of the other sims at the DRC. The technician muttered under his breath, "No way I could have gone that hard, even when I was eighteen, especially if my girl was that ugly."

Howard knew he was not supposed to hear, but turned back anyway. "Jane looks as good to Matt as the lead in *Vixens in Love* does to you."

"That's *his* problem," the technician retorted. Howard knew he had a picture of that particular blonde taped above his desk.

"I'm glad he has the urge back," the doctor said. "It shows the effectiveness of the HIVI in returning him to good health."

"Almost," the technician reminded him. "What I'm glad of is that Jane already carries the AIDS virus too, because no matter how good Matt feels, he's still got the virus in him and he can still spread it, right?"

"Yes," Howard said reluctantly. "That's the main drawback to HIVI at the moment: it can let carriers go on transmitting AIDS, giving it to people who will pass it on in turn."

"In some ways, you know, that strikes me as worse than no cure at all," the technician said.

Howard wished the man would shut up and let him go away. He was putting his finger on just the problem that most worried the doctor. Luckily, it had not occurred to any of the reporters in Philadelphia, or a triumphant news conference might have turned embarrassing in a hurry.

Being who he was, though, Howard could not simply shove the comment aside. He paused to pick his words with care. "It depends. As far as checking the epidemic goes, I suppose you're right. But if my blood test had just come back positive, I'd scream bloody murder if somebody said I couldn't have HIVI."

"I can't argue with you there," the technician admitted, and the doctor took advantage of the moment of agreement to leave.

A fresh batch of calc printouts was on his desk: analyses of the effectiveness of a variant of HIVI at restoring the immune system and protecting T-cells. The variant wasn't as good as the basic drug. Howard made a note to assign writing up the new datum to somebody so it could get into print. Negative information was information too—now some other lab would not have to waste time checking this new subtype.

It wouldn't be the sort of publication a news conference accompanied, though.

Howard put his head in his hands. He wished he'd never called the bloody conference in the first place. That was exactly the word for it: dozens of people had been hurt in what turned into a riot outside the Hall of the Popular Assembly. Censor Bryan had called for an investigation of the way the constabulary handled it, and Censor Jennings had promptly vetoed the call. It was the worst falling-out the two chief executives had had in their term.

Howard did not care about that; politics meant nothing to him. He cared very much about hurt people, though.

Had he known the protest outside would cause so many of them, he never would have gone to Philadelphia.

He sat up straight. No, that wasn't true. AIDS hurt more people than riots ever would. The only way to fight it was with research. Research took denaires, lots of them, and the best way to latch on to them was by shouting every piece of progress, even one as ambiguous as HIVI, to the housetops.

The intercom buzzed. He jumped, and was glad no one was with him to see it. "Mr. Tanaka is here to see you, sir," his secretary said.

"Oh, yes, of course. Thank you, Doris. Send him in." Howard ran fingers through his thick brown hair. Joseph Tanaka had no official standing, but he had been friends with Censor Jennings since they were at middle school together. "Jennings's eyes," the papers called him these days.

Doris opened the door for Tanaka. Howard rose to shake his hand. He had a strong grip, and looked a few years younger in person than in photos—he was, of course, almost exactly the censor's age. His sturdy, middle-aged oriental features somehow went well with the conservative blue velvet jacket and maroon ruffled shirt he wore.

"Good of you to take time from your busy schedule, Dr. Howard." Tanaka's voice was deep, almost gravelly, his manner straightforward.

"A pleasure." Howard waved to a chair. "Won't you sit down?"

Tanaka did not. "I was hoping you'd show me around first."

"Certainly." Straightforward indeed, Howard thought. "Follow me, then." He gave Tanaka a quick tour of the DRC laboratories, ending with the bank of screens that monitored the infected sims. The technician, fortunately, had sense enough to keep his mouth shut.

When they were back in Howard's office, Tanaka did at last take a seat. "Most interesting," he said, steepling his fingers, "especially the sims' quarters. I must say, you treat them well."

"Certainly we do," Howard said. "For one example, they

eat the same food as our staff buys at the cafeteria we passed through."

Tanaka gave a wry chuckle. "From what I know of cafeterias, that's not necessarily a recommendation. Still, I see your point. You do well by the sims, as I said already." He turned serious again. "Of course, you've also given them AIDS."

"Mr. Tanaka," Howard said stiffly, "this research program operates under laws passed by the Popular Assembly with funds appropriated by the Senate. Neither censor saw fit to affix his veto to the laws of the appropriation. I assure you, I am conforming to them in every particular."

"I do not doubt that for a moment, Dr. Howard," Tanaka said. "What I've come to see is the result of that conformity. After all, though they are not human beings, sims do have their own smaller measure of intelligence, and they did not consent to be experimented on."

Appalled, Howard burst out, "A sim cannot give informed consent! That's a fundamental principle of law."

"Not quite what I meant," Tanaka said. "I doubt they are eager to die, though, of a disease they almost certainly would not have contracted in the normal course of their lives. Many people not usually supportive of the sim justice movement—" He paused to let Howard make some uncomplimentary remark, but the doctor stayed quiet. Shrugging, Tanaka went on, "—still have qualms at their being infected with AIDS."

Howard had dealt with officials for years, and had no trouble translating what they said into what they meant. Tanaka was talking about votes. The doctor took a moment to make sure his reply informed without antagonizing: "They also have qualms, Mr. Tanaka, about being infected themselves, and two or three million of them have been. Of those, somewhere around a third—maybe more, as time goes by—will actually develop AIDS. And just about all of those will die, very unpleasantly. The people who show no symptoms are just as able to pass it on through sex as the ones who do—more able, because the ones without symptoms feel fine. Sims give me my best chance of fighting AIDS in people. How can I do anything but use them?"

"What would you do if there were no sims?" Tanaka asked after thinking a few seconds himself.

"The best I could," Howard answered. "Muddle along with shimpanses and a lot of *in vitro* work, I suppose. It wouldn't be the same. I think you've seen that here. A lot more people would die while I—and a lot of other researchers using sims, don't forget—struggled to translate the answers we eventually got into clinical terms. We don't have that problem with sims. Their biochemistry is almost identical to ours."

Tanaka nodded and rose, showing the meeting was done. He stuck out his hand. "Thank you very much, Dr. Howard. You've been most interesting."

"Have I? I'm glad. What will you tell Censor Jennings, then?"

Tanaka blinked. "You're very forthright."

"I'm concerned about my program, sir."

"Reluctantly, Dr. Howard, I have to say you needn't be. I don't think the Censor will be happy when I tell him that, but you've made your points well. You also might have given me another answer to my question just now, in which case I would have said something different to Censor Jennings."

Honestly puzzled, Howard asked, "What might I have said?"

"When I asked what you'd do without sims, you might have suggested going on with human defectives."

The doctor felt his face freeze. "Good day, Mr. Tanaka. Someone, I am certain, will show you out." He sat down abruptly.

"I understand your reaction, Dr. Howard. As I said, you passed the test nicely. The idea revolts me quite as much as it does you, I assure you. But I had to know."

"Good day," Howard repeated, unmollified. Nodding, Tanaka left. Howard was so filled with fury that he did not care whether he had hurt the DRC politically. He did not think he had; Tanaka plainly felt as he did.

He was also, he realized, furious at himself, and took a long while to figure out why. When he did, he wished he hadn't. If there were no sims, who could say what he might do to take a crack at AIDS? And who could say whether he would be able to look at himself in a mirror afterwards? He was not grateful to Tanaka for showing him a part of himself he would sooner have left unseen.

He got very little work done the rest of the day.

The air waggon pulled slowly to a stop outside Terminus. When it was not moving anymore, a steward opened the door. Ken Dixon got his shoulder bag out from under his seat, worked his way up the aisle. "Thanks for breaking the trail for me," Melody Porter said from behind him.

"My pleasure," he said, adding "Oof!" a moment later as another passenger stuck an accidental elbow in his belly. He turned his head back toward Melody. "You'll forgive me if I omit the gallant bow."

"This once," she said graciously. He snorted.

"Have a pleasant stay in Terminus," the steward said as Dixon walked by, and then again to Melody.

They walked out of the air waggon's cooled air and into the furious muggy heat of a Terminus August afternoon. "What's the matter?" Melody asked when Dixon suddenly stopped halfway down the descent ladder. In less polite voices, passengers behind them asked the same thing.

"Sorry. My spectacles just steamed up." Dixon took them off his nose, peered at them in nearsighted wonder, and stuck them in his hip pocket. Holding tightly to the rail, he went carefully down the rest of the ladder.

Once down on the ground, he was relieved to discover that the fog dissipated as his spectacles reached the same sweltering temperature as their surroundings. He put them back on. When they went inside the cooled station building, he let out a blissful sigh.

Melody echoed him, adding, "Philadelphia summer is bad, but this—"

"—Is worse," he finished. Walking twenty yards had left him covered with a sweaty film. He wiped his forehead with the back of his hand.

Through the station building's broad sweep of plate glass, he and Melody watched a human boss supervise the gang of sims that was loading baggage from the air waggon onto carts. He shook his head. "The seventeenth century, alive and well in the twentieth," he said scornfully.

"Well," someone with an amused voice said at his elbow, "you sound like the chap I'm looking for. Look like him, too," the young man added.

He looked the way the Philadelphia committee said he should: a tall man with a good many blacks in his ancestry who wore a thick mustache. "You're Patrick?" Dixon asked, as he had been told to do.

"Sorry, no. Stephen's the name," the fellow said. They nodded at each other. Amateurs' games, Dixon thought, but good enough—he hoped—for the moment. Later—later was another matter. He put it aside.

"Here comes the luggage." Melody had been watching the sims tossing bags onto the conveyor belt.

They walked over to it. Stephen nudged Dixon. "Is she really the one who's his great-granddaughter?" he whispered, not wanting her to hear.

"Great-great, yeah."

"Whoa." The respect in Stephen's voice and eyes was just this side of awe. Dixon's lingering doubts cleared up. No infiltrator could be that impressed over her ancestry.

He and Melody had boarded the air waggon early; their bags, naturally, were among the last ones out, having been buried beneath everyone else's. "So much for efficiency," Melody sighed when she had hers. Dixon's finally appeared a couple of minutes after that.

"Come on," Stephen said. He led them to an omnibus with PEACHTREE STREET on the destination placard. It roared off, a little more than half full, about ten minutes later. It was, Dixon discovered thankfully, cooled.

Stephen rose from his seat at a stop on Peachtree Street, in the midst of a neighborhood with many more apartment blocks than private houses. Dixon thought himself ready for the blast of heat that would greet him when he got off the omnibus, and was almost right.

"The collegium is over there," Stephen said, pointing west; Dixon could see a couple of tall buildings over the tops of the apartments. "In this neighborhood, no one will pay any attention to you; everybody will figure you're just a couple of new students here for the start of fall term."

"Good," Melody said briskly. She turned around, trying to orient herself. "Where's the DRC from here? That way?"

Stephen gave her a respectful glance. "Yes, northwest of here, maybe three or four miles."

"Good," she said again. "We'll be staying with you, I gather, until we get down to business?"

"That's right. People float in and out of my cube all the time; the landlord's used to it. As long as he gets paid on the first of every month and nobody screams too loud, he doesn't care. Half the cubes in his block are like that." Stephen started walking down the street. "Come on. It's this way."

Following, Dixon asked, "How alert are they likely to be at the DRC?"

"Not very, I hope. Since the word came down from Philadelphia that this was going to happen, Terminus hasn't heard much from us about justice for sims. We've been quiet, just letting everybody relax and think we've forgotten what we're for."

"Outstanding," Dixon said. "If they were alert, either this wouldn't work at all or a lot of people might end up hurt on account of us, which wouldn't do the cause any good."

"No," Stephen agreed. "But we have made the two connections we'll need most: one in the calc department, the other in food services."

"The calc department I can see, but why food services?"

Stephen told him why. He grinned. Melody laughed out loud.

Stephen turned off the street, led them into an apartment block and up three flights of stairs. By the time they got to the fourth floor, Dixon was sweating for reasons that had nothing to do with Terminus's climate. "My arms'll be as long as a shimpanse's if I have to carry these bags one more flight," he complained.

"You don't. We're here." Stephen had his key out and opened the door to his cube. "Here, this will help." He turned on the cooler. Nodding gratefully, Dixon set down his bags and shut the door behind him and Melody.

The cube was not big; the luggage Dixon had dropped and the two bedrolls on the floor effectively swallowed the living room. A table covered with what looked like floor plans was shoved into one corner. Melody made a beeline for that. Dixon was content just to stand and rest for a minute.

Stephen handed him a glass of iced coffee. He gulped it down fast enough to make his sinuses hurt. "Thanks," he said, squeezing his eyes shut to try to make the pain go away.

"No problem." Stephen's eyes traveled to the bedrolls. He lowered his voice a little. "I don't know what kind of arrangement the two of you have, but I'm not here all the time."

Dixon looked at Melody, who was engrossed in architectural drawings. "I don't quite know either," he said, also quietly. "I was sort of hoping this trip would let me find out."

"Like that, eh? All right. Like I said, I'll be gone a lot. I expect you'll have the chance to learn."

"Chance to learn what?" Melody looked up from the floor plans, beckoned. "Come over here, the two of you. Stephen, just how much support can we count on from your people here? If we can put folks in a couple of places at the same time, we may actually bring this off. If I read this right, we can get in and out *here* pretty fast."

They bent over the plans together.

The night guard's footsteps echoed down the quiet hallway. Except for him, it was empty. He was sleepy and bored. He turned a corner. Gray light from the bank of monitors lit the corridor ahead. The night technician was leaning back in his swivel chair, reading a paperback. He looked bored too.

"Hello, Edward," the guard said. "Slow here tonight."

"Isn't it, though, Lloyd?" The technician put the book down on his thigh, open, so he could keep his place. "Place is like a morgue when the calcs go haywire—everybody packs it in and goes home early."

Lloyd nodded, not quite happily. "Getting so no one can think anymore without the damn gadgets to help 'em." He glanced at the screens. "That's something sims don't have to worry about."

"Just swive and sleep and eat," Edward agreed. "It could be worse." Then, because he was a fair-minded man, he added, "A lot of times it is—especially when the new drugs go thumbs-down."

"AIDS." Like everyone else at the DRC, the guard made it a swear word. "How's he doing?"

Having been free of symptoms for eight months now on HIVI, Matt was a being to conjure with in these halls. Everyone worried over him. The technician perfectly understood Lloyd's concern. "He's fine, just worn out from the females again."

"Good." Lloyd yawned till the hinge of his jaw cracked like a knuckle. His eyes shifted from the monitors to a coffeepot on a hot plate. "I need another cup of that."

"I'll join you." Edward got up and poured for both of them.

"Thanks." The guard sipped. He made a face. "Give me some sugar, will you? It's bitter tonight—tastes like it's been sitting in the pot for a week."

"It is viler than usual, isn't it?" The technician added cream and sugar to his own brew.

Lloyd finished, tossed his cup at a trash can under the coffeepot. He missed, muttered to himself, and bent to pick up the cup. Then he ambled down the hall.

He yawned again, even wider than before. He glared back toward the technician's station. The coffee hadn't done him much good, had it?

He put a hand on the wall of the corridor. For some reason, he did not feel very steady on his feet. Before he knew what was happening, he found himself sliding to the tile floor. He opened his mouth to call for help. Only a snore came out.

In front of the monitors, the technician lolled in his chair, his head thrown back bonelessly. The paperback lay under the swivel chair's wheels, where it had fallen. Its cover was bent.

Terminus night was as hot as Terminus day, with the added pleasure of mosquitoes. Crouched on the wide lawn outside the DRC complex, Dixon was trying to keep his swearing to whispers as he slapped at bugs. "When do we go?" he asked for the fourth time, like a small child impatient to set out on a trip.

One of the lighted windows in the big building went dark for a moment, then lit again. "Now," Melody said at last. "Good luck to all of us."

People rose and ran forward, their feet scuffling softly on the grass. Automatic doors hissed open, leading into a passage that bent sharply. Out of sight from outside was a guard station. A guard slept in the chair; a cup of coffee had spilled on the desk in front of him.

The fluorescent lights overhead made Stephen's teeth gleam whitely as he grinned. "Food services," he said. Also grinning, Dixon nodded and gave him a thumbs-up.

"We split here," Melody declared, refusing to be distracted even for a moment. "Stephen, your group goes that way, toward elevator B. Bring back as much HIVI and as many syringes and needles as you can get your hands on."

"Right." He and two other young men dashed away.

"Out of here in fifteen minutes, or you get left behind," Melody called after them. Then she turned to Dixon and the young woman with him, whom they knew only as Dee. "Now we head up ourselves and get Matt."

The elevators right across from the guard station went up to the sim ward. Dixon thumbed the UP button. A door whooshed open. The three raiders—no, liberators, Dixon thought—crowded in.

He hit *14* a moment before Melody got it on the other panel. The door closed. Acceleration pressed against the soles of his shoes.

The door opened again. "How convenient," Melody said as they tumbled out; the bank of monitor screens was in the same position on floor 14 as the guard station on the ground floor. The man in the chair in front of them was as solidly out as the guard down below.

"Good—the screens have room numbers on them. That's the one thing I wasn't sure of," Dixon said. "Is that Matt?"

"Let's see," Melody said, coming up beside him and following his pointing finger. "Yes, that's him. Room— 1427B, is it? Let's go."

NO ENTRY WITHOUT AUTHORIZED ACCOMPANIMENT, read a large sign above closed double doors. Dixon tried them. They were locked. "Figured as much," he said. He stepped aside. "All yours, Dee."

She didn't speak; she never said much, as far as Dixon could tell. She was a locksmith by trade, though, and carried a set of picks on her belt. Her motions were quick and sure. In less than a minute, she had the doors open. "Come on," she said.

They went quietly, not wanting to disturb any of the sleeping sims but Matt. "1427B," Melody said, stopping. Dee took a step toward the door, but Melody was already trying it. Melody raised a hand in triumph, like a cricketeer after a century.

Matt woke to the sound of the opening door. His wide mouth fell open in surprise when he saw three strange humans coming in. *Who?* he signed. *What?*

"Henry Quick was my great-great-grandfather," Melody said, voice hardly above a whisper. Her fingers echoed the words.

"Hoo!" It was the sound sims made when they were impressed or interested. Dixon shook his head in wonder; he had lost track of how many times he had seen that reaction when Melody said who she was. Somehow all sims everywhere knew that Henry Quick had been the first man who worked to give them justice.

What? Matt signed again. *Why you here?*

"To make you free," Dixon said. As Melody had—as anyone did who communicated with sims—he repeated his spoken words with sign-talk. "Come with us. Do you want to spend the rest of your life cooped up in here?"

Matt shrugged. *Food good. Females here. Feel good now. Not sick.*

Dixon scowled. That wasn't the answer he was looking for. Melody asked quietly, "Do you want to be sick again? You probably will, if you stay here. Do you remember what it was like when you were sick?"

The question was not quite theoretical; like very young children, sims often let the past recede quickly. But Dixon saw that what Matt had undergone was not something he would easily forget. The sim's nostrils flared in alarm; under his brow-ridges, his eyes went wide. *No!* he signed, and vehemently shook his head. He climbed off the bed. *I come with you.*

"Good," Dee said. She turned and started down the hall. Melody and Matt followed. Dixon came with them a moment later, after leaving a souvenir on the bed to give Dr. Howard something to think about.

They hurried out through the double doors. Dee locked them again. This time, riding the elevator made Dixon feel briefly light.

"Hoo!" Matt said again when they were in the lobby. He pointed at the unconscious guard there, signed, *Not to be asleep.*

"That's what he thought," Dixon said. Matt looked at him in confusion. "Never mind. Come on."

They dashed out of the DRC and ran toward one of the two horselesses parked on the roadway close to the edge of the lawn. It was not, strictly speaking, a legal place to park, but traffic regulations were not likely to be enforced in the wee small hours.

One of the horselesses sped off. As it passed under a street lamp, Dixon saw it was crowded with people. Triumph flared in him. "They must have got the HIVI! And we've got Matt!"

The driver of the remaining horseless threw open the door across from him. *In*, Melody signed to Matt. She, Dixon, and Dee came piling after the sim. No sooner had Dee slammed the door than the driver roared away from the curb.

Dixon started to say something to the sim, but before he could, Melody leaned over and kissed him for a long time. When she finally let Dixon go, by some miracle he remembered what he had been about to tell Matt: "Free! You're free at last!"

That got him kissed again, which was, he thought dizzily, a long way from bad.

" 'Free,' " Dr. Peter Howard read. It was the last word of the pamphlet on Matt's bed, printed twice as big and black as any of the others. In Howard's mouth, it sounded obscene. Normally among the most self-controlled of men, he savagely crumpled the pamphlet and flung it to the floor.

The security officer who picked it up gave him a reproachful look. "There might have been useful evidence there, doctor."

"Oh, shut up," Howard snarled. "Where the hell were you people when this sim was stolen? Asleep on the job, that's where!"

"The guards were drugged, Dr. Howard," the security man corrected stiffly. "Our investigation into that part of the affair is just beginning."

"Wonderful." Howard turned away. Slowly, clumsily, he made his way down the hall. Getting out of the way for other people seemed more trouble than it was worth. It's as if I were one of the walking wounded, he thought—and then realized, a moment later, I am.

He sat behind his desk, but could not pretend, not today, that the broad expanse of walnut was a fortress wall to hold the outside world outside. In a bigger sense, he had used the whole DRC the same way. Well, the outside world had invaded with a vengeance.

And with such stupidity, he thought, filled with rage that was all the more consuming for having no outlet. He had only skimmed the pamphlet the thieves left behind to explain their handiwork, but he had seen and heard the phrases there often enough over the years.

His fists clenched till nails bit into flesh. At the pain, he opened them again; no matter how furious he was, he stayed careful about his hands. But it was not, was not, was *not* his fault that sims were as they were. In earlier days, he knew, people had thought other races of people to be inferior breeds. Sims did that much, at least, to stop man's inhumanity to man, by showing what an inferior breed really was like.

The security man stuck his head into the office, breaking Howard's chain of thought. "Outside greencoats are here to see you, sir," he said.

"Send them in," Howard sighed. Normally, Terminus's regular constabulary stayed away from the DRC. Normally, Howard thought—he would not get to use that word again any time soon.

No sooner had the greencoat—actually, the fellow was in ordinary clothes, blue breeches and a yellow tunic—come in than the phone chimed. "Excuse me," Howard said, thinking, everything happens at once. The greencoat nodded.

Howard picked up the phone. An excited voice said in his ear, "This is Butler, at the Terminus *Constitution*. We've had a report that a sim with AIDS has been taken from the Disease Research Center—Hello? Is that you, Dr. Howard? Are you there?"

"I'm here," Howard said. No point in breaking the connection. Like the greencoat in his office, this Butler was only the first of many.

Matt was confused. Dealing with people often left him feeling that way, but he had lived in his old home in the tower for a long time, and mostly knew what to expect. With these new people, he had no idea what was coming next.

Shaking his head, he got out of bed—the third new, strange, not quite comfortable bed he'd had in as many nights—and used the toilet. He had to strain to make the urine go through his penis, which was stiff with a morning erection. Stiffer than usual, even; he missed the females with whom he'd been living.

He flushed the toilet, sat down on it to comb his red-brown hair. That was another reason he missed the females: there was a big patch on his back that he could not reach. In the towers, sims by twos and threes would spend a lot of time combing each other all over. It was something to do.

He sniffed, and felt his broad nostrils expand with pleasure. Breakfast was cooking—sausages today, from the smell. He liked sausages.

He went out to the kitchen. The man and woman who had taken him from the tower were there, along with the strange man and woman whose house this was. They were all drinking coffee. They looked up as he came in.

Good morning, he signed.

"Good morning," the people replied, with mouths and hands. "Help yourself," added the woman who lived here. Emily was her name, Matt remembered.

He nodded his thanks. Along with the sausages were sweet rolls and slices of apple. He filled his plate, took a glass of water (he did not care for coffee).

Behind him, Emily's mate Isaac whistled and said, "Certainly nothing wrong with his appetite now."

"We've noticed that," replied Ken, one of the ones who had taken him away. "Hope it won't put you to too much trouble."

"Don't worry," Isaac said.

Matt sat down at the table and started to eat. Emily said,

"We're proud to help keep him out of the DRC, folks, and taking him was a grand gesture. But do you know what you'll do with him in the end?"

"We were thinking of getting him to one of the preserves and setting him loose there," Ken said, "but—" His voice trailed away.

"With the AIDS virus still in him, we can't do that, " Melody finished for him. "Not without spreading AIDS among the wild sims."

People often talked around sims as if they could not understand spoken words because they could not say them. Matt put down his fork so he could sign, *Feel good*.

"We know you do, Matt," Melody said gently, touching his hand for a moment with her small hairless one. "But no matter how good you feel, you *aren't* well. The sickness is still inside you."

She and Ken had said that before. It made no sense to Matt. If he did not feel sick, how could he be sick? *Feel good*, he repeated. He watched the humans roll their eyes and shrug. He shrugged too.

"There's another problem," Ken added. "He'll feel well only as long as we have HIVI for him." He looked down at his hands. "Maybe we should have thought a little longer about that, for his sake."

"We did the best we could," Melody said. "He's out now. They can't do any more experimenting on him. He's free, for as long as we can keep him that way."

Matt had heard almost identical talk every day since he left the towers. It was about him, he knew, but it did not seem to connect to him.

Then Isaac said something new: "I don't think we can keep him free. We can keep him away from the doctors, sure, but only he can make himself free."

Dixon scowled; Melody rose abruptly from the table. "We'll be taking off soon, I think." Even Matt, who did not use speech himself, could hear the anger in her voice.

He ate another sausage. *Free* was one of the many words people used that gave him trouble. Ideas like *bread* or *cat* or *green* or *jump* or *sideways* were easy enough to deal with. He could even count, though sometimes he had trouble remembering which number went with how many things or whether he had attached a number to each of the things in the group he happened to be counting.

But he could not eat *free* or see it or do it. The closest he could come to it in his own mind was *do whatever I want.* Right now he was full and felt well. He wouldn't have minded coupling, but Ken and Melody had taken him away from his females and he found human women ugly. Still, he was reasonably content. Did that make him *free?* He didn't know.

"Come on, Matt," Melody said. "We have to get moving. We've imposed on these good people quite enough, that's obvious." She walked out of the kitchen.

"Don't take it that way, Melody," Emily said. "Isaac just—"

"Never mind," Ken said, before anyone else could talk. "You put us up for the night, and we're grateful. We all share wanting to make things better for sims, and that's enough, isn't it?"

Nobody said anything. Matt wondered what the answer to the question was. In the towers, people had wanted answers to questions all the time, and were upset when they didn't get them. But Ken and Melody and Isaac and Emily were just leaving this one lying around. Matt shook his head at the vagaries of people.

Melody came back wearing rubber gloves and carrying a razor and a syringe. "Give me your arm, Matt," she said.

Not need, he protested. *Feel good.*

He had said the same thing back in the towers, and had the same success with it: none. "Give me your arm," Melody repeated. "You want to keep feeling good, don't you?"

He nodded resignedly and held out his right arm. The hair on its underside had been shaved a few days before he left the tower, but it was growing in again. The razor scraped it away, leaving a long, narrow stretch of pinkish-brown skin exposed. Now Melody could see exactly where to put the needle.

Matt's lips skinned back from his teeth in a grimace of pain. The people in the towers were much better at using the syringe. They hardly hurt him at all. Finally, the ordeal was done. Melody left the syringe on the table. "Boil it or put it in a glass full of bleach before you throw it away," she said to Emily and Isaac. "Make sure you get rid of that virus."

Not sick, nothing wrong, Matt signed, adding a moment later, *But arm hurts*.

"We're glad you feel all right," Melody said, smiling in a way that made her seem more appealing to Matt than she had before, "but the virus is still in your blood. We don't want to take any risk of its spreading."

Matt sighed. The people in the tower had talked that way, too, but it made no sense to him. *Blood is blood*, he signed.

"Never mind," Ken said again. "Let's get going."

Matt accompanied him and Melody out to the horseless in front of Emily's and Isaac's house. Isaac stayed behind inside. Emily waved from the porch. The morning sun glinted off a gold front tooth.

Ken started the horseless. He and Melody shared the front seat; Matt had the back to himself. "Springfield?" Ken asked as he pulled out into traffic.

"Springfield," Melody agreed. "I've got the town map here."

"We won't need that for a few hours," he said. "All I need to worry about now is finding my way to Via LXVI westbound."

Matt listened to the two people with half an ear at best. He watched houses, trees, open spaces go by. That wasn't very interesting, either. He'd done too much of it already, the last few days. After a while, one house, one tree, one open space looked like another. If anything could be more boring for him than traveling in a horseless, he had no idea what it was.

His eyes tried to glaze, but even that was denied him; it

was too early in the day for him to fall asleep. He played with his fingers for a bit. That soon palled. He started to stroke himself, then stopped. For some reason, he knew, people did not like anyone doing that out in the open.

He started to sing instead. His song had no words; his tongue and lips could not shape them. But the hoots and grunts he let out in their place had rhythm of a sort, a rhythm he made plainer by pounding on his thighs with the palm of his hands. His head bobbed happily. As far as he was concerned, it was a fine song.

He was the only one who thought so. Before very long, Ken burst out, "Will you please stop that infernal racket?"

Matt subsided; he was used to obeying people. But he was not pleased about it this time. He held up his hands so Ken could see them in the mirror. *Like my song*, he signed grumpily.

"Is that what you call it?" Ken said. "I don't."

Matt held up his hands again. *Not free to sing?* he asked. *Not free?*

Ken almost drove off the road. "Watch where you're going," Melody exclaimed. "What's the matter with you?" Ken told her what the matter was; she laughed and laughed. She turned round in her seat so she could sign with Matt as well as speak to him. "Sing all you like."

He opened his mouth to begin again, then paused. *Why laugh?* he asked.

"Because—because—" Melody stopped, finally resuming, "Because we do want to help sims be freer, but it still surprised us to have a sim—you—use the word to us."

Matt made an uncertain noise deep in his throat. That didn't seem very funny to him. He gave up and started to sing again. Ken made a noise remarkably similar to his, but he didn't say anything.

They got to Springfield before noon; Ken drove around a while, trying to find the next safe house. "Fancier part of town than I expected," he observed. The house was bigger than the ones where they had stayed before and the yard had a fence around it, but Matt, who was used to the immense

DRC towers, remained unimpressed. He yawned. If riding all day in a horseless was the way to freedom, he was beginning to doubt that he wanted any part of it.

His boredom fell away as he walked through the front gate. A female sim of about his own age was on her hands and knees in front of the house, weeding in a flower bed. *"Hoo!"* he said enthusiastically.

The female looked over her shoulder and smiled at him. *"Hoo!"* she said back. Her backside twitched a little.

"Uh-oh," Ken and Melody said at the same time. Matt paid little attention to them. Something else was on his mind.

A plump, middle-aged man came out on the front porch of the house. "Hello, my friends," he said. "I'm glad to see you. I'm Saul. Rhoda is on the phone, but she'll be out in a moment, I'm sure."

"Glad to see you, Saul." Ken nodded toward the female sim. "And who is this?"

"Lucy?" Saul frowned. Then he looked from her to Matt. Matt saw that Saul was not looking at his face. He looked down at himself. His enthusiasm was quite visible. "Oh," Saul said. "I see."

"Yes," Ken said. He did not sound happy.

"Well," Saul said, and let that hang for a while before resuming as if with happy inspiration, "let's go inside and eat lunch. After that we can see what comes up." He looked at Matt again, and broke into a laugh that sounded anything but cheerful.

The prospect of food was almost enough to divert Matt from Lucy. He went with Ken and Melody to join Saul inside, with only a brief sideways glance at the female sim.

Lucy put down the trowel she had been using and started to follow everyone else in. Matt felt a smile spread over his face. Food, a female—maybe this was what Ken and Melody meant by *freedom*. He had had this much back in the tower, but outside, at least, no one did hurtful things to him, save for the injection each morning. He'd had that before too, along with much else, none of it pleasant. Getting away from those proddings, pokings, and stickings made even long stretches of riding in a horseless seem not too bad.

But then he heard Saul say, "Lucy, why don't you stay outside and finish what you're doing? Rhoda will bring you something soon, I'm sure."

Matt let out an indignant grunt and sent a look of appeal to Ken and Melody. He was surprised and dismayed when they sided with Saul. "Come on, Matt," Ken said. "Lunch first. We'll worry about everything else later."

Sulkily, Lucy went back to work. Before she did, though, she gave Matt a glance full of promise from beneath her brow-ridges. He let himself be steered into the house, but all he noticed about lunch was that there was a lot of it. He ended up not being hungry anymore, but with no idea of what he'd eaten.

After a while, Lucy did come in, to use the toilet. Before she could get into the same room as Matt, Rhoda found something for her to do out in the back yard. Again Ken and Melody failed to interfere. Matt glowered at them. This did not strike him as anything like *freedom*.

Finally he had waited as long as he could. He got up and started toward the back of the house. "The toilet isn't through that door," Ken said sharply.

Matt snorted. *Not want toilet*, he signed. *Want—* His forearm pumped graphically.

"No!" All the people in the room spoke together.

The flat refusal brought Matt up short, and also made him angry. *Yes*, he signed, nodding so vigorously that his long, chinless jaw thumped against his chest. *Want to couple. Not couple since leave tower. Want to. You, you couple, Yes?* He pointed at Saul and Rhoda.

Rhoda was even rounder than her husband. She turned pink at the question, but answered, "Yes, of course we do." Saul nodded.

Matt turned to Ken and Melody. *You, you couple, yes?*

They both turned pink, and looked away from each other for a moment. "Yes, we do," Ken admitted at last. He still did not look at Melody until she reached out and took his hand in hers.

Now female for me, Matt signed. *I couple too.* He headed for the back door again.

"No!" everyone said again.

Now he stared at them in disbelief. *Not free to couple?* he signed. *Not free?* That had worked just this morning; he was sure it would again.

But it failed. "No, Matt," Melody told him. "I'm sorry, but you're not free to couple."

Not free? Matt signed, wondering if he had heard correctly. *Why not free?* When his hands had finished signing, they curled of themselves into fists. He saw Melody—and everyone else—look alarmed at that. Sims were stronger than people.

Their fear did not stop them from arguing with him, though. Ken said, "You can't couple with Lucy because you still have the AIDS virus in you. If you couple with her, you'll give her the same sickness you have."

Not sick, Matt protested. *Feel fine. Feel fine long time now. You give medicine—hurt arm—so I feel fine, yes?*

"You feel fine, yes," Melody said, "but what makes you sick is still in you, and can go out when you couple. And we have no medicine for Lucy. I'm sorry, Matt." She spread her hands in a gesture sims and people shared.

Matt only shook his head in reply. What she said made no sense to him. If he felt well, how could he have anything inside him that made him sick? And when he mated, the only thing that came out of him was jism. Jism was just jism. How could it make a female sick?

Besides— *In tower*, he signed, *couple with many females. They not sick now. Why this female here get sick, if they not sick now?* He grinned, pleased at his own cleverness: it was a bigger mental effort than he usually made.

The people seemed to understand that too. Ken rolled his eyes—something else that was not part of sign-talk but that Matt understood—and said to no one in particular, "Just what we need, a sim who cites precedent on us."

That Matt did not follow. He did not waste time on it in any case, for Melody was saying to him, "The female sims in the DRC—in the tower—had the AIDS virus in them too, so it didn't matter if you coupled with them. They were already ill the same way you are."

They not ill. They feel fine, Matt signed. *Feel good*. His hips moved involuntarily as he remembered how good the females back at the tower had felt. He wanted that feeling again.

Melody still would not let him go. "Matt," she persisted, "those females in the tower were getting medicine too, just like you, weren't they?"

Yes, and they feel fine, Matt answered.

"This is getting us nowhere," Saul broke in. "If you're thinking of letting him couple with Lucy, you two, Rhoda and I will have to ask you to leave."

"We never would have come here if we'd known you had a female sim," Ken said. They glared at each other. Hoping he was forgotten, Matt started toward the back of the house again.

"Wait!" Melody said. Resentfully, he turned back. He was tired of her trying to tell him things that obviously weren't so. What she said, though, did not look to have anything to do with his lust for Lucy: "You remember that I'm Henry Quick's great-great-granddaughter, don't you, Matt?"

He nodded. That was one reason, and a big one, why he'd gone along when she and Ken and Dee came bursting into his room in the tower. No one connected with Henry Quick could mean harm to a sim. He was sure of that.

"Then please believe me, in Henry Quick's name, when I tell you that you shouldn't couple with Lucy, or with any other female sim out here," Melody said earnestly. "Please, Matt."

He looked away from her. He did not think she was lying. He wished he did. *Not understand*, he signed.

She sighed. "I know, Matt. Will you do as I ask anyhow?"

Yes, he signed, giving up with more than a twinge of regret—this Lucy was quite a desirable female. *Hand all right?* he asked.

"Is that sarcasm?" Saul asked.

"Hush," Melody said. "Of course not." She turned back to Matt. "Yes, of course using your hand is all right. . . . You might go into another room first."

Matt went, thinking grumpily that people from outside the towers, even if they were related to Henry Quick, complained about every little thing. Then he thought of Lucy again, and the heat of that thought drove from his mind any worries about people.

That evening, Dixon sat up on the guest-room bed he shared with Melody. "Poor miserable bastard," he said as he peeled off the rubber he was wearing. "I wonder if I should have offered him one of these."

"That never occurred to me." Melody sat up too—languor afterward was not her style. She looked interested. "Do you think he could have used one?"

Dixon had been half joking, or more than half. Now he gave it some serious thought, and regretfully shook his head. "I doubt it. I massacred a fair number of them learning how, and I suspect he wouldn't care if he tore one putting it on. Sims aren't careful over details like that."

"No, they aren't," Melody admitted, adding, "A lot of people aren't, either."

"I suppose not, " Dixon said. "But if a man didn't like a rubber, he probably wouldn't take it off halfway through and go on without it. I'm afraid Matt might. That's the other reason I didn't think I ought to try to give him one."

"I'll tell you why *I* like rubbers." Melody waited for Dixon to let out a questioning grunt. Then she said, "Because with them, *you* have to go clean up."

"Harumph." In almost high dudgeon, he did just that.

When he came back to the bed, Melody was wearing a nightshirt and a serious expression. "Ken, why did you get into the sim justice movement in the first place?"

"What brought that on?" he asked, blinking, as he sat down beside her.

"Oh, I don't know." Rather to his relief, she did not meet his eyes. But she did go on even so: "I suppose it's just that you seem to keep emphasizing the ways sims are different

from people, and less than people, not the ways we're al
the same.''

"Melody, they *are* different from us," he said, as gently a
he could. Her mouth went wide and thin, a sure dange
sign. All the same, he continued, "No matter how muc
you want justice for sims, that doesn't mean you'll ever se
one elected censor, or even see one learn to read. I've know
people—not you," he added hastily, "who sometimes seen
to forget that."

"I don't think you answered me. Everything you sai
sounds as though it ought to put you on the other side.'
Now she did look at him, in the same way she might hav
at a roach on her salad plate.

"Oh, for heaven's sake," he said in some exasperation
"Doesn't my being here count for anything? Look, as far a
I can see, we have a responsibility to sims, just because the
aren't as smart as we are and can't stand against us withou
people on their side. That's always been true, I suppose, bu
it's especially true now that we have machines to drudge fo
us instead of sims. We don't need to exploit them anymore
and we shouldn't. All right? Do I pass? Can we go to sleep?'

She seemed taken aback at his vehemence, and needed ;
moment to collect herself and nod. "All right," she said
and turned out the light.

"Good." He lay down beside her. His outburst hac
startled him a little, too. He thought about what he'd said
He believed all of it. That was not the problem.

The problem, he eventually realized, was that he hadn'
given Melody all his reasons. One of them was the hope o
being just where he was now, in bed with her.

Would he have worked for sims' justice without tha
hope? He looked inside himself and decided he would. Tha
appeased his conscience and let him slide toward sleep
More time on the road was coming tomorrow.

Doris dumped the morning's pile of mail on Dr. Howard's
desk, then went back to her own station outside his office
Howard went quickly through the stack, dividing it into

things he had to deal with now, things that could wait, and things that could go straight into the trash. The wastebasket gave a resounding metallic *clunk* as he got rid of the latter stack.

An insta-picture of a sim fell out of an envelope as Howard opened it. Swearing, the doctor pulled out the sheet that accompanied the photo. The lead line shouted, MATT IS STILL FREE!

Howard jabbed the intercom button with his thumb. When Doris came on, he growled, "Fetch me Coleman. We've got another one."

"Yes, Dr. Howard."

While he waited for the security chief to get there, he read through the sheet. It was much like the others that had come to the DRC—and the copies that had gone to television outlets and papers all across the Federated Commonwealths. Whoever had Matt knew how to keep reminding the country about it.

Even some of the phrases were ones he had seen before: "no longer a victim of experimentation," "freed from the shadow of certain death in the laboratory." Howard's mouth quirked sourly. That last was an out-and-out lie. He knew it, and he expected that the people who had stolen Matt knew it too. He hoped they did.

The intercom buzzed. Coleman came in without waiting for Doris to go through the formalities; he and Howard had been seeing a lot of each other lately. Coleman was in his fifties, with red hair going white at the temples. His movements were quick and jerky, as if he had abundant energy seeking some kind, any kind, of outlet.

He fairly snatched the picture and sheet out of Howard's hand, then made a grab for the envelope still sitting on the doctor's desk. "Posted in Philadelphia," he noted, adding a moment later, "Different printer from the one for the text. Probably came to somebody who sent it on to us. Makes it hard to trace."

" 'Impossible' would seem a better word," Howard said. If he hoped to get a rise out of the security officer, he was disappointed. All Coleman did was nod. "Nothing we can do with it," he said gloomily. "I'll pass it on to the Terminus greencoats, but no reason to think they'll find anymore on it than on any of the others."

"Meanwhile, of course, all the commentators and reporters in the country go right on giving it to us," Howard growled.

"Nothing I can do about that," Coleman said. "Long as these folks care to, they'll feed the newsies whatever they want."

"Oh, get the hell out of here," the doctor shouted at him. Unruffled, Coleman took the photo, the sheet of paper, and the envelope and left. The door closed softly behind him.

Howard stared down at his hands, ashamed of his angry outburst. Matt had been gone more than a month now, and no one was having any luck tracking him down. No one even knew what commonwealth he was in. The FCA was just too big, had too many people—and sims—to make finding ones who did not want to be found easy.

The doctor was also aware that Coleman had not been quite right. Howard knew to the hundredth of a cubic inch how much HIVI the thieves had stolen. He knew almost to the day how long that HIVI would hold off the AIDS virus in Matt.

He also knew what would happen when the HIVI was gone. For Matt's sake, he hoped the people who had him did too.

The coughing from the next room went on and on and on. Ken Dixon looked at Melody, who was looking at the closed door. Worry had drawn her mouth down, put two deep lines between her eyes and other, fainter ones on her forehead. She looked, he thought, the way she would when she was forty. It was not the kind of thought he usually had. That endless cough, though, left him with mortality on his mind.

"The antibiotic isn't helping much," he said reluctantly. In fact, it wasn't helping at all. He and Melody both knew that, although she had not yet admitted it out loud.

He thought she would not answer him this time, either. But she did, saying, "No," in a low voice.

"It's probably not a bacterial pneumonia, then," he said. "It's the one caused by protozoans."

"Yes," Melody said, as low as before.

"Which means Matt's immune system is going south again, or he never would have come down with it," Dixon said. He wished Melody would make things easier by helping with the chain of logic, but after her two one-word comments she went back to moodily staring at the bedroom door. He would have to say it himself, then: "Which means the AIDS virus is loose in him again."

"Yes," Melody said—whispered, really. As quietly as she had spoken, she began to cry; Dixon did not realize it until he saw tear tracks glistening on her cheeks. "Oh, Ken," she said, and then sobbed out loud for the first time, "we tried—so—hard!"

"I know. Oh, how I know." His voice was heavy. He would have lightened it, but could not. He was tasting defeat now, for the first time in his life. The young think things come easily, as if by right, that the world shapes itself to the bidding of their will. One by one, generation by generation, they learn how small a part of truth that is, how the world shapes them far more than they it.

When Melody said, "What are we going to do?" he knew what he had to answer. Knowing hurt worse than staying blind would have.

He said, "We're going to give Matt back to the DRC."

"What?" She stared at him.

"That's the only place he can get more HIVI, and without it he won't go on too long. If this round of pneumonia doesn't finish him, the next one will, or some other infection he won't be able to fight off and we can't treat. Come on, Melody, is it so or not?"

"Yes," she said grimly. AIDS was not a quick or easy way to go; too many thousands of deaths had left everyone knowing that. "But they'll only go on using him as a lab rat—"

"A live one," Dixon broke in, "at least for a while, and

with the HIVI he feels all right, for as long as it stays effective.''

"However long that is." Melody was still fighting the idea.

"Longer than he has with us."

She flinched. "The cause—"

"If you think that cause is worth more than what happens to one sim in particular, how are you any different from Dr. Howard?"

"That's a low blow, Ken." But she did not give him any direct reply. For some time, she did not give him any reply at all. She finally said, "Let's see what Matt has to say about it. If he wants to go back—oh, shit." It was not much of a concession, but Dixon knew it was as much as he would get.

They went to the closed door. Melody, usually impetuous, stayed behind Dixon, as if to say this was not her plan. He opened the door. They both frowned at the stale sickroom smell that met them.

Matt lay on his back on the bed. He lifted his head a couple of inches when they came in, then let it fall back to the pillow, as though the effort of holding it up was too much for him. For the moment, though, he was breathing well.

He had lost weight, but had no appetite; a bowl of soup, almost full, stood untouched on the nightstand. His eyes were the only live things in his thin face. He looked, Dixon thought, like a camp survivor from the Russo-Prussian War. Dixon knew the comparison was a cliché. Nonetheless, it fit all too well.

Once inside the bedroom, Melody took the lead; Dixon's idea might have been her own, once she was with Matt. "You've stopped coughing," she said quietly. "Are you feeling any better?"

Tired, the sim signed. *So tired*. His arms flopped down on the mattress as soon as he was done using his hands. Then one of them came up again. *Medicine?* he asked. *Medicine that helps?*

"I'm sorry, Matt. We have none, and don't know where to

get any," Melody said. Dixon winced at Matt's shrug of resignation. Melody went on, "They do have that kind of medicine at the towers, Matt, if you want to go back." Somehow she held her voice steady.

Back home? Matt signed, which only made Dixon feel worse—he had not thought he could. The sim's somber features brightened. *Medicine back home?* He tried to sit up and eventually succeeded, though it set off another spasm of coughing, this one fortunately brief. *Females too, yes?* he signed with a sidelong look at Dixon and Melody. *Tired of hand.*

That set Melody laughing so hard she had trouble stopping. Finally, at Dixon's quizzical look, she explained, "I read in my great-great-grandfather's diary that the only reason he ever came home from a trapping run was that he got bored with his hand."

"Oh." Dixon laughed too, a little, before turning serious again. "Matt seems to have made his choice." That brought Melody up short; after a moment, she gave a reluctant nod. He went on, "Now we have to figure out how to give him back without giving ourselves away to the greencoats. . . ."

The intercom buzzed. "Yes, Doris?" Dr. Howard said.

"Call for you, sir," his secretary said. "Won't give a name, won't speak to anyone but you. He says it's about Matt."

"Put him on," Howard said wearily. He'd had enough lunatic calls since Matt was taken to last him a lifetime, but there was always the off chance. . . . He picked up the phone. "Yes? This is Dr. Peter Howard. Go ahead."

The man on the other end of the line sounded young and nervous, but what he said made Howard sit straighter in his chair: "If I were a fake, would I have any way of knowing that the last three pamphlets you got were red, green, and gray, in that order?"

"No," the doctor said, excitement rising in him. "I don't believe you would. This is about Matt, you say? Where is he? Is he well? Is he alive?" The stolen HIVI should have been used up some time ago. After it was gone, anything might have happened.

"No, he's not very well, but he is alive," the caller said. "As a matter of fact, he's sitting on a bench on the corner of Peachtree and Sherman, waiting for somebody to come pick him up. We're giving him back to you."

If that was true—! Relief left Howard limp. "Thank you," he whispered.

"You're anything but welcome," the young man said bitterly. "You made him sick, but you're the only one who can slow down the AIDS in him now, so we don't have any choice but to give him back. I wish we did."

"People will be better because of what we've done to him," Howard said.

"Will Matt? He didn't get a choice."

"You had him some little while yourself. Did you let him make all his own choices?" The silence at the other end of the connection answered that for Howard. "You can't with a sim, can you?" the doctor said. "Believe me, I know that."

"Go to hell," the young man said. "I'm breaking off now. You're probably tracking this call." The connection went blank.

"Thank you for giving him back, anyhow," Howard said to the dead line. Then he gathered himself and rang Coleman. He was not surprised to find that the security chief had already given orders for picking up Matt, and for going after the caller.

Howard found himself hoping the young man would get away. That did surprise him.

"It's no good, Ken," Melody said. They were sitting side by side at the edge of the hotel bed, but he had known long before she spoke that they would not be making love in it tonight. The way she'd sat stiffly, not looking at him, in the passenger seat of the horseless as he drove away from calling the DRC had been plenty to tell him that. Now she went on, "After today, in fact, we'd probably be better traveling separately."

"Why?" he said. Down deep he knew why, though, and proved it to himself by continuing, "You agreed we had to give Matt back."

"I know I did. It was the only thing we could do, and I hated it. I don't see how I'll ever do anything but hate it, either, and being with you just keeps reminding me of it. I'm sorry."

"The rewards of being right," he said.

That earned him a glare. "Call it whatever you like. But if we stay together, I think I'll end up hating you too. I'd sooner break clean now."

"However you like," he said tonelessly. He suspected she would end up hating him anyway, convincing herself that everything that had gone wrong was his fault. It was already too late for him to do anything about that.

He and Melody slept with their backs to each other. The small space of mattress between them might as well have been a chasm.

The IV that slowly dripped into Matt's arm for a while gave him familiar pain. He slept again on a familiar bed in a familiar room. His breakfast came on a familiar tray at a familiar time. After so much strangeness, all that was reassuring.

Aside from the temporary nuisance of the IV, he felt much better. The towers had the medicines to cure the sicknesses he had come down with on his travels, and the special medicine to help keep him from falling sick so easily again.

He had females once more, when he felt well enough for them. That was good, after doing so long without. When the couplings were done, they would ask him in sign-talk about his adventures on the outside. He answered as best he could. They were curious, and it helped pass the time.

Go in horseless, like on television, he would sign, and point to himself. That never failed to draw awed murmurs and excited "*Hoo*"s from whatever female he was with.

Better than here. Here everything the same all the time,

one of the females signed wistfully.

He shrugged and yawned, baring his large yellow teeth. *After while, going in horseless same all the time too,* he answered, full of the ennui of the experienced traveler.

One afternoon, the female called Jane asked, *Why people take you from here?*

People want to help make sims free, he signed back. *People want to make me free.*

"Hoo," Jane said softly. *You go outside tower, you free?*

Matt thought that over. No matter how often Ken and Melody had used the word, he still could not quite grasp what they meant by it. *Not sure,* he signed. Then, slowly, he shook his head. *No, not free. People outside like people here. Say they let sims do what sims want, but really only let sims do what sims want when they want that too.*

"Ah," Jane said, and nodded. She understood that perfectly. After a while, they coupled again. Then a nurse came to take Matt away.

More needles? he signed. The nurse nodded. He sighed and went with her. The afternoon moved on toward twilight.